Books by Gene Wolfe

The Island of Doctor Death and Other Stories
    and Other Stories
The Shadow of the Torturer
The Claw of the Conciliator

Published by TIMESCAPE/POCKET BOOKS

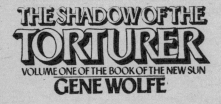

THE SHADOW OF THE TORTURER

VOLUME ONE OF THE BOOK OF THE NEW SUN

GENE WOLFE

A TIMESCAPE BOOK

PUBLISHED BY POCKET BOOKS NEW YORK

This novel is a work of fiction. Names, characters, places and incidents are either the product of the author's imagination or are used fictitiously, and any resemblance to actual persons, living or dead, events or locales is entirely coincidental.

 A Timescape Book published by
POCKET BOOKS, a Simon & Schuster division of
GULF & WESTERN CORPORATION
1230 Avenue of the Americas, New York, N.Y. 10020

Copyright © 1980 by Gene Wolfe

Library of Congress Catalog Card Number: 79-22371

ISBN: 0-671-45070-0

First Timescape Books printing May, 1981

10 9 8 7 6 5 4 3 2

POCKET and colophon are trademarks of Simon & Schuster.

Use of the TIMESCAPE trademark is by exclusive license
from Gregory Benford, the trademark owner.

Also available in Simon and Schuster trade edtion.

Printed in the U.S.A.

A thousand ages in thy sight
  Are like an evening gone;
Short as the watch that ends the night
  Before the rising sun.

THE SHADOW OF THE
TORTURER

I

Resurrection and Death

IT IS POSSIBLE I ALREADY HAD SOME PRESENTIMENT OF MY future. The locked and rusted gate that stood before us, with wisps of river fog threading its spikes like the mountain paths, remains in my mind now as the symbol of my exile. That is why I have begun this account of it with the aftermath of our swim, in which I, the torturer's apprentice Severian, had so nearly drowned.

"The guard has gone." Thus my friend Roche spoke to Drotte, who had already seen it for himself.

Doubtfully, the boy Eata suggested that we go around. A lift of his thin, freckled arm indicated the thousands of paces of wall stretching across the slum and sweeping up the hill until at last they met the high curtain wall of the Citadel. It was a walk I would take, much later.

"And try to get through the barbican without a safe-conduct? They'd send to Master Gurloes."

"But why would the guard leave?"

"It doesn't matter." Drotte rattled the gate. "Eata, see if you can slip between the bars."

Drotte was our captain, and Eata put an arm and a leg through the iron palings, but it was immediately clear that there was no hope of his getting his body to follow.

"Someone's coming," Roche whispered. Drotte jerked Eata out.

I looked down the street. Lanterns swung there among the fogmuffled sounds of feet and voices. I would have hidden, but Roche held me, saying, "Wait, I see pikes."

"Do you think it's the guard returning?"

He shook his head. "Too many."

1

"A dozen men at least," Drotte said.

Still wet from Gyoll we waited. In the recesses of my mind we stand shivering there even now. Just as all that appears imperishable tends toward its own destruction, those moments that at the time seem the most fleeting recreate themselves—not only in my memory (which in the final accounting loses nothing) but in the throbbing of my heart and the prickling of my hair, making themselves new just as our Commonwealth reconstitutes itself each morning in the shrill tones of its own clarions.

The men had no armor, as I could soon see by the sickly yellow light of the lanterns; but they had pikes, as Drotte had said, and staves and hatchets. Their leader wore a long, double-edged knife in his belt. What interested me more was the massive key threaded on a cord around his neck; it looked as if it might fit the lock of the gate.

Little Eata fidgeted with nervousness, and the leader saw us and lifted his lantern over his head. "We're waiting to get in, goodman," Drotte called. He was the taller, but he made his dark face humble and respectful.

"Not until dawn," the leader said gruffly. "You young fellows had better get home."

"Goodman, the guard was supposed to let us in, but he's not here."

"You won't be getting in tonight." The leader put his hand on the hilt of his knife before taking a step closer. For a moment I was afraid he knew who we were.

Drotte moved away, and the rest of us stayed behind him. "Who are you, goodman? You're not soldiers."

"We're the volunteers," one of the others said. "We come to protect our own dead."

"Then you can let us in."

The leader had turned away. "We let no one inside but ourselves." His key squealed in the lock, and the gate creaked back. Before anyone could stop him Eata darted through. Someone cursed, and the leader and two others sprinted after Eata, but he was too fleet for them. We saw his tow-colored hair and patched shirt zigzag among the sunken graves of paupers, then disappear in the thicket of statuary higher up. Drotte tried to pursue him, but two men grabbed his arms.

"We have to find him. We won't rob you of your dead."

"Why do you want to go in, then?" one volunteer asked.

"To gather herbs," Drotte told him. "We are physicians' gallipots. Don't you want the sick healed?"

The volunteer stared at him. The man with the key had dropped his lantern when he ran after Eata, and there were only two left. In their dim light the volunteer looked stupid and innocent; I suppose he was a laborer of some kind.

Drotte continued, "You must know that for certain simples to attain their highest virtues they must be pulled from grave soil by moonlight. It will frost soon and kill everything, but our masters require supplies for the winter. The three of them arranged for us to enter tonight, and I borrowed that lad from his father to help me."

"You don't have anything to put simples in."

I still admire Drotte for what he did next. He said, "We are to bind them in sheaves to dry," and without the least hesitation drew a length of common string from his pocket.

"I see," the volunteer said. It was plain he did not. Roche and I edged nearer the gate.

Drotte actually stepped back from it. "If you won't let us gather the herbs, we'd better go. I don't think we could ever find that boy in there now."

"No you don't. We have to get him out."

"All right," Drotte said reluctantly, and we stepped through, the volunteers following. Certain mystes aver that the real world has been constructed by the human mind, since our ways are governed by the artificial categories into which we place essentially undifferentiated things, things weaker than our words for them. I understood the principles intuitively that night as I heard the last volunteer swing the gate closed behind us.

A man who had not spoken before said, "I'm going to watch over my mother. We've wasted too much time already. They could have her a league off by now."

Several of the others muttered agreement, and the group began to scatter, one lantern moving to the left and the other to the right. We went up the center path (the one we always took in returning to the fallen section of the Citadel wall) with the remaining volunteers.

It is my nature, my joy and my curse, to forget nothing. Every rattling chain and whistling wind, every sight, smell, and taste, remains changeless in my mind, and though I know it is not so with everyone, I cannot imagine what it can mean to be otherwise, as if one had slept when in fact an experience is merely remote. Those few steps we took upon the whited path rise before me now: It was cold and growing colder; we had no light, and fog had begun to roll in from Gyoll in earnest. A few birds had come to roost in the pines and cypresses, and flapped uneasily from tree to tree. I remember the feel of my own hands as I rubbed my arms, and the lantern bobbing among the steles some distance off, and how the fog brought out the smell of the river water in my shirt, and the pungency of the new-turned earth. I had almost died that day, choking in the netted roots; the night was to mark the beginning of my manhood.

There was a shot, a thing I had never seen before, the bolt of violet energy splitting the darkness like a wedge, so that it closed with a thunderclap. Somewhere a monument fell with a crash. Silence then . . . in which everything around me seemed to dissolve. We began to run. Men were shouting, far off. I heard the ring of steel on stone, as if someone had struck one of the grave markers with a badelaire. I dashed along a path that was (or at least then seemed) completely unfamiliar, a ribbon of broken bone just wide enough for two to walk abreast that wound down into a little dale. In the fog I could see nothing but the dark bulk of the memorials to either side. Then, as suddenly as if it had been snatched away, the path was no longer beneath my feet—I suppose I must have failed to notice some turning. I swerved to dodge an oblesque that appeared to shoot up before me, and collided full tilt with a man in a black coat.

He was solid as a tree; the impact took me off my feet and knocked my breath away. I heard him muttering execrations, then a whispering sound as he swung some weapon. Another voice called, "What was that?"

"Somebody ran into me. Gone now, whoever he was."

I lay still.

A woman said, "Open the lamp." Her voice was like a dove's call, but there was urgency in it.

The man I had run against answered, "They would be on us like a pack of dholes, Madame."

"They will be soon in any case—Vodalus fired. You must have heard it."

"Be more likely to keep them off."

In an accent I was too inexperienced to recognize as an exultant's, the man who had spoken first said, "I wish I hadn't brought it. We shouldn't need it against this sort of people." He was much nearer now, and in a moment I could see him through the fog, very tall, slender, and hatless, standing near the heavier man I had run into. Muffled in black, a third figure was apparently the woman. In losing my wind I had also lost the strength of my limbs, but I managed to roll behind the base of a statue, and once secure there I peered out at them again.

My eyes had grown accustomed to the dark. I could distinguish the woman's heart-shaped face and note that she was nearly as tall as the slender man she had called Vodalus. The heavy man had disappeared, but I heard him say, "More rope." His voice indicated that he was no more than a step or two away from the spot where I crouched, but he seemed to have vanished like water cast into a well. Then I saw something dark (it must have been the crown of his hat) move near the slender man's feet, and understood that that was almost precisely what had become of him—there was a hole there, and he was in it.

The woman asked, "How is she?"

"Fresh as a flower, Madame. Hardly a breath of stink on her, and nothing to worry about." More agilely than I would have thought possible, he sprung out. "Now give me one end and you take the other, Liege, and we'll have her out like a carrot."

The woman said something I could not hear, and the slender man told her, "You didn't have to come, Thea. How would it look to the others if I took none of the risks?" He and the heavy man grunted as they pulled, and I saw something white appear at their feet. They bent to lift it. As though an amschaspand had touched them with his radiant wand, the fog swirled and parted to let a beam of green moonlight fall. They had the corpse of a woman. Her hair, which had been dark, was in some disorder now about her livid face; she wore a long gown of some pale fabric.

"You see," the heavy man said, "just as I told you, Liege, Madame, nineteen times of a score there's nothin' to it. We've only to get her over the wall now."

The words were no sooner out of his mouth than I heard someone shout. Three of the volunteers were coming down the path over the rim of the dale. "Hold them off, Liege," the heavy man growled, shouldering the corpse. "I'll take care of this, and get Madame to safety."

"Take it," Vodalus said. The pistol he handed over caught the moonlight like a mirror.

The heavy man gasped at it. "I've never used one, Liege . . ."

"Take it, you may need it." Vodalus stooped, then rose holding what appeared to be a dark stick. There was a rattle of metal on wood, and in place of the stick a bright and narrow blade. He called, *"Guard yourselves!"*

As if a dove had momentarily commanded an arctother, the woman took the shining pistol from the heavy man's hand, and together they backed into the fog.

The three volunteers had hesitated. Now one moved to the right and another to the left, so as to attack from three sides. The man in the center (still on the white path of broken bones) had a pike, and one of the others an ax.

The third was the leader Drotte had spoken with outside the gate. "Who are you?" he called to Vodalus, "and what power of Erebus's gives you the right to come here and do something like this?"

Vodalus did not reply, but the point of his sword looked from one to another like an eye.

The leader grated, "All together now and we'll have him." But they advanced hesitantly, and before they could close Vodalus sprang forward. I saw his blade flash in the faint light and heard it scrape the head of the pike—a metallic slithering, as though a steel serpent glided across a log of iron. The pikeman yelled and jumped back; Vodalus leaped backward too (I think for fear the other two would get behind him), then seemed to lose his balance and fell.

All this took place in dark and fog. I saw it, but for the most part the men were no more than ambient shadows—as the woman with the heart-shaped face had been. Yet something touched me. Perhaps it was Vodalus's willingness to die to protect her that made the woman seem precious to me; certainly it was that willingness that kindled my admiration for him. Many times since then, when I have stood upon a shaky platform in some market-town square with *Terminus Est* at rest before me and a miserable vagrant kneeling at my feet, when I have heard in hissing whispers the hate of the crowd and sensed what was far less welcome, the admiration of those who find an unclean joy in pains and deaths not their own, I have recalled Vodalus at the graveside, and raised my own blade half pretending that when it fell I would be striking for him.

He stumbled, as I have said. In that instant I believe my whole life teetered in the scales with his.

The flanking volunteers ran toward him, but he had held onto his weapon. I saw the bright blade flash up, though its owner was still on the ground. I remember thinking what a fine thing it would have been to have had such a sword on the day Drotte became captain of apprentices, and then likening Vodalus to myself.

The axman, toward whom he had thrust, drew back; the other drove forward with his long knife. I was on my feet by then, watching the fight over the shoulder of a chalcedony angel, and I saw the knife come down, missing Vodalus by a thumb's width as he writhed away and burying itself to the hilt in the ground. Vodalus slashed at the leader then, but he was too near for the length of his blade. The leader, instead of backing off, released his weapon and clutched him like a wrestler. They were at the very edge of the opened grave—I suppose Vodalus had tripped over the soil excavated from it.

The second volunteer raised his ax, then hesitated. His leader was nearest him; he circled to get a clear stroke until he was less than a pace from where I hid. While he shifted his ground I saw Vodalus wrench the knife free and drive it into the leader's throat. The ax rose to strike; I grasped the helve just below the head almost by reflex, and found myself at once in the struggle, kicking, then striking.

Quite suddenly it was over. The volunteer whose bloodied weapon I held was dead. The leader of the volunteers was writhing at our feet. The pikeman was gone; his pike lay harmlessly across the path. Vodalus retrieved a black wand from the grass nearby and sheathed his sword in it. "Who are you?"

"Severian. I am a torturer. Or rather, I am an apprentice of the torturers, Liege. Of the Order of the Seekers for Truth and Penitence." I drew a deep breath. "I am a Vodalarius. One of the thousands of Vodalarii of whose existence you are unaware." It was a term I had scarcely heard.

"Here." He laid something in my palm: a small coin so smooth it seemed greased. I remained clutching it beside the violated grave and watched him stride away. The fog swallowed him long before he reached the rim, and a few moments later a silver flier as sharp as a dart screamed overhead.

The knife had somehow fallen from the dead man's neck. Perhaps he had pulled it out in his agony. When I bent to pick it up, I discovered that the coin was still in my hand and thrust it into my pocket.

We believe that we invent symbols. The truth is that they invent us; we are their creatures, shaped by their hard, defining edges. When soldiers take their oath they are given a coin, an asimi stamped with the profile of the Autarch. Their acceptance of that coin is their acceptance of the special duties and burdens of military life—they are soldiers from that moment, though they may know nothing of the management of arms. I did not know that then, but it is a profound mistake to believe that we must know of such things to be influenced by them, and in fact to believe so is to believe in the most debased and superstitious kind of magic. The would-be sorcerer alone has faith in the efficacy of pure knowledge; rational people know that things act of themselves or not at all.

Thus I knew nothing, as the coin dropped into my pocket, of the dogmas of the movement Vodalus led, but I soon learned them all, for they were in the air. With him I hated the Autarchy, though I had no notion of what might replace it. With him I despised the exultants who failed to rise against the Autarch and bound the fairest of their daughters to him in ceremonial concubinage. With him I detested the people for their lack of discipline and a common purpose. Of those values that Master Malrubius (who had been master of apprentices when I was a boy) had tried to teach me, and that Master Palaemon still tried to impart, I accepted only one: loyalty to the guild. In that I was quite correct—it was, as I sensed, perfectly feasible for me to serve Vodalus and remain a torturer. It was in this fashion that I began the long journey by which I have backed into the throne.

II

Severian

MEMORY OPPRESSES ME. HAVING BEEN REARED AMONG THE torturers, I have never known my father or my mother. No more did my brother apprentices know theirs. From time to time, but most particularly when winter draws on, poor wretches come clamoring to the Corpse Door, hoping to be admitted to our ancient guild. Often they regale Brother Porter with accounts of the torments they will willingly inflict in payment for warmth and food; occasionally they fetch animals as samples of their work.

All are turned away. Traditions from our days of glory, antedating the present degenerate age, and the one before it, and the one before that, an age whose name is hardly remembered now by scholars, forbid recruitment from such as they. Even at the time I write of, when the guild had shrunk to two masters and less than a score of journeymen, those traditions were honored.

From my earliest memory I remember all. That first recollection is of piling pebbles in the Old Yard. It lies south and west of the Witches' Keep, and is separated from the Grand Court. The curtain wall our guild was to help defend was ruinous even then, with a wide gap between the Red

Tower and the Bear, where I used to climb the fallen slabs of unsmeltable gray metal to look out over the necropolis that descends that side of Citadel Hill.

When I was older, it became my playground. The winding paths were patrolled during daylight hours, but the sentries were largely concerned for the fresher graves on the lower ground, and knowing us to belong to the torturers, they seldom had much stomach for expelling us from our lurking places in the cypress groves.

Our necropolis is said to be the oldest in Nessus. That is certainly false, but the very existence of the error testifies to a real antiquity, though the autarchs were not buried there even when the Citadel was their stronghold, and the great families—then as now—preferred to inter their long-limbed dead in vaults on their own estates. But the armigers and optimates of the city favored the highest slopes, near the Citadel wall; and the poorer commons lay below them until the farthest reaches of the bottom lands, pressing against the tenements that came to line Gyoll, held potter's fields. As a boy I seldom went so far alone, or half so far.

There were always the three of us—Drotte, Roche, and I. Later Eata, the next oldest among the apprentices. None of us were born among the torturers, for none are. It is said that in ancient times there were both men and women in the guild, and that sons and daughters were born to them and brought up in the mystery, as is now the case among the lamp-makers and the goldsmiths and many other guilds. But Ymar the Almost Just, observing how cruel the women were and how often they exceeded the punishments he had decreed, ordered that there should be women among the torturers no more.

Since that time our numbers have been repaired solely from the children of those who fall into our hands. In our Matachin Tower, a certain bar of iron thrusts from a bulkhead at the height of a man's groin. Male children small enough to stand upright beneath it are nurtured as our own; and when a woman big with child is sent to us we open her and if the babe draws breath engage a wet-nurse if it be a boy. The females are rendered to the witches. So it has been since the days of Ymar, and those days are now by many hundreds of years forgotten.

Thus none of us knows our descent. Each would be an exultant if he could, and it is a fact that many persons of high lineage are given over to us. As boys each of us formed his own conjectures, and each attempted to question the older brothers among the journeymen, though they were locked in their own bitternesses and told us little. Eata, believing himself descended of that family, drew the arms of one of the great northern clans on the ceiling above his cot in the year of which I speak.

For my part, I had already adopted as my own the device graved in bronze above the door of a certain mausoleum. They were a fountain rising above waters, and a ship *volant*, and below these a rose. The door itself had been sprung long ago; two empty coffins lay on the floor. Three more, too heavy for me to shift and still intact, waited on the shelves along one wall. Neither the closed coffins nor the open ones constituted the attraction of the place, though I sometimes rested on what remained of the soft, faded padding of the latter. Rather, it was the smallness of the room, the thick walls of masonry, and the single, narrow window with its one bar, together with the faithless door (so massively heavy) that remained eternally ajar.

Through window and door I could look out unseen on all the bright life of tree and shrub and grass outside. The linnets and rabbits that fled when I approached could neither hear nor scent me there. I watched the storm crow build her nest and rear her young two cubits from my face. I saw the fox trot by with upraised brush; and once that giant fox, taller than all but the tallest hounds, that men call the maned wolf, loped by at dusk on some unguessable errand from the ruined quarters of the south. The caracara coursed vipers for me, and the hawk lifted his wings to the wind from the top of a pine.

A moment suffices to describe these things, for which I watched so long. The decades of a saros would not be long enough for me to write all they meant to the ragged apprentice boy I was. Two thoughts (that were nearly dreams) obsessed me and made them infinitely precious. The first was that at some not-distant time, time itself would stop . . . the colored days that had so long been drawn forth like a chain of conjuror's scarves come to an end, the sullen sun wink out at last. The second was that there existed somewhere a miraculous light—which I sometimes conceived of as a candle, sometimes as a flambeau—that engendered life in whatever objects it fell upon, so that a leaf plucked from a bush grew slender legs and waving feelers, and a rough brown brush opened black eyes and scurried up a tree.

Yet sometimes, particularly in the sleepy hours around noon, there was little to watch. Then I turned again to the blazon over the door and wondered what a ship, a rose, and a fountain had to do with me, and stared at the funeral bronze I had found and cleaned and set up in a corner. The dead man lay at full length, his heavy-lidded eyes closed. In the light that pierced the little window I examined his face and meditated on my own as I saw it in the polished metal. My straight nose, deep-set eyes, and sunken cheeks were much like his, and I longed to know if he too had dark hair.

In the winter I seldom came to the necropolis, but in the summer that violated mausoleum and others provided me with places of observation and cool repose. Drotte and Roche and Eata came too, though I never guided them to my favorite retreat, and they, I knew, had secret places of their own. When we were together we seldom crept into tombs at all. Instead we made swords of sticks and held running battles, or threw pinecones at the soldiers, or scratched boards on the soil of new graves and played draughts with stones, and ropes and snails, and high-toss-cockle.

We amused ourselves in the maze that was the Citadel too, and swam in the great cistern under the Bell Keep. It was cold and damp there even in summer, under its vaulted ceiling beside the circular pool of endlessly deep, dark water. But it was hardly worse in winter, and it had the supreme advantage of being forbidden, so we could slip down to it with delicious stealth when we were assumed to be elsewhere, and not kindle our torches until we had closed the barred hatch behind us. Then, when the flames shot up from the burning pitch, how our shadows danced up those clammy walls!

As I have already mentioned, our other swimming place was in Gyoll, which winds through Nessus like a great, weary snake. When warm weather came, we trooped through the necropolis on our way there—first past the old exalted sepulchers nearest the Citadel wall, then between the vainglorious death houses of the optimates, then through the stony forest of common monuments (we trying to appear highly respectable when we had to pass the burly guards leaning on their polearms). And at last across the plain, bare mounds that marked the interments of the poor, mounds that sank to puddles after the first rain.

At the lowest margin of the necropolis stood the iron gate I have already described. Through it the bodies intended for the potter's field were borne. When we passed those rusting portals we felt we were for the first time truly outside the Citadel, and thus in undeniable disobedience of the rules that were supposed to govern our comings and goings. We believed (or pretended to believe) we would be tortured if our older brothers discovered the violation; in actuality, we would have suffered nothing worse than a beating—such is the kindness of the torturers, whom I was subsequently to betray.

We were in greater danger from the inhabitants of the many-storied tenements that lined the filthy street down which we walked. I sometimes think the reason the guild has endured so long is that it serves as a focus for the hatred of the people, drawing it from the Autarch, the exultants, and the army, and even in some degree from the pale cacogens who sometimes visit Urth from the farther stars.

The same presentment that told the guards our identity often seemed to inform the residents of the tenements; slops were thrown at us from upper windows occasionally, and an angry mutter followed us. But the fear that engendered this hatred also protected us. No real violence was done to us, and once or twice, when it was known that some tyrannical wildgrave or venal burgess had been delivered to the mercy of the guild, we received shouted suggestions as to his disposal—most of them obscene and many impossible.

At the place where we swam, Gyoll had lost its natural banks hundreds of years ago. Here it was a two-chain-wide expanse of blue nenuphars penned between walls of stone. Steps intended for boat landings led down into the river at several points; on a warm day each flight would be held by a gang of ten or fifteen brawling youths. The four of us lacked the strength to displace these groups, but they could not (or at least would not) deny us admission, though whichever we chose to join would threaten us as we approached and taunt us when we were in their midst. Soon, however, all would drift away, leaving us in sole possession until the next swimming day.

I have chosen to describe all this now because I never went again after the day on which I saved Vodalus. Drotte and Roche believed it was because I was afraid we would be locked out. Eata guessed, I think—before they come too near to being men, boys often have an almost female insight. It was because of the nenuphars.

The necropolis has never seemed a city of death to me; I know its purple roses (which other people think so hideous) shelter hundreds of smaller animals and birds. The executions I have seen performed and have performed myself so often are no more than a trade, a butchery of human beings who are for the most part less innocent and less valuable than cattle. When I think of my own death, or of the death of someone who has been kind to me, or even of the death of the sun, the image that comes to my mind is that of the nenuphar, with its glossy, pale leaves and azure flower. Under flower and leaves are black roots as fine and strong as hair, reaching down into the dark waters.

As young men we thought nothing of these plants. We splashed and floated among them, pushed them aside, and ignored them. Their perfume countered to some degree the foul odor of the water. On the day I was to save Vodalus I dove beneath their crowded pads as I had done a thousand times.

I did not come up. Somehow I had entered a region where the roots seemed far thicker than I had ever encountered them before. I was caught in a hundred nets at once. My eyes were open, but I could see nothing—only the black web of the roots. I swam, and could feel that though my arms and legs moved among their millions of fine tendrils, my body did not. I grasped them by the handful and tore them apart, but when I had torn them I was immobilized as ever. My lungs seemed to rise in my throat to choke me, as if they would burst of themselves out into the water. The desire to draw breath, to suck in the dark, cold fluid around me, was overwhelming.

I no longer knew in what direction the surface lay, and I was no longer conscious of the water as water. The strength had left my limbs. I was no longer afraid, though I knew I was dying, or perhaps already dead. There was a loud and very unpleasant ringing in my ears, and I began to see visions.

Master Malrubius, who had died several years before, was waking us by drumming on the bulkhead with a spoon: that was the metallic din I heard. I lay in my cot unable to rise, though Drotte and Roche and the younger boys were all up, yawning and fumbling for their clothes. Master Malrubius's cloak was thrown back; I could see the loose skin of his chest and belly where the muscle and fat had been destroyed by time. There was a triangle of hair there, and it was as gray as mildew. I tried to call to him to tell him I was awake, but I could make no sound. He began to walk along the bulkhead, still striking it with his spoon. After what seemed a very long time he reached the port, stopped and leaned out. I knew he was looking for me in the Old Yard below.

Yet he could not see far enough. I was in one of the cells below the examination room. I lay there on my back, looking up at the gray ceiling. A woman cried but I could not see her, and I was less conscious of her sobs than of the ringing, ringing, ringing of the spoon. Darkness closed over me, but out of the darkness came the face of a woman, as immense as the green face of the moon. It was not she who wept—I could hear the sobs still, and this face was untroubled, and indeed filled with that kind of beauty that hardly admits of expression. Her hands reached toward me, and I at once became a fledgling I had taken from its nest the year before in the hope of taming it to perch on my finger, for her hands were each as long as the coffins in which I sometimes rested in my secret mausoleum. They grasped me, pulled me up, then flung me down, away from her face and from the sound of sobbing, down into the blackness until at last I struck what I took to be the bottom mud and burst through it into a world of light rimmed with black.

Still I could not breathe. I no longer wished to, and my chest no longer moved of itself. I was sliding through the water, though I did not know how. (Later I learned that

Drotte had seized me by the hair.) At once I lay on the cold, slimy stones with Roche, then Drotte, then Roche again, breathing into my mouth. I was enveloped in eyes as one is enveloped in the repetitious patterns of a kaleidoscope, and thought that some defect of my own vision was multiplying Eata's eyes.

At last I pulled away from Roche and vomited great quantities of black water. After that I was better. I could sit up, and breathe again in a crippled way, and though I had no strength and my hands shook, I could move my arms. The eyes around me belonged to real people, the denizens of the riverside tenements. A woman brought a bowl of some hot drink—I could not be sure if it was soup or tea, only that it was scalding and somewhat salty, and smelled of smoke. I pretended to drink it, and afterward found that I had slight burns on my lips and tongue.

"Were you trying to do that?" Drotte asked. "How did you come up?"

I shook my head.

Someone in the crowd said, "He shot right out of the water!"

Roche helped me steady my hand. "We thought you'd come up somewhere else. That you were playing a joke on us."

I said, "I saw Malrubius."

An old man, a boatman from his tar-stained clothes, took Roche by the shoulder. "Who's that?"

"Used to be Master of Apprentices. He's dead."

"Not a woman?" The old man was holding Roche but looking at me.

"No, no," Roche told him. "There are no women in our guild."

Despite the hot drink and the warmth of the day, I was cold. One of the youths we sometimes fought brought a dusty blanket, and I wrapped myself in it; but it was so long before I was strong enough to walk again that by the time we reached the gate of the necropolis, the statue of Night atop the khan on the opposite bank was a minute scratch of black against the sun's field of flame, and the gate itself stood closed and locked.

III

The Autarch's Face

IT WAS MIDMORNING OF THE NEXT DAY BEFORE I THOUGHT TO look at the coin Vodalus had given me. After serving the journeymen in the refectory we had breakfasted as usual, met Master Palaemon in our classroom, and after a brief preparatory lecture followed him to the lower levels to view the work of the preceding night.

But perhaps before I write further I should explain something more of the nature of our Matachin Tower. It is situated toward the back of the Citadel, upon the western side. At ground level are the studies of our masters, where consultations with the officers of justice and the heads of other guilds are conducted. Our common room is above them, with its back to the kitchen. Above that is the refectory, which serves us as an assembly hall as well as an eating place. Above it are the private cabins of the masters, in better days much more numerous. Above these are the journeymen's cabins, and above them the apprentices' dormitory and classroom, and a series of attics and abandoned cubicles. Near the very top is the gun room, whose remaining pieces we of the guild are charged with serving should the Citadel suffer attack.

The real work of our guild is carried out below all this. Just underground lies the examination room; beneath it, and thus outside the tower proper (for the examination room was the propulsion chamber of the original structure) stretches the labyrinth of the oubliette. There are three usable levels, reached by a central stairwell. The cells are plain, dry and

17

clean, equipped with a small table, a chair, and narrow bed fixed in the center of the floor.

The lights of the oubliette are of that ancient kind that is said to burn forever, though some have now gone out. In the gloom of those corridors, my feelings that morning were not gloomy but joyous—here I would labor when I became a journeyman, here I would practice the ancient art and raise myself to the rank of master, here I would lay the foundation for the restoration of our guild to its former glory. The very air of the place seemed to wrap me like a blanket that had been warmed before some clean-scented fire.

We halted before the door of a cell, and the journeyman on duty rattled his key in the lock. Inside, the client lifted her head, opening dark eyes very wide. Master Palaemon wore the sable-trimmed cloak and velvet mask of his rank; I suppose that these, or the protruding optical device that permitted him to see, must have frightened her. She did not speak, and of course none of us spoke to her.

"Here," Master Palaemon began in his driest tone, "we have something outside the routine of judicial punishment and well illustrative of modern technique. The client was put to the question last night—perhaps some of you heard her. Twenty minims of tincture were given before the excruciation, and ten after. The dose was only partially effective in preventing shock and loss of consciousness, so the proceedings were terminated after flaying the right leg, as you will see." He gestured to Drotte, who began unwrapping the bandages.

"Half boot?" Roche asked.

"No, full boot. She has been a maidservant, and Master Gurloes says he has found them strong-skinned. In this instance he was proved correct. A simple circular incision was made below the knee, and its edge taken with eight clamps. Careful work by Master Gurloes, Odo, Mennas, and Eigil permitted the removal of everything between the knee and the toes without further help from the knife."

We gathered around Drotte, the younger boys pushing in as they pretended they knew the points to look for. The arteries and major veins were all intact, but there was a slow generalized welling of blood. I helped Drotte apply fresh dressings.

Just as we were about to leave the woman said, "I don't know. Only, oh, can't you believe I wouldn't tell you if I did? She's gone with Vodalus of the Wood, I don't know where." Outside, feigning ignorance, I asked Master Palaemon who Vodalus of the Wood was.

"How often have I explained that nothing said by a client under questioning is heard by you?"

"Many times, Master."

"But to no effect. Soon it will be masking day, and Drotte and Roche will be journeymen, and you captain of apprentices. Is this the example you'll set the boys?"

"No, Master."

Behind the old man's back, Drotte gave me a look that meant he knew much about Vodalus and would tell me at a convenient time.

"Once the journeymen of our guild were deafened. Would you have those days again? Take your hands from your pockets when I speak to you, Severian."

I had put them there because I knew it would distract his anger, but as I drew them out I realized I had been fumbling the coin Vodalus had given me the night before. In the remembered terror of the fight I had forgotten it; now I was in agony to look at it—and could not, with Master Palaemon's bright lens fixed on me.

"When a client speaks, Severian, you hear nothing. Nothing whatsoever. Think of mice, whose squeaking conveys no meaning to men."

I squinted to indicate that I was thinking of mice.

All the long, weary way up the stair to our classroom, I ached to look at the thin disc of metal I clutched; but I knew that if I were to do so the boy behind me (as it happened, one of the younger apprentices, Eusignius) would see it. In the classroom, where Master Palaemon droned over a ten-day corpse, the coin was like a coal of fire, and I dared not look.

It was afternoon before I found privacy, hiding myself in the ruins of the curtain wall among the shining mosses, then hesitating with my fist poised in a ray of sun because I was afraid that when I saw it at last the disappointment would be more than I could bear.

Not because I cared for its value. Though I was already a man, I had had so little money that any coin would have seemed a fortune to me. Rather it was that the coin (so mysterious now, but not likely to remain so) was my only link with the night before, my only connection with Vodalus and the beautiful, hooded woman and the heavy man who had struck at me with his shovel, my only booty from the fight at the opened grave. My life in the guild was the only life I had known, and it seemed as drab as my ragged shirt in comparison with the flash of the exultant's sword blade and the sound of the shot echoing among the stones. All that might be gone when I opened my hand.

In the end I looked, having drained the dregs of pleasant dread. The coin was a gold chrisos, and I closed my hand once more, fearing that I had only mistaken a brass orichalk, and waited until I found my courage again.

It was the first time I had ever touched a piece of gold. Orichalks I had seen in some plenty, and I had even possessed a few of my own. Silver asimi I had glimpsed once or twice. But chrisos I knew only in the same dim way I knew of the existence of a world outside our city of Nessus, and of continents other than our own to the north and east and west.

This one bore what I at first thought was a woman's face—a woman crowned, neither young nor old, but silent and perfect in the citrine metal. At last I turned my treasure over, and then indeed I caught my breath; stamped on the reverse was just such a flying ship as I had seen in the arms above the door of my secret mausoleum. It seemed beyond explanation—so much so that at the time I did not even trouble to speculate about it, so sure was I that any speculation would be fruitless. Instead, I thrust the coin back into my pocket and went, in a species of trance, to rejoin my fellow apprentices.

To carry the coin about with me was out of the question. As soon as there was an opportunity to do so, I slipped into the necropolis alone and sought out my mausoleum. The weather had turned that day—I pushed through drenching shrubbery and trudged over long, aged grass that had begun to flatten itself for winter. When I reached my retreat it was no longer the cool, inviting cave of summer but an icy trap where I sensed the nearness of enemies too vague for names, opponents of Vodalus who surely knew by now that I was his sworn supporter; as soon as I entered they would rush forward to swing the back door shut on newly oiled hinges. I knew that it was nonsense, of course. Yet I also knew there was truth in it, that it was a proximity in time I felt. In a few months or a few years I might reach the point at which those enemies waited for me; when I had swung the ax I had chosen to fight, a thing a torturer does not normally do.

There was a loose stone in the floor almost at the foot of my funeral bronze. I pried it up and put the chrisos under it, then muttered an incantation I had learned years before from Roche, a few lines of verse that would hold hidden objects safe:

> "Where I put you, there you lie,
> Never let a stranger spy,
> Like glass grow to any eye,
> Not of me.
>
> Here be safe, never leave it,
> Should a hand come, deceive it,
> Let strange eyes not believe it,
> Till I see."

For the charm to be really effective one had to walk around the spot at midnight carrying a corpse-candle, but I found myself laughing at the thought—which suggested Drotte's mummery about simples drawn at midnight from graves—and decided to rely on the verse alone, though I was somewhat astonished to discover that I was now old enough not to be ashamed of it.

Days passed, and the memory of my visit to the mausoleum remained vivid enough to dissuade me from making another to verify that my treasure was safe, though at times I longed to do so. Then came the first snow, turning the ruins of the curtain wall into an almost impassably slippery barrier, and the familiar necropolis into a strange wilderness of deceptive hummocks, in which monuments were suddenly too large under their coats of new snow, and the trees and bushes crushed to half size by theirs.

It is the nature of apprenticeship in our guild that, though easy at first, its burdens grow greater and greater as one comes to manhood. The smallest boys do no work at all. At the age of six, when work begins, it is at first no more than running up and down the stairs of the Matachin Tower with messages, and the little apprentice, proud of being entrusted with them, hardly feels the labor. As time progresses, however, his work becomes more and more onerous. His duties take him to other parts of the Citadel—to the soldiers in the barbican, where he learns that the military apprentices have drums and trumpets and ophicleids and boots and sometimes gilded cuirasses; to the Bear Tower, where he sees boys no older than himself learning to handle wonderful fighting animals of all kinds, mastiffs with heads as large as a lion's, diatrymae taller than a man, with beaks sheathed in steel; and to a hundred other such places where he discovers for the first time that his guild is hated and despised even by those (indeed, most of all by those) who make use of its services. Soon there is scrubbing and kitchen work. Brother Cook performs such cooking as might be interesting or pleasurable, and the apprentice is left to pare vegetables, serve the journeymen, and carry an endless succession of stacks of trays down the stairs to the oubliette.

I did not know it at the time, but soon this apprentice life of mine, which had been growing harder for as long as I could remember, would reverse its course and become less drudging and more pleasant. In the years before he is to become a journeyman, a senior apprentice does little but supervise the work of his juniors. His food and even his dress improve. The younger journeymen begin to treat him almost as an equal, and he has, above all, the elevating burden of responsibility and the pleasure of issuing and enforcing orders.

When his elevation comes, he is an adult. He does no work but that for which he has been trained; and he is free to leave the Citadel when his duties are over, for which recreation he is supplied with liberal funds. Should he eventually rise to mastership (an honor that requires the affirmative votes of all the living masters), he will be able to pick and choose such assignments as may interest or amuse him, and direct the affairs of the guild itself.

But you must understand that in the year I have been writing of, the year in which I saved the life of Vodalus, I was unconscious of all that. Winter (I was told) had ended the campaigning season in the north, and thus brought the

Autarch and his chief officers and advisors back to the seats of justice. "And so," as Roche explained, "we have all these new clients. And more to come . . . dozens, maybe hundreds. We might have to reopen the fourth level." He waved a freckled hand to show that he at least was ready to do whatever might be necessary.

"Is he here?" I asked. "The Autarch? Here in the Citadel? In the Great Keep?"

"Of course not. If he ever came, you'd know it, wouldn't you? There'd be parades and inspections and all kinds of goings on. There's a suite for him there but the door hasn't been opened in a hundred years. He'll be in the hidden palace—the House Absolute—north of the city someplace."

"Don't you know where?"

Roche grew defensive. "You can't say where it is because there's nothing there except the House Absolute itself. It's where it is. To the north, on the other bank."

"Beyond the Wall?"

He smiled on my ignorance. "Far past it. Weeks, if you walked. Naturally the Autarch could get here by flier in an instant if he wanted to. The Flag Tower—that's where the flier would land."

But our new clients did not come in fliers. The less important arrived in coffles of ten to twenty men and women, chained one behind the other by the neck. They were guarded by dimarchi, hard-bitten troopers in armor that looked as if it had been made for use and used. Each client carried a copper cylinder supposedly containing his or her papers and thus his or her fate. All of them had broken the seals and read those papers, of course; and some had destroyed them or exchanged them for another's. Those who arrived without papers would be held until some further word concerning their disposition was received—probably for the remainder of their lives. Those who had exchanged papers with someone else had exchanged fates; they would be held or released, tortured or executed, in another's stead.

The more important arrived in armored carriages. The steel sides and barred windows of these vehicles were not intended to prevent escape so much as to thwart rescue, and no sooner had the first of them thundered around the east side of the Witches' Tower and entered the Old Yard than the whole guild was filled with rumors of daring raids contemplated or attempted by Vodalus. For all my fellow apprentices and most of the journeymen believed that many of these clients were his henchmen, confederates, and allies. I would not have released them for that reason—it would have brought disgrace on the guild, which for all my attachment to him and his movement I was unready to do, and would have been impossible anyway. But I hoped to provide those I considered my comrades-in-arms with such small comforts as lay within my power: extra food stolen from the trays of less deserving clients and occasionally a bit of meat smuggled from the kitchen.

One blustering day I was given the opportunity to learn who they were. I was scrubbing the floor in Master Gurloes's study when he was called away on some errand, leaving his table stacked with newly arrived dossiers. I hurried over as soon as the door had clanged behind him, and was able to skim most of them before I heard his heavy tread on the stair again. Not one—*not one*—of the prisoners whose papers I had read had been an adherent of Vodalus. There were merchants who had tried to make rich profits on supplies needed by the army, camp followers who had spied for the Ascians, and a sprinkling of sordid civil criminals. Nothing else.

When I carried my bucket out to empty in the stone sink in the Old Yard, I saw one of the armored carriages halted there with its long-maned team steaming and stamping, and the guards in their fur-trimmed helmets sheepishly accepting our smoking goblets of mulled wine. I caught the name Vodalus in the air; but at that moment it seemed I was the only one who heard it, and suddenly I felt Vodalus had been only an eidolon created by my imagination from the fog, and only the man I had slain with his own ax real. The dossiers I had fumbled through a moment before seemed blown like leaves against my face.

It was in this instant of confusion that I realized for the first time that I am in some degree insane. It could be argued that it was the most harrowing of my life. I had lied often to Master Gurloes and Master Palaemon, to Master Malrubius while he still lived, to Drotte because he was captain, to

Roche because he was older and stronger than I, and to Eata and the other smaller apprentices because I hoped to make them respect me. Now I could no longer be sure my own mind was not lying to me; all my falsehoods were recoiling on me, and I who remembered everything could not be certain those memories were more than my own dreams. I recalled the moonlit face of Vodalus; but then, I had wanted to see it. I recalled his voice as he spoke to me, but I had desired to hear it, and the woman's voice too.

One freezing night, I crept back to the mausoleum and took out the chrisos again. The worn, serene, androgynous face on its obverse was not the face of Vodalus.

IV

Triskele

I HAD BEEN POKING A STICK UP A FROZEN DRAIN AS PUNISHMENT from some petty infraction, and I found him where the keepers of the Bear Tower throw their refuse, the bodies of the torn animals killed in practice. Our guild buries its own dead beside the wall and our clients in the lower reaches of the necropolis, but the keepers of the Bear Tower leave theirs to be taken away by others. He was the smallest of those dead.

There are encounters that change nothing. Urth turns her aged face to the sun and he beams upon her snows; they scintillate and coruscate until each little point of ice hanging from the swelling sides of the towers seems the Claw of the Conciliator, the most precious of gems. Then everyone except the wisest believes that the snow must melt and give way to a protracted summer beyond summer.

Nothing of that sort occurs. The paradise endures for a

watch or two, then shadows blue as watered milk lengthen on the snow, which shifts and dances under the spur of an east wind. Night comes, and all is as it was.

My finding Triskele was like that. I felt that it could have and should have changed everything, but it was only the episode of a few months, and when it was over and he was gone, it was only another winter passed and the Feast of Holy Katharine come again, and nothing had changed. I wish I could tell you how pitiful he looked when I touched him, and how cheerful.

He lay on his side, covered with blood. It was as hard as tar in the cold, and still bright red because the cold had preserved it. I went over and put my hand on his head—I don't know why. He seemed as dead as the rest, but he opened one eye then and rolled it at me, and there was a confidence in it that the worst was over now—I have carried my part, it seemed to say, and borne up, and done all I could do; now it is your turn to do your duty by me.

If it had been summer, I think I would have let him die. As it was I had not seen a living animal, not so much as a garbage-eating thylacodon, in some time. I stroked him again and he licked my hand, and I could not turn away after that.

I picked him up (surprised at how heavy he was) and looked about trying to decide what to do with him. He would be discovered in our dormitory before the candle had burned a finger's width, I knew. The Citadel is immense and immensely complicated, with little-visited rooms and passages in its towers, in the buildings that have been erected between the towers, and in the galleries delved under them. Yet I could not think of any such place that I could reach without being seen half a dozen times on the way, and in the end I carried the poor brute into the quarters of our own guild.

I then had to get him past the journeyman who stood guard at the head of the stair leading to the cell tiers. My first idea was to put him in the basket in which we took down the client's clean bedding. It was a laundry day, and it would have been easy enough to make one more trip than was actually required; the chance that the journeyman-guard would notice anything amiss seemed remote, but it would have involved waiting more than a watch for the scrubbed linen to dry and risking the questions of the brother on duty in the third tier, who would see me descending to the deserted fourth.

Instead I laid the dog in the examination room—he was too weak to move—and offered to take the guard's place at the head of the ramp. He was happy enough to seize the opportunity to relieve himself and handed over his wide-bladed carnificial sword (which I in theory was not supposed to touch) and his fuligin cloak (which I was forbidden to wear, though I was already taller than most of the journeymen) so that from a distance it would appear that there had been no substitution. I put on the cloak and as soon as he was gone stood the sword in a corner and got my dog. All our guild cloaks are voluminous, and this one was more so than most since the brother I had replaced was large of frame. Furthermore, the hue fuligin, which is darker than black, admirably erases all folds, bunchings, and gatherings so far as the eye is concerned, showing only a featureless dark. With the hood pulled up, I must have appeared to the journeymen at their tables in the tiers (if they looked toward the stair and saw me at all) as a brother somewhat more portly than most descending to the lower levels. Even the man on duty in the third, where the clients who had lost all reason howled and shook their chains, could have seen nothing unusual in another journeyman going down to the fourth when there were rumors that it was to be refurbished—or in an apprentice running down shortly after the journeyman went up again; no doubt he had forgotten something there and the apprentice had been sent to fetch it.

It was not a prepossessing place. About half of the old lights still burned, but mud had seeped into the corridors until it lay to the thickness of one's hand. A duty table stood where it had been left, perhaps two hundred years before; the wood had rotted and the whole thing fell at a touch.

Yet the water had never been high here, and the farther end of the corridor I chose was free even of the mud. I laid my dog on a client's bed and cleaned him as well as I could with sponges I had carried down from the examination room.

Under the crusted blood his fur was short, stiff, and tawny. His tail had been cut so short that what remained was wider than it was long. His ears had been cut almost completely away, leaving only stiff points shorter than the first joint of my thumb. In his last fight his chest had been laid open. I could see the wide muscles like drowsy constrictors of pale red. His right foreleg was gone—the upper half crushed to a pulp. I cut it away after I had sutured up his chest as well as I could, and it began to bleed again. I found the artery and tied it, then folded the skin under (as Master Palaemon had taught us) to make a neat stump.

Triskele licked my hand from time to time as I worked, and when I had made the last stitch began slowly licking that, as if he were a bear and could lick a new leg into shape. His jaws were as big as an arctother's and his canines as long as my index finger, but his gums were white; there was no more strength in those jaws now than in a skeleton's hands. His eyes were yellow and held a certain clean madness.

That evening I traded tasks with the boy who was to bring the clients their meals. There were always extra trays because some clients would not eat, and now I carried two of these down to Triskele, wondering if he were still alive.

He was. He had somehow climbed out of the bed where I had laid him and crawled—he could not stand—to the edge of the mud, where a little water had gathered. That was where I found him. There was soup and dark bread and two carafes of water. He drank one bowl of soup, but when I tried to feed him the bread I found he could not chew it enough to swallow; I soaked it in the other bowl of soup for him, then filled the bowl again and again with water until both carafes were empty.

When I lay on my cot almost at the top of our tower, I thought that I could hear his labored breathing. Several times I sat up, listening; each time the sound faded away, only to return when I had lain flat for a time. Perhaps it was only the beating of my heart. If I had found him a year, two years, before, he would have been a divinity to me. I would have told Drotte and the rest, and he would have been a divinity to us all. Now I knew him for the poor animal he was, and yet I could not let him die because it would have been a breaking of faith with something in myself. I had been a man (if I was truly a man) such a short time; I could not endure to think that I had become a man so different from the boy I had been. I could remember each moment of my past, every vagrant thought and sight, every dream. How could I destroy that past? I held up my hands and tried to look at them—I knew the veins stood out on their backs now. It is when those veins stand out that one is a man.

In a dream I walked through the fourth level again, and found a huge friend there with dripping jaws. It spoke to me.

Next morning I served the clients again, and stole food to take down to the dog, though I hoped that he was dead. He was not. He lifted his muzzle and seemed to grin at me with a mouth so wide it appeared his head might fall in two halves, though he did not try to stand. I fed him and as I was about to leave was struck by the misery of his condition. He was dependent on me. Me! He had been valued; trainers had coached him as runners are coached for a race; he had walked in pride, his enormous chest, as wide as a man's, set on two legs like pillars. Now he lived like a ghost. His very name had been washed away in his own blood.

When I had time, I visited the Bear Tower and struck up such friendships as I could with the beast handlers there. They have their own guild, and though it is a lesser guild than ours, it has much stange lore. To a degree that astonished me, I found it to be the same lore, though I did not, of course, penetrate to their arcanum. In the elevation of their masters, the candidate stands under a metal grate trod by a bleeding bull; at some point in life each brother takes a lioness or bear-sow in marriage, after which he shuns human women.

All of which is only to say that there exists between them and the animals they bring to the pits a bond much like that between our clients and ourselves. Now I have traveled much farther from our tower, but I have found always that the pattern of our guild is repeated mindlessly (like the repetitions of Father Inire's mirrors in the House Absolute) in the societies of every trade, so that they are all of them torturers, just as we. His quarry stands to the hunter as our clients to us; those who buy to the tradesman; the enemies of the Commonwealth to the soldier; the governed to the governors; men to women. All love that which they destroy.

A week after I had carried him down, I found only Triskele's hobbling footprints in the mud. He was gone, but I set out after him, sure that one of the journeymen would have mentioned it to me if he had come up the ramp. Soon the footprints led to a narrow door that opened on a welter of lightless corridors of whose existence I had been utterly unaware. In the dark I could no longer track him, but I pressed on nevertheless, thinking that he might catch my scent in the stale air and come to me. Soon I was lost, and went forward only because I did not know how to go back.

I have no way of knowing how old those tunnels are. I suspect, though I can hardly say why, that they antedate the Citadel above them, ancient though it is. It comes to us from the very end of the age when the urge to flight, the outward urge that sought new suns not ours, remained, though the means to achieve that flight were sinking like dying fires. Remote as that time is, from which hardly one name is recalled, we still remember it. Before it there must have been another time, a time of burrowing, of the creation of dark galleries, that is now utterly forgotten.

However that may be, I was frightened there. I ran—and sometimes ran into walls—until at last I saw a spot of pale daylight and clambered out through a hole hardly big enough for my head and shoulders.

I found myself crawling onto the ice-covered pedestal of one of those old, faceted dials whose multitudinous faces give each a different time. No doubt because the frost of these latter ages entering the tunnel below had heaved its foundation, it had slipped sidewise until it stood at such an angle that it might have been one of its own gnomons, drawing the silent passage of the short winter day across the unmarked snow.

The space about it had been a garden in summer, but not such a one as our necropolis, with half-wild trees and rolling, meadowed lawns. Roses had blossomed here in kraters set upon a tessellated pavement. Statues of beasts stood with their backs to the four walls of the court, eyes turned to watch the canted dial: hulking barylambdas; arctothers, the monarchs of bears; glyptodons; smilodons with fangs like glaives. All were dusted now with snow. I looked for Triskele's tracks, but he had not come here.

The walls of the court held high, narrow windows. I could see no light through them, and no motion. The spear-towers of the Citadel rose on every side, so that I knew I had not left it—instead, I seemed to be somewhere near its heart, where I had never been. Shaking with cold I crossed to the nearest door and pounded on it. I had the feeling that I might wander forever in the tunnels below without ever finding another way to the surface, and I was resolved to smash one of the windows if need be rather than return that way. There was no sound within, though I beat my fist against the door panels again and again.

There is really no describing the sensation of being watched. I have heard it called a prickling at the back of the neck, and even a consciousness of eyes that seem to float in darkness, but it is neither—at least, not for me. It is something akin to a sourceless embarrassment, coupled with the feeling that I must not turn around, because to turn will be to appear a fool, answering the promptings of baseless intuition. Eventually, of course, one does. I turned with the vague impression that someone had followed me through the hole at the base of the dial.

Instead I saw a young woman wrapped in furs standing before a door at the opposite side of the court. I waved to her and began to walk toward her (hurriedly, because I was so cold). She advanced toward me then, and we met on the farther side of the dial. She asked who I was and what I was doing there, and I told her as well as I could. The face circled by her fur hood was exquisitely molded, and the hood itself, and her coat and fur-trimmed boots, were soft-looking and rich, so that I was miserably conscious as I spoke to her of my own patched shirt and trousers and my muddy feet.

Her name was Valeria. "We do not have your dog here," she said. "You may search, if you do not believe me."

"I never thought you did. I only want to go back where I belong, to the Matachin Tower, without having to go down there again."

"You're very brave. I have seen that hole since I was a little girl, but I never dared go in."

"I'd like to go in," I said. "I mean, inside there."

She opened the door through which she had come and led me into a tapestried room where stiff, ancient chairs seemed as fixed in their places as the statues in the frozen court. A diminutive fire smoked in a grate against one wall. We went to it, and she took off her coat while I spread my hands to the warmth.

"Wasn't it cold in the tunnels?"

"Not as cold as outside. Besides, I was running and there was no wind."

"I see. How strange that they should come up in the Atrium of Time." She looked younger than I, but there was an antique quality about her metal-trimmed dress and the shadow of her dark hair that made her seem older than Master Palaemon, a dweller in forgotten yesterdays.

"Is that what you call it? The Atrium of Time? Because of the dials, I suppose."

"No, the dials were put there because we call it that. Do you like the dead languages? They have mottoes. *Lux dei vitae viam monstrat,*' that's 'The beam of the New Sun lights the way of life.' *'Felicibus brevis, miseris hora longa.'* 'Men wait long for happiness.' *'Aspice ut aspiciar.'*'"

I had to tell her with some shame that I knew no tongue beyond the one we spoke, and little of that.

Before I left we talked a sentry's watch or more. Her family occupied these towers. They had waited, at first, to leave Urth with the autarch of their era, then had waited because there was nothing left for them but waiting. They had given many castellans to the Citadel, but the last had died generations ago; they were poor now, and their towers were in ruins. Valeria had never gone above the lower floors.

"Some of the towers were built more strongly than others," I said. "The Witches' Keep is decayed inside too."

"Is there really such a place? My nurse told me of it when I was little—to frighten me—but I thought it was only a tale. There was supposed to be a Tower of Torment too, where all who enter die in agony."

I told her that, at least, was a fable.

"The great days of these towers are more fabulous to me," she said. "No one of my blood carries a sword now against the enemies of the Commonwealth, or stands hostage for us at the Well of Orchids."

"Perhaps one of your sisters will be summoned soon," I said, for I did not want, for some reason, to think of her going herself.

"I am all the sisters we breed," she answered. "And all the sons."

An old servant brought us tea and small, hard cakes. Not real tea, but the maté of the north, which we sometimes give our clients because it is so cheap.

Valeria smiled. "You see, you have found some comfort here. You are worried about your poor dog because he is lame. But he, too, may have found hospitality. You love him, so another may love him. You love him, so you may love another."

I agreed, but secretly thought that I would never have another dog, which has proved true.

I did not see Triskele again for almost a week. Then one day as I was carrying a letter to the barbican, he came bounding up to me. He had learned to run on his single front leg, like an acrobat who does handstands on a gilded ball.

After that I saw him once or twice a month for as long as the snow lasted. I never knew whom he had found, who was feeding him and caring for him; but I like to think it was someone who took him away with him in the spring, perhaps north to the cities of tents and the campaigns among the mountains.

V

The Picture-Cleaner and Others

THE FEAST OF HOLY KATHARINE IS THE GREATEST OF DAYS FOR our guild, the festival by which we are recalled to our heritage, the time when journeymen become masters (if they ever do) and apprentices become journeymen. I will leave my description of the ceremonies of that day until I have occasion to tell of my own elevation; but in the year I am recounting, the year of the fight by the graveside, Drotte and Roche were elevated, leaving me captain of apprentices.

The full weight of that office did not impress itself on me until the ritual was nearly over. I was sitting in the ruined chapel enjoying the pageantry and only just conscious (in the same pleasant way I was anticipating the feast) that I would be senior to all the rest when the last of it was done.

By slow degrees, however, a feeling of disquiet seized me. I was miserable before I knew I was no longer happy, and bowed with responsibility when I did not yet fully understand I held it. I remembered how much difficulty Drotte had encountered in keeping us in order. I would have to do it now without his strength, and with no one to be to me what Roche had been to him—a lieutenant of his own age. When the final chant crashed to a close and Master Gurloes and Master Palaemon in their gold-traced masks had slow-stepped through the door, and the old journeymen had hoisted Drotte and Roche, the new journeymen, on their shoulders (already fumbling in the sabretaches at their belts for the fireworks they would set off outside), I had steeled myself and even formed a rudimentary plan.

We apprentices were to serve the feast, and before we did so were to doff the relatively new and clean clothes we had been given for the ceremony. After the last cracker had popped and the matrosses, in their annual gesture of amity, had torn the sky with the largest piece of ordinance in the Great Keep, I hustled my charges—already, or so I thought, beginning to look at me resentfully—back to our dormitory, closed the door, and pushed a cot against it.

Eata was the oldest except for myself, and fortunately for me I had been friendly enough in the past that he suspected nothing until it was too late to make effective resistance. I got him by the throat and banged his head half a dozen times against the bulkhead, then kicked his feet from under him. "Now," I said, "are you going to be my second? Answer!"

He could not speak, but he nodded.

"Good. I'll get Timon. You take the next biggest."

In the space of a hundred breaths (and very quick breaths they were) the boys had been kicked into submission. It was three weeks before any of them dared to disobey me, and

then there was no mass rebellion, only individual malin-
gering.

As captain of apprentices I had new functions, as well as
more freedom than I had ever enjoyed before. It was I who
saw that the journeymen on duty got their meals hot, and who
supervised the boys who toiled under the stacks of trays
intended for our clients. In the kitchen I drove my charges to
their tasks, and in the classroom I coached them in their
studies; I was employed to a much greater degree than
previously in carrying messages to distant parts of the
Citadel, and even in a small way in conducting the guild's
business. Thus I became acquainted with all the thorough-
fares and with many an unfrequented corner—granaries with
lofty bins and demonic cats; wind-swept ramparts overlooking gangrenous slums; and the pinakotheken, with their great
hallway topped by a vaulted roof of window-pierced brick,
floored with flagstones strewn with carpets, and bound by
walls from which dark arches opened to strings of chambers
lined—as the hallway itself was—with innumerable pictures.

Many of these were so old and smoke-grimed that I could
not discern their subjects, and there were others whose
meaning I could not guess—a dancer whose wings seemed
leeches, a silent-looking woman who gripped a double-bladed
dagger and sat beneath a mortuary mask. After I had walked
at least a league among these enigmatic paintings one day, I
came upon an old man perched on a high ladder. I wanted to
ask my way, but he seemed so absorbed in his work that I
hesitated to disturb him.

The picture he was cleaning showed an armored figure
standing in a desolate landscape. It had no weapon, but held a
staff bearing a strange, stiff banner. The visor of this figure's
helmet was entirely of gold, without eye slits or ventilation; in
its polished surface the deathly desert could be seen in
reflection, and nothing more.

This warrior of a dead world affected me deeply, though I
could not say why or even just what emotion it was I felt. In
some obscure way, I wanted to take down the picture and
carry it—not into our necropolis but into one of those
mountain forests of which our necropolis was (as I under-

stood even then) an idealized but vitiated image. It should have stood among trees, the edge of its frame resting on young grass.

"—and so," a voice behind me said, "they all escaped. Vodalus had what he had come for, you see."

"You," snapped the other. "What are you doing here?"

I turned and saw two armigers dressed in bright clothes that came as near to exultants' as they dared have them. I said, "I have a communication for the archivist," and held up the envelope.

"Very well," said the armiger who had spoken to me. "Do you know the location of the archives?"

"I was about to ask, sieur."

"Then you are not the proper messenger to take the letter, are you? Give it to me and I'll give it to a page."

"I can't, sieur. It is my task to deliver it."

The other armiger said, "You needn't be so hard on this young man, Racho."

"You don't know what he is, do you?"

"And you do?"

The one called Racho nodded. "From what part of this Citadel are you, messenger?"

"From the Matachin Tower. Master Gurloes sends me to the archivist."

The other armiger's face tightened. "You are a torturer, then."

"Only an apprentice, sieur."

"I don't wonder then that my friend wants you out of his sight. Follow the gallery to the third door, make your turn and continue about a hundred paces, climb the stair to the second landing and take the corridor south to the double doors at the end."

"Thank you," I said, and took a step in the direction he had indicated.

"Wait a bit. If you go now, we'll have to look at you."

Racho said, "I'd as soon have him ahead of us as behind us."

I waited nonetheless, with one hand resting on the leg of the ladder, for the two of them to turn a corner.

Like one of those half-spiritual friends who in dreams

address us from the clouds, the old man said, "So you're a torturer, are you? Do you know, I've never been to your place." He had a weak glance, reminding me of the turtles we sometimes frightened on the banks of Gyoll, and a nose and chin that nearly met.

"Grant I never see you there," I said politely.

"Nothing to fear now. What could you do with a man like me? My heart would stop like that!" He dropped his sponge into his bucket and attempted to snap his wet fingers, though no sound came. "Know where it is, though. Behind the Witches' Keep. Isn't that right?"

"Yes," I said, a trifle surprised that the witches were better known than we.

"Thought so. Nobody never talks about it, though. You're angry about those armigers and I don't blame you. But you ought to know how it is with them. They're supposed to be like exultants, only they're not. They're afraid to die, afraid to hurt, and afraid to act like it. It's hard on them."

"They should be done away with," I said. "Vodalus would set them quarrying. They're only a carryover from some past age—what possible help can they give the world?"

The old man cocked his head. "Why, what help was they to begin? Do you know?"

When I admitted I did not, he scrambled down from the ladder like an aged monkey, seeming all arms and legs and wrinkled neck; his hands were as long as my feet, the crooked fingers laced with blue veins. "I'm Rudesind the curator. You know old Ultan, I take it? No, course not. If you did, you'd know the way to the library."

I said, "I've never been in this part of the Citadel before."

"Never been here? Why, this is the best part. Art, music, and books. We've a Fechin here that shows three girls dressing another one with flowers that's so real you expect the bees to come out of it. A Quartillosa, too. Not popular anymore, Quartillosa isn't, or we wouldn't have him here. But the day he was born he was a better draughtsman than the drippers and spitters they're wild for today. We get what the House Absolute don't want, you see. That means we get the old ones, and they're the best, mostly. Come in here dirty from having hung so long, and I clean them up.

Sometimes I clean them again, after they've hung here a time. We've got a Fechin here. It's the truth! Or you take this one now. Like it?"

It seemed safe to say I did.

"*Third* time for it. When I was new come, I was old Branwallader's apprentice and he taught me how to clean. This was the one he used, because he said it wasn't worth nothing. He begun down here in this corner. When he'd done about as much as you could cover with one hand, he turned it over to me and I did the rest. Back when my wife still lived I cleaned it again. That would be after our second girl was born. It wasn't all that dark, but I had things on my mind and wanted something to do. Today I took the notion to clean it again. And it needs it—see how nice it's brightening up? There's your blue Urth coming over his shoulder again, fresh as the Autarch's fish."

All this time the name of Vodalus was echoing in my mind. I felt certain the old man had come down from his ladder only because I had mentioned it, and I wanted to ask him about it. But try as I might, I could find to way to bring the conversation around to it. When I had been silent a moment too long and was afraid he was about to mount his ladder and begin cleaning again, I managed to say, "Is that the moon? I have been told it's more fertile."

"Now it is, yes. This was done before they got it irrigated. See that gray-brown? In those times, that's what you'd see if you looked up at her. Not green like she is now. Didn't seem so big either, because it wasn't so close in—that's what old Branwallader used to say. Now there's trees enough on it to hide Nilammon, as the saw goes."

I seized my opportunity. "Or Vodalus."

Rudesind cackled. "Or him, that's right enough. Your bunch must be rubbing their hands waiting to have him. Got something special planned?"

If the guild had particular excruciations reserved for specific individuals, I knew nothing of it; but I endeavored to look wise and said, "We'll think of something."

"I suppose you will. A bit ago, though, I thought you was for him. Still you'll have to wait if he's hiding in the Forests of Lune." Rudesind looked up at the picture with obvious appreciation before turning back to me. "I'm forgetting. You want to visit our Master Ultan. Go back to that arch you just come by—"

"I know the way," I said. "The armiger told me."

The old curator blew those directions to the winds with a puff of sour breath. "What he laid down would only get you to the Reading Room. From there it'd take you a watch to get to Ultan, if ever you did. No, step back to that arch. Go through and all the way to the end of the big room there, and down the stair. You'll come to a locked door—pound till somebody lets you in. That's the bottom of the stacks, and that's where Ultan has his study."

Since Rudesind was watching I followed his directions, though I had not liked the part about the locked door, and steps downward suggested I might be nearing those ancient tunnels where I had wandered looking for Triskele.

On the whole I felt far less confident than when I was in those parts of the Citadel that I knew. I have learned since that strangers who visit it are awed by its size; but it is only a mote in the city spread about it, and we who grew up within the gray curtain wall, and have learned the names and relationships of the hundred or so landmarks necessary to those who would find their way in it, are by that very knowledge discomfited when we find ourselves away from the familiar regions.

So it was with me as I walked through the arch the old man had indicated. Like the rest of that vaulted hall it was of dull, reddish brick, but it was upheld by two pillars whose capitals bore the faces of sleepers, and I found the silent lips and pale, closed eyes more terrible than the agonized masks painted on the metal of our own tower.

Each picture in the room beyond contained a book. Sometimes they were many, or prominent; some I had to study for some time before I saw the corner of a binding thrusting from the pocket of a woman's skirt or realized that some strangely wrought spool held words spun like thread.

The steps were narrow and steep and without railings; they twisted as they descended, so that I had not gone down more than thirty before the light of the room above was nearly cut off. At last I was forced to put my hands before me and feel my way for fear I would break my head on the door.

My questing fingers never encountered it. Instead the steps

ended (and I nearly fell in stepping off a step that was not there), and I was left to grope across an uneven floor in total darkness.

"Who's there?" a voice called. It was a strangely resonant one, like the sound of a bell tolled inside a cave.

VI

The Master of the Curators

"WHO'S THERE?" ECHOED IN THE DARK. AS BOLDLY AS I COULD, I said, "Someone with a message."

"Let me hear it then."

My eyes were growing used to the dark at last, and I could just make out a dim and very lofty shape moving among dark, ragged shapes that were taller still. "It is a letter, sieur," I answered. "Are you Master Ultan the curator?"

"None other." He was standing before me now. What I had at first thought was a whitish garment now appeared to be a beard reaching nearly to his waist. I was as tall already as many men who are called so, but he was a head and a half taller than I, a true exultant.

"Then here you are, sieur," I said, and held out the letter.

He did not take it. "Whose apprentice are you?" Again I seemed to hear bronze, and quite suddenly I felt that he and I were dead, and that the darkness surrounding us was grave soil pressing in about our eyes, grave soil through which the bell called us to worship at whatever shrines may exist below ground. The livid woman I had seen dragged from her grave rose before me so vividly that I seemed to see her face in the almost luminous whiteness of the figure who spoke. "Whose apprentice?" he asked again.

"No one's. That is, I am an apprentice of our guild. Master

Gurloes sent me, sieur. Master Palaemon teaches us apprentices, mostly."

"But not grammar." Very slowly the tall man's hand groped toward the letter.

"Oh yes, grammar too." I felt like a child talking to this man, who had already been old when I was born. "Master Palaemon says we must be able to read and write and calculate, because when we are masters in our time, we'll have to send letters and receive the instructions of the courts, and keep records and accounts."

"Like this," the dim figure before me intoned. "Letters such as this."

"Yes, sieur. Just so."

"And what does this say?"

"I don't know. It's sealed, sieur."

"If I open it—" (I heard the brittle wax snap under the pressure of his fingers) "—will you read it to me?"

"It's dark in here, sieur," I said doubtfully.

"Then we'll have to have Cyby. Excuse me." In the gloom I could barely see him turn away and raise his hands to form a trumpet. *"Cy-by! Cy-by!"* The name rang through the dark corridors I sensed all about me as the iron tongue struck the echoing bronze on one side, then the other.

There was an answering call from far off. For some time we waited in silence.

At last I saw light down a narrow alley bordered (as it seemed) by precipitous walls of uneven stone. It came nearer—a five-branched candlestick carried by a stocky, very erect man of forty or so with a flat, pale face. The bearded man beside me said, "There you are at last, Cyby. Have you brought a light?"

"Yes, Master. Who is this?"

"A messenger with a letter." In a more ceremonious tone, Master Ultan said to me, "This is my own apprentice, Cyby. We have a guild too, we curators, of whom the librarians are a division. I am the only master librarian here, and it is our custom to assign our apprentices to our senior members. Cyby has been mine for some years now."

I told Cyby that I was honored to meet him, and asked, somewhat timidly, what the feast day of the curators was—a question that must have been suggested by the thought that a great many of them must have gone by without Cyby's being elevated to journeyman.

"It is now passed," Master Ultan said. He looked toward me as he spoke, and in the candlelight I could see that his eyes were the color of watered milk. "In early spring. It is a beautiful day. The trees put out their new leaves then, in most years."

There were no trees in the Grand Court, but I nodded; then, realizing he could not see me, I said, "Yes, beautiful with soft breezes."

"Precisely. You are a young man after my own heart." He put his hand on my shoulder—I could not help noticing that his fingers were dark with dust. "Cyby, too, is a young man after my heart. He will be chief librarian here when I am gone. We have a procession, you know, we curators. Down Iubar Street. He walks beside me then, the two of us robed in gray. What is the tinct of your own guild?"

"Fuligin," I told him. "The color that is darker than black."

"There are trees—sycamores and oaks, rock maples and duckfoot trees said to be the oldest on Urth. The trees spread their shade on either side of Iubar Street, and there are more on the esplanades down the center. Shopkeepers come to their doors to see the quaint curators, you know, and of course the booksellers and antique dealers cheer us. I suppose we are one of the spring sights of Nessus, in our little way."

"It must be very impressive," I said.

"It is, it is. The cathedral is very fine too, once we reach it. There are banks of tapers, as though the sun were shining on the night sea. And candles in blue glass to symbolize the Claw. Enfolded in light, we conduct our ceremonies before the high altar. Tell me, does your own guild go to the cathedral?"

I explained that we used the chapel here in the Citadel, and expressed surprise that the librarians and other curators left its walls.

"We are entitled to, you see. The library itself does—doesn't it, Cyby?"

"Indeed it does, Master." Cyby had a high square forehead, from which his graying hair was in retreat. It made his face seem small and a trifle babyish; I could understand how Ultan, who must occasionally have run his fingers over it as Master Palaemon sometimes ran his over mine, could think him still almost a boy.

"You are in close contact, then, with your opposite numbers in the city," I said.

The old man stroked his beard. "The closest, for we are they. This library is the city library, and the library of the House Absolute too, for that matter. And many others."

"Do you mean that the rabble of the city is permitted to enter the Citadel to use your library?"

"No," said Ultan. "I mean that the library itself extends beyond the walls of the Citadel. Nor, I think, is it the only institution here that does so. It is thus that the contents of our fortress are so much larger than their container."

He took me by the shoulder as he spoke, and we began to walk down one of the long, narrow paths between the towering bookcases. Cyby followed us holding up his candelabrum—I suppose more for his benefit than mine, but it permitted me to see well enough to keep from colliding with the dark oak shelves we passed. "Your eyes have not yet failed you," Master Ultan said after a time. "Do you apprehend any termination to this aisle?"

"No, sieur," I said, and in fact I did not. As far as the candlelight flew there was only row upon row of books stretching from the floor to the high ceiling. Some of the shelves were disordered, some straight; once or twice I saw evidence that rats had been nesting among the books, rearranging them to make snug two- and three-level homes for themselves and smearing dung on the covers to form the rude characters of their speech.

But always there were books and more books: rows of spines in calf, morocco, binder's cloth, paper, and a hundred other substances I could not identify, some flashing with gilt, many lettered in black, a few with paper labels so old and yellowed that they were as brown as dead leaves.

"'Of the trail of ink there is no end,'" Master Ultan told me. "Or so a wise man said. He lived long ago—what would he say if he could see us now? Another said, 'A man will give his life to the turning over of a collection of books,' but I would like to meet the man who could turn over this one, on any topic."

"I was looking at the bindings," I answered, feeling rather foolish.

"How fortunate for you. Yet I am glad. I can no longer see them, but I remember the pleasure I once had in doing it. That would be just after I had become master librarian. I suppose I was about fifty. I had, you know, been an apprentice for many, many years."

"Is that so, sieur?"

"Indeed it is. My master was Gerbold, and for decades it appeared that he would never die. Year followed straggling year for me, and all that time I read—I suppose few have ever read so. I began, as most young people do, by reading the books I enjoyed. But I found that narrowed my pleasure, in time, until I spent most of my hours searching for such books. Then I devised a plan of study for myself, tracing obscure sciences, one after another, from the dawn of knowledge to the present. Eventually I exhausted even that, and beginning at the great ebony case that stands in the center of the room we of the library have maintained for three hundred years against the return of the Autarch Sulpicius (and into which, in consequence, no one ever comes) I read outward for a period of fifteen years, often finishing two books in one day."

Behind us, Cyby murmured, "Marvelous, sieur." I suspected that he had heard the story many times.

"Then the unlooked-for seized me by the coat. Master Gerbold died. Thirty years before I had been ideally suited by reason of predilection, education, experience, youth, family connections, and ambition to succeed him. At the time I actually did so, no one could have been less fit. I had waited so long that waiting was all I understood, and I possessed a mind suffocated beneath the weight of inutile facts. But I forced myself to take charge, and spent more hours than I could expect you to believe now in attempting to recall the plans and maxims I had laid down so many years ago for my eventual succession."

He paused, and I knew he was delving again in a mind larger and darker than even his great library. "But my old habit of reading dogged me still. I lost to books days and even weeks, during which I should have been considering the operations of the establishment that looked to me for leadership. Then, as suddenly as the striking of a clock, a new passion came to me, displacing the old. You will already have guessed what it was."

I told him I had not.

"I was reading—or so I thought—on the seat of that bow window on the forty-ninth floor that overlooks—I have forgotten, Cyby. What is it that it overlooks?"

"The upholsterers' garden, sieur."

"Yes, I recall it now—that little square of green and brown. I believe they dry rosemary there to put in pillows. I was sitting there, as I said, and had been for several watches, when it came to me that I was reading no longer. For some time I was hard put to say what I had been doing. When I tried, I could only think of certain odors and textures and colors that seemed to have no connection with anything discussed in the volume I held. At last I realized that instead of reading it, I had been observing it as a physical object. The red I recalled came from the ribbon sewn to the headband so that I might mark my place. The texture that tickled my fingers still was that of the paper on which the book was printed. The smell in my nostrils was old leather, still bearing the traces of birch oil. It was only then, when I saw the books themselves, that I began to understand their care."

His grip on my shoulder tightened. "We have books here bound in the hides of echidnes, krakens, and beasts so long extinct that those whose studies they are, are for the most part of the opinion that no trace of them survives unfossilized. We have books bound wholly in metals of unknown alloy, and books whose bindings are covered with thickset gems. We have books cased in perfumed woods shipped across the inconceivable gulf between creations—books doubly precious because no one on Urth can read them.

"We have books whose papers are matted of plants from which spring curious alkaloids, so that the reader, in turning their pages, is taken unaware by bizarre fantasies and chimeric dreams. Books whose pages are not paper at all, but delicate wafers of white jade, ivory, and shell; books too whose leaves are the desiccated leaves of unknown plants. Books we have also that are not books at all to the eye: scrolls and tablets and recordings on a hundred different substances.

There is a cube of crystal here—though I can no longer tell you where—no larger than the ball of your thumb that contains more books than the library itself does. Though a harlot might dangle it from one ear for an ornament, there are not volumes enough in the world to counterweight the other. All these I came to know, and I made safeguarding them my life's devotion.

"For seven years I busied myself with that; and then, just when the pressing and superficial problems of preservation were disposed of, and we were on the point of beginning the first general survey of the library since its foundation, my eyes began to gutter in their sockets. He who had given all books into my keeping made me blind so that I should know in whose keeping the keepers stand."

"If you can't read the letter I brought, sieur," I said, "I will be glad to read it to you."

"You are right," Master Ultan muttered. "I had forgotten it. Cyby will read it—he reads well. Here, Cyby."

I held the candelabrum for him, and Cyby unfolded the crackling parchment, held it up like a proclamation, and began to read, the three of us standing in a little circle of candlelight while all the books crowded around.

"'From Master Gurloes of the Order of the Seekers for Truth and Penitence—'"

"What," said Master Ultan. "Are you a torturer, young man?"

I told him I was, and there occurred a silence so long that Cyby began to read the letter a second time: "'From Master Gurloes of the Order of the Seekers—'"

"Wait," Ultan said. Cyby paused again; I stood as I had, holding the light and feeling the blood mounting to my cheeks. At last Master Ultan spoke again, and his voice was as matter-of-fact as it had been in telling me Cyby read well. "I can hardly recall my own admission to our guild. You are familiar, I suppose, with the method by which we recruit our numbers?"

I admitted I was not.

"In every library, by ancient precept, is a room reserved for children. In it are kept bright picture books such as children delight in, and a few simple tales of wonder and adventure. Many children come to these rooms, and so long as they remain within their confines, no interest is taken in them."

He hesitated, and though I could discern no expression on his face, I received the impression that he feared what he was about to say might cause Cyby pain.

"From time to time, however, a librarian remarks a solitary child, still of tender years, who wanders from the children's room . . . and at last deserts it entirely. Such a child eventually discovers, on some low but obscure shelf, *The Book of Gold.* You have never seen this book, and you will never see it, being past the age at which it is met."

"It must be very beautiful," I said.

"It is indeed. Unless my memory betrays me, the cover is of black buckram, considerably faded at the spine. Several of the signatures are coming out, and certain of the plates have been taken. But it is a remarkably lovely book. I wish that I might find it again, though all books are shut to me now.

"The child, as I said, in time discovers *The Book of Gold.* Then the librarians come—like vampires, some say, but others say like the fairy godparents at a christening. They speak to the child, and the child joins them. Henceforth he is in the library wherever he may be, and soon his parents know him no more. I suppose it is much the same among the torturers."

"We take such children as fall into our hands," I said, "and are very young."

"We do the same," old Ultan muttered. "So we have little right to condemn you. Read on, Cyby."

" 'From Master Gurloes of the Order of the Seekers for Truth and Penitence, to the Archivist of the Citadel: Greetings, Brother.

" 'By the will of a court we have in our keeping the exulted person of the Chatelaine Thecla; and by its further will we would furnish to the Chatelaine Thecla in her confinement such comforts as lie not beyond reason and prudence. That she may while away the moments until her time with us is come—or rather, as she has instructed me to say, until the heart of the Autarch, whose forebearance knows not walls nor seas, is softened toward her, as she prays—she asks that you, consonant with your office, provide her with certain books, which books are—' "

"You may omit the titles, Cyby," Ultan said. "How many are there?"

"Four, sieur."

"No trouble then. Proceed."

" 'For this, Archivist, we are much obligated to you.' Signed, 'Gurloes, Master of the Honorable Order commonly called the Guild of Torturers.' "

"Are you familiar with any of the titles on Master Gurloes's list, Cyby?"

"With three, sieur."

"Very good. Fetch them, please. What is the fourth? *The Book of the Wonders of Urth and Sky*, sieur."

"Better and better—there is a copy not two chains from here. When you have your volumes, you may meet us at the door through which this young man, whom I fear we have already detained too long, entered the stacks."

I attempted to return the candelabrum to Cyby, but he indicated by a sign that I was to keep it and trotted off down a narrow aisle. Ultan was stalking away in the opposite direction, moving as surely as if he possessed vision. "I recollect it well," he said. "The binding is of brown cordwain, all edges are gilt, and there are etchings by Gwinoc, hand-tinted. It is on the third shelf from the floor, and leans against a folio in green cloth—I believe it is Blaithmaic's *Lives of the Seventeen Megatherians.*"

Largely to let him know I had not left him (though no doubt his sharp ears caught my footfalls behind him), I asked, "What is it, sieur? The Urth and sky book, I mean."

"Why," he said, "don't you know better than to ask that question of a librarian? Our concern, young man, is with the books themselves, not with their contents."

I caught the amusement in his tone. "I think you know the contents of every book here, sieur."

"Hardly. But *Wonders of Urth and Sky* was a standard work, three or four hundred years ago. It relates most of the familiar legends of ancient times. To me the most interesting is that of the Historians, which tells of a time in which every legend could be traced to half-forgotten fact. You see the paradox, I assume. Did that legend itself exist at that time? And if not, how came it into existence?"

"Aren't there any great serpents, sieur, or flying women?"

"Oh, yes," Master Ultan answered, stooping as he spoke. "But not in the legend of the Historians." Triumphantly, he held up a small volume bound in flaking leather. "Have a look at this, young man, and see if I've got the right one."

I had to set the candelabrum on the floor and crouch beside it. The book in my hands was so old and stiff and musty that it seemed impossible that it had been opened within the past century, but the title page confirmed the old man's boast. A subtitle announced: "Being a Collection from Printed Sources of Universal Secrets of Such Age That Their Meaning Has Become Obscured of Time."

"Well," asked Master Ultan, "was I right or no?"

I opened the book at random and read, ". . . by which means a picture might be graven with such skill that the whole of it, should it be destroyed, might be recreated from a small part, and that small part might be any part."

I suppose it was the word *graven* that suggested to me the events I had witnessed on the night I had received my chrisos. "Master," I answered, "you are phenomenal."

"No, but I am seldom mistaken."

"You, of all men, will excuse me when I tell you I tarried a moment to read a few lines of this book. Master, you know of the corpse-eaters, surely. I have heard it said that by devouring the flesh of the dead, together with a certain pharmacon, they are able to relive the lives of their victims."

"It is unwise to know too much about these practices," the archivist murmured, "though when I think of sharing the mind of a historian like Loman, or Hermas . . ." In his years of blindness he must have forgotten how nakedly our faces can betray our deepest feelings. By the light of the candles I saw his twisted in such an agony of desire that out of decency I turned away; his voice remained as calm as some solemn bell. "But from what I once read, you are correct, though I do not now recall that the book you hold treats of it."

"Master," I said, "I give you my word I would never suspect you of such a thing. But tell me this—suppose two collaborate in the robbing of a grave, and one takes the right hand for his share, and the other the left. Does he who ate the right hand have but half the dead man's life, and the other the rest? And if so, what if a third were to come and devour a foot?"

"It's a pity you are a torturer," Ultan said. "You might have been a philosopher. No, as I understand this noxious matter, each has the entire life."

"Then a man's whole life is in his right hand and in his left as well. Is it in each finger too?"

"I believe each participant must consume more than a mouthful for the practice to be effective. But I suppose that in theory at least, what you say is correct. The entire life is in each finger."

We were already walking back in the direction we had come. Since the aisle was too narrow for us to pass one another, I now carried the candelabrum before him, and a stranger, seeing us, would surely have thought I lighted his way. "But Master," I said, "how can that be? By the same argument, the life must reside in each joint of every finger, and surely that is impossible."

"How big is a man's life?" asked Ultan.

"I have no way of knowing, but isn't it larger than that?"

"You see it from the beginning, and anticipate much. I, recollecting it from its termination, know how little there has been. I suppose that is why the depraved creatures who devour the bodies of the dead seek more. Let me ask you this—are you aware that a son often strikingly resembles his father?"

"I have heard it said, yes. And I believe it," I answered. I could not help thinking as I did of the parents I would never know.

"Then it is possible, you will agree, since each son may resemble his father, for a face to endure through many generations. That is, if the son resembles the father, and *his* son resembles him, and that son's son resembles him, then the fourth in line, the great-grandson, resembles his great-grandfather."

"Yes," I said.

"Yet the seed of all of them was contained in a drachm of sticky fluid. If they did not come from there, from where did they come?"

I could make no answer to that, and walked along in puzzlement until we reached the door through which I had entered this lowest level of the great library. Here we met Cyby carrying the other books mentioned in Master

Gurloes's letter. I took them from him, bade goodbye to
Master Ultan, and very gratefully left the stifling atmosphere
of the library stacks. To the upper levels of that place I
returned several times; but I never again entered that
tomblike cellar, or ever wished to.

One of the three volumes Cyby had brought was as large as
the top of a small table, a cubit in width and a scant ell in
height; from the arms impressed upon its saffian cover, I
supposed it to be the history of some old noble family. The
others were much smaller. A green book hardly larger than
my hand and no thicker than my index finger appeared to be a
collection of devotions, full of enameled pictures of ascetic
pantocrators and hypostases with black halos and gemlike
robes. I stopped for a time to look at them, sharing a little,
forgotten garden full of winter sunshine with a dry fountain.

Before I had so much as opened any of the other volumes, I
felt that pressure of time that is perhaps the surest indication
we have left childhood behind. I had already been two
watches at least on a simple errand, and soon the light would
fade. I gathered up the books and hurried along, though I did
not know it, to meet my destiny and eventually myself in the
Chatelaine Thecla.

VII

The Traitress

IT WAS ALREADY TIME FOR ME TO CARRY THEIR MEALS TO THE
journeymen on duty in the oubliette. Drotte was in charge of
the first level, and I brought his last because I wanted to talk
to him before I went up again. The truth was that my head
was still swimming with thoughts engendered by my visit to
the archivist, and I wanted to tell him about them.

He was nowhere to be seen. I put his tray and the four

books on his table and shouted for him. A moment later I
heard his answering call from a cell not far off. I ran there and
looked through the grilled window set at eye level in the door;
the client, a wasted-looking woman of middle age, was
stretched on her cot. Drotte leaned over her, and there was
blood on the floor.

He was too occupied to turn his head. "Is that you,
Severian?"

"Yes. I've got your supper, and books for the Chatelaine
Thecla. Can I do anything to help?"

"She'll be all right. Tore her dressings off and tried to bleed
herself to death, but I got her in time. Leave my tray on my
table, will you? And you might finish shoving their food at the
rest for me, if you've got a moment."

I hesitated. Apprentices were not supposed to deal with
those committed to the guild's care.

"Go ahead. All you have to do is poke the trays through
the slots."

"I brought the books."

"Poke those through the slot too."

For a moment more I watched him as he bent over the livid
woman on the cot; then I turned away, found the undistribu-
ted trays, and began to do as he had asked. Most of the clients
in the cells were still strong enough to rise and take the food
as I passed it through. A few were not, and I left their trays
outside their doors for Drotte to carry in later. There were
several aristocratic-looking women, but none who seemed
likely to be the Chatelaine Thecla, a newly come exultant who
was—at least for the time being—to be treated with defer-
ence.

As I should have guessed, she was in the last cell. It had
been furnished with a carpet in addition to the usual bed,
chair, and small table; in place of the customary rags she wore
a white gown with wide sleeves. The ends of those sleeves and
the hem of the skirt were sadly soiled now, but the gown still
preserved an air of elegance as foreign to me as it was to the
cell itself. When I first saw her, she was embroidering by the
light of a candle brightened by a silver reflector; but she must
have felt my eyes upon her. It would gratify me now to say
there was no fear in her face, yet it would not be true. There
was terror there, though controlled nearly to invisibility.

"It's all right," I said. "I've brought your food."

She nodded and thanked me, then rose and came to the door. She was taller even than I had expected, nearly too tall to stand upright in the cell. Her face, though it was triangular rather than heart-shaped, reminded me of the woman who had been with Vodalus in the necropolis. Perhaps it was her great violet eyes, with their lids shaded with blue, and the black hair that, forming a V far down her forehead, suggested the hood of a cloak. Whatever the reason, I loved her at once—loved her, at least, insofar as a stupid boy can love. But being only a stupid boy, I did not know it.

Her white hand, cold, slightly damp, and impossibly narrow, touched mine as she took the tray from me. "That's ordinary food," I told her. "I think you can get some that's better if you ask."

"You're not wearing a mask," she said. "Yours is the first human face I've seen here."

"I'm only an apprentice. I won't be masked until next year."

She smiled, and I felt as I had when I had been in the Atrium of Time and had come inside to a warm room and food. She had narrow, very white teeth in a wide mouth; her eyes, each as deep as the cistern beneath the Bell Keep, shone when she smiled.

"I'm sorry," I said. "I didn't hear you."

The smile came again and she tilted her lovely head to one side. "I told you how happy I was to see your face, and asked if you would bring my meals in the future, and what this was you brought me."

"No. No, I won't be. Only today, because Drotte is occupied." I tried to recall what her meal had been (she had put the tray on her little table, where I could not see its contents through the grill). I could not, though I nearly burst my brain with the effort. At last I said lamely, "You'd probably better eat it. But I think you can get better food if you ask Drotte."

"Why, I intend to eat it. People have always complimented me on my slender figure, but believe me, I eat like a dire wolf." She picked up the tray and held it out to me, as though she knew I would need every help in unraveling the mystery of its contents.

"Those are leeks, Chatelaine," I said. "Those green things. The brown ones are lentils. And that's bread."

" 'Chatelaine'? You needn't be so formal. You're my jailer, and can call me anything you choose." There was merriment in the deep eyes now.

"I have no wish to insult you," I told her. "Would you rather I called you something else?"

"Call me Thecla—that's my name. Titles are for formal occasions, names for informal ones, and this is that or nothing. I suppose it will be very formal though, when I receive my punishment?"

"It is, usually, for exultants."

"There will be an exarch, I should think, if you will let him in. All in scarlet patches. Several others too—perhaps the Starost Egino. Are you certain this is bread?" She poked it with one long finger, so white I thought for a moment that the bread might soil it.

"Yes," I said. "The Chatelaine has eaten bread before, surely?"

"Not like this." She picked the meager slice up and tore it with her teeth, quickly and cleanly. "It isn't bad, though. You say they'll bring me better food if I ask for it?"

"I think so, Chatelaine."

"Thecla. I asked for books—two days ago when I came. But I haven't got them."

"I have them," I told her. "Right here." I ran back to Drotte's table and got them, and passed the smallest through the slot.

"Oh, wonderful! Are there others?"

"Three more." The brown book went through the slot as well, but the other two, the green book and the folio volume with arms on its cover, were too wide. "Drotte will open your door later and give them to you," I said.

"Can't you? It's terrible to look through this and see them, and not be able to touch them."

"I'm not even supposed to feed you. Drotte should do it."

"But you did. Besides, you brought them. Weren't you supposed to give them to me?"

I could argue only weakly, knowing she was right in principle. The rule against apprentices working in the oubli- ette was intended to prevent escapes; and I knew that tall though she was, this slender woman could never overpower me, and that should she do so she would have no chance of making her way out without being challenged. I went to the door of the cell where Drotte still labored over the client who had tried to take her own life, and returned with his keys.

Standing before her, with her own cell door closed and locked behind me, I found myself unable to speak. I put the books on her table beside the candlestand and her food pan and carafe of water; there was hardly room for them. When it was done I stood waiting, knowing I should leave and yet unable to go.

"Won't you sit down?"

I sat on her bed, leaving her the chair.

"If this were my suite in the House Absolute, I could offer you better comfort. Unfortunately, you never called while I was there."

I shook my head.

"Here I have no refreshment to offer you but this. Do you like lentils?"

"I won't eat that, Chatelaine. I'll have my own supper soon, and there's hardly enough for you."

"True." She picked up a leek, and then as if she did not know what else to do with it dropped it down her throat like a mountebank swallowing a viper. "What will you have?"

"Leeks and lentils, bread and mutton."

"Ah, the torturers get mutton—that's the difference. What's your name, Master Torturer?"

"Severian. It won't help, Chatelaine. It won't make any difference."

She smiled. "What won't?"

"Making friends with me. I couldn't give you your freedom. And I wouldn't—not if I had no friend but you in all the world."

"I didn't think you could, Severian."

"Then why do you bother to talk to me?"

She sighed, and all the gladness went out of her face, as the sunlight leaves the stone where a beggar seeks to warm himself. "Who else have I to talk to, Severian? It may be that I will talk to you for a time, for a few days or a few weeks, and die. I know what you're thinking—that if I were back in my suite I would never spare a glance for you. But you're wrong.

One can't talk to everyone because there are so many everyones, but the day before I was taken I talked for some time with the man who held my mount. I spoke to him because I had to wait, you see, and then he said something that interested me."

"You won't see me again. Drotte will bring your food."

"And not you? Ask him if he will let you do it." She took my hands in hers, and they were like ice.

"I'll try," I said.

"Do. Do try. Tell him I want better meals than this, and you to serve me—wait, I'll ask him myself. To whom does he answer?"

"Master Gurloes."

"I'll tell the other—is it Drotte?—that I want to speak to him. You're right, they'll have to do it. The Autarch might release me—they don't know." Her eyes flashed.

"I'll tell Drotte you want to see him when he's not busy," I said, and stood up.

"Wait. Aren't you going to ask me why I'm here?"

"I know why you're here," I said as I swung back the door. "To be tortured, eventually, like the others." It was a cruel thing to say, and I said it without reflection as young men do, only because it was what was in my mind. Yet it was true, and I was glad in some way, as I turned the key in the lock, that I had said it.

We had had exultants for clients often before. Most, when they arrived, had some understanding of their situation, as the Chatelaine Thecla did now. But when a few days' d passed and they were not put to torment, their hope cast down their reason and they began to talk of release—how friends and family would maneuver to gain their freedom, and of what they would do when they were free.

One would withdraw to his estates and trouble the Autarch's court no more. Another would volunteer to lead a muster of lansquenets in the north. Then the journeymen on duty in the oubliette would hear tales of hunting dogs and remote heaths, and country games, unknown elsewhere, played beneath immemorial trees. The women were more realistic for the most part, but even they in time spoke of highly placed lovers (cast aside now for months or years) who would never abandon them, and then of bearing children or adopting waifs. One knew when these never-to-be-born children were given names that clothing would not be far behind: a new wardrobe on their release, the old clothes to be burned; they talked of colors, of inventing new fashions and reviving old ones.

At last the time would come, to men and women alike, when instead of a journeyman with food, Master Gurloes would appear trailing three or four journeymen and perhaps an examiner and a fulgurator. I wanted to preserve the Chatelaine Thecla from such hopes if I could. I hung Drotte's keys on their accustomed nail in the wall, and when I passed the cell in which he was now swabbing blood from the floor told him that the chatelaine desired to speak with him.

On the next day but one, I was summoned to Master Gurloes. I had expected to stand, as we apprentices usually did, with hands behind back before his table; but he told me to sit, and removing his gold-traced mask, leaned toward me in a way that implied a common cause and friendly footing.

"A week ago, or a little less, I sent you to the archivist," he said.

I nodded.

"When you brought the books, I take it you delivered them to the client yourself. Is that right?"

I explained what had happened.

"Nothing wrong there. I don't want you to think I'm going to order extra fatigues for what you did, much less have you bent over a chair. You're nearly a journeyman yourself already—when I was your age, they had me cranking the alternator. The thing is, you see, Severian, the client is highly placed." His voice sank to a rough whisper. "Quite highly connected."

I said that I understood that.

"Not just an armiger family. High blood." He turned, and after searching the disorderly shelves behind his chair produced a squat book. "Have you any notion how many exulted families there are? This lists only the ones that are still going. A compendium of the extinguished ones would take an encyclopedia, I suppose. I've extinguished a few of them myself."

He laughed and I laughed with him.

"It gives about half a page to each. There are seven hundred and forty-six pages."

I nodded to show I understood.

"Most of them have nobody at court—can't afford it, or are afraid of it. Those are the small ones. The greater families must: the Autarch wants a concubine he can lay hands on if they start misbehaving. Now the Autarch can't play quadrille with five hundred women. There are maybe twenty. The rest talk to each other, and dance, and don't see him closer than a chain off once in a month."

I asked (trying to hold my voice steady) if the Autarch actually bedded these concubines.

Master Gurloes rolled his eyes and pulled at his jaw with one huge hand. "Well now, for decency's sake they have these khaibits, what they call the shadow women, that are common girls that look like the chatelaines. I don't know where they get them, but they're supposed to stand in place of the others. Of course they're not so tall." He chuckled. "I said stand in place, but when they're laying down the tallness probably doesn't make much difference. They do say, though, that oftentimes it works the other way than it's supposed to. Instead of those shadow girls doing duty for their mistresses, the mistresses do it for them. But the present Autarch, whose every deed, I may say, is sweeter than honey in the mouths of this honorable guild and don't you forget it—in his case, I may say, from what I understand it is more than somewhat doubtful if he has the pleasure of any of them."

Relief flooded my heart. "I never knew that. It's very interesting, Master."

Master Gurloes inclined his head to acknowledge that it was indeed, and laced his fingers over his belly. "Someday you may have the ordering of the guild yourself. You'll need to know these things. When I was your age—or a trifle younger, I suppose—I used to fancy I was of exulted blood. Some have been, you know."

It struck me, and not for the first time, that Master Gurloes and Master Palaemon too must have known whence all the apprentices and younger journeymen had come, having approved their admissions originally.

"Whether I am or no, I cannot say. I have the physique of a rider, I think, and I am somewhat over the average in height despite a hard boyhood. For it was harder, much harder, forty years ago, I'll tell you."

"So I have been told, Master."

He sighed, the kind of wheezing noise a leather pillow sometimes makes when one sits on it. "But with the passage of time I have come to understand that the Increate, in choosing for me a career in our guild, was acting for my benefit. Doubtless I had acquired merit in a previous life, as I hope I have in this one."

Master Gurloes fell silent, looking (it seemed to me) at the jumble of papers on his table, the instructions of jurists and the dossiers of clients. At last, when I was about to ask if he had anything further to tell me, he said, "In all my years, I have never known of a member of the guild put to torment. Of them, several hundred, I suppose."

I ventured the commonplace saying that it was better to be a toad hidden under a stone than a butterfly crushed beneath it.

"We of the guild are more than toads, I think. But I should have added that though I have seen five hundred or more exultants in our cells, I have never, until now, had charge of a member of that inner circle of concubines closest to the Autarch."

"The Chatelaine Thecla belonged to it? You implied that a moment ago, Master."

He nodded gloomily. "It wouldn't be so bad if she were to be put to torment at once, but that isn't to be. It may be years. It may be never."

"You believe she may be released, Master?"

"She's a pawn in the Autarch's game with Vodalus—even I know that much. Her sister, the Chatelaine Thea, has fled the House Absolute to become his leman. They will bargain with Thecla for a time at least, and while they do, we must give her good fare. Yet not too good."

"I see," I said. I was acutely uncomfortable not knowing what the Chatelaine Thecla had told Drotte, and what Drotte had told Master Gurloes.

"She's asked for better food, and I've made arrangements to supply it. She's asked for company as well, and when we told her visitors would not be permitted, she urged that one of us, at least, should keep her company sometimes."

Master Gurloes paused to wipe his shining face with the edge of his cloak. I said, "I understand." I was fairly certain that I indeed understood what was to come next.

"Because she had seen your face, she asked for you. I told her you'll sit with her while she eats. I don't ask your agreement—not only because you're subject to my instructions, but because I know you're loyal. What I do ask is that you be careful not to displease her, and not to please her too much."

"I will do my best." I was surprised to hear my own steady voice.

Master Gurloes smiled as if I had eased him. "You've a good head, Severian, though it's a young one yet. Have you been with a woman?"

When we apprentices talked, it was the custom to invent fables on this topic, but I was not among apprentices now, and I shook my head.

"You've never been to the witches? That may be for the best. They supplied my own instruction in the warm commerce, but I'm not sure I'd send them another such as I was. It's likely, though, that the Chatelaine wants her bed warmed. You're not to do it for her. Her pregnancy would be no ordinary one—it might force a delay in her torment and bring disgrace on the guild. You follow me?"

I nodded.

"Boys your age are troubled. I'll have somebody take you where such ills are speedily cured."

"As you wish, Master."

"What? You don't thank me?"

"Thank you, Master," I said.

Gurloes was one of the most complex men I have known, because he was a complex man trying to be simple. Not a simple, but a complex man's idea of simplicity. Just as a courtier forms himself into something brilliant and involved, midway between a dancing master and a diplomacist, with a touch of assassin if needed, so Master Gurloes had shaped himself to be the dull creature a pursuivant or bailiff expected to see when he summoned the head of our guild, and that is the only thing a real torturer cannot be. The strain showed; though every part of Gurloes was as it should have been, none of the parts fit. He drank heavily and suffered from nightmares, but he had the nightmares when he had been drinking, as if the wine, instead of bolting the doors of his mind, threw them open and left him staggering about in the last hours of the night, trying to catch a glimpse of a sun that had not yet appeared, a sun that would banish the phantoms from his big cabin and permit him to dress and send the journeymen to their business. Sometimes he went to the top of our tower, above the guns, and waited there talking to himself, peering through glass said to be harder than flint for the first beams. He was the only one in our guild—Master Palaemon not excepted—who was unafraid of the energies there and the unseen mouths that spoke sometimes to human beings and sometimes to other mouths in other towers and keeps. He loved music, but he thumped the arm of his chair to it and tapped his foot, and did so most vigorously to the kind he liked best, whose rhythms were too subtle for any regular cadence. He ate too much and too seldom, read when he thought no one knew of it, and visited certain of our clients, including one on the third level, to talk of things none of us eavesdropping in the corridor outside could understand. His eyes were refulgent, brighter than any woman's. He mispronounced quite common words: *urticate, salpinx, bordereau.* I cannot tell you how bad he looked when I returned to the Citadel recently, how bad he looks now.

VIII

The Conversationalist

NEXT DAY, FOR THE FIRST TIME, I CARRIED THECLA'S SUPPER TO her. For a watch I remained with her, frequently observed through the slot in the cell door by Drotte. We played word games, at which she was far better than I, and after a while talked of those things those who have returned are said to say lie beyond death, she recounting what she had read in the smallest of the books I had brought her—not only the accepted views of the hierophants, but various eccentric and heretic theories.

"When I am free," she said, "I shall found my own sect. I will tell everyone that its wisdom was revealed to me during my sojourn among the torturers. They'll listen to that."

I asked what her teachings would be.

"That there is no agathodaemon or afterlife. That the mind is extinguished in death as in sleep, yet more so."

"But who will you say revealed that to you?"

She shook her head, then rested her pointed chin upon one hand, a pose that showed off the graceful line of her neck admirably. "I haven't decided yet. An angel of ice, perhaps. Or a ghost. Which do you think best?"

"Isn't there a contradiction in that?"

"Precisely." Her voice was rich with the pleasure the question gave her. "In that contradiction will reside the appeal of this new belief. One can't found a novel theology on Nothing, and nothing is so secure a foundation as a contradiction. Look at the great successes of the past—they say their deities are the masters of all the universes, and yet that they require grandmothers to defend them, as if they were children frightened by poultry. Or that the authority that punishes no one while there exists a chance for reformation will punish everyone when there is no possibility anyone will become the better for it."

I said, "These things are too complex for me."

"No they're not. You're as intelligent as most young men, I think. But I suppose you torturers have no religion. Do they make you swear to give it up?"

"Not at all. We've a celestial patroness and observances, just like any other guild."

"We don't," she said. For a moment she seemed to brood on that. "Only the guilds do, you know, and the army, which is a kind of guild. We'd be better off, I think, if we did. Still all the days of feast and nights of vigil have become shows, opportunities to wear new dresses. Do you like this?" She stood and extended her arms to show the soiled gown.

"It's very pretty," I ventured. "The embroidery, and the way the little pearls are sewed on."

"It's the only thing I have here—what I was wearing when I was taken. It's for dinner, really. After late afternoon and before early evening."

I said I was sure Master Gurloes would have others brought if she asked.

"I already have, and he says he sent some people to the House Absolute to fetch them for me, but they were unable to find it, which means that the House Absolute is trying to pretend I don't exist. Anyway, it's possible all my clothes have been sent to our chateau in the north, or one of the villas. He's going to have his secretary write them for me."

"Do you know who he sent?" I asked. "The House Absolute must be nearly as big as our Citadel, and I would think it would be impossible for anyone to miss."

"On the contrary, it's quite easy. Since it can't be seen, you can be there and never know it if you're not lucky. Besides, with the roads closed, all they have to do is alert their spies to give a particular party incorrect direction, and they have spies everywhere."

I started to ask how it was possible for the House Absolute (which I had always imagined a vast palace of gleaming towers and domed halls) to be invisible; but Thecla was already thinking of something else altogether, stroking a bracelet formed like a kraken, a kraken whose tentacles wrapped the white flesh of her arm; its eyes were cabochon emeralds. "They let me keep this, and it's quite valuable. Platinum, not silver. I was surprised."

"There's no one here who can be bribed."

"It might be sold in Nessus to buy clothing. Have any of my friends tried to see me? Do you know, Severian?"

I shook my head. "They would not be admitted."

"I understand, but someone might try. Do you know that most of the people in the House Absolute don't know this place exists? I see you don't believe me."

"You mean they don't know of the Citadel?"

"They're aware of that, of course. Parts of it are open to everyone, and anyway you can't miss seeing the spires if you get down into the southern end of the living city, no matter which side of Gyoll you're on." She slapped the metal wall of her cell with one hand. "They don't know of *this*—or at least, a great many of them would deny it still exists."

She was a great, great chatelaine, and I was something worse than a slave (I mean in the eyes of the common people, who do not really understand the functions of our guild). Yet when the time had passed and Drotte tapped the ringing door, it was I who rose and left the cell and soon climbed into the clean air of evening, and Thecla who stayed behind to listen to the moans and screams of the others. (Though her cell was some distance from the stairwell, the laughter from the third level was audible still when there was no one there to talk with her.)

In our dormitory that night I asked if anyone knew the names of the journeymen Master Gurloes had sent in search of the House Absolute. No one did, but my question stirred an animated discussion. Although none of the boys had seen the place or so much as spoken with anyone who had, all had heard stories. Most were of fabled wealth—gold plates and silk saddle blankets and that sort of thing. More interesting were the descriptions of the Autarch, who would have had to be a kind of monster to fit them all; he was said to be tall when standing, of common size seated, aged, young, a woman dressed as a man, and so on. More fantastic still were the tales of his vizier, the famous Father Inire, who looked like a monkey and was the oldest man in the world.

We had just begun trading wonders in good earnest when there was a knock at the door. The youngest opened it, and I saw Roche—dressed not in the fuligin breeches and cloak the regulations of the guild decree, but in common, though new and fashionable, trousers, shirt, and coat. He motioned to me, and when I came to the door to speak to him, he indicated that I was to follow him.

After we had gone some way down the stair, he said, "I'm afraid I frightened the little fellow. He doesn't know who I am."

"Not in those clothes," I told him. "He'd recall you if he saw you dressed the way you used to be."

That pleased him and he laughed. "Do you know, it felt so strange, having to bang on that door. Today is what? The eighteenth—it's been under three weeks. How are things going for you?"

"Well enough."

"You seem to have the gang in hand. Eata's your second, isn't he? He won't make a journeyman for four years, so he'll be captain for three after you. It's good for him to have the experience, and I'm sorry now you didn't have more before you had to take the job on. I stood in your way, but I never thought about it at the time."

"Roche, where are we going?"

"Well, first we're going down to my cabin to get you dressed. Are you looking forward to becoming a journeyman yourself, Severian?"

These last words were thrown over his shoulder as he clattered down the steps ahead of me, and he did not wait for an answer.

My costume was much like his, though of different colors. There were overcoats and caps for us too. "You'll be glad for them," he said as I put mine on. "It's cold out and starting to snow." He handed me a scarf and told me to take off my worn shoes and put on a pair of boots.

"They're journeymen's boots," I protested. "I can't wear those."

"Go ahead. Everyone wears black boots. Nobody will notice. Do they fit?"

They were too large, so he made me draw a pair of his stockings on over my own.

"Now, I'm supposed to keep the purse, but since there's always a chance we may be separated, it would be better if you have a few asimi." He dropped coins into my palm. "Ready? Let's go. I'd like to be back in time for some sleep if we can."

We left the tower, and muffled in our strange clothing rounded the Witches' Keep to take the covered walk leading past the Martello to the court called Broken. Roche had been right: it was starting to snow, fluffy flakes as big as the end of my thumb sifting so slowly through the air that it seemed they must have been falling for years. There was no wind, and we could hear the creaking our boots made in breaking through the familiar world's new, thin disguise.

"You're in luck," Roche told me. "I don't know how you worked this, but thank you."

"Worked what?"

"A trip to the Echopraxia and a woman for each of us. I know you know—Master Gurloes told me he'd already notified you."

"I had forgotten, and anyway I wasn't sure he meant it. Are we going to walk? It must be a long way."

"Not as long as you probably think, but I told you we have funds. There will be fiacres at the Bitter Gate. There always are—people are continually coming and going, though you wouldn't think it back in our little corner."

To make conversation, I told him what the Chatelaine Thecla had said: that many people in the House Absolute did not know we existed.

"That's so, I'm sure. When you're brought up in the guild it seems like the center of the world. But when you're a little older—this is what I've found myself, and I know I can rely on you not to tell tales—something pops in your head, and you discover it isn't the linchpin of this universe after all, only a well-paid, unpopular business you happen to have fallen into."

As Roche had predicted there were coaches, three of them, waiting in the Broken Court. One was an exultant's with blazonings painted on the doors and palfreniers in fanciful liveries, but the other two were fiacres, small and plain. The drivers in their low fur caps were bending over a fire they had kindled on the cobbles. Seen at a distance through the falling snow it seemed no bigger than a spark.

Roche waved an arm and shouted, and a driver vaulted into the seat, cracked his whip, and came rattling to meet us. When we were inside, I asked Roche if he knew who we were, and he said, "We're two optimates who had business in the Citadel and are bound now for the Echopraxia and an evening of pleasure. That's all he knows and all he needs to know."

I wondered if Roche were much more experienced at such pleasures than I was myself. It seemed unlikely. In the hope of discovering whether he had visited our destination before, I asked where the Echopraxia lay.

"In the Algedonic Quarter. Have you heard of it?"

I nodded and said that Master Palaemon had once mentioned that it was one of the oldest parts of the city.

"Not really. There are parts farther south that are older still, a waste of stone where only omophagists live. The Citadel used to stand some distance north of Nessus, did you know that?"

I shook my head.

"The city keeps creeping upriver. The armigers and optimates want purer water—not that they drink it, but for their fishponds, and for bathing and boating. Then too, anyone living too near the sea is always somewhat suspect. So the lowest parts, where the water's the worst, are gradually given up. In the end the law goes, and those who stay behind are afraid to kindle a fire for fear of what the smoke may draw down on them."

I was looking out the window. We had already passed through a gate unknown to me, dashing by helmeted guards; but we were still within the Citadel, descending a narrow close between two rows of shuttered windows.

"When you are a journeyman you can go into the city any time you want, provided you're not on duty."

I knew that already, of course; but I asked Roche if he found it pleasant.

"Not pleasant, exactly . . . I've only gone twice, to tell you the truth. Not pleasant, but interesting. They know who you are, naturally."

"You said the driver didn't."

"Well, he probably doesn't. Those drivers go all over Nessus. He may live anywhere, and not get to the Citadel more than once a year. But the locals know. The soldiers tell. They always know, and they always tell, that's what everybody says. They can wear their uniforms when they go out."

"These windows are all dark. I don't think there's anyone in this part of the Citadel at all."

"Everything's getting smaller. Not much anybody can do about that. Less food means fewer people until the New Sun comes."

Despite the cold, I felt stifled in the fiacre. "Is it much farther?" I asked.

Roche chuckled. "You're bound to be nervous."

"No, I'm not."

"Certainly you are. Just don't let it bother you. It's natural. Don't be nervous about being nervous, if you see what I mean."

"I'm quite calm."

"It can be quick, if that's what you want. You don't have to talk to the woman if you don't want to. She doesn't care. Of course, she'll talk if that's what you like. You're paying—in this case I am, but the principle's the same. She'll do what you want, within reason. If you strike her or use a grip, they'll charge more."

"Do people do that?"

"You know, amateurs. I didn't think you'd want to, and I don't think anybody in the guild does it, unless perhaps they're drunk." He paused. "The women are breaking the law, so they can't complain."

With the fiacre sliding alarmingly, we wheeled out of the close and into a still narrower one that ran crookedly east.

IX

The House Azure

OUR DESTINATION WAS ONE OF THOSE ACCRETIVE STRUCTURES seen in the older parts of the city (but so far as I know, only there) in which the accumulation and interconnection of what were originally separate buildings produce a confusion of jutting wings and architectural styles, with peaks and turrets where the first builders had intended nothing more than rooftops. The snow had fallen more heavily here—or perhaps had only been falling while we rode. It surrounded the high portico with shapeless mounds of white, softened and blurred the outlines of the entrance, made pillows of the window ledges, and masking and robing the wooden caryatids who supported the roof, seemed to promise silence, safety, and secrecy.

There were dim yellow lights in the lower windows. The upper stories were dark. In spite of the drifted snow, someone within must have heard our feet outside. The door, large and old and no longer in the best condition, swung back before Roche could knock. We entered and found ourselves in a narrow little room like a jewel box, in which the walls and ceiling were covered with blue satin quilting. The person who had admitted us wore thick-soled shoes and a yellow robe; his short, white hair was smoothed back from a wide but rounded brow above a beardless and unlined face. As I passed him in the doorway, I discovered that I was looking into his eyes as I might have looked into a window. Those eyes could truly have been of glass, so unveined and polished they seemed— like a sky of summer drought.

"You are in good fortune," he said, and handed us each a goblet. "There is no one here but yourselves."

Roche answered, "I'm sure the girls are lonesome."

"They are. You smile . . . I see you do not believe me, but it is so. They complain when too many attend their court, but they are sad, too, when no one comes. Each will try to fascinate you tonight. You'll see. They'll want to boast when you are gone that you chose them. Besides, you are both handsome young men." He paused, and though he did not stare, seemed to look at Roche more closely. "You have been here previously, have you not? I remember your red hair and high color. Far to the south, in the narrow lands, the savages paint a fire spirit much like you. And your friend has the face of an exultant . . . that is what my young women like best of all. I see why you brought him here." His voice might have been a man's tenor or a woman's contralto.

Another door opened. It had a stained-glass insert showing the Temptation. We went into a room that seemed (no doubt in part because of the constriction of the one we had just left) more spacious than the building could well sustain. The high ceiling was festooned with what appeared to be white silk, giving it the air of a pavilion. Two walls were lined with colonnades—these were false, the pretended columns being only half-round pilasters pressed against their blue-painted surfaces, and the architrave no more than a molding; but so long as we remained near the center, the effect was impressive and nearly perfect.

At the farther end of this chamber, opposite the windows, was a high-backed chair like a throne. Our host seated himself in it, and almost at once I heard a chime somewhere in the interior of the house. In two lesser chairs, Roche and I waited in silence while its clear echoes died. There was no sound from outside, yet I could sense the falling snow. My wine promised to hold the cold at bay, and in a few swallows I saw the bottom of the cup. It was as though I were awaiting the beginning of some ceremony in the ruined chapel, but at once less real and more serious.

"The Chatelaine Barbea," our host announced.

A tall woman entered. So poised was she, and so beautifully and daringly dressed, that it was several moments before I realized she could be no more than seventeen. Her face was oval and perfect, with limpid eyes, a small, straight nose, and a tiny mouth painted to appear smaller still. Her hair was so near to burnished gold that it might have been a wig of golden wires.

She posed herself a step or two before us and slowly began to revolve, striking a hundred graceful attitudes. At the time I had never seen a professional dancer; even now I do not believe I have seen one so beautiful as she. I cannot convey what I felt then, watching her in that strange room.

"All the beauties of the court are here for you," our host said. "Here in the House Azure, by night flown here from the walls of gold to find their dissipation in your pleasure."

Half hypnotized as I was, I thought this fantastic assertion had been put forward seriously. I said, "Surely that's not true."

"You came for pleasure, did you not? If a dream adds to your enjoyment, why dispute it?" All this time the girl with the golden hair continued her slow, unaccompanied dance.

Moment flowed into moment.

"Do you like her?" our host asked. "Do you choose her?"

I was about to say—to shout rather, feeling everything in me that had ever yearned for a woman yearning then—that I did. Before I could catch my breath, Roche said, "Let's see some of the others." The girl ended her dance at once, made an obeisance, and left the room.

"You may have more than one, you know. Separately or together. We have some very large beds." The door opened again. "The Chatelaine Gracia."

Though this girl seemed quite different, there was much about her that reminded me of the "Chatelaine Barbea" who had come before her. Her hair was as white as the flakes that floated past the windows, making her youthful face seem younger still, and her dark complexion darker. She had (or seemed to have) larger breasts and more generous hips. Yet I felt it was almost possible that it was the same woman after all, that she had changed clothing, changed wigs, dusked her face with cosmetics in the few seconds between the other's exit and her entrance. It was absurd, yet there was an element of truth in it, as in so many absurdities. There was something in the eyes of both women, in the expression of their mouths, their carriage and the fluidity of their gestures, that was one.

It recalled something I had seen elsewhere (I could not remember where), and yet it was new, and I felt somehow that the other thing, that which I had known earlier, was to be preferred.

"That will do for me," Roche said. "Now we must find something for my friend here." The dark girl, who had not danced as the other had, but had only stood, smiling very slightly, curtsying and turning in the center of the room, now permitted her smile to widen a trifle, went to Roche, seated herself on the arm of his chair, and began whispering to him.

As the door opened a third time, our host said, "The Chatelaine Thecla."

It seemed really she, just as I had remembered her—how she had escaped I could not guess. In the end it was reason rather than observation that told me I was mistaken. What differences I could have detected with the two standing side by side I cannot say, though certainly this woman was somewhat shorter.

"It is she you wish, then," our host said. I could not recall speaking.

Roche stepped forward with a leather purse, announcing that he would pay for both of us. I watched the coins as he drew them out, waiting to see the gleam of a chrisos. It was not there—there were only a few asimi.

The "Chatelaine Thecla" touched my hand. The scent she wore was stronger than the faint perfume of the real Thecla; still it was the same scent, making me think of a rose burning. "Come," she said.

I followed her. There was a corridor, dimly lit and not clean, then a narrow stair. I asked how many of the court were here, and she paused, looking down at me obliquely. Something there was in her face that might have been vanity satisfied, love, or that more obscure emotion we feel when what had been a contest becomes a performance. "Tonight, very few. Because of the snow. I came in a sleigh with Gracia."

I nodded. I thought I knew well enough that she had come only from one of the mean lanes about the house in which we were that night, and most likely on foot, with a shawl over her hair and the cold striking through old shoes. Yet what she said I found more meaningful than reality: I could sense the sweating destriers leaping through the falling snow faster than any machine, the whistling wind, the young, beautiful, jaded women bundled inside in sable and lynx, dark against red velvet cushions.

"Aren't you coming?"

She had already reached the top of the stair, nearly out of sight. Someone spoke to her, calling her "my dearest sister," and when I had gone up a few steps more I saw it was a woman very like the one who had been with Vodalus, she of the heart-shaped face and black hood. This woman paid no heed to me, and as soon as I gave her room to do so hurried down the stair.

"You see now what you might have had if you'd only waited for one more to come out." A smile I had learned to know elsewhere lurked at one corner of my paphian's mouth.

"I would have chosen you still."

"Now *that* is truly amusing—come on, come with me, you don't want to stand in this drafty hall forever. You kept a perfectly straight face, but your eyes rolled like a calf's. She's pretty, isn't she."

The woman who looked like Thecla opened a door, and we were in a tiny bedroom with an immense bed. A cold thurible hung from the ceiling by a silver-gilt chain; a lampstand supporting a pint-tinted light stood in one corner. There was a tiny dressing table with a mirror, a narrow wardrobe, and hardly room enough for us to move.

"Would you like to undress me?"

I nodded and reached for her.

"Then I warn you, you must be careful of my clothes." She turned away from me. "This fastens at the back. Begin at the top, at the back of my neck. If you get excited and tear something, he'll make you pay for it—don't say you haven't been told."

My fingers found a tiny catch and loosed it. "I would think, Chatelaine Thecla, that you would have plenty of clothes."

"I do. But do you think I want to return to the House Absolute in a torn gown?"

"You must have others here."

"A few, but I can't keep much in this place. Someone takes things when I'm gone."

The stuff between my fingers, which had looked so bright

and rich in the colonnaded blue room below, was thin and cheap. "No satins, I suppose," I said as I unfastened the next catch. "No sables and no diamonds."

"Of course not."

I took a step away from her. (It brought my back almost to the door.) There was nothing of Thecla about her. All that had been a chance resemblance, some gestures, a similarity in dress. I was standing in a small, cold room looking at the neck and bare shoulders of some poor young woman whose parents, perhaps, accepted their share of Roche's meager silver gratefully and pretended not to know where their daughter went at night.

"You are not the Chatelaine Thecla," I said. "What am I doing here with you?"

There was surely more in my voice than I had intended. She turned to face me, the thin cloth of her gown sliding away from her breasts. I saw fear flicker across her face as though directed by a mirror; she must have been in this situation before, and it must have turned out badly for her. "I am Thecla," she said. "If you want me to be."

I raised my hand and she added quickly, "There are people here to protect me. All I have to do is scream. You may hit me once, but you won't hit me twice."

"No," I told her.

"Yes there are. Three men."

"There is no one. This whole floor is empty and cold—don't you think I've noticed how quiet it is? Roche and his girl stayed below, and perhaps got a better room there because he paid. The woman we saw at the top of the stair was leaving and wanted to speak to you first. Look." I took her by the waist and lifted her into the air. "Scream. No one will come." She was silent. I dropped her on the bed, and after a moment sat down beside her.

"You are angry because I'm not Thecla. But I would have been Thecla for you. I will be still." She slipped the strange coat from my shoulders and let it fall. "You're very strong."

"No I'm not." I knew that some of the boys who were afraid of me were already stronger than I.

"Very strong. Aren't you strong enough to master reality, even for a little while?"

"What do you mean?"

"Weak people believe what is forced on them. Strong people what they wish to believe, forcing that to be real. What is the Autarch but a man who believes himself Autarch and makes others believe by the strength of it?"

"You are not the Chatelaine Thecla," I told her.

"But don't you see, neither is she. The Chatelaine Thecla, whom I doubt you've ever laid eyes on—No, I see I'm wrong. Have you been to the House Absolute?"

Her hands, small and warm, were on my own right hand, pressing. I shook my head.

"Sometimes clients say they have. I always find pleasure in hearing them."

"Have they been? Really?"

She shrugged. "I was saying that the Chatelaine Thecla is not the Chatelaine Thecla. Not the Chatelaine Thecla of your mind, which is the only Chatelaine Thecla you care about. Neither am I. What, then, is the difference between us?"

"None, I suppose."

While I was undressing I said, "Nevertheless, we all seek to discover what is real. Why is it? Perhaps we are drawn to the theocenter. That's what the hierophants say, that only that is true."

She kissed my thighs, knowing she had won. "Are you really ready to find it? You must be clothed in favor, remember. Otherwise you will be given over to the torturers. You wouldn't like that."

"No," I said, and took her head between my hands.

X

The Last Year

I THINK IT WAS MASTER GURLOES'S INTENTION THAT I SHOULD be brought to that house often, so I would not become too much attracted to Thecla. In actuality I permitted Roche to pocket the money and never went there again. The pain had been too pleasurable, the pleasure too painful; so that I feared that in time my mind would no longer be the thing I knew.

Then too, before Roche and I had left the house, the whitehaired man (catching my eye) had drawn from the bosom of his robe what I had at first thought was an icon but soon saw to be a golden vial in the shape of a phallus. He had smiled, and because there had been nothing but friendship in his smile it had frightened me.

Some days passed before I could rid my thoughts of Thecla of certain impressions belonging to the false Thecla who had initiated me into the anacreontic diversions and fruitions of men and women. Possibly this had an effect opposite to that Master Gurloes intended, but I do not think so. I believe I was never less inclined to love the unfortunate woman than when I carried in my memory the recent impressions of having enjoyed her freely; it was as I saw it more and more clearly for the untruth it was that I felt myself drawn to redress the fact, and drawn through her (though I was hardly conscious of it at the time) to the world of ancient knowledge and privilege she represented.

The books I had carried to her became my university, she my oracle. I am not an educated man—from Master

Palaemon I learned little more than to read, write, and cipher, with a few facts concerning the physical world and the requisites of our mystery. If educated men have sometimes thought me, if not their equal, at least one whose company did not shame them, that is owing solely to Thecla: the Thecla I remember, the Thecla who lives in me, and the four books.

What we read together and what we said of it to one another, I shall not tell; to recount the least of it would wear out this brief night. All that winter while snow whitened the Old Yard, I came up from the oubliette as if from sleep, and started to see the tracks my feet left behind me and my shadow on the snow. Thecla was sad that winter, yet she delighted in talking to me of the secrets of the past, of the conjectures formed of higher spheres, and of the arms and histories of heroes millennia dead.

Spring came, and with it the purple-striped and white-dotted lilies of the necropolis. I carried them to her, and she said my beard had shot up like them, and I should be bluer of cheek than the run of common men, and the next day begged my pardon for it, saying I was that already. With the warm weather and (I think) the blossoms I brought, her spirits lifted. When we traced the insignia of old houses, she talked of friends of her own station and the marriages they had made, good and bad, and how such and such a one had exchanged her future for a ruined stronghold because she had seen it in a dream; and how another, who had played at dolls with her when they were children, was the mistress now of so many thousands of leagues. "And there must be a new Autarch and perhaps an Autarchia sometime, you know, Severian. Things can go on as they have for a long while. But not forever."

"I know little of the court, Chatelaine."

"The less you know, the happier you will be." She paused, white teeth nibbling her delicately curved lower lip. "When my mother was in labor, she had the servants carry her to the Vatic Fountain, whose virtue is to reveal what is to come. It prophesied I should sit a throne. Thea has always envied me that. Still, the Autarch . . ."

"Yes?"

"It would be better if I didn't say too much. The Autarch is not like other people. No matter how I may talk sometimes, on all of Urth there is no one like him."

"I know that."

"Then that is enough for you. Look here," she held up the brown book. "Here it says, 'It was the thought of Thadelaeus the Great that the democracy'—that means the People—'desired to be ruled by some power superior to itself, and of Yrierix the Sage that the commonality would never permit one differing from themselves to hold high office. Notwithstanding this, each is called The Perfect Master.'"

I did not see what she meant, and said nothing.

"No one really knows what the Autarch will do. That's what it all comes down to. Or Father Inire either. When I first came to court I was told, as a great secret, that it was Father Inire who really determined the policy of the Commonwealth. When I had been there two years, a man very highly placed—I can't even tell you his name—said it was the Autarch who ruled, though to those in the House Absolute it might seem that it was Father Inire. And last year a woman whose judgment I trust more than any man's confided that it really made no difference, because they were both as unfathomable as the pelagic deeps, and if one decided things while the moon waxed and the other when the wind was in the east, no one could tell the difference anyway. I thought that was wise counsel until I realized she was only repeating something I had said to her myself half a year before." Thecla fell silent, reclining on the narrow bed, her dark hair spread on the pillow.

"At least," I said, "you were right to have confidence in that woman. She had taken her opinions from a trustworthy source."

As if she had not heard me, she murmured, "But it's all true, Severian. No one knows what they may do. I might be freed tomorrow. It's quite possible. They must know by now that I am here. Don't look at me like that. My friends will speak with Father Inire. Perhaps some may even mention me to the Autarch. You know why I was taken, don't you?"

"Something about your sister."

"My half-sister Thea is with Vodalus. They say she is his paramour, and I think it extremely likely."

I recalled the beautiful woman at the top of the stairs in the House Azure and said, "I think I saw your half-sister once. It was in the necropolis. There was an exultant with her who carried a canesword and was very handsome. He told me he was Vodalus. The woman had a heart-shaped face and a voice that made me think of doves. Was that she?"

"I suppose so. They want her to betray him to save me, and I know she won't. But when they discover that, why shouldn't they let me go?"

I spoke of something else until she laughed and said, "You are so intellectual, Severian. When you're made a journeyman, you'll be the most cerebral torturer in history—a frightful thought."

"I was under the impression you enjoyed such discussions, Chatelaine."

"Only now, because I can't get out. Though it may come as a shock to you, when I was free I seldom devoted time to metaphysics. I went dancing instead, and pursued the peccary with pardine limers. The learning you admire was acquired when I was a girl, and sat with my tutor under the threat of the stick."

"We need not talk of such things, Chatelaine, if you would rather we not."

She stood and thrust her face into the center of the bouquet I had picked for her. "Flowers are better theology than folios, Severian. Is it beautiful in the necropolis where you got these? You aren't bringing me the flowers from graves, are you? Cut flowers someone brought?"

"No. These were planted long ago. They come up every year."

At the slot in the door, Drotte said, "Time to go," and I stood up.

"Do you think you may see her again? The Chatelaine Thea, my sister?"

"I don't think so, Chatelaine."

"If you should, Severian, will you tell her about me? They may not have been able to communicate with her. There will be no treason in that—you'll be doing the Autarch's work."

"I will, Chatelaine." I was stepping through the doorway.

"She won't betray Vodalus, I know, but there may be some compromise."

Drotte closed the door and turned the key. It had not escaped me that Thecla had not asked how her sister and Vodalus had come to be in our ancient—and by such people as themselves, forgotten—necropolis. The corridor, with its lines of metal doors and coldsweating walls, seemed dark after the lamp in the cell. Drotte began to talk of an expedition he and Roche had made to a lion pit across Gyoll; over the sound of his voice I heard Thecla calling faintly, "Remind her of the time we sewed Josepha's doll."

The lilies faded as lilies do, and the dark death roses came into bloom. I cut them and carried them to Thecla, nigrescent purple flecked with scarlet. She smiled and recited:

"Here Rose the Graced, not Rose the Chaste, reposes.
The scent that rises is no scent of roses."

"If their odor offends you, Chatelaine . . ."

"Not at all, it is very sweet. I was only quoting something my grandmother used to say. The woman was infamous when she was a girl, or so she told me, and all the children chanted that rhyme when she died. Actually I suspect it is much older, and lost in time, like the beginnings of all the good and bad things. Men are said to desire women, Severian. Why do they despise the women they obtain?"

"I don't believe all do, Chatelaine."

"That beautiful Rose gave herself, and suffered such mockery for it that I know of it, though her dreams long ago turned to dust with her smooth flesh. Come here and sit by me."

I did as I was told, and she slipped her hands under the frayed bottom of my shirt and drew it over my head. I protested, but found myself unable to resist.

"What are you ashamed of? You who have no breasts to hide. I've never seen such white skin coupled with dark hair . . . Do you think my own skin white?"

"Very white, Chatelaine."

"So do others, but it is dun next to yours. You must flee the sun when you're a torturer, Severian. You'll burn terribly."

Her hair, which she often let fall free, today was bound about her head in a dark aureole. She had never more closely resembled her half-sister Thea, and I felt such desire for her that I seemed to be spilling my blood upon the floor, growing weaker and fainter with each contraction of my heart.

"Why are you pounding on my door?" Her smile told me she knew.

"I must go."

"You'd better put your shirt back on before you leave—you wouldn't want your friend to see you like that."

That night, though I knew it was in vain, I went to the necropolis and spent several watches in wandering among the silent houses of the dead. The next night I returned, and the next, but on the fourth Roche took me into the city, and in a drinking den I heard someone who seemed to know say that Vodalus was far to the north, hiding among the frost-pinched forests and raiding kafilas.

Days passed. Thecla was certain now, since she had been held in safety so long, that she would never be put to torment, and had Drotte bring her materials for writing and drawing, with which she planned a villa she meant to build on the southern shore of Lake Diuturna, which is said to be the most remote part of the Commonwealth, as well as the most beautiful. I took parties of apprentices to swim, thinking that to be my duty, though I could never dive in deep water without fear.

Then, suddenly as it seemed, the weather was too cold for swimming; one morning there was sparkling frost on the worn flagstones of the Old Yard, and fresh pork appeared on our plates at dinner, a sure sign that the cold had reached the hills below the city. Master Gurloes and Master Palaemon summoned me.

Master Gurloes said, "From several quarters we have had good reports of you, Severian, and now your apprenticeship is nearly served."

Nearly whispering, Master Palaemon added, "Your boyhood is behind you, your manhood ahead of you." There was affection in his voice.

"Just so," Master Gurloes continued. "The feast of our patroness draws near. I suppose you have given thought to it?"

I nodded. "Eata will be captain after me."

"And you?"

I did not understand what was meant; Master Palaemon, seeing that, asked gently, "What will you be, Severian? A torturer? You may leave the guild, you know, if you prefer."

I told him firmly—and as though I were slightly shocked by the suggestion—that I had never considered it. It was a lie. I had known, as all the apprentices knew, that one was not firmly and finally a member of the guild until one consented as an adult to the connection. Furthermore, though I loved the guild I hated it too—not because of the pain it inflicted on clients who must sometimes have been innocent, and who must often have been punished beyond anything that could be justified by their offences; but because it seemed to me inefficient and ineffectual, serving a power that was not only ineffectual but remote. I do not know how better to express my feelings about it than by saying that I hated it for starving and humiliating me and loved it because it was my home, hated and loved it because it was the exemplar of old things, because it was weak, and because it seemed indestructible.

Naturally I expressed none of this to Master Palaemon, though I might have if Master Gurloes had not been present. Still, it seemed incredible that my profession of loyalty, made in rags, could be taken seriously; yet it was.

"Whether you have considered leaving us or not," Master Palaemon told me, "it is an option open to you. Many would say that only a fool would serve out the hard years of apprenticeship and refuse to become a journeyman of his guild when his apprenticeship was past. But you may do so if you wish."

"Where would I go?" That, though I could not tell them so, was the real reason I was staying. I knew that a vast world lay outside the walls of the Citadel—indeed, outside the walls of our tower. But I could not imagine that I could ever have any place in it. Faced with a choice between slavery and the emptiness of freedom, I added, "I have been reared in our guild," for fear they would answer my question.

"Yes," Master Gurloes said in his most formal manner. "But you are no torturer yet. You have not put on fuligin."

Master Palaemon's hand, dry and wrinkled as a mummy's, groped until it found mine. "Among the initiates of religion it is said, 'You are an epopt always.' The reference is not only to knowledge but to their chrism, whose mark, being invisible, is ineradicable. You know our chrism."

I nodded again.

"Less even than theirs can it be washed away. Should you leave now, men will only say, 'He was nurtured by the torturers.' But when you have been anointed they will say, 'He is a torturer.' You may follow the plow or the drum, but still you will hear, 'He is a torturer.' Do you understand that?"

"I wish to hear nothing else."

"That is well," Master Gurloes said, and suddenly they both smiled, Master Palaemon showing his few old crooked teeth, and Master Gurloes his square yellow ones, like the teeth of a dead nag. "Then it is time that we explained to you the final secret." (I can hear the emphasis his voice gave the words even as I write.) "For it would be well for you to think upon it before the ceremony."

Then he and Master Palaemon expounded to me that secret which lies at the heart of the guild and is the more sacred because no liturgy celebrates it, and it lies naked in the lap of the Pancreator.

And they swore me never to reveal it save—as they did—to one about to enter upon the mysteries of the guild. I have since broken that oath, as I have many others.

XI

The Feast

THE DAY OF OUR PATRONESS FALLS IN THE FADING OF WINTER.
Then do we make merry: the journeymen perform the sword
dance in procession, leaping and fantastic; the masters light
the ruined chapel in the Grand Court with a thousand
perfumed candles, and we ready our feast.

In the guild, the annual observance is counted as *lofty* (in
which a journeyman is elevated to mastership), *lesser* (in
which one apprentice at least is created journeyman), or *least*
(in which no elevation takes place). Since no journeyman rose
to mastership in the year in which I was made a journeyman—
which is not to be wondered at, since such occasions are rarer
than the decades—the ceremony of my masking was a lesser
feast.

Even so, weeks were spent in preparation. I have heard it
said that no less than one hundred and thirty-five guilds have
members laboring within the Citadel walls. Of these, some
(as we have seen among the curators) are too few to keep
their patron's feast in the chapel, but must join their brothers
in the city. Those more numerous celebrate with such pomp
as they may to raise the esteem in which they are held. Of this
kind are the soldiers upon Hadrian's day, the matrosses on
Barbara's, the witches on Mag's, and many others. By
pageantry and wonders, and freely given food and drink, they
seek to have as many as may be from outside their guilds
attend their ceremonies.

Not so is it among the torturers. No one from without the
guild has dined with us at Holy Katharine's feast for more
than three hundred years, when a lieutenant of the guard (so

it is said) dared to come for a wager. There are many idle tales of what befell him—as that we made him seat himself at our table upon a chair of glowing iron. None of them are true. By the lore of our guild, he was made welcome and well feasted; but because we did not, over our meat and Katharine cake, talk of the pain we had inflicted, or devise new modes of torment, or curse those whose flesh we had torn for dying too soon, he grew ever more anxious, imagining that we sought to lull his fears so we might entrap him subsequently. Thus thinking, he ate little and drank much, and returning to his own quarters fell and struck his head in such a way that he evermore upon occasion lost his wits and suffered great pain. In time he put the muzzle of his own weapon into his mouth, but it was none of our doing.

None but torturers, then, come to the chapel on Holy Katharine's day. Yet each year (knowing we are watched from high windows) we prepare as do all the rest, and more grandly. Outside the chapel our wines burn like gems in the light of a hundred flambeaux; our beeves steam and wallow in ponds of gravy, rolling baked-lemon eyes; capybaras and agoutis, posed in the stances of life and bearing fur in which toasted cocoanut mingles with their own flayed skin, clamber on logs of ham and scale boulders of new-baked bread.

Our masters, of whom, when I was made journeyman, there were only two, arrive in sedan chairs whose curtains are woven of blossoms, and tread carpets patterned of colored sands, carpets telling of the traditions of the guild and laid grain by grain by the journeymen in days of toil and destroyed at once by the feet of the masters.

Within the chapel wait a great spiked wheel, a maid, and a sword. That wheel I knew well, for as an apprentice I had several times assisted in setting it up and taking it down. It was stored in the topmost part of the tower, just under the gun room, when it was not in use. The sword—though it seemed a true headsman's blade from a pace or two away— was no more than a wooden batten provided with an old hilt and brightened with tinsel.

Of the maid I can tell you nothing. When I was very young, I did not even wonder about her; those are the earliest feasts I can remember. When I was a little older and Gildas (who was long since a journeyman at the time of which I write) was captain of apprentices, I thought her perhaps one of the witches. When I grew a year older, I knew such disrespect would not be tolerated.

Perhaps she was a servant from some remote part of the Citadel. Perhaps she was a resident of the city, who for gain or because of some old connection with our guild consented to play the part; I do not know. I only know that each feast found her in her place, and so far as I could judge, unchanged. She was tall and slender, though not so tall nor so slender as Thecla, dark of complexion, dark of eye, raven of hair. Hers was such a face as I have never seen elsewhere, like a pool of pure water found in the midst of a wood.

She stood between the wheel and the sword while Master Palaemon (as the older of our masters) told us of the founding of the guild, and of our precursors in the years before the ice came—this part was different each year, as his scholarship decided. Silent she stood too while we sang the Fearful Song, the hymn of the guild, which apprentices must get by heart but which is sung only on that one day of the year. Silent she stood too while we knelt among the broken pews and prayed.

Then Master Gurloes and Master Palaemon, aided by several of the older journeymen, began her legend. Sometimes one spoke alone. Sometimes all chanted together. Sometimes two spoke to different effect while the others played flutes they had carved of thighbones, or the three-stringed rebéc that shrieks like a man.

When they reached that part of the narration at which our patroness is condemned by Maxentius, four masked journeymen rushed out to seize her. So silent and serene before, she resisted now, struggled and cried out. But as they bore her toward it, the wheel appeared to blur and change. In the light of the candles, it seemed at first that serpents, green pythons with jeweled heads of scarlet and citrine and white, writhed from it. Then it was seen that these were flowers, roses in the bud. When the maid was but a step away they bloomed (they were of paper, concealed, as I well knew, within the segments of the wheel). Feigning fear, the journeymen drew back; but the narrators, Gurloes, Palaemon, and the others, speaking together as Maxentius, urged them on.

Then I, still unmasked and in the dress of an apprentice, stepped forward and said: "Resistance avails nothing. You are to be broken on the wheel, but we would do you no further indignity."

The maid gave no answer but reached out and touched the wheel, which at once fell to pieces, collapsing with a clatter to the floor, all its roses gone.

"Behead her," demanded Maxentius, and I took up the sword. It was very heavy.

She knelt before me. "You are a counselor of Omniscience," I said. "Though I must slay you, I beg you spare my life."

For the first time the maid spoke, saying, "Strike and fear not."

I lifted the sword. I remember that for a moment I feared it would overbalance me.

When I think back on that time, it is that moment I recall first; to remember more, I must work forward or backward from that. In memory it seems to me I stand always so, in gray shirt and ragged trousers, with the blade poised above my head. While I raised it, I was an apprentice; when it descended, I would be a journeyman of the Order of the Seekers for Truth and Penitence.

It is our rule that the executioner must stand between his victim and the light; the maid's head lay in shadow on the block. I knew that the sword in falling would do her no harm—I would direct it to one side, tripping an ingenious mechanism that would elevate a wax head smeared with blood while the maid draped her own with a fuligin cloth. Still I hesitated to give the blow.

She spoke again from the floor at my feet, and her voice seemed to ring in my ears. "Strike and fear not." With such strength as I was capable of, I sent the false blade down. For an instant it seemed to me that it met resistance; then it thudded into the block, which fell into two. The maid's head, all bloody, tumbled forward toward the watching brothers. Master Gurloes lifted it by the hair and Master Palaemon cupped his left hand to receive the blood.

"With this, our chrism," he said, "I anoint you, Severian, our brother forever." His index finger traced the mark upon my forehead.

"So be it," said Master Gurloes, and all the journeymen save I.

The maid stood. I knew even as I watched her that her head was only concealed in the cloth; but it seemed there was nothing there. I felt dizzy and tired.

She took the wax head from Master Gurloes and pretended to replace it on her shoulders, slipping it by some sleight into the fuligin cloth, then standing before us radiant and whole. I knelt before her, and the others withdrew.

She raised the sword with which I had so lately struck off her head; the blade was bloody now from some contact with the wax. "You are of the torturers," she said. I felt the sword touch either shoulder, and at once eager hands were drawing the head mask of the guild over my face and lifting me. Before I well knew what had occurred, I was on the shoulders of two journeymen—it was only afterward that I learned they were Drotte and Roche, though I should have guessed it. They were bearing me up the processional aisle through the center of the chapel, while everyone cheered and shouted.

We were no sooner outside than the fireworks began: crackers about our feet and even around our ears, torpedoes banging against the thousand-year-old walls of the chapel, rockets red and yellow and green leaping into the air. A gun from the Great Keep split the night.

All the brave meats I have described were on the tables in the court; I sat at the head between Master Palaemon and Master Gurloes, and drank too much (very little, for me, has always been too much), and was cheered and toasted. What became of the maid I do not know. She disappeared as she has each Katharine's Day I can remember. I have not seen her again.

How I reached my bed I have no notion. Those who drink much have told me that they sometimes forget all that befell them in the latter part of the night, and perhaps it was so with me. But I think it more likely that I (who never forget anything, who, if I may for once confess the truth, though I seem to boast, do not truly understand what others mean when they say *forget*, for it seems to me that all experience becomes a part of my being) only slept and was carried there.

However it may be, I woke not in the familiar low room that was our dormitory, but in a cabin so small it was much higher than wide, a journeyman's cabin, and because I was the most junior of the journeymen, the least desirable in the tower, a portless cubbyhole no larger than a cell.

My bed seemed to toss beneath me. I gripped the sides and sat up and it was still, but as soon as my head touched the pillow once more the swaying began again. I felt I was wide awake—then that I was awake again but had been sleeping only a moment before. I was conscious that someone was in the tiny cabin with me, and for some reason I could not have explained I thought it was the young woman who had taken the part of our patroness.

I sat up in the tossing bed. Dim light filtered beneath the door; there was no one there.

When I lay down again, the room was filled with Thecla's perfume. The false Thecla from the House Azure had come, then. I got out of bed, and nearly falling opened the door. There was no one in the passage outside.

A chamber pot waited beneath the bed, and I pulled it out and filled it with my spew, rich meats swimming in wine mixed with bile. Somehow I felt what I had done was treason, as if by casting out all that the guild had given me that night I had cast out the guild itself. Coughing and sobbing I knelt beside the bed, and at last, after wiping my mouth clean, lay down again.

No doubt I slept. I saw the chapel, but it was not the ruin I knew. The roof was whole and high and straight, and from it there hung ruby lamps. The pews were whole and gleamed with polish; the ancient stone altar was swatched in cloth of gold. Behind the altar rose a wonderful mosaic of blue; but it was blank, as if a fragment of sky without cloud or star had been torn away and spread upon the curving wall.

I walked toward it down the aisle, and as I did so I was struck by how much lighter it was than the true sky, whose blue is nearly black even on the brightest day. Yet how much more beautiful this was! It thrilled me to look at it. I felt I was floating in air, borne up by the beauty of it, looking down upon the altar, down into the cup of crimson wine, down upon shewbread and antique knife. I smiled . . .

And woke. In my sleep I had heard footsteps in the passage outside, and I knew I had recognized them, though I could not just then recall whose steps they were. Struggling, I brought back the sound; it was no human tread, only the padding of soft feet, and an almost imperceptible scraping.

I heard it again, so faint that for a time I thought I had confused my memory with reality; but it was real, slowly coming up the passage, slowly going back. The mere lifting of my head brought a wave of nausea; I let it fall again, telling myself that whoever might pace back and forth, it was no affair of mine. The perfume had vanished, and sick though I was, I felt I needed to fear unreality no longer—I was back in the world of solid objects and plain light. My door opened a trifle and Master Malrubius looked in as though to make certain I was all right. I waved to him and he shut the door again. It was some time before I recalled that he had died while I was still a boy.

XII

The Traitor

THE NEXT DAY MY HEAD ACHED AND I WAS ILL. BUT AS I WAS (by a long-standing tradition) spared from the cleaning of the Grand Court and the chapel, where most of the brothers were, I was needed in the oubliette. For a few moments at least the morning calm of the corridors soothed me. Then the apprentices came clattering down (the boy Eata, not quite so small now, with a puffed lip and the gleam of triumph in his eye), bringing the clients' breakfast—cold meats mostly, salvage from the ruins of the banquet. I had to explain to several clients that this was the only day of the year on which they would get meat, and went along assuring one after another that there would be no excruciations—the feast day itself and the day after are exempt, and even when a sentence demands torment on those days, it is postponed. The

Chatelaine Thecla was still asleep. I did not wake her, but unlocked her cell and carried her food in and put it on her table.

About midmorning I again heard the echoes of footsteps. Coming to the landing, I saw two cataphracts, an anagnost reading prayers, Master Gurloes, and a young woman. Master Gurloes asked if I had an empty cell, and I began to describe those that were vacant.

"Then take this prisoner. I have already signed for her."

I nodded and grasped the woman by the arm; the cataphracts released her and turned away like silver automata.

The elaboration of her sateen costume (somewhat dirty and torn now) showed that she was an optimate. An armigette would have worn finer stuffs in simpler lines, and no one from the poorer classes could have dressed so well. The anagnost tried to follow us down the corridor, but Master Gurloes prevented him. I heard the soldiers' steel-shod feet on the steps.

"When am I . . .?" It had a rising, somehow terrorized inflection.

"To be taken to the examination room?"

She clung to my arm now as though I were her father or her lover. "Will I be?"

"Yes, Madame."

"How do you know?"

"All who are brought here are, Madame."

"Always? Isn't anybody ever released?"

"Occasionally."

"Then I might be too, mightn't I?" The hope in her voice now made me think of a flower growing in shadow.

"It's possible, but it's very unlikely."

"Don't you want to know what I've done?"

"No," I said. As it happened, the cell next to Thecla's was vacant; for a moment I wondered if I should put this woman there. She would be company (the two could speak through the slots in their doors), but her questions and the opening and closing of the cell might wake Thecla now. I decided to do it—the companionship, I felt, would more than compensate for a little lost sleep.

"I was affianced to an officer, and I found he was maintaining a jade. When he wouldn't give her up, I paid bravos to fire her thatch. She lost a featherbed, a few sticks of furniture, and some clothes. Is that a crime for which I should be tortured?"

"I don't know, Madame."

"My name is Marcellina. What is yours?"

I turned the key to her cell while I debated answering her. Thecla, whom I could hear stirring now, would doubtless tell her in any event. "Severian," I said.

"And you get your bread by breaking bones. It must give you good dreams by night."

Thecla's eyes, widely spaced and as deep as wells, were at the slot in her door. "Who is that with you, Severian?"

"A new prisoner, Chatelaine."

"A woman? I know she is—I heard her voice. From the House Absolute?"

"No, Chatelaine." Not knowing how long it might be before the two would be able to see each other again, I made Marcellina stand before Thecla's door.

"Another woman. Isn't that unusual? How many do you have, Severian?"

"Eight on this level now, Chatelaine."

"I would think you would often have more than that."

"We rarely have more than four, Chatelaine."

Marcellina asked, "How long will I have to stay here?"

"Not long. Few stay here long, Madame."

With an unhealthy seriousness, Thecla said, "I am about to be released, you understand. He knows."

Our guild's new client looked at what could be seen of her with increased interest. "Are you really about to be set free, Chatelaine?"

"He knows. He's mailed letters for me—haven't you, Severian? And he's been saying goodbye for these last few days. He's really rather a sweet boy in his way."

I said, "You must go in now, Madame. You may continue to talk, if you like."

I was relieved after I had served the clients their suppers. Drotte met me on the stair and suggested I go to bed.

"It's the mask," I told him. "You're not used to seeing me with it on."

"I can see your eyes, and that's all I need to see. Can't you recognize all the brothers by their eyes, and tell whether they're angry, or in the mood for a joke? You ought to go to bed."

I told him I had something to do first, and went to Master Gurloes's study. He was absent, as I had hoped he would be, and among the papers on his table I found what I had, in some fashion I cannot explain, known would be there: an order for Thecla's excruciation.

I could not sleep after that. Instead I went (for the last time, though I did not know it) to the tomb in which I had played as a boy. The funeral bronze of the old exultant was dull for lack of rubbing, and a few more leaves had drifted through the half-open door; otherwise it was unchanged. I had once told Thecla of the place, and now I imagined her with me. She had escaped by my aid, and I promised her that no one would find her here, and that I would bring her food, and when the hunt had cooled I would help her secure passage on a merchant dhow, by which she could make her way unnoticed down the winding coils of Gyoll to the delta and the sea.

Were I such a hero as we had read of together in old romances, I would have released her that very evening, overpowering or drugging the brothers on watch. I was not, and I possessed no drugs and no weapon more formidable than a knife taken from the kitchen.

And if the truth is to be known, between my inmost being and the desperate attempt there stood the words I had heard that morning—the morning after my elevation. The Chatelaine Thecla had said I was "rather a sweet boy," and some already mature part of me knew that even if I succeeded against all odds, I would still be *rather a sweet boy*. At the time I thought it mattered.

The next morning Master Gurloes ordered me to assist him in performing the excruciation. Roche came with us.

I unlocked her cell. She did not understand at first why we had come, and asked me if she had a visitor, or if she were to be discharged.

By the time we reached our destination she knew. Many men faint, but she did not. Courteously, Master Gurloes asked if she would like an explanation of the various mechanisms.

"Do you mean the ones you are going to employ?" There was a tremor in her voice, but it was not marked.

"No, no, I wouldn't do that. Just the curious machines you will be seeing as we pass through. Some are quite old, and most are hardly ever used."

Thecla looked about her before answering. The examination room—our workroom—is not divided into cells, but is a unified space, pillared with the tubes of the ancient engines and cluttered with the tools of our mystery. "The one to which I will be subjected—is that old too?"

"The most hallowed of all," Master Gurloes replied. He waited for her to say something more, and when she did not, proceeded with his descriptions. "The kite I'm certain you must be familiar with—everyone knows of it. Behind it there . . . if you'll take a step this way you'll be able to see it better . . . is what we call the apparatus. It is supposed to letter whatever slogan is demanded in the client's flesh, but it is seldom in working order. I see you're looking at the old post. It's no more than it seems, just a stake to immobilize the hands, and a thirteen-thonged scourge for correction. It used to stand in the Old Yard, but the witches complained, and the castellan made us move it down here. That was about a century ago."

"Who are the witches?"

"I'm afraid we don't have time to go into that now. Severian can tell you when you're back in your cell."

She looked at me as if to say "Am I really going back, eventually?" and I took advantage of my position on the side opposite Master Gurloes to clasp her icy hand.

"Beyond that—"

"Wait. Can I choose? Is there any way I can persuade you to . . . do one thing instead of another?" Her voice was still brave, but weaker now.

Gurloes shook his head. "We have no say in the matter, Chatelaine. Nor do you. We carry out the sentences that are delivered to us, doing no more than we are told, and no less, and making no changes." Embarrassed, he cleared his throat. "The next one's interesting, I think. We call it Allowin's necklace. The client is strapped into that chair, and the pad is adjusted against his breastbone. Each breath he draws thereafter tightens the chain, so that the more he breathes, the less breath he can take. In theory it can go on forever, with very shallow breaths and very small tightenings."

"How horrible. What is that behind it? That tangle of wire, and the great glass globe over the table?"

"Ah," said Master Gurloes. "We call this the revolutionary. The subject lies here. Will you, Chatelaine?"

For a long moment Thecla stood poised. She was taller than any of us, but with that terrible fear in her face, her height was no longer imposing.

"If you do not," Master Gurloes continued, "our journeymen will have to force you. You would not like that, Chatelaine."

Thecla whispered, "I thought you were going to show me all of them."

"Only until we reached this spot, Chatelaine. It's better if the client's mind is occupied. Now lie down, please. I won't be asking again."

She lay down at once, quickly and gracefully, as I had often seen her stretch herself in her cell. The straps Roche and I buckled about her were so old and cracked that I wondered if they would hold.

There were cables to be wound from one part of the examination room to another, rheostats and magnetic amplifiers to be adjusted. Antique lights like blood-red eyes gleamed on the control panel, and a droning like the song of some huge insect filled the entire chamber. For a few moments, the ancient engine of the tower lived again. One cable was loose, and sparks as blue as burning brandy played about its bronze fittings.

"Lightning," Master Gurloes said as he rammed the loose cable home. "There's another word for it, but I forget. Anyway, the revolutionary here runs by lightning. It's not as if you were going to be struck, of course, Chatelaine. But lightning's the thing that makes it go.

"Severian, push up your handle there until this needle's here." A coil that had been as cold as a snake when I had touched it a moment before was warm now.

"What does it do?"

"I couldn't describe it, Chatelaine. Anyway, I've never had it done, you see." Gurloes's hand touched a knob on the control panel and Thecla was bathed in white light that stole the color from all it fell upon. She screamed; I have heard screaming all my life, but that was the worst, though not the loudest; it seemed to go on and on like the shrieking of a cartwheel.

She was not unconscious when the white light died. Her eyes were open, staring upward; but she did not appear to see my hand, or to feel it when I touched her. Her breathing was shallow and rapid.

Roche asked, "Shall we wait until she can walk?" I could see he was thinking how awkward so tall a woman would be to carry.

"Take her now," Master Gurloes said. We got out the travail.

When all my other work was complete, I came into her cell to see her. She was fully aware by then, though she could not stand. "I ought to hate you," she said.

I had to lean over her to catch the words. "It's all right," I said.

"But I don't. Not for your sake . . . if I hate my last friend, what would be left?"

There was nothing to say to that, so I said nothing.

"Do you know what it was like? It was a long time before I could think of it."

Her right hand was creeping upward, toward her eyes. I caught it and forced it back.

"I thought I saw my worst enemy, a kind of demon. And it was me."

Her scalp was bleeding. I put clean lint there and taped it down, though I knew it would soon be gone. Curling, dark hairs were entangled in her fingers.

"Since then, I can't control my hands . . . I can if I think about it, if I know what they're doing. But it is so hard, and I'm getting tired." She rolled her head away and spat blood. "I bite myself. Bite the lining of my cheeks, and my tongue and lips. Once my hands tried to strangle me, and I thought oh good, I will die now. But I only lost consciousness, and they must have lost their strength, because I woke. It's like that machine, isn't it?"

I said, "Allowin's necklace."

"But worse. My hands are trying to blind me now, to tear my eyelids away. Will I be blind?"

"Yes," I said.

"How long before I die?"

"A month, perhaps. The thing in you that hates you will weaken as you weaken. The revolutionary brought it to life, but its energy is your energy, and in the end you will die together."

"Severian . . ."

"Yes?"

"I see," she said. And then, "It is a thing from Erebus, from Abaia, a fit companion for me. Vodalus . . ."

I leaned closer, but I could not hear. At last I said, "I tried to save you. I wanted to. I stole a knife, and spent the night watching for a chance. But only a master can take a prisoner from a cell, and I would have had to kill—"

"Your friends."

"Yes, my friends."

Her hands were moving again, and blood trickled from her mouth. "Will you bring me the knife?"

"I have it here," I said, and drew it from under my cloak. It was a common cook's knife with a span or so of blade.

"It looks sharp."

"It is," I said. "I know how to treat an edge, and I sharpened it carefully." That was the last thing I said to her. I put the knife into her right hand and went out.

For a time, I knew, her will would hold it back. A thousand times one thought recurred: I could reenter her cell, take back the knife, and no one would know. I would be able to live out my life in the guild.

If her throat rattled, I did not hear it; but after I had stared at the door of her cell for a long while, a little crimson rivulet crept from under it. I went to Master Gurloes then, and told him what I had done.

XIII

The Lictor of Thrax

FOR THE NEXT TEN DAYS I LIVED THE LIFE OF A CLIENT, IN A CELL of the topmost level (not far, in fact, from that which had been Thecla's). In order that the guild should not be accused of having detained me without legal process, the door was left unlocked; but there were two journeymen with swords outside my door, and I never stepped from it save for a brief time on the second day when I was brought to Master Palaemon to tell my story again. That was my trial, if you like. For the remainder of the time, the guild pondered my sentence.

It is said that it is the peculiar quality of time to conserve fact, and that it does so by rendering our past falsehoods true. So it was with me. I had lied in saying that I loved the guild—that I desired nothing but to remain in its embrace. Now I found those lies become truths. The life of a journeyman and even that of an apprentice seemed infinitely attractive. Not only because I was certain I was to die, but truly attractive in themselves, because I had lost them. I saw the brothers now from the viewpoint of a client, and so I saw them as powerful, the active principles of an inimical and nearly perfect machine.

Knowing that my case was hopeless, I learned in my own person what Master Malrubius had once impressed on me when I was a child: that hope is a psychological mechanism unaffected by external realities. I was young and adequately fed; I was permitted to sleep and therefore I hoped. Again and again, waking and sleeping, I dreamed that just as I was to die Vodalus would come. Not alone as I had seen him fight in the necropolis, but at the head of an army that would sweep the decay of centuries away and make us once more the masters of the stars. Often I thought to hear tread of that army ringing in the corridors; sometimes I carried my candle to the little slot in the door because I thought I had seen the face of Vodalus outside in the dark.

As I have said, I supposed I would be killed. The question that occupied my mind most during those slow days was that of means. I had learned all the arts of the torturer; now I thought of them—sometimes one by one, as we had been taught them, sometimes all together in a revelation of pain. To live day after day in a cell below ground, thinking of torment, is torment itself.

On the eleventh day I was summoned by Master Palaemon. I saw the red light of the sun again, and breathed that wet wind that tells in winter that spring is almost come. But, oh, how much it cost me to walk past the open tower door and looking out see the corpse door in the curtain wall, and old Brother Porter lounging there.

Master Palaemon's study seemed very large when I entered it and yet very precious to me—as though the dusty books and papers were my own. He asked me to sit. He was not masked and seemed older than I remembered him. "We have discussed your case," he said. "Master Gurloes and I. We have had to take the other journeymen into our confidence, and even the apprentices. It is better that they know the truth. Most agree that you are deserving of death."

He waited for me to comment, but I did not.

"And yet there was much said in your defense. Several of the journeymen urged in private meetings, to me and to Master Gurloes as well, that you be permitted to die without pain."

I cannot say why, but it became of central importance to me to know how many of these friends I had, and I asked.

"More than two, and more than three. The exact number does not matter. Do you not believe that you deserve to die painfully?"

"By the revolutionary," I said, hoping that if I asked that death as a favor it would not be granted.

"Yes, that would be fitting. But . . ."

And here he paused. The moment passed, then two. The first brass-backed fly of the new summer buzzed against the port. I wanted to crush it, to catch and release it, to shout at Master Palaemon to speak, to flee from the room; but I could do none of these things. I sat, instead, in the old wooden chair beside his table, feeling that I was already dead but still must die.

"We cannot kill you, you see. I have had a most difficult time convincing Gurloes of that, yet it is so. If we slay you without judicial order, we are no better than you: you have been false to us, but we will have been false to the law. Furthermore, we would be putting the guild in jeopardy forever—an Inquisitor would call it murder."

He waited for me to comment, and I said, "But for what I have done . . ."

"The sentence would be just. Yes. Still, we have no right in law to take life on our own authority. Those who have that right are properly jealous of it. If we were to go to them, the verdict would be sure. But were we to go, the repute of the guild would be publicly and irrevocably stained. Much of the trust now reposed in us would be gone, and permanently. We might confidently expect our affairs to be supervised by others in the future. Would you enjoy seeing our clients guarded by soldiers, Severian?"

The vision I had in Gyoll when I had so nearly drowned rose before me, and it possessed (as it had then) a sullen yet strong attraction. "I would rather take my own life," I said. "I will feign to swim, and die in mid-channel, far from help."

The shadow of a sour smile crossed Master Palaemon's ruined face. "I am glad you made that offer only to me. Master Gurloes would have taken far too much pleasure in pointing out that at least a month must pass before swimming can be made credible."

"I am sincere. I sought a painless death, but it was death I sought, and not an extension of life."

"Even if it were midsummer, what you propose could not be permitted. An Inquisitor might still conclude that we contrived your death. Fortunately for you, we have agreed upon a less incriminating solution. Do you know anything of the condition of our mystery in the provincial towns?"

I shook my head.

"It is but low. Nowhere but in Nessus—nowhere but here in the Citadel—is there a chapter of our guild. Lesser places have no more than a carnifex, who takes life and performs such excruciations as the judicators there decree. Such a man is universally hated and feared. Do you understand?"

"Such a position," I answered, "is too high for me." There was no falsehood in what I said; I despised myself, at that moment, far more than I did the guild. Since then I have recalled those words often, though they were but my own, and they have been a comfort to me in many troubles.

"There is a town called Thrax, the City of Windowless Rooms," Master Palaemon continued. "The archon there—his name is Abdiesus—has written the House Absolute. A marshall there has transmitted the letter to the Castellar, and from him I have it. They are in sore need in Thrax of the functionary I have described. In the past they have pardoned condemned men on the condition that they accept the post. Now the countryside is rotten with treachery, and since the position entails a certain degree of trust, they are reluctant to do so again."

I said, "I understand."

"Twice before members of the guild have been dispatched to outlying towns, though whether those were such cases as this the chronicles do not say. Nevertheless, they furnish a precedent now, and an escape from the maze. You are to go to Thrax, Severian. I have prepared a letter that will introduce you to the archon and his magistrates. It describes you as highly skilled in our mystery. For such a place, it will not be a falsehood."

I nodded, being already resigned to what I was to do. Yet while I sat there, maintaining the expressionless face of a journeyman whose only will is to obey, a new shame burned in me. Though it was not so hot as the one for the disgrace I had brought upon the guild, still it was fresher, and hurt the more because I had not yet grown accustomed to the sickness of it as I had the other. It was this: that I was glad to go—that my feet already longed for the feel of grass, my eyes for strange sights, my lungs for the new, clear air of far, unmanned places.

I asked Master Palaemon where the town of Thrax might be.

"Down Gyoll," he said. "Near the sea." Then he stopped as old men will, and said, "No, no, what am I thinking of? Up Gyoll, of course," and for me hundreds of leagues of marching waves, and the sand, and the seabirds' crying all faded away. Master Palaemon took a map from his cabinet and unrolled it for me, bending over it until the lens by which he saw such things nearly touched the parchment. "There," he said, and showed me a dot on the margin of the young river, at the lower cataracts. "If you had funds you might travel by boat. As it is, you must walk."

"I understand," I said, and though I remembered the thin piece of gold Vodalus had given me, safe in its hiding place, I knew I could not take advantage of whatever wealth it might represent. It was the guild's will to cast me out with no more money than a young journeyman might be expected to possess, and for prudence's sake as well as honor's, so I must go.

Yet I knew it was unfair. If I had not glimpsed the woman with the heart-shaped face and earned that small gold coin, it is more than possible I would never have carried the knife to Thecla and forfeited my place in the guild. In a sense, that coin had bought my life.

Very well—I would leave my old life behind me . . .

"Severian!" Master Palaemon exclaimed. "You are not listening to me. You were never an inattentive pupil in our classes."

"I'm sorry. I was thinking about a great many things."

"No doubt." For the first time he really smiled, and for an instant looked his old self, the Master Palaemon of my boyhood. "Yet I was giving you such good advice for your journey. Now you must do without it, but doubtless you would have forgotten everything anyway. You know of the roads?"

"I know they must not be used. Nothing more."

"The Autarch Maruthas closed them. That was when I was your age. Travel encouraged sedition, and he wished goods to enter and leave the city by the river, where they might be easily taxed. The law has remained in force since, and there is a redoubt, so I've heard, every fifty leagues. Still the roads remain. Though they are in poor repair, it is said some use them by night."

"I see," I said. Closed or not, the roads might make for an easier passage than traveling across the countryside as the law demanded.

"I doubt you do. I mean to warn you against them. They are patrolled by uhlans under orders to kill anyone found upon them, and since they have permission to loot the bodies of those they slay, they are not much inclined to ask excuses."

"I understand," I told him, and in private wondered how he came to know so much of travel.

"Good. The day is half spent now. If you like, you may sleep here tonight and depart in the morning."

"Sleep in my cell, you mean."

He nodded. Though I knew he could scarcely see my face, I felt that something in him was studying me.

"I will leave now, then." I tried to think of what I would have to do before I turned my back on our tower forever; nothing came to me, yet it seemed there must surely be something. "May I have a watch in which to prepare? When the time is up, I will go."

"That's easily granted. But before you leave, I want you to return here—I have something to give you. Will you do it?"

"Of course, Master, if you want me to."

"And Severian, be careful. There are many in the guild who are your friends—who wish this had never happened. But there are others who feel you have betrayed our trust and deserve agony and death."

"Thank you, Master," I said. "The second group is correct."

My few possessions were already in my cell. I bundled them together and found the whole bundle so small I could put it in the sabretache hanging from my belt. Moved by love, and regret for what had been, I went to Thecla's cell.

It was empty still. Her blood had been scrubbed from the floor, but a wide, dark spot of blood-rust had etched the metal. Her clothing was gone, and her cosmetics. The four books I had carried to her a year before remained, stacked with others on the little table. I could not resist the temptation to take one; there were so many in the library that they would never miss a single volume. My hand had stretched forth before I realized I did not know which to choose. The book of heraldry was the most beautiful, but it was too large by far to carry about the country. The book of theology was the smallest of all, but the brown book was hardly larger. In the end it was that I took, with its tales from vanished worlds.

I climbed the stair of our tower then, past the storeroom to the gun room where the seige pieces lounged in cradles of pure force. Then higher still to the room of the glass roof, with its gray screens and strangely contorted chairs, and up a slender ladder until I stood on the slippery panes themselves, where my presence scattered blackbirds across the sky like flecks of soot and our fuligin pennon streamed and snapped from the staff over my head.

Below me the Old Yard seemed small and even cramped, but infinitely comfortable and homey. The breach in the curtain wall was greater than I had ever realized, though to either side of it the Red Tower and the Bear Tower still stood proud and strong. Nearest our own, the witches' tower was slender, dark, and tall; for a moment the wind blew a snatch of their wild laughter to me and I felt the old fear, though we of the torturers have always been on the most friendly terms with the witches, our sisters.

Beyond the wall, the great necropolis rolled down the long slope toward Gyoll, whose waters I could glimpse between the half-rotted buildings on its banks. Across the flood of the river the rounded dome of the khan seemed no more than a pebble, the city about it an expanse of many-colored sand trodden by the master torturers of old.

I saw a caique, with high, sharp prow and stern, and a bellying sail, making south with the dark current; and against my will I followed it for a time—to the delta and the swamps, and at last to the flashing sea where that great beast Abaia, carried from the farther shores of the universe in anteglacial days, wallows until the moment comes for him and his kind to devour the continents.

Then I abandoned all thoughts of the south and her ice-choked sea and turned north to the mountains and the rising of the river. For a long time (I do not know how long, though the sun seemed in a new place when I took notice of its position again) I looked to the north. The mountains I could see with my mind's eye, but not with the body's: only the rolling expanse of the city with its million roofs. And to tell the truth, the great silver columns of the Keep and its surrounding spires blocked half my view. Yet I cared nothing for them, and indeed hardly saw them. North lay the House Absolute and the cataracts, and Thrax, City of Windowless Rooms. North lay the wide pampas, a hundred trackless forests, and the rotting jungles at the waist of the world.

When I had thought on all those things until I was half mad, I came down to Master Palaemon's study again and told him I was ready to depart.

XIV

Terminus Est

"I HAVE A GIFT FOR YOU," MASTER PALAEMON SAID. "CONSIDering your youth and strength, I don't believe you will find it too heavy."

"I am deserving of no gifts."

"That is so. But you must recall, Severian, that when a gift is deserved, it is not a gift but a payment. The only true gifts are such as you now receive. I cannot forgive you for what you have done, but I cannot forget what you were. Since Master Gurloes rose to journeyman, I have had no better scholar." He rose and walked stiffly to the alcove, where I heard him say, "Ah, she is not overburdensome for me yet."

He was lifting something so dark it was swallowed by the shadows. I said, "Let me assist you, Master."

"No need, no need. Light to raise, weighty to descend. Such is the mark of a good one."

Upon his table he laid a night-black case nearly long enough for a coffin, but much narrower. When he opened its silver catches, they rang like bells.

"I am not giving you the casket, which would only impede you. Here is the blade, her sheath to protect her when you are traveling, and a baldric."

It was in my hands before I fully understood what it was he gave me. The sheath of sable manskin covered it nearly to the pommel. I drew it off (it was soft as glove leather), and beheld the sword herself.

I shall not bore you with a catalog of her virtues and beauties; you would have to see her and hold her to judge her justly. Her bitter blade was an ell in length, straight and square-pointed as such a sword's should be. Man-edge and woman-edge could part a hair to within a span of the guard, which was of thick silver with a carven head at either end. Her grip was onyx bound with silver bands, two spans long and terminated with an opal. Art had been lavished upon her; but it is the function of art to render attractive and significant those things that without it would not be so, and so art had nothing to give her. The words *Terminus Est* had been engraved upon her blade in curious and beautiful letters, and I had learned enough of ancient languages since leaving the Atrium of Time to know that they meant *This Is the Line of Division*.

"She is well honed, I promise you," Master Palaemon said, seeing me test the man-edge with my thumb. "For the sake of those given over to you, see you keep her so. My question is whether she is not too ponderous a mate for you. Raise her and see."

I clasped *Terminus Est* as I had the false sword at my elevation, and lifted her above my head, taking care not to strike the ceiling. She shifted as though I wrestled a serpent.

"You have no difficulty?"

"No, Master. But she writhed when I poised her."

"There is a channel in the spine of her blade, and in it runs a river of hydrargyrum—a metal heavier than iron, though it flows like water. Thus the balance is shifted toward the hands when the blade is high, but to the tip when it falls. Often you will have to wait the completion of a final prayer, or a hand signal from the quaesitor. Your sword must not slack or tremble—But you know all that. I need not tell you to respect such an instrument. May the Moira favor you, Severian."

I took the whetstone from its pocket in the sheath and

dropped it into my sabretache, folded the letter he had given me to the archon of Thrax, wrapped it in a scrap of oiled silk, and committed it to the sword's care. Then I took my leave of him.

With the broad blade slung behind my left shoulder, I made my way through the corpse door and out into the windy garden of the necropolis. The sentry at the lowest gate, nearest the river, allowed me to pass without challenge, though with many a strange look, and I threaded the narrow streets to the Water Way, that runs with Gyoll.

Now I must write something that still shames me, even after all that has occurred. The watches of that afternoon were the happiest of my life. All my old hatred of the guild had vanished, and my love for it, for Master Palaemon, my brothers, and even the apprentices, my love for its lore and usages, my love which had never wholly died, was all that remained. I was leaving all those things I loved, after having disgraced them utterly. I should have wept.

I did not. Something in me soared, and when the wind whipped my cloak out behind me like wings, I felt I might have flown. We are forbidden to smile in the presence of any but our masters, brothers, clients, and apprentices. I did not wish to wear my mask, but I had to pull up my hood and bow my head lest the passersby see my face. Wrongly I thought I would perish on the way. Wrongly I thought I should never return to the Citadel and our tower; but wrongly too I believed that there were many more such days to come, and I smiled.

In my ignorance, I had supposed that before dark I would have left the city behind me, and that I would be able to sleep in relative safety beneath some tree. In actuality, I had not so much as outwalked the older and poorer parts before the west was lifted to cover the sun. To ask hospitality in one of the tottering buildings that bordered the Water Way, or attempt to rest in some corner, would have been an invitation to death. And so I trudged along under stars brightened by the wind, no longer a torturer in the eyes of the few who passed me, but only a somberly clad traveler who shouldered a dark paterissa.

From time to time boats glided through the weed-choked water while the wind drew music from their rigging. The poorer sort showed no lights and seemed hardly more than floating debris; but several times I beheld rich thalamegii with bow and stern lamps to show off their gilding. These kept to the center of the channel for fear of attack, yet I could hear the song of their sweepsmen across the water:

> Row, brothers, row!
> The current is against us.
> Row, brothers, row!
> Yet God is for us.
> Row, brothers, row!
> The wind is against us.
> Row, brothers, row!
> Yet God is for us.

And so on. Even when the lamps were no more than sparks a league or more upriver, the sound came on the wind. As I was later to see, they pull the shaft with the refrain, and put it back again with the alternate phrases, and so make their way watch upon watch.

When it seemed that it must soon be day, I saw upon the broad, black ribbon of the river a line of sparks that were not the lights of vessels but fixed fires stretching from bank to bank. It was a bridge, and after tramping long through the dark I reached it. Leaving the lapping tongues of the river, I mounted a flight of broken steps from the Water Way to the more elevated street of the bridge, and at once found myself an actor in a new scene.

The bridge was as well lighted as the Water Way had been shadowed. There were flambeaux on staggering poles every ten strides or so, and at intervals of about a hundred strides, bartizans whose guardroom windows glared like fireworks clung to the bridge piers. Carriages with lanterns rattled along, and most of the people who thronged the walkway were accompanied by linkboys or carried lights themselves. There were vendors who shouted the wares they displayed in trays hung from their necks, externs who gabbled in rude tongues, and beggars who showed their sores, feigned to play flageolets and ophicleides, and pinched their children to make them weep.

I confess I was much interested by all this, though my training prohibited me from gawking at it. With my hood drawn well over my head, and my eyes resolutely to the front, I passed among the crowd as if indifferent to it; but for a short time at least I felt my fatigue melt away, and my strides were, I think, the longer and swifter because I wanted to remain where I was.

The guards in the bartizans were not city roundsmen but peltasts in half-armor, bearing transparent shields. I was almost at the western bank when two stepped forward to bar my way with their blazing spears. "It is a serious crime to wear the costume you affect. If you intend some jape or artifice, you endanger yourself for its sake."

I said, "I am entitled to the habit of my guild."

"You seriously claim you are a carnifex, then? Is that a sword you carry?"

"It is, but I am no such thing. I am a journeyman of the Order of the Seekers for Truth and Penitence."

There was a silence. A hundred people or so had surrounded us in the few moments required for them to ask, and me to answer, their question. I saw the peltast who had not spoken glance at the other as if to say *he means it,* and then at the crowd.

"Come inside. The lochage wishes to speak with you."

They waited while I preceded them through the narrow door. The interior boasted only one small room, with a table and a few chairs. I mounted a little stair much worn by booted feet. In the room above, a man in a cuirass was writing at a high desk. My captors had followed me up, and when we stood before him, the one who had spoken previously said, "This is the man."

"I am aware of that," the lochage answered without looking up.

"He calls himself a journeyman of the guild of torturers."

For a moment the quill, which had skated along steadily before, paused. "I had never thought to encounter such a thing outside the pages of some book, but I dare say he speaks no more than the truth."

"Ought we to release him then?" the soldier asked.

"Not quite yet."

Now the lochage wiped his quill, sanded the letter over which he had labored, and looked up at us. I said, "Your subordinates stopped me because they doubted my right to the cloak I wear."

"They stopped you because I ordered it, and I ordered it because you were creating a disturbance, according to the report of the eastern turrets. If you are of the guild of torturers—which to be honest I had supposed reformed out of existence long ago—you have spent your life in the—What do you call it?"

"The Matachin Tower."

He snapped his fingers, and looked as though he were both amused and chagrined. "I mean the place where your tower stands."

"The Citadel."

"Yes, the Old Citadel. It's east of the river, as I recall, and just at the northern edge of the Algedonic Quarter. I was taken there to see the Donjon when I was a cadet. How often have you gone out into the city?"

I thought of our swimming expeditions and said, "Often."

"Dressed as you are now?"

I shook my head.

"If you're going to do that, pull back that hood. I can only see the tip of your nose wiggle." The lochage slid from his stool and strode to a window overlooking the bridge. "How many people do you think there are in Nessus?"

"I have no idea."

"No more do I, Torturer. No more does anyone. Every attempt to count them has failed, as has every attempt to tax them systematically. The city grows and changes every night, like writing chalked on a wall. Houses are built in the streets by clever people who take up the cobbles in the dark and claim the ground—did you know that? The exultant Talarican, whose madness manifested itself as a consuming interest in the lowest aspects of human existence, claimed that the persons who live by devouring the garbage of others number two gross thousands. That there are ten thousand begging acrobats, of whom nearly half are women. That if a pauper were to leap from the parapet of this bridge each time we draw breath, we should live forever, because the city breeds and breaks men faster than we respire. Among such a throng, there is no alternative to peace. Disturbances cannot be tolerated, because disturbances cannot be extinguished. Do you follow me?"

"There is the alternative of order. But yes, until that is achieved, I understand."

The lochage sighed and turned to face me. "If you understand that at least, good. It will be necessary, then, for you to obtain more conventional clothing."

"I cannot return to the Citadel."

"Then get out of sight tonight and buy something tomorrow. Have you funds?"

"A trifle, yes."

"Good. Buy something. Or steal, or strip the clothes from the next unfortunate you shorten with that thing. I'd have one of my fellows take you to an inn, but that would mean more staring and whispering still. There's been some kind of trouble on the river, and they're telling each other too many ghost stories out there already. Now the wind's dying and a fog's coming in—that will make it worse. Where are you going?"

"I am appointed to the town of Thrax."

The peltast who had spoken before said, "Do you believe him, Lochage? He's shown no proof that he's what he claims."

The lochage was looking out the window again, and now I too saw the threads of ochre mist. "If you can't use your head, use your nose," he said. "What odors entered with him?"

The peltast smiled uncertainly.

"Rusting iron, cold sweat, putrescent blood. An impostor would smell of new cloth, or rags picked from a truck. If you don't wake to your business soon, Petronax, you'll be north fighting the Ascians."

The peltast said, "But Lochage—" shooting such a look of hatred toward me that I thought he might attempt to do me some harm when I left the bartizan.

"Show this fellow you are indeed of the torturers' guild."

The peltast was relaxed, so there was no great difficulty. I knocked his shield aside with my right arm, putting my left foot on his right to pin him while I crushed that nerve in the neck that induces convulsions.

XV

Baldanders

THE CITY AT THE WESTERN END OF THE BRIDGE WAS VERY different from the one I had left. At first there were flambeaux at the corners, and nearly as much coming and going of coaches and drays as there had been on the bridge itself. Before quitting the bartizan, I had asked the lochage's advice about a place to spend what remained of the night; now, feeling the fatigue that had deserted me only briefly, I plodded along watching for the inn sign.

After a time the dark seemed to thicken with each step I took, and somewhere I must have taken the wrong turning. Unwilling to retrace my way, I tried to maintain a generally northerly route, comforting myself with the thought that though I might be lost, each stride carried me nearer Thrax. At last I discovered a small inn. I saw no sign and perhaps it had none, but I smelled cooking and heard the clink of tumblers, and I went in, throwing open the door and dropping into an old chair that stood near it without paying much attention to where I had come or whose company I had entered.

When I had been sitting there long enough to get my breath and was wishing for a place where I could take off my boots (though I was far from ready to get up to look for one), three men who had been drinking in a corner got up and left; and an old man, seeing, I suppose, that I was going to be bad for his business, came over and asked what I wanted. I told him I required a room.

"We have none."

I said, "That's just as well—I have no money to pay anyway."

"Then you will have to leave."

I shook my head. "Not yet. I'm too tired." (Other journeymen had told me of playing this trick in the city.)

"You're the carnifex, ain't you? You take their heads off."

"Bring me two of those fish I smell and you won't have anything but the heads left."

"I can call the City Guard. They'll have you out."

I knew from his tone that he did not believe what he said, so I told him to call away, but to bring me the fish in the meantime, and he went off grumbling. I sat up straighter then, with *Terminus Est* (which I had had to take from my shoulder to sit down) upright between my knees. There were five men still in the room with me, but none of them would meet my eye, and two soon left.

The old man returned with a small fish that had expired upon a slice of coarse bread, and said, "Eat this and go."

He stood and watched me while I had my supper. When I had finished it, I asked where I could sleep.

"No rooms. I told you."

If a palace had stood with open doors half a chain away, I do not think I could have driven myself to leave that inn to go to it. I said, "I'll sleep in this chair, then. You're not likely to have more trade tonight anyway."

"Wait," he said, and left me. I heard him talking to a woman in another room.

When I woke, he was shaking me by the shoulder. "Will you sleep three in a bed?"

"With whom?"

"Two optimates, I swear to you. Very nice men, traveling together."

The woman in the kitchen shouted something I could not understand.

"Did you hear that?" the old man continued. "One of them's not even come in yet. This time of night, he probably won't come at all. There'll be just the two of you."

"If these men have rented a bedchamber—"

"They won't object, I promise. Truth is, Carnifex, they're behind. Three nights here, and only paid for the first."

So I was to be used as an eviction notice. That did not disturb me much, and in fact it seemed somewhat promising—if the man sleeping there tonight left, I would have the room to myself. I clambered to my feet and followed the old man up a crooked stair.

The room we entered was not locked, but it was as dark as a tomb. I could hear heavy breathing. "Goodman!" the old fellow bawled, forgetting he had said his tenant was an optimate. "What-do-you-call-yourself? Baldy? Baldanders? I brought company for you. If you won't pay your rate, you got to take in boarders."

There was no reply.

"Here, Master Carnifex," the old man said to me, "I'll make you a light." He puffed at a bit of punk until it was bright enough to ignite a stub of candle.

The room was small, and held no furniture but a bed. In it, asleep on his side (as it appeared) with his back toward us and his legs drawn up, was the largest man I had ever seen—a man who might fairly have been called a giant.

"Aren't you going to wake, Goodman Baldanders, and see who your lodgemate might be?"

I wanted to go to bed and told the old man to leave us. He objected, but I pushed him out of the room and as soon as he was gone sat down on the unoccupied side of the bed and pulled off my boots and stockings. The weak light of the candle confirmed that I had developed several blisters. I took off my cloak and spread it on the worn counterpane. For a moment I considered whether I should take off my belt and trousers or sleep in them; prudence and weariness together urged the latter, and I noticed that the giant seemed fully dressed. With a feeling of inexpressible fatigue and relief I blew out the candle and lay down to spend the first night outside the Matachin Tower that I could recall.

"Never."

The tone was so deep and resonant (almost like the lowest notes of an organ) that I was not certain at first what the meaning of the word had been, or even if it had been a word at all. I mumbled, "What did you say?"

"Baldanders."

"I know—the innkeeper told me. I'm Severian." I was lying on my back, with *Terminus Est* (which I had brought into the bed for safekeeping) between us. In the dark, I could not tell whether my companion had rolled to face me or not, yet I was certain I would have felt any motion of that enormous frame.

"You—strike off."

"You heard us when we came in then. I thought you were asleep." My lips shaped themselves to say I was no carnifex, but a journeyman of the torturers' guild. Then I recalled my disgrace, and that Thrax has sent for an executioner. I said, "Yes, I'm a headsman, but you need not fear me. I only do what I am feed to do."

"Tomorrow, then."

"Yes, tomorrow will be time enough for us to meet and talk."

And then I dreamed, though it may have been that Baldanders' words, too, were a dream. Yet I do not think so, and if they were, it was a different dream.

I bestrode a great, leather-winged being under a lowering sky. Just equipoised between the rack of cloud and a twilit land we slid down a hill of air. Hardly once, it seemed to me, the finger-winged soarer flapped her long pinions. The dying sun was before us, and it seemed we matched the speed of Urth, for it stood unmoving at the horizon, though we flew on and on.

At last I saw a change in the land, and at first I thought it a desert. Far off, no cities or farms or woods or fields appeared, but only a level waste, a blackened purple in color, featureless and nearly static. The leathern-winged one observed it as well, or perhaps snatched some odor from the air. I felt iron muscles beneath me grow tense, and there were three stro' together.

The purple waste showed flecks of white. Af became aware that its seeming stillness was uniformity—it was the same everywhere in motion—the sea—the World-River Uroboros—cradling Urth.

Then for the first time I looked behind me, seeing all the country of humankind swallowed in the night.

When it was gone, and there was everywhere beneath us the waste of rolling water and nothing more, the beast turned her head to regard me. Her beak was the beak of an ibis, her face the face of a hag; on her head was a miter of bone. For an instant we regarded each other, and I seemed to know her thought: *You dream; but were you to wake from your waking, I would be there.*

Her motion changed as a lugger's does when the sailors make it to come about on the opposite tack. One pinion dipped, the other rose until it pointed toward the sky, and I scrabbled at the scaled hide and plummeted into the sea.

The shock of the impact woke me. I twitched in every joint, and heard the giant mutter in his sleep. In much the same way I murmured too, and groped to find if my sword still lay at my side, and slept again.

The water closed over me, yet I did not drown. I felt I might breathe water, yet I did not breathe. Everything was so clear that I felt I fell through an emptiness more translucent than air.

Far off loomed great shapes—things hundreds of times larger than a man. Some seemed ships, and some clouds; one was a living head without a body; one had a hundred heads. A blue haze obscured them, and I saw below me a country of sand, carved by the currents. A palace stood there that was greater than our Citadel, but it was ruinous, its halls as unroofed as its gardens; through it moved immense figures, white as leprosy.

Nearer I fell, and they turned up their faces to me, faces such as I had seen once beneath Gyoll; they were women, naked, with hair of sea-foam green and eyes of coral. Laughing, they watched me fall, and their laughter came bubbling up to me. Their teeth were white and pointed, each a finger's length.

I fell nearer. Their hands reached up to me and stroked me as a mother strokes her child. The gardens of the palace held sponges and sea anemones and countless other beauties to which I could put no name. The great women circled me round, and I was only a doll before them. "Who are you?" I asked. "And what do you do here?"

"We are the brides of Abaia. The sweethearts and playthings, the toys and valentines of Abaia. The land could not hold us. Our breasts are battering rams, our buttocks would break the backs of bulls. Here we feed, floating and growing, until we are great enough to mate with Abaia, who will one day devour the continents."

"And who am I?"

Then they laughed all together, and their laughter was like surf upon a beach of glass. "We will show you," they said. "We will show you!" One took me by each hand, as sisters take their sister's child, and lifted me up, and swam with me through the garden. Their fingers were webbed, and as long as my arm from shoulder to elbow.

They halted, settling through the water like carracks sinking, until their feet and mine touched the strand. There stood before us a low wall, and on it a little stage and curtain, such as are used for children's entertainments.

Our roiling of the water seemed to flutter the kerchief-sized cloth. It rippled and swayed, and began to draw back as though teased by an unseen hand. At once there appeared the tiny figure of a man of sticks. His limbs were twigs, still showing bark and green bud. His body was a quarter-span of branch, big through as my thumb, and his head a knot whose whorls formed his eyes and mouth. He carried a club (which he brandished at us) and moved as if he were alive.

When the wooden man had jumped for us, and struck the little stage with his weapon to show his ferocity, there appeared the figure of a boy armed with a sword. This marionette was as finely finished as the other was crude—it might have been a real child reduced to the size of a mouse.

After both had bowed to us, the tiny figures fought. The wooden man performed prodigious leaps and seemed to fill the stage with the blows of his cudgel; the boy danced like a dust mote in a sunbeam to avoid it, darting at the wooden man to slash with his pin-sized blade.

At last the wooden figure collapsed. The boy strode over as if to set his foot upon its chest; but before he could do so, the wooden figure floated from the stage, and turning limply and lazily rose until it vanished from sight, leaving behind the boy, and the cudgel and the sword—both broken. I seemed to hear (no doubt it was really the squeaking of cartwheels on the street outside) a flourish of toy trumpets.

I woke because a third person had come into the room. He was a small, brisk man with fiery red hair, well and even foppishly dressed. When he saw me awake, he threw back the shutters that had covered the window, bringing red sunlight streaming in.

"My partner," he said, "sleeps soundly always. His snoring didn't deafen you?"

"I slept well myself," I told him. "And if he snored, I didn't hear him."

That seemed to please the small man, who showed a good many gold teeth when he smiled. "He does. He snores to shake Urth, I assure you. Happy you got your rest anyway." He extended a delicate, well-cared-for hand. "I am Dr. Talos."

"The Journeyman Severian." I threw off the thin coverings and stood up to take it.

"You wear black, I see. What guild is that?"

"It is the fuligin of the torturers."

"Ah!" He cocked his head to one side like a thrush, and hopped about to look at me from various angles. "You're a tall fellow—that's a shame—but all that sooty stuff is very impressive."

"We find it practical," I said. "The oubliette is a dirty place, and fuligin doesn't show bloodstains."

"You have humor! That's excellent! There are few advantages, I'll tell you, that profit a man more than humor. Humor will draw a crowd. Humor will calm a mob or reassure a nursery school. Humor will get you on and get you off, and pull in asimis like a magnet."

I had only the vaguest idea of what he was saying, but seeing that he was in an affable mood, I ventured, "I hope I didn't discommode you? The landlord said I was to sleep here, and there was room for another person in the bed."

"No, no, not at all! I never came back—found a better place to pass the night. I sleep very little, I may as well tell you, and I'm a light sleeper too. But I had a good night of it, an excellent night. Where are you going this morning, optimate?"

I was fumbling under the bed for my boots. "First to look for some breakfast, I suppose. After that, out of the city, to the north."

"Excellent! No doubt my partner would appreciate a breakfast—it will do him a world of good. And we're traveling north. After a most successful tour of the city, you know. Going back home now. Played the east bank down, and playing the west up. Perhaps we'll stop at the House Absolute on our way north. That's the dream, you know, in the profession. Play the Autarch's palace. Or come back, if you've already played there. Chrisos by the hatful."

"I've met one other person, at least, who dreamed of going back."

"Don't put on that long face—you must tell me about him sometime. But now, if we're to go to breakfast—*Baldanders!* Wake up! Come, Baldanders, come! Wake up!" He danced to the foot of the bed and grasped the giant by an ankle. "Baldanders! Don't take him by the shoulder, optimate!" (I had made no motion to do so.) "He thrashes about sometimes. BALDANDERS!"

The giant murmured and stirred.

"A new day, Baldanders! Still alive! Time to eat and defecate and make love—all that! Up now, or we'll never get home."

There was no sign that the giant had heard him. It was as if the murmur of the moment before had been only a protest voiced in a dream, or his death rattle. Dr. Talos seized the foul blankets with both hands and swept them back.

The monstrous shape of his partner lay revealed. He was even taller than I had supposed, nearly too tall for the bed, though he slept with his knees drawn almost to his chin. His shoulders were an ell across, high and hunched. His face I could not see; it lay buried in his pillow. There were strange scars about his neck and ears.

"Baldanders!"

His hair was grizzled, and despite the innkeeper's pretended error, very thick.

"Baldanders! Your pardon, optimate, but may I borrow that sword?"

"No," I said. "You may not."

"Oh, I'm not going to kill him, or anything of that sort. I only want to use the flat of it."

I shook my head, and when Dr. Talos saw I was still adamant, he began to rummage about the room. "Left my stick downstairs. Vile custom, they'll thieve it. I should learn to limp, I really should. There's nothing here at all."

He darted out the door, and was back in a moment carrying an ironwood walking stick with a gilt-brass knob. "Now then! *Baldanders!*" The strokes fell upon the giant's broad back like the big raindrops that precede a thunderstorm.

Quite suddenly, the giant sat up. "I'm awake, Doctor." His face was large and coarse, but sensitive and sad as well. "Have you decided to kill me at last?"

"What are you talking about, Baldanders? Oh, you mean the optimate here. He's not going to do you any hurt—he shared the bed with you, and now he's going to join us at breakfast."

"He slept here, Doctor?"

Dr. Talos and I both nodded.

"Then I know whence my dreams rose."

I was still saturated with the sight of the huge women beneath the monstered sea, and so I asked what his dreams had been, though I was somewhat in awe of him.

"Of caverns below, where stone teeth dripped blood . . . Of arms dismembered found on sanded paths, and things that shook chains in the dark." He sat at the edge of the bed, cleaning sparse and surprisingly small teeth with one great finger.

Dr. Talos said, "Come on, both of you. If we're to eat and talk and get anything done today—why, we must be at it. Much to say and much to do."

Baldanders spat into the corner.

XVI

The Rag Shop

IT WAS ON THAT WALK THROUGH THE STREETS OF STILL SLUMBER-
ing Nessus that my grief, which was to obsess me so often,
first gripped me with all its force. When I had been
imprisoned in our oubliette, the enormity of what I had done,
and the enormity of the redress I felt sure I would make soon
under Master Gurloes's hands, had dulled it. The day before,
when I had swung down the Water Way, the joy of freedom
and the poignancy of exile had driven it away. Now it seemed
to me that there was no fact in all the world beyond the fact of
Thecla's death. Each patch of darkness among the shadows
reminded me of her hair; every glint of white recalled her
skin. I could hardly restrain myself from rushing back to the
Citadel to see if she might not still be sitting in her cell,
reading by the light of the silver lamp.

We found a cafe whose tables were set along the margin of
the street. It was still sufficiently early that there was very
little traffic. A dead man (he had, I think, been suffocated
with a lambrequin, there being those who practice that art)
lay at the corner. Dr. Talos went through his pockets, but
came back with empty hands.

"Now then," he said. "We must think. We must contrive a
plan."

A waitress brought mugs of mocha, and Baldanders pushed
one toward him. He stirred it with his forefinger.

"Friend Severian, perhaps I should elucidate our situation.
Baldanders—he is my only patient—and I hail from the
region about Lake Diuturna. Our home burned, and needing

121

a trifle of money to set it right again we decided to venture abroad. My friend is a man of amazing strength. I assemble a crowd, he breaks some timbers and lifts ten men at once, and I sell my cures. Little enough, you will say. But there's more. I've a play, and we've assembled properties. When the situation is favorable, he and I enact certain scenes and even invite the participation of some of the audience. Now, friend, you say you are going north, and from your bed last night I take it you are not in funds. May I propose a joint venture?"

Baldanders, who appeared to have understood only the first part of his companion's speech, said slowly, "It is not entirely destroyed. The walls are stone, very thick. Some of the vaults escaped."

"Quite correct. We plan to restore the dear old place. But see our dilemma—we're now halfway on the return leg of our tour, and our accumulated capital is still far from sufficient. What I propose—"

The waitress, a thin young woman with straggling hair, came carrying a bowl of gruel for Baldanders, bread and fruit for me, and a pastry for Dr. Talos. "What an attractive girl!" he said.

She smiled at him.

"Can you sit down? We seem to be your only customers."

After glancing in the direction of the kitchen, she shrugged and pulled over a chair.

"You might enjoy a bit of this—I'll be too busy talking to eat such a dry concoction. And a sip of mocha, if you don't object to drinking after me."

She said, "You'd think he'd let us eat for nothing, wouldn't you? But he won't. Charges everything at full price."

"Ah! You're not the owner's daughter, then. I feared you were. Or his wife. How can he have allowed such a blossom to flourish unplucked?"

"I've only worked here about a month. The money they leave on the table's all I get. Take you three, now. If you don't give me anything, I will have served you for nothing."

"Quite so, quite so! But what about this? What if we attempt to render you a rich gift, and you refuse it?" Dr. Talos leaned toward her as he said this, and it struck me that his face was not only that of a fox (a comparison that was perhaps too easy to make because his bristling reddish eyebrows and sharp nose suggested it at once) but that of a stuffed fox. I have heard those who dig for their livelihood say there is no land anywhere in which they can trench without turning up the shards of the past. No matter where the spade turns the soil, it uncovers broken pavements and corroding metal; and scholars write that the kind of sand that artists call polychrome (because flecks of every color are mixed with its whiteness) is actually not sand at all, but the glass of the past, now pounded to powder by aeons of tumbling in the clamorous sea. If there are layers of reality beneath the reality we see, even as there are layers of history beneath the ground we walk upon, then in one of those more profound realities, Dr. Talos's face was a fox's mask on a wall, and I marveled to see it turn and bend now toward the woman, achieving by those motions, which made expression and thought appear to play across it with the shadows of the nose and brows, an amazing and realistic appearance of vivacity. "Would you refuse it?" he asked again, and I shook myself as though waking.

"What do you mean?" the woman wanted to know. "One of you is a carnifex. Are you talking about the gift of death? The Autarch, whose pores outshine the stars themselves, protects the lives of his subjects."

"The gift of death? Oh, no!" Dr. Talos laughed. "No, my dear, you've had that all your life. So has he. We wouldn't pretend to give you what is already yours. The gift we offer is beauty, with the fame and wealth that derive from it."

"If you're selling something, I haven't got any money."

"Selling? Not at all! Quite the contrary, we are offering you new employment. I am a thaumaturge, and these optimates are actors. Have you never wanted to go on the stage?"

"I thought you looked funny, the three of you."

"We stand in need of an ingenue. You may claim the position, if you wish. But you must come with us now—we've no time to waste, and we won't come this way again."

"Becoming an actress won't make me beautiful."

"I will make you beautiful because we require you as an actress. It is one of my powers." He stood up. "Now or not at all. Will you come?"

The waitress rose too, still looking at his face. "I have to go to my room . . ."

"What do you own but dross? I must cast the glamour and teach you your lines, all in a day. I will not wait."

"Give me the money for your breakfasts, and I'll tell him I'm leaving."

"Nonsense! As a member of our company, you must assist in conserving the funds we will require for your costumes. Not to mention that you ate my pastry. Pay for it yourself."

For an instant she hesitated. Baldanders said, "You may trust him. The doctor has his own way of looking at the world, but he lies less than people believe."

The deep, slow voice seemed to reassure her. "All right," she said, "I'll go."

In a few moments, the four of us were several streets away, walking past shops that were still for the most part shuttered. When we had gone some distance, Dr. Talos announced, "And now, my dear friends, we must separate. I will devote my time to the enhancement of this sylph. Baldanders, you must get our collapsing proscenium and the other properties from the inn where you and Severian spent the night—I trust that will present no difficulties. Severian, we will perform, I think, at Ctesiphon's Cross. Do you know the spot?"

I nodded, though I had no notion of where it might be. The truth was that I had no intention of rejoining them.

Now, as Dr. Talos quick-stepped away with the waitress trotting behind him, I found myself alone with Baldanders on the deserted street. Anxious that he leave too, I asked him where he meant to go. It was more like talking to a monument than speaking with a man.

"There is a park near the river where one may sleep by day, though not by night. When it is nearly dark, I will awaken and collect our belongings."

"I'm afraid I'm not sleepy. I'm going to look around the city."

"I will see you then, at Ctesiphon's Cross."

For some reason I felt he knew what was in my mind. "Yes," I said. "Of course."

His eyes were dull as an ox's as he turned away to lumber with long steps toward Gyoll. Since Baldanders's park lay east and Dr. Talos had taken the waitress west, I resolved to walk north and so continue my journey toward Thrax, the City of Windowless Rooms.

Meanwhile, Nessus, the City Imperishable (the city in which I had lived all my life, though I had seen so little of it), lay all about me. Along a wide, flint-paved avenue I walked, not knowing or caring whether it was a side street or the principal one of the quarter. There were raised paths for pedestrians at either side, and a third in the center, where it served to divide the northbound traffic from the southbound.

To the left and right, buildings seemed to spring from the ground like grain too closely planted, shouldering one another for a place; and what buildings they were—nothing so large as the Great Keep and nothing so old; none, I think, with walls like the metal walls of our tower, five paces through; yet the Citadel had nothing to compare with them in color or originality of conception, nothing so novel and fantastic as each of these structures was, though each stood among a hundred others. As is the fashion in some parts of the city, most of these buildings had shops in their lower levels, though they had not been built for the shops but as guildhalls, basilicas, arenas, conservatories, treasuries, oratories, artellos, asylums, manufactures, conventicles, hospices, lazarets, mills, refectories, deadhouses, abattoirs, and playhouses. Their architecture reflected these functions, and a thousand conflicting tastes. Turrets and minarets bristled; lanterns, domes, and rotundas soothed; flights of steps as steep as ladders ascended sheer walls; and balconies wrapped facades and sheltered them in the par-terre privacies of citrons and pomegranates.

I was wondering at these hanging gardens amid the forest of pink and white marble, red sardonyx, blue-gray, and cream, and black bricks, and green and yellow and tyrian tiles, when the sight of a lansquenet guarding the entrance to a casern reminded me of the promise I had made the officer of the peltasts the night before. Since I had little money and was well aware that I would require the warmth of my guild cloak by night, the best plan seemed to be to buy a voluminous mantle of some cheap stuff that could be worn over it. Shops were opening, but those that sold clothing all appeared to sell what would not fit my purpose, and at prices greater than I could afford.

The idea of working at my profession before I reached Thrax had not yet occurred to me; if it had, I would have dismissed it, supposing that there would be so little call for a torturer's services that it would be impractical for me to seek out those who required them. I believed, in short, that the three asimis, and the orichalks and aes in my pocket would have to carry me all the way to Thrax; and I had no idea of the size of the rewards that would be proffered me. Thus I stared at balmacaans and surtouts, dolmans and jerkins of paduasoy, matelasse, and a hundred other costly fabrics without ever going into the places that displayed them, or even stopping to examine them.

Soon my attention was seduced by other goods. Though I knew nothing of it at the time, thousands of mercenaries were outfitting themselves for the summer campaign. There were bright military capes and saddle blankets, saddles with armored pommels to protect the loins, red forage caps, long-shafted khetens, fans of silver foil for signaling, bows curved and recurved for use by cavalry, arrows in matched sets of ten and twenty, bow cases of boiled leather decorated with gilt studs and mother-of-pearl, and archers' guards to protect the left wrist from the bowstring. When I saw all these, I remembered what Master Palaemon had said before my masking about following the drum; and although I had held the matrosses of the Citadel in some contempt, I seemed to hear the long rattle of the call to parade, and the bright challenge the trumpets sent from the battlements.

Just when I had been wholly distracted from my search, a slender woman of twenty or a little more came out of one of the dark shops to unfasten the gratings. She wore a pavonine brocade gown of amazing richness and raggedness, and as I watched her, the sun touched a rent just below her waist, turning the skin there to palest gold.

I cannot explain the desire I felt for her, then and afterward. Of the many women I have known, she was, perhaps, the least beautiful—less graceful than her I have loved most, less voluptuous than another, less reginal far than Thecla. She was of average height, with a short nose, wide cheekbones, and the elongated brown eyes that often accompany them. I saw her lift the grating, and I loved her with a love that was deadly and yet not serious.

Of course I went to her. I could no more have resisted her than I could have resisted the blind greed of Urth if I had tumbled over a cliff. I did not know what to say to her, and I was terrified that she would recoil in horror at the sight of my sword and fuligin cloak. But she smiled and actually seemed to admire my appearance. After a moment, when I said nothing, she asked what I wanted; and I asked if she knew where I might buy a mantle.

"Are you sure you need one?" Her voice was deeper than I had expected. "You've such a beautiful cloak now. May I touch it?"

"Please. If you wish to."

She took up the edge and rubbed the fabric gently between her palms. "I've never seen such a black—so dark you can't see folds in it. It makes my hand look as though it's disappeared. And that sword. Is that an opal?"

"Would you like to examine that too?"

"No, no. Not at all. But if you really want a mantle . . ." She gestured toward the window, and I saw that it was filled with articles of worn clothing of every kind, jelabs, capotes, smocks, cymars, and so on. "Very inexpensive. Really reasonable. If you'll just go in, I'm sure you'll find what you want." I entered through a jingling door, but the young woman did not (as I had so much hoped she would) follow me inside.

The interior was dim, yet as soon as I looked about I thought I understood why the woman had not been disturbed by my appearance. The man behind the counter was more frightening than any torturer. His face was a skeleton's or nearly so, a face with dark pits for eyes, shrunken cheeks, and a lipless mouth. If it had not moved and spoken, I would not have believed he was a living man at all, but a corpse left erect behind the counter in fulfilment of the morbid wish of some past owner.

XVII

The Challenge

YET IT DID MOVE, TURNING TO LOOK AT ME AS I CAME IN; AND IT did speak. "Very fine. Yes, very fine. Your cloak, optimate—may I see it?"

I walked across a floor of worn and uneven tiles to him. A slash of red sunshine alive with swarming dust stood stiff as a blade between us.

"Your garment, optimate." I caught up my cloak and extended my left hand, and he touched the fabric much as the young woman had outside. "Yes, very fine. Soft. Wool-like, yet softer, much softer. A blend of linen and vicuna? And wonderful color. A torturer's vesture. One doubts the real ones were half so fine, but who can argue with a textile like that?" He ducked beneath his counter and emerged with a handful of rags. "Might I examine the sword? I'll be extremely careful, I promise you."

I unsheathed *Terminus Est* and laid her on the rags. He bent over her, neither touching her nor speaking. By that time my eyes had become accustomed to the dimness of the shop, and I noticed a narrow black ribbon that stretched forward a finger's width from the hair above his ears. "You are wearing a mask," I said.

"Three chrisos. For the sword. Another for the cloak."

"I didn't come here to sell," I told him. "Take it off."

"If you like. All right, four chrisos for the sword." He lifted his hands and the death's-head fell into them. His real face, flat-cheeked and tanned, was remarkably like that of the young woman I had seen outside.

"I want to buy a mantle."

"Five chrisos for it. That's positively my last offer. You'll have to give me a day to raise the money."

"I told you, this sword is not for sale." I picked up *Terminus Est* and resheathed her.

"Six." Reaching across the counter, he took me by the arm. "That's more than it's worth. Listen, it's your last chance. I mean it. Six."

"I came in to buy a mantle. Your sister, as I would assume she was, said you would have one at a reasonable price."

He sighed. "All right, I'll sell you a mantle. Will you tell me first where you got that sword?"

"It was given me by a master of our guild." I saw an expression I could not quite identify flicker across his face, and I asked, "You don't believe me?"

"I do believe you, that's the trouble. Just what are you?"

"A journeyman of the torturers. We don't often get to this side of the river, or come this far north. But are you really so surprised?"

He nodded. "It's like encountering a psychopomp. Can I ask why you're in this quarter of the city?"

"You may, but it's the last question I'm going to answer. I'm on my way to Thrax, to take up an assignment there."

"Thank you," he said. "I won't pry any more. I don't have to, really. Now since you'll want to surprise your friends when you take off your mantle—am I right?—it ought to be of some color that will contrast with your vesture. White might be good, but it's a rather dramatic color itself, and terribly hard to keep clean. What about a dull brown?"

"The ribbons that held your mask," I said. "They're still there."

He was dragging down boxes from behind his counter and did not reply. After a moment or two we were interrupted by the tinkling of the bell above the door. The new customer was a youth whose face was hidden in an inlaid close helmet, of which down-curving and intertwined horns formed the visor. He wore armor of lacquered leather; a golden chimera with the blank, staring face of a madwoman fluttered on his breastplate.

"Yes, hipparch." The shopkeeper dropped his boxes to make a servile bow. "How may I assist you?"

A gauntleted hand reached toward me, the fingers pinched as though to give me a coin.

"Take it," the shopkeeper said in a frightened whisper. "Whatever it is."

I extended my own hand, and received a shining black seed the size of a raisin. I heard the shopkeeper gasp; the armored figure turned and went out.

When he was gone, I laid the seed on the counter. The shopkeeper squeaked, "Don't try to pass it to me!" and backed away.

"What is it?"

"You don't know? The stone of the avern. What have you done to offend an officer of the Household Troops?"

"Nothing. Why did he give me this?"

"You've been challenged. You're called out."

"To monomachy? Impossible. I'm not of the contending class."

His shrug was more eloquent than words. "You'll have to fight, or they'll have you assassinated. The only question is whether you've really offended the hipparch, or if there's some highly placed official of the House Absolute behind this."

As clearly as I saw the shopkeeper, I saw Vodalus in the necropolis standing his ground against the three volunteer guards; and though all prudence told me to toss aside the avern stone and flee the city, I could not do it. Someone— perhaps the Autarch himself or shadowy Father Inire—had learned the truth about Thecla's death, and now sought to destroy me without disgracing the guild. Very well, I would fight. If I were victorious he might reconsider; if I were killed, that would be no more than just. Still thinking of Vodalus's slender blade, I said, "The only sword I understand is this one."

"You won't engage with swords—in fact, it would be best if you left that with me."

"Absolutely not."

He sighed again. "I see you know nothing about these matters, yet you are going to fight for your life at twilight. Very well, you are my customer, and I've never yet abandoned a customer. You wanted a mantle. Here." He strode to the back of his shop and came forward carrying a garment the color of dead leaves. "Try this one. It will be four orichalks if it fits."

A mantle so large and loose could not but fit unless it was grossly short or long. The price seemed excessive, but I paid, and in donning the mantle took one step further toward becoming the actor that day seemed to wish to force me to become. Indeed, I was already taking part in more dramas than I realized.

"Now then," the shopkeeper said, "I must stay here to look after things, but I'll send my sister to help you get your avern. She has often gone to the Sanguinary Field, so perhaps she can also teach you the rudiments of combat with it."

"Did someone speak of me?" The young woman I had met at the front of the shop now came from one of the dark storerooms at its rear. With her upturned nose and strangely tilted eyes, she looked so much like her brother I felt sure they were twins, but the slender figure and delicate features that seemed incongruent in him were compelling in her. Her brother must have explained what had befallen me. I do not know, because I did not hear it. I was looking only at her.

Now I begin again. It has been a long time (twice I have heard the guard changed outside my study door) since I wrote the lines you read only a moment before. I am not certain it is right to record these scenes, which perhaps are important only to me, in so much detail. I might easily have condensed everything: I saw a shop and went in; I was challenged by an officer of the Septentrions; the shopkeeper sent his sister to help me pluck the poisoned flower. I have spent weary days in reading the histories of my predecessors, and they consist of little but such accounts. For example, of Ymar:

Disguising himself, he ventured into the countryside, where he spied a muni meditating beneath a plane tree. The Autarch joined him and sat with his back to the trunk until Urth had begun to spurn the sun. Troopers bearing an oriflamme galloped past, a merchant drove a mule staggering under gold, a beautiful woman rode the shoulders of eunuchs, and at last a dog trotted through the dust. Ymar rose and followed the dog, laughing.

Supposing this anecdote to be true, how easy it is to explain: the Autarch had demonstrated that he chose his active life by an act of will, and not because of the seductions of the world.

But Thecla had had many teachers, each of whom would explain the same fact in a different way. Here, then, a second teacher might say that the Autarch was proof against those things that attract common men, but powerless to control his love of the hunt.

And a third, that the Autarch wished to show his contempt for the muni, who had remained silent when he might have poured forth enlightenment and received more. That he could not do by leaving when there was none to share the road, since solitude has great attractions for the wise. Nor could he when the soldiers passed, nor the merchant with his wealth, nor the woman, for unenlightened men desire all those things, and the muni would have thought him one more such man.

And a fourth, that the Autarch accompanied the dog because it went forth alone, the soldiers having other soldiers, the merchant his mule and the mule his merchant, and the woman her slaves; while the muni did not go forth.

Yet why did Ymar laugh? Who shall say? Did the merchant follow the soldiers to buy their booty? Did the woman follow the merchant to sell her kisses and her loins? Was the dog of the hunting kind, or such a short-limbed one as women keep to bark lest someone fondle them while they sleep? Who now shall say? Ymar is dead, and such memories of his as lived for a time in the blood of his successors are long faded.

So mine in time shall fade too. Of this I feel sure: not one of the explanations for the behavior of Ymar was correct. The truth, whatever it may have been, was simpler and more subtle. Of me it might be asked why I accepted the shopkeeper's sister as my companion—I who in all my life had had no true companion. And who, reading only of "the shopkeeper's sister," would understand why I remained with her after what is, at this point in my own story, about to happen? No one, surely.

I have said that I cannot explain my desire for her, and it is true. I loved her with a love thirsty and desperate. I felt that we two might commit some act so atrocious that the world, seeing us, would find it irresistible.

No intellect is needed to see those figures who wait beyond the void of death—every child is aware of them, blazing with glories dark or bright, wrapped in authority older than the universe. They are the stuff of our earliest dreams, as of our dying visions. Rightly we feel our lives guided by them, and rightly too we feel how little we matter to them, the builders of the unimaginable, the fighters of wars beyond the totality of existence.

The difficulty lies in learning that we ourselves encompass forces equally great. We say, "I will," and "I will not," and imagine ourselves (though we obey the orders of some prosaic person every day) our own masters, when the truth is that our masters are sleeping. One wakes within us and we are ridden like beasts, though the rider is but some hitherto unguessed part of ourselves.

Perhaps, indeed, that is the explanation of the story of Ymar. Who can say?

However that may be, I let the shopkeeper's sister help me adjust the mantle. It could be drawn tightly about the neck, and when it was worn so, my fuligin guild cloak was invisible beneath it. Still without revealing myself, I could reach through the front or through slits at the sides. I unfastened *Terminus Est* from her baldric and carried her like a staff for as long as I wore that mantle, and because her sheath covered most of her guard and was tipped with dark iron, many of the people who saw me no doubt thought it was one.

It was the only time in my life when I have covered the habit of the guild with a disguise. I have heard it said that one always feels a fool in them, whether they succeed or not, and surely I felt a fool in that one. And yet it was hardly a disguise at all. Those wide, old-fashioned mantles originated with shepherds (who wear them still), and were passed from them to the military in the days when the fighting with the Ascians took place here in the cool south. From the army they were taken up by religious pilgrims, who no doubt found a garment that could be converted into a more-or-less-satisfactory little tent very practical. The decline of religion has no doubt done much to extinguish them in Nessus, where I never saw any other than the one I wore myself. If I had known more about them when I put on mine in the rag shop, I would have bought a soft, wide-brimmed hat to go with it; but I did not, and the shopkeeper's sister told me I looked a good palmer. No doubt she said it with that twinkle of mockery with which she said everything else, but I was concerned with my appearance and failed to notice it. I told her and her brother that I wished I knew more of religion.

Both smiled, and the brother said, "If you mention it first, no one will want to talk about it. Besides, you can get the reputation of being a good fellow by wearing that and *not* talking about it. When you meet someone you don't want to talk to at all, beg alms."

So I became, in appearance at least, a pilgrim bound for some vague northern shrine. Have I said that time turns our lies into truths?

XVIII

The Destruction of the Altar

THE HUSH OF EARLY MORNING HAD VANISHED WHILE I WAS IN the rag shop. Wains and drays rumbled by in an avalanche of beasts, wood, and iron; the shopkeeper's sister and I had no more than stepped out of the door than I heard a flier skimming among the towers of the city. I looked up in time to see it, sleek as a raindrop on a windowpane.

"That's probably the officer who called you out," she remarked. "He'll be on his way back to the House Absolute. A hipparch of the Septentrion Guard—isn't that what Agilus said?"

"Is that your brother? Yes, something like that. What is your own name?"

"Agia. And you know nothing of monomachy? And have me for an instructor? Well, high Hypogeon help you. We'll have to go to the Botanic Gardens to begin with and cut you an avern. Fortunately they're not too far from here. Do you have enough money for us to take a fiacre?"

"I suppose so. If it is necessary."

"Then you're really not an armiger in costume. You're a—whatever you are."

"A torturer. Yes. When am I supposed to meet the hipparch?"

"Not until late afternoon, when the fighting begins at the Sanguinary Field and the avern opens its flower. We've plenty of time, but I think we'd better use it in getting you one and teaching you how to fight with it." A fiacre drawn by a pair of onegars was dodging toward us, and she waved to it. "You're going to be killed, you know."

"From what you say, it seems very likely."

"It's practically certain, so don't worry about your money." Agia stepped out into the traffic, looking for a moment (so finely chiseled was that delicate face, so graceful the curve of her body as she lifted an arm) like a memorial statue to the unknown woman on foot. I thought she was certain to be killed herself. The fiacre drew up to her with the skittish animals dancing to one side as though she were a thyacine, and she vaulted in. Light as she was, her weight made the little vehicle rock. I climbed in beside her, where we sat with our hips pressed together. The driver glanced back at us, Agia said, "The landing for the Botanic Gardens," and we jolted off. "So dying doesn't bother you—that's refreshing."

I braced myself with a hand on the back of the driver's bench. "Surely that's not unusual. There must be thousands, and perhaps millions of people like me. People accustomed to death, who feel that the only part of their lives that really mattered is over."

The sun was now just above the tallest spires, and the flooding light that turned the dusty pavement to red gold made me feel philosophical. In the brown book in my sabretache there was the tale of an angel (perhaps actually one of the winged women warriors who are said to serve the Autarch) who, coming to Urth on some petty mission or other, was struck by a child's arrow and died. With her gleaming robes all dyed by her heart's blood even as the boulevards were stained by the expiring life of the sun, she encountered Gabriel himself. His sword blazed in one hand, his great two-headed ax swung in the other, and across his back, suspended on the rainbow, hung the very battle horn of Heaven. "Where wend you, little one," asked Gabriel, "with your breast more scarlet than the robin's?" "I am killed," the angel said, "and I return to merge my substance once more with the Pancreator." "Do not be absurd. You are an angel, a pure spirit, and cannot die." "But I am dead," said the angel, "nevertheless. You have observed the wasting of my blood— do you not observe also that it no longer issues in straining spurtings, but only seeps sluggishly? Note the pallor of my countenance. Is not the touch of an angel warm and bright? Take my hand and you will imagine you hold a horror new dragged from some stagnant pool. Taste my breath—is it not fetid, foul, and nidorous?" Gabriel answered nothing, and at last the angel said, "Brother and better, even if I have not convinced you with all my proofs, I pray you stand aside. I would rid the universe of my presence." "I am convinced indeed," Gabriel said, stepping from the other's way. "It is only that I was thinking that had I known we might perish, I would not at all times have been so bold."

To Agia I said, "I feel like the archangel in the story—if I had known I could spend my life so easily and so soon, I would not—probably—have done it. Do you know the legend? But I have made my decisions now, and there's nothing more to say or do. This afternoon the Septentrion will kill me with what? A plant? A flower? In some way I don't understand. A short time ago, I thought I could go to a place called Thrax and live there whatever life there was to be lived. Well, last night I roomed with a giant. One is not more fantastical than the other."

She did not reply, and after a time I asked, "What is that building over there? The one with the vermilion roof and the forked columns? I think there's allspice pounded in the mortar. At least, I smell something of that sort from it."

"The mensal of the monachs. Do you know you are a frightening man? When you entered our shop, I thought you only another young armiger in motley. Then when I found you really were a torturer, I thought it couldn't really be so bad after all—that you were only a young man like other young men."

"And you have known a great many young men, I imagine." The truth was that I was hoping she had. I wanted her to be more experienced than I; and though I did not for an instant think myself pure, I wished to think her less pure still.

"But there is something more to you after all. You have the face of someone who stands to inherit two palatinates and an isle somewhere I never heard of, and the manners of a shoemaker, and when you say you're not afraid to die, you think you mean it, and under that you believe you don't. But you do, at the very bottom. It wouldn't bother you a bit to chop off my head either, would it?"

Around us swirled traffic of every sort: machines, wheeled and wheelless vehicles pulled by animals and slaves, walkers, and riders on the backs of dromedaries, oxen, metamynodons, and hackneys. Now an open fiacre like our own drew up beside us. Agia leaned toward the couple it carried and shouted, "We'll distance you!"

"Where bound?" the man called back, and I recognized Sieur Racho, whom I had once met when I had been sent to Master Ultan for books.

I gripped Agia by the arm. "Are you mad, or is he?"

"The Garden Landing, for a chrisos!"

The other vehicle tore away with ours behind it. "Faster!" Agia shouted to our driver. Then to me: "Have you a dagger? It's best to put the point to his back, so he can say he drove under threat of annihilation if we're stopped."

"Why are you doing this?"

"As a test. No one will believe your disguise. But everyone will believe you're an armiger in fancy dress. I've just proved it." (We careened about a dray loaded with sand.) "Besides, we'll win. I know this driver and his team's fresh. The other's been carting that whore for half the night."

I realized then that I would be expected to give Agia the money if we won, and that the other woman would claim my (nonexistent) chrisos from Racho if they did. Yet how sweet to humble him! Speed and the nearness of death (for I felt certain I would indeed be slain by the hipparch) made me more reckless than I had ever been in my life. I drew *Terminus Est*, and thanks to the length of her blade I could reach the onegars easily. Their flanks were already soaked with sweat, and the shallow cuts I made there must have burned like flames. "That's better than any dagger," I told Agia.

The crowd parted like water before the drivers' whips, mothers clasping their children as they fled, soldiers vaulting on their spears to the safety of windowsills. The conditions of the race favored us: the fiacre ahead to some extent cleared our path, and it was more impeded by other vehicles than we. Still we gained only slowly, and to get a few ells' advantage, our driver, who no doubt anticipated a rich tip if he won, sent the onegars hurtling up a flight of broad chalcedony steps. Marbles and monuments, pillars and pilasters, seemed thrown at our faces. We crashed through the green wall of a hedge as high as a house, overturned a cartload of comfits, dove through an arch and down a stair wound in a half turn, and were in the street again without ever knowing whose patio we had violated.

A baker's barrow drawn by sheep ambled into the narrow space between our vehicle and the other, and our big rear wheel jolted it, sending a shower of fresh bread into the street and throwing Agia's slight body against mine so pleasantly that I put an arm about it and held it there. I had clasped women so before—Thecla often, and hired bodies in the town. There was new bittersweetness in this, born of the cruel attraction Agia held for me. "I'm glad you did that," she said in my ear. "I hate men who grab me," and covered my face with kisses.

The driver looked back with a grin of triumph, letting the maddened team choose its own path. "Gone down the Twisted Way—got them now—across the common and reach them by a hundred ells."

The fiacre reeled and plunged into a narrow gateway in a barrier of shrubbery. An immense building loomed before us. The driver tried to turn his animals, but it was too late. We hit its side; it gave like the fabric of a dream, and we were in a cavernous space, dimly lit and smelling of hay. Ahead was a stepped altar as large as a cottage and dotted with blue lights. I saw it and realized I was seeing it too well—our driver had been swept out of his seat or had jumped clear. Agia shrieked.

We crashed into the altar. There was a confusion of flying objects impossible to describe, the sense of everything whirling and tumbling and never colliding, as in the chaos before creation. The ground seemed to leap at me; it struck with an impact that set my ears humming.

I had been holding *Terminus Est*, I think, while I flew through the air, but she was no longer in my hand. When I tried to get up to look for her, I had no breath and no strength. Somewhere far off, a man shouted. I rolled on my side, then managed to get my lifeless legs beneath me.

We seemed to be near the center of the building, which was as big around as the Great Keep and yet completely empty: without interior walls, stairs, or furniture of any kind. Through the golden, dusty air I could see crooked pillars that seemed of painted wood. Lamps, mere points of light, hung a chain or more overhead. Far above them, a many-colored roof rippled and snapped in a wind I could not feel.

I stood on straw, and straw was spread everywhere in an endless yellow carpet, like the field of a titan after harvest. All about me were the battens of which the altar had been constructed: fragments of thin wood braved with gold leaf and set with turquoises and violet amethysts. With some vague idea of finding my sword, I began to walk, stumbling almost at once over the smashed body of the fiacre. One onegar lay not far from it; I recall thinking it must have broken its neck. Someone called, "Torturer!" and I looked around and saw Agia—standing erect, though shakily. I asked if she were all right.

"Alive, anyway, but we must leave this place at once. Is that animal dead?"

I nodded.

"I could have ridden on it. Now you'll have to carry me if you can. I don't think my right leg will bear my weight." She tottered as she spoke, and I had to spring to her and catch her to keep her from falling. "Now we have to go," she said. "Look around . . . can you see a door? Quickly!"

I could not. "Why is it so urgent that we leave?"

"Use your nose if you can't use your eyes to see this floor."

I sniffed. The odor in the air was no longer straw, but straw burning; at almost the same instant I saw the flames, bright in the gloom, but still so small that a few moments before they must have been mere sparks. I tried to run, but could manage nothing better than a limping walk. "Where are we?"

"It's the Cathedral of the Pelerines—some call it the Cathedral of the Claw. The Pelerines are a band of priestesses who travel the continent. They never—"

Agia broke off because we were approaching a cluster of scarlet-clad people. Or perhaps they were approaching us, for they seemed to me to have appeared in the middle distance without warning. The men had shaven heads and held gleaming scimitars curved like the young moon and blazing with gilding; a woman with the towering height of an exultant cradled a sheathed two-handed sword: my own *Terminus Est*. She wore a hood and a narrow cape that trailed long tassels.

Agia began, "Our animals ran wild, Holy Domnicellae . . ."

"That is of no moment," the woman who held my sword said. There was much beauty in her, but it was not the beauty of women who quench desire. "This belongs to the man carrying you. Tell him to set you on your feet and take it. You can walk."

"A little. Do as she says, Torturer."

"Don't you know his name?"

"He told me, but I've forgotten."

I said, "Severian," and steadied her with one hand while I accepted *Terminus Est* with the other.

"Use it to end quarrels," the woman in scarlet said. "Not to begin them."

"The straw floor of this great tent is on fire, Chatelaine. Do you know it?"

"It will be extinguished. The sisters and our servants are crushing the embers now." She paused, her gaze flickering from Agia to me and back to Agia again. "In the remains of our high altar, which your vehicle destroyed, we found only one thing that seemed yours, and likely to be of value to you—that sword. We have returned it. Will you now also return to us anything of value to us you may have found?"

I remembered the amethysts. "I found nothing of value, Chatelaine." Agia shook her head, and I continued, "There were splinters of wood set with precious stones, but I left them where they had fallen."

The men shifted the hilts of their weapons in their hands and sought good footing, but the tall woman stood motionless, staring at me, then at Agia, then at me once more. "Come to me, Severian."

I came forward, a matter of three or four paces. It was a great temptation to draw *Terminus Est* as a defense against the men's blades, but I resisted it. Their mistress took my wrists in her hands and looked into my eyes. Her own were calm, and in the strange light seemed hard as beryls. "There is no guilt in him," she said.

One of the men muttered, "You are mistaken, Domnicellae."

"No guilt, I say. Step back, Severian, and let the woman come forward."

I did as she told me, and Agia limped to within a long pace of her. When she would not come nearer, the tall woman came to her and took her wrists as she had mine. After a moment, she glanced toward the other women who had waited behind the swordsmen. Before I realized what was happening, two of them seized Agia's gown and drew it over her head and away. One said, "Nothing, Mother."

"I think this the day foretold."

Her hands crossed over her breasts, Agia whispered to me, "These Pelerines are insane. Everyone knows it, and if I had had more time I would have told you so."

The tall woman said, "Return her rags. The Claw has not vanished in living memory, but it does so at will and it would be neither possible nor permissible for us to stop it."

One of the women murmured, "We may find it in the wreckage still, Mother." A second added, "Should they not be made to pay?" "Let us kill them," a man said.

The tall woman gave no indication that she had heard any of them. She was already leaving us, seeming to glide across the straw. The women followed her, looking at one another, and the men lowered their gleaming blades and backed away.

Agia was struggling into her gown. I asked her what she knew of the Claw, and who these Pelerines were.

"Get me out of here, Severian, and I'll tell you. It isn't lucky to talk of them in their own place. Is that a tear in the wall over there?"

We walked in the direction she had indicated, stumbling sometimes in the soft straw. There was no opening, but I was able to lift the edge of the silken wall enough for us to slip under.

XIX

The Botanic Gardens

THE SUNLIGHT WAS BLINDING; IT SEEMED AS IF WE HAD STEPPED from twilight into full day. Golden particles of straw swam in the crisp air about us.

"That's better," Agia said. "Wait a moment now and let me get my bearings. I think the Adamnian Steps will be to our right. Our driver wouldn't have gone down them—or perhaps he would, the fellow was mad—but they should take us to the landing by the shortest route. Give me your arm again, Severian. My leg's not quite recovered."

We were walking on grass now, and I saw that the tent-cathedral had been pitched on a champian surrounded by semi-fortified houses; its insubstantial belfries looked down upon their parapets. A wide, paved street bordered the open lawn, and when we reached it I asked again who the Pelerines were.

Agia looked sidelong at me. "You must forgive me, but I don't find it easy to talk of professional virgins to a man who's just seen me naked. Though under other circumstances it might be different." She drew a deep breath. "I don't really know a great deal about them, but we have some of their habits in the shop, and I asked my brother about them once, and after that paid attention to whatever I heard. It's a popular costume for masques—all that red.

"Anyway, they are an order of conventionals, as no doubt you've already discerned. The red is for the descending light of the New Sun, and they descend on landowners, traveling around the country with their cathedral and seizing enough to set it up. Their order claims to possess the most valuable relic in existence, the Claw of the Conciliator, so the red may be for the Wounds of the Claw as well."

Trying to be facetious I said, "I didn't know he had claws."

"It isn't a real claw—it's said to be a gem. You must have heard of it. I don't understand why it's called the Claw, and I doubt that those priestesses do themselves. But assuming it to have had some real association with the Conciliator, you can appreciate its importance. After all, our knowledge of him now is purely historical—meaning that we either confirm or deny that he was in contact with our race in the remote past. If the Claw is what the Pelerines represent it to be, then he once lived, though he may be dead now."

A startled glance from a woman carrying a dulcimer told me the mantle I had bought from Agia's brother was in disarray, permitting the fuligin of my guild cloak (which must have looked like mere empty darkness to the poor woman) to be seen through the opening. As I rearranged it and reclasped the fibula I said, "Like all these religious arguments, this one gets less significant as we continue. Supposing the Conciliator to have walked among us eons ago, and to be dead now, of what importance is he save to historians and fanatics? I value his legend as a part of the sacred past, but it seems to me that it is the legend that matters today, and not the Conciliator's dust."

Agia rubbed her hands, seeming to warm them in the sunlight. "Supposing him—we turn at this corner, Severian, you may see the head of the stair, if you'll look, there where the statues of the eponyms stand—supposing him to have lived, he was by definition the Master of Power. Which means the transcendence of reality, and includes the negation of time. Isn't that correct?"

I nodded.

"Then there is nothing to prevent him, from a position, say, of thirty thousand years ago, coming into what we call the present. Dead or not, if he ever existed, he could be around the next bend of the street or the next turn of the week."

We had reached the beginning of the stair. The steps were of stone as white as salt, sometimes so gradual that several strides were needed to go from one descent to the next, sometimes almost as abrupt as a ladder. Confectioners, sellers of apes, and the like had set up their stands here and there. For whatever reason, it was very pleasant to discuss mysteries with Agia while descending these steps, and I said, "All this because those women say they possess one of his glittering fingernails. I suppose it performs miraculous cures?"

"On occasion, so they claim. It also forgives injuries, raises the dead, draws new races of beings from the soil, purifies lust, and so on. All the things he is supposed to have done himself."

"You're laughing at me now."

"No, only laughing at the sunshine—you know what it is supposed to do to women's faces."

"Make them brown."

"Make them ugly. To begin with, it dries the skin and creates wrinkles and so on. Then too, it shows up every little defect. Urvasi loved Pururavas, you know, before she saw him in a bright light. Anyway, I felt it on my face, and I was thinking, 'I don't care for *you*. I'm still too young to worry about you, and next year I'll get a wide hat from our stock.'"

Agia's face was far from perfect now in the clear sunshine, but she had nothing to fear from it. My hunger fed at least as ravenously upon her imperfections. She possessed the hopeful, hopeless courage of the poor, which is perhaps the most appealing of all human qualities; and I rejoiced in the flaws that made her more real to me.

"Anyway," she continued, squeezing my hand, "I have to admit I've never understood why people like the Pelerines always think ordinary people have to have their lust purified. In my experience, they control it well enough by themselves, and just about every day, too. What most of us need is to find someone we can unbottle it with."

"Then you care that I love you." I was only half joking.

"Every woman cares if she's loved, and the more men who love her, the better! But I don't choose to love you in return, if that's what you mean. It would be so easy today, going around the city with you like this. But then if you're killed this evening, I'll feel badly for a fortnight."

"So will I," I said.

"No you won't. You won't even care. Not about that or anything, not ever again. Being dead doesn't hurt, as you of all people should know."

"I'm almost inclined to think this whole affair is some trick of yours, or of your brother's. You were outside when the Septentrion came—did you tell him something to inflame him against me? Is he your lover?"

Agia laughed at that, her teeth flashing in the sun. "Look at me. I have a brocade gown, but you've seen what's beneath it. My feet are bare. Do you see rings or earrings? A silver lamia twined about my neck? Are my arms constricted with circlets of gold? If not, you may safely assume I have no officer of the Household Troops for my paramour. There's an old sailor, ugly and poor, who presses me to live with him. Other than that, well, Agilus and I own our shop. It was bequeathed to us by our mother, and it's free of debt only because we can find no one who's enough of a fool to lend anything on it. Sometimes we rip up something from our stock and sell it to the paper-makers so we can buy a bowl of lentils to divide between us."

"You should eat well tonight anyway," I told her. "I gave your brother a good price for this mantle."

"What?" Her good humor seemed to have returned. She took a step back and feigned astonishment with an open mouth. "You won't buy me a supper this evening? After I've spent the day counseling you and guiding you about?"

"Involving me in the destruction of the altar those Pelerines had erected."

"I'm sorry about that. I really am. I didn't want you to tire your legs—you'll need them when you fight. Then those others came up, and I thought I saw a chance for you to make some money."

Her look had left my face and come to rest on one of the brutal busts that flanked the stair. I asked, "Is that really all there was to it?"

"To confess the truth, I wanted them to go on thinking you might be an armiger. Armigers go about in fancy dress so much because they're always going to fetes and tournaments, and you have the face. That's why I thought so myself when I first saw you. And you see, if you were, then I was someone that somebody like that, an armiger and probably the bastard of an exultant, might care for. Even if it was only a kind of joke. I had no way of knowing what would happen."

"I understand," I said. Suddenly laughter overcame me. "What fools we must have looked, jolting along in the fiacre."

"If you understand, then kiss me."

I stared at her.

"Kiss me! How many chances have you left? I'll give you more, what you want—" She paused, then laughed too. "After supper, perhaps. If we can find a private spot, though it won't be good for your fighting." She threw herself into my arms then, rising on her toes to press my lips. Her breasts were firm and high, and I could feel the motion of her hips.

"There now." She pushed me away. "Look down there, Severian. Between the pylons. What do you see?"

Water glimmered like a mirror in the sun. "The river."

"Yes, Gyoll. Now to the left. Because there are so many nenuphars, the island is hard to see. But the lawn is a lighter, brighter green. Don't you see the glass? Where it catches the light?"

"I see something. Is the building all glass?"

She nodded. "That's the Botanic Gardens, where we're going. They'll let you cut your avern there—all you have to do is demand it as your right."

We made the rest of the descent in silence. The Adamnian Steps wind back and forth across a long hillside, and they are a favored place for strollers, who often hire a ride to the top and descend. I saw many couples finely dressed, men with the marks of old difficulties scarring their faces, and romping children. Saddening me more, I saw too from several points the dark towers of the Citadel on the opposite bank, and on the second or third such sighting it came to me that when I had swum from the eastern bank, diving from the water-stairs and fighting with the tenement children, I had once or twice noticed this narrow line of white on the other shore, so far upstream as to be nearly beyond sight.

The Botanic Gardens stood on an island near the bank, enclosed in a building of glass (a thing I had not seen before and did not know could exist). There were no towers or battlements: only the faceted tholus, climbing until it lost itself against the sky and its momentary brilliancies were confounded with the faint stars. I asked Agia if we would have time to see the gardens—and then, before she could reply, told her that I would see them whether there was time or not. The fact was that I had no compunction about arriving late for my death, and was beginning to have difficulty in taking seriously a combat fought with flowers.

"If you wish to spend your last afternoon visiting the gardens, so be it," she said. "I come here myself often. It's free, being maintained by the Autarch, and entertaining if you're not too squeamish."

We went up steps of glass, palely green. I asked Agia if the enormous building existed only to provide blooms and fruit.

She shook her head, laughing, and motioned toward the wide arch before us. "On either side of this corridor are chambers, and each chamber is a bioscape. I warn you though that because the corridor is shorter than the building itself, the chambers will widen as we go into them more deeply. Some people find that disconcerting."

We entered, and in so doing stepped into such silence as must have been in the morning of the world, before the fathers of men first hammered out brazen gongs, built squealing cartwheels, and splashed Gyoll with striding oars. The air was fragrant, damp, and a trifle warmer than it had been outside. The walls to either side of the tessellated floor were also of glass, but so thick that sight could scarcely penetrate them; leaves and flowers and even soaring trees seen through these walls wavered as though glimpsed through water. On one broad door I read:

THE GARDEN OF SLEEP

"You may enter whichever you like," an old man said, rising from his chair in a corner. "And as many as you like."

Agia shook her head. "We won't have time for more than one or two."

"Is it your first visit? Newcomers generally enjoy the Garden of Pantomime."

He wore a faded robe that reminded me of something I could not place. I asked if it were the habit of some guild.

"Indeed it is. We are the curators—have you never met one of our brotherhood previously?"

"Twice, I believe."

"There are only a few of us, but our charge is the most important that society boasts—the preservation of all that is gone. Have you seen the Garden of Antiquities?"

"Not yet," I said.

"You should! If this is your first visit, I would advise you to begin with the Garden of Antiquities. Hundreds and hundreds of extinct plants, including some that have not been seen for tens of millions of years."

Agia said, "That purple creeper you're so proud of—I met it growing wild on a hillside in Cobblers Common."

The curator shook his head sadly. "We lost spores, I'm afraid. We know about it . . . A roof pane broke, and they blew away." The unhappiness quickly left his lined face, draining away as the troubles of simple people do. He smiled. "It's likely to do well now. All its enemies are as dead as the disorders its leaves cured."

A rumbling made me turn. Two workmen were wheeling a cart through one of the doorways, and I asked what they were doing.

"That's the Sand Garden. They're rebuilding it. Cactuses and yucca—that kind of thing. I'm afraid there's not much to see there now."

I took Agia by the hand, saying, "Come on, I'd like to look at the work." She smiled at the curator and gave a half shrug, but followed docilely enough.

Sand there was, but no garden. We stepped into a seemingly unlimited space dotted with boulders. More stone rose in cliffs behind us, concealing the wall through which we had come. Just beside the doorway spread one large plant, half bush, half vine, with cruel, curved thorns; I assumed that it was the last of the old flora, not yet removed. There was no other vegetation, and no sign of the restocking the curator had implied except for the twin tracks of the workmen's cart, winding off among the rocks.

"This isn't much," Agia said. "Why don't you let me take you to the Garden of Delectation?"

"The door is open behind us—why is it I feel I can't leave this place?"

She looked at me sidelong. "Everyone feels like that in these gardens sooner or later, though usually not so quickly. It would be better for you if we stepped outside now." She said something else as well, something I could not catch. Far off, I seemed to hear surf pounding on the edge of the world.

"Wait . . ." I said. But Agia drew me out into the corridor again. Our feet carried away as much sand as a child might hold in the palm of one hand.

"We really don't have much time left now," Agia told me. "Let me show you the Garden of Delectation, then we'll pluck your avern and go."

"It can't be much later than midmorning."

"It's past noon. We were more than a watch just in the Sand Garden."

"Now I know you're lying to me."

For an instant I saw a flash of anger in her face. Then it was spread over with an unction of philosophical irony, the secretion of her injured self-esteem. I was far stronger than she, and poor though I was, richer; she told herself now (I felt I could almost hear her voice whispering in her own ear) that by accepting such insults she mastered me.

"Severian, you argued and argued, and in the end I had to drag you away. The gardens affect people like that—certain suggestible people. They say the Autarch wants some people to remain in each to accent the reality of the scene, and so his archimage, Father Inire, has invested them with a conjuration. But since you were so drawn to that one, it's not likely any of the others will affect you so much."

"I felt I belonged there," I said. "That I was to meet someone . . . and that a certain woman was there, nearby, but concealed from sight."

We were passing another door, on which was written:

THE JUNGLE GARDEN

When Agia did not answer me, I said, "You tell me the others won't affect me, so let's go in here."

"If we waste our time with that, we won't get to the Garden of Delectation at all."

"Only for a moment." Because she was so determined to take me into the garden she had selected, without seeing any of the others, I had grown frightened of what I might find there, or bring with me.

The heavy door of the Jungle Garden swung toward us, bringing a rush of steaming air. Beyond, the light was dim and green. Lianas half obscured the entrance, and a great tree, rotted to punk, had fallen across the path a few strides away. Its trunk still bore a small sign: *Caesalpinia sappan.*

"The real jungle is dying in the north as the sun cools," Agia said. "A man I know says it has been dying so for many centuries. Here, the old jungle stands preserved as it was when the sun was young. Come in. You wanted to see this place."

I stepped inside. Behind us the door swung shut and vanished.

XX

Father Inire's Mirrors

As Agia had said, the real jungles sickened far to the north. I had never seen them, yet the Jungle Garden made me feel I had. Even now, as I sit at my writing table in the House Absolute, some distant noise brings back to my ears the screams of the magenta-breasted, cynaeous-backed parrot that flapped from tree to tree, watching us with white-rimmed and disapproving eyes—though this is no doubt because my mind was already turned to that haunted place. Through its screaming, a new sound—a new voice—came from some red world still unconquered by thought.

"What is it?" I touched Agia's arm.

"A smilodon. But he's far away and only wants to frighten the deer so they'll blunder into his jaws. He'd run from you and your sword much faster than you could run from him." Her gown had been torn by a branch, exposing one breast. The incident had left her in no good mood.

"Where does the path lead? And how can the cat be so far off when all this is only one room of the building we saw from the top of the Adamnian Steps?"

"I've never gone so deeply into this garden. You were the one who wanted to come."

"Answer my questions," I said, and took her by the shoulder.

"If this path is like the others—I mean, in the other gardens—it runs in a wide loop that will eventually return us to the door by which we came in. There's no reason to be afraid."

"The door vanished when I shut it."

"Only trickery. Haven't you seen those pictures in which a pietist exhibits a meditating face when you're on one side of the room, but stares at you when you cross to the opposite wall? We'll see the door when we approach it from the other direction."

A snake with carnelian eyes came gliding onto the path, lifted a venomous head to look at us, then slipped away. I heard Agia's gasp and said, "Who's afraid now? Will that snake flee you as quickly as you would flee it? Now answer my question about the smilodon. Is it really far away? And if so, how can that be?"

"I don't know. Do you think there are answers to everything here? Is that true in the place you come from?"

I recalled the Citadel and the age-old usages of the guilds. "No," I said. "There are inexplicable offices and customs in my home, though in these decadent times they are falling out of use. There are towers no one has ever entered, too, and lost rooms, and tunnels whose entrances have not been seen."

"Then can't you understand that it's the same way here? When we were at the top of the steps and you looked down and saw these gardens, could you make out the entire building?"

"No," I admitted. "There were pylons and spires in the way, and the corner of the embankment."

"And even so, could you delimit what you saw?"

I shrugged. "The glass made it difficult to tell where the edges of the building were."

"Then how can you ask the questions you do? Or if you

have to ask them, can't you understand that I don't necessarily have the answers? From the sound of the smilodon's roar, I knew he was far off. Perhaps he is not here at all, or perhaps the distance is of time."

"When I looked down on this building, I saw a faceted dome. Now when I look up, I see only the sky between the leaves and vines."

"The surfaces of the facets are large. It may be that their edges are concealed by the limbs," Agia said.

We walked on, wading a trickle of water in which a reptile with evil teeth and a finned back soaked himself. I unsheathed *Terminus Est*, fearing he would dart at our feet. "I grant," I told her, "that the trees grow too thickly here to permit me to see far to either side. But look here, through the opening where this freshet runs. Upstream I can see only more jungle. Downstream there is the gleam of water, as though it empties into a lake."

"I warned you that the rooms open out, and that you might find that disturbing. It is also said that the walls of these places are specula, whose reflective power creates the appearance of vast space."

"I once knew a woman who had met Father Inire. She told me a tale about him. Would you like to hear it?"

"Suit yourself."

Actually it was I who wanted to hear the story, and I did suit myself: I told it to myself in the recesses of my mind, hearing it there hardly less than I had heard it first when Thecla's hands, white and cold as lilies taken from a grave filled with rain, lay clasped between my own.

"I was thirteen, Severian, and I had a friend named Domnina. She was a pretty girl who looked several years younger than she really was. Perhaps that's why he took a fancy to her.

"I know you know nothing of the House Absolute. You must take my word for it that at one place in the Hall of Meaning there are two mirrors. Each is three or four ells wide, and each extends to the ceiling. There's nothing between the two except a few dozen strides of marble floor. In other words, anyone who walks down the Hall of Meaning sees himself infinitely multiplied there. Each mirror reflects the images in its twin.

"Naturally, it's an attractive spot when you're a girl and fancy yourself something of a beauty. Domnina and I were playing there one night, turning around and around to show off new camisias. We had moved a couple of big candelabra so one was on the left of one mirror and the other on the left of the facing one—at opposite corners if you see what I mean.

"We were so busy looking at ourselves that we didn't notice Father Inire until he was only a step away. Ordinarily, you understand, we would have run and hidden when we saw him coming, though he was scarcely taller than we. He wore iridescent robes that seemed to fade into gray when I looked at them, as if they had been dyed in mist. 'You must be wary, children, of looking at yourselves like that,' he said. 'There's an imp who waits in silvered glass and creeps into the eyes of those who look into it.'

"I knew what he meant, and blushed. But Domnina said, 'I think I've seen him. Is he shaped like a tear, all gleaming?'

"Father Inire did not hesitate before he answered her, or even blink—still, I understood that he was startled. He said, 'No, that is someone else, dulcinea. Can you see him plainly? No? Then come into my presence chamber tomorrow a little after Nones, and I'll show him to you.'

"We were frightened when he left. Domnina swore a hundred times that she would not go. I applauded her resolution and tried to strengthen her in it. More to the point, we arranged that she should stay with me that night and the next day.

"It was all for nothing. A little before the appointed time, a servant in a livery neither of us had ever seen came for poor Domnina.

"A few days before I had been given a set of paper figures. There were soubrettes, columbines, coryphees, harlequinas, figurantes, and so on—the usual thing. I remember that I waited on the window seat all afternoon for Domnina, toying with these little people, coloring their costumes with wax pencils, arranging them in various ways and inventing games she and I would play when she came back.

"At last my nurse called me to supper. By that time I

thought Father Inire had killed Domnina, or that he had sent her back to her mother with an order that she must never visit us again. Just as I was finishing my soup there was a knock. I heard mother's servitrix go to answer the door, then Domnina burst in. I'll never forget her face—it was as white as the faces of the dolls. She cried and my nurse comforted her, and eventually we got the story out of her.

"The man who had been sent for her had taken her through halls she hadn't known existed. That, you understand, Severian, was frightening in itself. We both thought ourselves perfectly familiar with our wing of the House Absolute. Eventually he had led her into what must have been the presence chamber. She said it was a large room with hangings of a solid, dark red and almost no furniture except for vases taller than a man and wider than she could spread her arms.

"In the center was what she at first took to be a room within the room. The walls were octagonal and painted with labryinths. Over it, just visible from where she stood at the entrance to the presence chamber, burned the brightest lamp she had ever seen. It was blue-white, she said, and so brilliant an eagle could not have kept his eyes on it.

"She had heard the click of the bolt when the door had been closed behind her. There was no other exit she could see. She ran to the curtains hoping to find another door behind them, but as soon as she pulled one aside, one of the eight walls painted with labryinths opened and Father Inire stepped out. Behind him she saw what she called a bottomless hole filled with light.

" 'There you are,' he said. 'You've come just in time. Child, the fish is nearly caught. You can watch the setting of the hook, and learn by what means his golden scales are to be meshed in our landing net.' He took her arm and led her into the octagonal enclosure."

At this point I was forced to interrupt my tale to help Agia through a section of the path almost completely overgrown. "You're talking to yourself," she said. "I can hear you muttering behind me."

"I'm telling myself the story I mentioned to you. You seemed to have no wish to hear it, and I wanted to listen to it again—besides, it concerns the specula of Father Inire, and may contain hints useful to us."

"Domnina drew away. In the center of the enclosure, just under the lamp, was a haze of yellow light. It was never still, she said. It moved up and down and from side to side with rapid flickerings, never leaving a space that might have been four spans high and four long. It did indeed remind her of a fish. Much more than the faint flagae she had glimpsed in the mirrors of the Hall of Meaning ever had—a fish swimming in air, confined to an invisible bowl. Father Inire drew the wall of the octagon closed behind them. It was a mirror in which she could see his face and hand and shining, indefinite robes reflected. Her own form too, and the fish's . . . but there seemed to be another girl—her own face peering over her shoulder; then another and another and another, each with a smaller face behind it. And so on *ad infinitum,* an endless chain of fainter Domnina-faces.

"She realized when she saw them that the wall of the octagonal enclosure through which she had passed faced another mirror. In fact, all the others were mirrors. The light of the blue-white lamp was caught by them all and reflected from one to another as boys might pass silver balls, interlacing and intertwining in an interminable dance. In the center, the fish flickered to and fro, a thing formed, as it seemed, by the convergence of the light.

"'Here you see him,' Father Inire said. 'The ancients, who knew this process at least as well as we and perhaps better, considered the Fish the least important and most common of the inhabitants of specula. With their false belief that the creatures they summoned were ever present in the depths of the glass, we need not concern ourselves. In time they turned to a more serious question: By what means may travel be effected when the point of departure is at an astronomical distance from the place of arrival?'

"'Can I put my hand through him?'

"'At this stage you may, child. Later I would not advise it.'

"She did so, and felt a sliding warmth. 'Is this how the cacogens come?'

"'Has your mother ever taken you riding in her flier?'

" 'Of course.'

" 'And you have seen the toy fliers older children make on the pleasance at night, with paper hulls and parchment lanterns. What you see here is to the means used to travel between suns as those toy fliers are to real ones. Yet we can call up the Fish with these, and perhaps other things too. And just as the boys' fliers sometimes set the roof of a pavilion ablaze, so our mirrors, though their concentration is not powerful, are not without danger.'

" 'I thought that to travel to the stars you'd have to sit on the mirror.'

"Father Inire smiled. It was the first time she had seen him smile, and though she knew he meant only that she had amused and pleased him (perhaps more than a grown woman could have) it was not pleasant. 'No, no. Let me outline the problem to you. When something moves very, very fast—as fast as you see all the familiar things in your nursery when your governess lights your candle—it grows heavy. Not larger, you understand, but only heavier. It is attracted to Urth or any other world more strongly. If it were to move swiftly enough, it would become a world itself, pulling other things to it. Nothing ever does, but if something did, that is what would happen. Yet even the light from your candle does not move swiftly enough to travel between the suns.'

"(The Fish flickered up and down, forward and back.)

" 'Couldn't you make a bigger candle?' I feel sure Domnina was thinking of the paschal candle she saw each spring, thicker than a man's thigh.

" 'Such a candle could be made, but its light would fly no more swiftly. Yet even though light is so weightless we have given its name to that condition, it presses against what it falls on, just as wind, which we cannot see, pushes the arms of a mill. See now what happens when we provide light to mirrors set face to face: The image they reflect travels from one to the other and returns. Suppose it meets itself in returning—what do you suppose happens then?'

"Domnina laughed despite her fear, and said she could not guess.

" 'Why it cancels itself. Think of two little girls running across a lawn without looking where they're going. When they meet, there are no more little girls running. But if the mirrors are well made and the distances between them are correct, the images do not meet. Instead, one comes behind the other. That has no effect when the light comes from a candle or a common star, because both the earlier light and the later light that would otherwise tend to drive it forward are only random white light, like the random waves a little girl might make by flinging a handful of pebbles into a lily pond. But if the light is from a coherent source, and forms the image reflected from an optically exact mirror, the orientation of the wave fronts is the same because the image is the same. Since nothing can exceed the speed of light in our universe, the accelerated light leaves it and enters another. When it slows again, it reenters ours—naturally at another place.'

" 'Is it just a reflection?' Domnina asked. She was looking at the Fish.

" 'Eventually it will be a real being, if we do not darken the lamp or shift the mirrors. For a reflected image to exist without an object to originate it violates the laws of our universe, and therefore an object will be brought into existence.' "

"Look," Agia said, "we're coming to something."

The shade of the tropical trees was so intense that spots of sunshine on the path seemed to blaze like molten gold. I squinted to peer beyond their burning shafts of light.

"A house set on stilts of yellow wood. It's thatched with palm fronds. Can't you see it?"

Something moved, and the hut seemed to spring at my eyes as it emerged from the pattern of greens, yellows, and blacks. A shadowed splotch became a doorway; two sloping lines, the angle of the roof. A man in light-colored clothes stood on a tiny veranda looking down the path at us. I straightened my mantle.

"You don't have to do that," Agia said. "It doesn't matter in here. If you're hot, take it off."

I removed the mantle and folded it over my left arm. The man on the veranda turned with an expression of unmistakable terror and went into the hut.

XXI

The Hut in the Jungle

A LADDER LED TO THE VERANDA. IT WAS MADE OF THE SAME knobby-jointed wood as the hut, lashed together with vegetable fiber. "You're not going up that?" Agia protested.

"If we're going to see what's to be seen here we must," I said. "And recalling the state of your undergarments, I thought you might feel more comfortable if I preceded you."

She surprised me by blushing. "It will only lead to such a house as was used in the hot parts of the world in ancient days. You'll soon be bored, believe me."

"Then we can come down, and we will have lost very little time." I swung myself up the ladder. It sagged and creaked alarmingly, but I knew that in a public pleasureground it was impossible that it should be really dangerous. When I was halfway up, I felt Agia behind me.

The interior was hardly larger than one of our cells, but there all resemblance ceased. In our oubliette, the overwhelming impression was of solidity and mass. The metal plates of the walls echoed even the slightest sounds; the floors rang beneath the tread of the journeymen and gave not a hairsbreadth under the walker's weight; the ceiling could never fall—but if it should, it would crush everything below it.

If it is true that each of us has an antipolaric brother somewhere, a bright twin if we are dark, a dark twin if we are bright, then that hut was surely such a changeling to one of our cells. There were windows on all sides save the one through which we entered by the open door, and they had neither bars nor panes nor any other sort of closing. Floor and walls and window frames were of the branches of the

158

yellow tree; branches not planed to boards but left in the round so that I could, in places, see sunlight through the walls, and if I had dropped a worn orichalk, it would very likely have come to rest on the ground below. There was no ceiling, only a triangular space beneath the roof where pans and food bags hung.

A woman was reading aloud in a corner, with a naked man crouched at her feet. The man we had seen from the path stood at the window opposite the door, looking out. I felt that he knew we had come (and even if he had not seen us a few moments before, he must certainly have felt the hut shake when we climbed the ladder), but that he wished to pretend he did not. There is something in the line of the back when a man turns so as not to see, and it was evident in his.

The woman read: "Then he went up from the plain to Mt. Nebo, the headland that faces the city, and the Compassionating showed him the whole country, all the land as far as the Western Sea. Then he said to him: 'This is the land I swore to your fathers I should give their sons. You have seen it, but you shall not set your feet upon it.' So there he died, and was buried in the ravine."

The naked man at her feet nodded. "It is even so with our own masters, Preceptress. With the smallest finger it is given. But the thumb is hooked into it, and a man has only to take the gift, and dig in the floor of his house, and cover all with a mat, than the thumb begins to pull and bit by bit the gift rises from the earth and ascends into the sky and is seen no more."

The woman seemed impatient with this, and began, "No, Isangoma—" But the man at the window interrupted her without turning around. "Be quiet, Marie. I want to hear what he has to say. You can explain later."

"   nephew of mine," the naked man continued, "a member of my own fire circle, had no fish. And so he took up his gowdalie and went to a certain pool. So quietly did he lean over the water he might have been a tree." The naked man leaped up as he said this, and posed his sinewy frame as though to spear the woman's feet with a shaft of air. "Long, long he stood . . . until the monkeys no longer feared him and returned to drop sticks in the water, and the hesperorn fluttered to her nest. A big fish came out of his den in the sunken trunks. My nephew watched him circle, slowly,

slowly. He swam near the surface, and then when my nephew was about to drive home the three-toothed spear, there was no longer a fish to be seen, but a lovely woman. At first my nephew thought the fish was the fish-king, who had changed his form that he might not be speared. Then he saw the fish moving beneath the woman's face, and knew that he saw a reflection. He looked up at once, but there was nothing to be seen but the whisk of the vines. The woman was gone!" The naked man looked up, mimicking very well the amazement of the fisherman. "That night my nephew went to the Numen, the Proud One, and slit the throat of a young oreodont, saying—"

Agia whispered to me, "In the name of the Theoanthropos, how long do you mean to stay here? This could go on all day."

"Let me look about the hut," I whispered back, "and we'll go."

"Mighty is the Proud One, sacred all his names. Everything found beneath leaves is his, the storms are carried in his arms, the poison holds no death unless his curse is pronounced over it!"

The woman said, "I don't think we need all these praises of your fetish, Isangoma. My husband wishes to hear your story. Very well, but tell it and spare us your litanies."

"The Proud One protects his supplicant! Would not he be shamed if one who adores him were to die?"

"Isangoma!"

From the window, the man said, "He's afraid, Marie. Can't you hear it in his voice?"

"There is no fear for those who wear the sign of the Proud One! His breath is the mist that hides the infant uakaris from the claws of the margay!"

"Robert, if you won't do something about this,   will. Isangoma, be silent. Or leave and never return here again."

"The Proud One knows Isangoma loves the Preceptress. He would save her if he could."

"Save me from what? Do you think there's one of your dreadful beasts here? If there were, Robert would shoot it with his gun."

"The tokoloshe, Preceptress. The tokoloshe come. But the

Proud One in his condensation will protect us. He is the mighty commander of all tokoloshe! When he roars, they hide beneath the fallen leaves."

"Robert, I think he's lost his mind."

"He has eyes, Marie, and you don't."

"What do you mean by that? And why do you keep looking out that window?"

Quite slowly, the man turned to face us. For a moment he looked at Agia and me, then he turned away. His expression was the one I have seen our clients wear when Master Gurloes showed them the instruments to be used in their anacrisis.

"Robert, for goodness' sake tell me what's wrong with you."

"As Isangoma says, the tokoloshe are here. Not his, I think, but ours. Death and the Lady. Have you heard of them, Marie?"

The woman shook her head. She had risen from her seat and opened the lid of a small chest.

"You wouldn't have, I suppose. It's a picture—an artistic theme, rather. Pictures by several artists. Isangoma, I don't think your Proud One has much authority over these tokoloshe. These come from Paris, where I used to be a student, to remonstrate with me for giving up art for this."

The woman said, "You have a fever, Robert. That's obvious. I'm going to give you something, and you'll feel better soon."

The man looked toward us again, at Agia's face and my own, as though he did not wish to do so but found himself unable to control the motion of his eyes. "If I am ill, Marie, then the diseased know things the well have overlooked. Isangoma knows they're here too, don't forget. Didn't you feel the floor tremble while you were reading to him? That was when they came in, I think."

"I've just poured you a glass of water so you can swallow your quinine. There are no ripples in it."

"What are they, Isangoma? Tokoloshe—but what are tokoloshe?"

"Bad spirits, Preceptor. When man think bad thought or woman do bad thing, there is another tokoloshe. He stay behind. Man think: *No one know, everyone dead.* But tokoloshe remain until end of world. Then everyone will see, know what that man did."

The woman said, "What a horrible idea."

Her husband's hands clenched the yellow stick of the windowsill. "Don't you see they are only the results of what we do? They are the spirits of the future, and we make them ourselves."

"They are a lot of pagan nonsense, that's what I see, Robert. Listen. Your vision is so sharp, can't you listen for a moment?"

"I am listening. What do you want to say?"

"Nothing. I only want you to listen. What do you hear?"

The hut fell silent. I listened too, and could not have not listened if I had wanted to. Outside the monkeys chattered, and the parrots screamed as before. Then I heard, over the jungle noises, a faint humming, as though an insect as large as a boat were flying far away.

"What is it?" the man asked.

"The mail plane. If you're lucky, you should be able to see it soon."

The man craned his neck out the window, and I, curious to see what he was looking for, went to the window on his left and looked out as well. The foliage was so thick that at first it seemed impossible to see anything, but he was staring almost straight up past the edge of the thatch, and I found a patch of blue there.

The humming grew louder. Into view came the strangest flier I have ever seen. It was winged, as if it had been built by some race that had not yet realized that since it would not flap wings like a bird in any case, there was no reason its lift, like a kite's, could not come from its hull. There was a bulbous swelling on each argent pinion, and a third at the front of the hull; the light seemed to glimmer before these swellings.

"In three days we could be at the landing strip, Robert. The next time it comes, we would be waiting."

"If the Lord has sent us here—"

"Yes, Preceptor, we must do what the Proud One wishes! There is none like he! Preceptress, let me dance to the Proud

One, and sing his song. Then it may be the tokoloshe will depart."

The naked man snatched her book from the woman and began to beat it with the flat of his hand—rhythmic claps as though he played a tambour. His feet scraped the uneven floor, and his voice, beginning with a melodic stridulation, became the voice of a child:

> "In the night when all is silent,
> Hear him screaming in the treetops!
> See him dancing in the fire!
> He lives in the arrow poison,
> Tiny as a yellow firefly!
> Brighter than a falling star!
> Hairy men walk in the forest—"

Agia said, "I'm leaving, Severian," and stepped through the doorway behind us. "If you want to stay and watch this, you can. But you'll have to get your avern yourself, and find your way to the Sanguinary Fields. Do you know what will happen if you fail to appear?"

"They'll employ assassins, you said."

"And the assassins will employ the snake called yellow-beard. Not on you, at first. On your family, if you have any, and your friends. Since I've been with you all over our quarter of the city, that probably means me."

> "He comes when the sun is setting,
> See his feet upon the water!
> Tracks of flame across the water!"

The chant continued, but the chanter knew we were going: his singsong held a note of triumph. I waited until Agia had reached the ground, then followed her.

She said, "I thought you'd never leave. Now that you're here, do you really like this place so much?" The metallic colors of her torn gown seemed as angry as she herself against the cool green of the unnaturally dark leaves.

"No," I said. "But I find it interesting. Did you see their flier?"

"When you and the inmate looked out the windows? I wasn't such a fool."

"It was like no other I've ever seen. I should have been looking at the roof facets of this building, but instead I saw the flier *he* expected to see. At least, that's what it seemed like. Something from somewhere else. A little while ago I wanted to tell you about a friend of a friend of mine who was caught in Father Inire's mirrors. She found herself in another world, and even when she returned to Thecla—that was my friend's name—she wasn't quite sure she had found her way back to her real point of origin. I wonder if we aren't still in the world those people left, instead of them in ours."

Agia had already started down the path. Flecks of sunlight seemed to turn her brown hair to dark gold as she looked over her shoulder to say, "I told you certain visitors are attracted to certain bioscapes."

I trotted to catch up with her.

"As time goes on, their minds bend to conform to their surroundings, and it may be they bend ours   well. It was probably an ordinary flier you saw."

"He saw us. So did the savage."

"From what I've heard, the further an inhabitant's consciousness must be warped, the more residual perceptions are likely to remain. When I meet monsters, wild men, and so forth in these gardens, I find they're a lot more likely to be at least partially aware of me than the others are."

"Explain the man," I said.

"I didn't build this place, Severian. All I know is that if you turn around on the path now, that last place we saw probably won't be there. Listen, I want you to promise me that when we get out of here, you'll let me take you straight to the Garden of Endless Sleep. We don't have time left for anything else, not even the Garden of Delectation. And you're not really the kind of person who ought to go sightseeing in here."

"Because I wanted to stay in the Sand Garden?"

"Partly, yes. You're going to make trouble for me here sooner or later, I think."

As she said that, we rounded one of the path's seemingly endless sinuosities. A log tagged with a small white rectangle that could only be a species sign lay across the path, and through the crowding leaves on our left I could see the wall, its greenish glass forming an unobtrusive backdrop for the foliage. Agia had already taken a step past the door when I shifted *Terminus Est* to the other hand and opened it for her.

XXII

Dorcas

When I had first heard of the flower, I had imagined averns would be grown on benches, in rows like those in the conservatory of the Citadel. Later, when Agia had told me more about the Botanic Gardens, I conceived of a place like the necropolis where I had frolicked as a boy, with trees and crumbling tombs, and walkways paved with bones.

The reality was very different—a dark lake in an infinite fen. Our feet sank in sedge, and a cold wind whistled past with nothing, as it seemed, to stop it before it reached the sea. Rushes grew beside the track on which we walked, and once or twice   water bird passed overhead, black against a misted sky.

I had been telling Agia about Thecla. Now she touched my arm. "You can see them from here, though we'll have to go half around the lake to pluck one. Look where I'm pointing . . . that smudge of white."

"They don't look dangerous from here."

"They've done for a great many people, I can assure you. Some of them are interred in this garden, I imagine."

So there were graves after all. I asked where the mausoleums stood.

"There aren't any. No coffins either, or mortuary urns, or any of that clutter. Look at the water slopping at your boots."

I did. It was as brown as tea.

"It has the property of preserving corpses. The bodies are weighed by forcing lead shot down their throats, then sunk here with their positions mapped so they can be fished up again later if anyone wants to look at them."

I would readily have sworn that there was no one within a league of where we stood. Or at least (if the segments of the glass building really confined the spaces they enclosed as they were supposed to do) within the borders of the Garden of Endless Sleep. But Agia had no sooner said what she did than the head and shoulders of an old man appeared over the top of some reeds a dozen paces off. " 'Tis not true," he called. "I know they say so, but 'tisn't right."

Agia, who had allowed the torn bodice of her gown to hang as it would, quickly drew it up again. "I didn't know I was talking to anyone but my escort here."

·   The old man ignored the rebuke. No doubt his thoughts were already too involved with the remark he had overheard for him to pay much heed. "I've the figure here—would you like to see it? You, young sieur—you've an education, anyone can tell that. Will you look?" He appeared to be carrying a staff. I watched its head rise and fall several times before I understood that he was poling toward us.

"More trouble," Agia said. "We'd better go."

I asked if it might not be possible for the old man to ferry us across the lake, thus saving us the long walk around.

He shook his head. "Too heavy for my little boat. There's but room for Cas and me here. You great folk would capsize us."

The prow came into sight, and I saw that what he said was true: the skiff was so small it seemed almost too much to ask of it that it keep the old man himself afloat, though he was bowed and shrunken by age (he appeared older even than Master Palaemon) until he could hardly have weighed more than a boy of ten. There was no one in it with him.

"Your pardon, sieur," he said. "But I can't come no nearer. Wet she may be, but she gets too dry for me, or you couldn't walk upon it. Can you step here by the edge so's I can show you my figure?"

I was curious to see what it was he wanted of us, so I did as he asked, Agia following me reluctantly.

"Here now." Reaching into his tunic he pulled out a small scroll. "Here is the position. Have a look, young sieur."

The scroll was headed with some name and   long

description of where this person had lived, whose wife she was, and what her husband had done for a living; all of which I only pretended to glance at, I am afraid. Below the description were a crude map and two numbers.

"Now you see, sieur, it ought to be easy enough. First number there, that's paces *over* from the Fulstrum. Second number's paces *up*. Now would you believe that for all these years I've been trying to find her, and never found her yet?" Looking at Agia, he drew himself up until he stood almost normally.

"I'd believe it," Agia said. "And if it will satisfy you, I'm sorry to hear it. But it has nothing to do with us."

She turned to go, but the old man thrust out his pole to prevent my following her. "Don't you heed what they say. They put them where the figure shows, but they don't stay there. Some has been see'd in the river, even." He looked vaguely toward the horizon. "Out there."

I told him I doubted that was possible.

"All the water here, where'd you think it come from? There's a conduit underground that brings it, and if it didn't this whole place'd dry out. When they get to moving about, what's to prevent one from swimming through? What's to prevent twenty? Can't be any current to speak of. You and her—you come to get a avern, did you? You know why they planted 'em here to begin with?"

I shook my head.

"For the manatees. They're in the river, and used to swim in through the conduit. It scared the kin to see their faces bobbing in the lake, so Father Inire had the gardeners plant the averns. I was here and saw it. Just a little man he is, with a wry neck and bow legs. If a manatee comes now, those flowers kill it in the night. One morning I come looking for Cas like I always do unless I've something else I have to take care of, and there was two curators on the shore with a harpoon. Dead manatee in the lake, they said. I went out with my hook and got it, and it wasn't no manatee, but a man. He'd spit up his lead, or they hadn't put enough in. Looked as good as you or her, and better than me."

"Had he been dead long?"

"No way of telling, for the water here pickles them. You'll hear it said it turns their skin to leather, and so it does. But don't think of the sole of your boot when you hear it. More like a woman's glove."

Agia was far ahead of us, and I began to walk after her. The old man followed us, poling his skiff parallel to the floating path of sedge.

"I told them I'd had better luck in one day for them than I've had in forty years for myself. Here's what I use." He held up an iron grapple on a length of rope. "Not that I haven't caught aplenty, all kinds. But not Cas. I started where the figure showed, year after she died. She wasn't there, so I kept working my way out. After five years of that I was a ways far away—that's what I thought then—from what it said. I got to be afraid she might be there after all, so I begun over. First where it said, then working out. Ten years of that. I got to be afraid again, so what I do now is start in the morning where it says, and make my first cast there. After that I go to where I stopped the last time, and circle out some more. She's not where it says—I know that, I know everyone that's there now, and some of them I've pulled up a hundred times. But she's wandering, and I keep thinking maybe she'll come home."

"She was your wife?"

The old man nodded, and to my surprise said nothing.

"Why do you want to recover her body?"

Still he said nothing. His pole made no sound as it slipped in and out of the water; the skiff left only the faintest of wakes behind it, tiny ripples that lapped the side of the sedge track like the tongues of kittens.

"Are you sure you would know her, after so long a time, if you found her?"

"Yes . . . yes." He nodded, slowly at first, then vigorously. "You're thinking I may have hooked her already. Drug her up, looked her in the face, and throwed her back in. Ain't you? It ain't possible. Not know Cas? You wondered why I want her back. One reason is the memory I have of her—the one that's strongest—is of this brown water closing over her face. Her eyes shut. Do you know about that?"

"I'm not certain I know what you mean."

"They've a cement they put on the lids. It's supposed to hold them down forever, but when the water hit them, they opened. Explain that. It's what I remember, what comes into my mind when I try to sleep. This brown water rolling over her face, and her eyes opening blue through the brown. I have to go to sleep five, six times every night, what with the waking up. Before I lie down here myself I'd like to have another picture there—her face coming back up, even if it's only on the end of my hook. You follow what I say?"

I thought of Thecla and the trickle of blood from beneath the door of her cell, and I nodded.

"Then there's the other thing. Cas and I, we had a little shop. Cloisonné-work, mostly. Her father and brother had the trade of making it, and they set us up on Signal Street, just past the middle, next to the auction house. The building's still there, though nobody lives in it. I'd go over to the inlaws and carry the boxes home on my back, and pull them open, and put the pieces on our shelves. Cas priced 'em, sold, and kept everything so clean! You know how long we did that? Run our little place?"

I shook my head.

"Four years, less a month and a week. Then she died. Cas died. It wasn't long before it was all gone, but it was the biggest part of my life. I've got a place to sleep in a loft now. A man I knew years before, though that was years after Cas was gone, he lets me sleep there. There isn't a piece of cloisonné in it, or a garment, or so much as a nail from the old shop. I tried to keep a locket and Cas's combs, but everything's gone. Tell me this, now. How am I to know it wasn't no dream?"

It seemed to me that the old man might be spell-caught, as the people in the house of yellow wood had been; so I said, "I have no way of knowing. Perhaps, as you say, it was a dream. I think you torment yourself too much."

His mood changed in an instant, as I have seen the moods of young children do, and he laughed. "It's easy to see, sieur, that despite the outfit under that mantle, you're no torturer. I do truly wish I could ferry you and your doxie. Since I can't, there's a fellow farther along that has a bigger boat. He comes here pretty often, and he talks to me sometimes like you did. Tell him I hope he'll take you across."

I thanked him and hurried after Agia, who by this time was a great distance ahead. She was limping, and I recalled how far she had walked today after wrenching her leg. As I was about to overtake her and give her my arm, I made one of those missteps that seem disastrous and enormously humiliating at the time, though one laughs at them afterward; and in so doing I set in motion one of the strangest incidents of my admittedly strange career. I began to run, and in running came too near the inner side of a curve in the track.

At one moment I was bounding along on the springy sedge—at the next I was floundering in icy brown water, much impeded by my mantle. For the space of a breath I knew again the terror of drowning; then I righted myself and got my face above water. The habits developed on all those summer swims in Gyoll reasserted themselves: I blew the water from my nose and mouth, took a deep breath, and pushed my sopping hood back from my face.

I was no sooner calm than I realized that I had dropped *Terminus Est,* and at that moment losing that blade seemed more terrible than the chance of death. I dove, not even troubling to kick off my boots, forcing my way through an umber fluid that was not water purely, but water laced and thickened with the fibrous stems of the reeds. These stems, though they multiplied the threat of drowning many times, saved *Terminus Est* for me—she would surely have outraced me to the bottom and buried herself in the mud there despite the meager air retained in her sheath, if her fall had not been obstructed. As it was, eight or ten cubits beneath the surface one frantically groping hand encountered the blessed, familiar shape of her onyx grip.

At the same instant, my other hand touched an object of a completely different kind. It was another human hand, and its grasp (for it had seized my own the moment I touched it) coincided so perfectly with the recovery of *Terminus Est* that it seemed the hand's owner was returning my property to me, like the tall mistress of the Pelerines. I felt a surge of lunatic gratitude, then fear returned tenfold: the hand was pulling my own, drawing me down.

XXIII

Hildegrin

WITH WHAT MUST SURELY HAVE BEEN THE LAST STRENGTH I possessed, I managed to throw *Terminus Est* onto the floating track of sedge and grasp its ragged margin before I sank again.

Someone caught me by the wrist. I looked up expecting Agia; it was not she but a woman younger still, with streaming yellow hair. I strove to thank her, but water, not words, poured from my mouth. She tugged and I struggled, and at last I lay wholly supported on the sedge, so weak I could do nothing more.

I must have rested there at least as long as it takes to say the angelus, and perhaps longer. I was conscious of the cold, which grew worse, and of the sagging of the whole fabric of rotting plants, which bent beneath my weight until I was half submerged again. I breathed in great gasps that failed to satisfy my lungs, and coughed water; water trickled from my nostrils too. Someone (it was a man's voice, a loud one I seemed to have heard a long time before) said, "Pull him over or he'll sink." I was lifted by my belt. In a few moments more I was able to stand, though my legs trembled so I feared I would fall.

Agia was there, and the blond girl who had helped me onto the sedge, and a big, beef-faced man. Agia asked what had happened, and half-conscious though I was I noticed how pale she was.

"Give him time," the big man said. "He'll be all right soon enough." And then, "Who in Phlegethon are you?"

He was looking at the girl, who seemed as dazed as I felt. She made a stammering sound, "D-d-d-d," then hung her

171

head and was silent. From hair to heels she was smeared with mud, and what clothing she had seemed no better than rags.

The big man asked Agia, "Where did that one come from?"

"I don't know. When I looked back to see what was keeping Severian, she was pulling him onto this floating path."

"Good thing she did, too. Good for him, anyway. Is she mad? Or chant-caught here, you think?"

I said, "Whatever she is, she saved me. Can't you give her something to cover herself with? She must be freezing." I was freezing myself, now that I was alive enough to notice it.

The big man shook his head, and seemed to draw his heavy coat about him more closely. "Not unless she gets clean I won't. And she won't unless she's put back in the water, and stirred around, too. But I've something here that's the next best thing, and maybe better." From one of his coat pockets he took a metal flask shaped like a dog, which he handed to me.

A bone in the dog's mouth proved to be the stopper. I offered the flask to the blond girl, who at first seemed not to know what to do with it. Agia took it from her and held it to her lips until she had taken several swallows, then handed it back to me. The contents seemed to be plum brandy; its fiery impact washed away the bitterness of the fen water very pleasantly. By the time I replaced the bone in the dog's mouth, his belly was, I think, better than half empty.

"Now then," said the big man, "I think you people ought to tell me who you are and what you're doing here—and don't none of you say you've just come to see the sights of the garden. I see enough gawkers these days to know them before they come in hailing distance." He looked at me. "That's a good big whittle you've got there, to begin with."

Agia said, "The armiger is in costume. He has been challenged, and has come to cut an avern."

"He's in costume and you aren't, I suppose. Do you think I don't know stage brocade? And bare feet too, when I see them?"

"I never said I was not in costume, nor that I was of his rank. As for my shoes, I left them outside so as not to ruin them in this water."

The big man nodded in a way that gave no clue as to whether he believed her or not. "Now you, goldy-hair. The embroidered baggage here has already said she don't know you. And from the look of him, I don't believe her fish—that you pulled out for her, and a good piece of work that was, too—knows any more than I do. Maybe not that much. So who are you?"

The blond girl swallowed. "Dorcas."

"And how'd you get here, Dorcas? And how'd you get in the water? For that's where you've been, plainly. You couldn't of got that wet just pulling out our young friend."

The brandy had brought a flush to the girl's cheeks, but her face was as vacant and bewildered as before, or nearly so. "I don't know," she whispered.

Agia asked, "You don't remember coming here?"

Dorcas shook her head.

"Then what's the last thing you do remember?"

There was a long silence. The wind seemed to be blowing harder than ever, and despite the drink, I was miserably cold. At last Dorcas murmured, "Sitting by a window . . . There were pretty things in the window. Trays and boxes, and a rood."

The big man said, "Pretty things? Well, if you was there, I'm assured there was."

"She's mad," Agia said. "Either someone's been taking care of her and she's wandered away, or no one is taking care of her, which seems more likely from the state of her clothes, and she wandered in here when the curators weren't looking."

"It may be somebody's cracked her over the head, took her things, and threw her in here thinking she was gone. There's more ways in, Mistress Slops, than the curator knows of. Or maybe somebody brought her in to be sunk when she was only sick and sleepin'. In a com'er, as they call it, and the water woke her up."

"Surely whoever brought her in would have seen her."

"They can stay under a long time in a com'er, so I've heard. But whichever way it was, it don't much matter now. Here she is, and it's up to her, I should say, to find out where she come from and who she is."

I had dropped the brown mantle and was trying to wring

my guild cloak dry; but I looked up when Agia said, "You've been asking all of us who we are. Who are you?"

"You've every right to know," the big man said. "Every right in the world, and I'll give you better bona fides than any of you have given me. Only after I does so, I must be about my own business. I come because I saw the young armiger here drowning, like any good man would. But I've my own affairs to take care of, the same as the next."

With that he pulled off his tall hat, and reaching inside produced a greasy card about twice the size of the calling cards I had occasionally seen in the Citadel. He handed it to Agia, and I peered over her shoulder. In florid script, the legend read:

HILDEGRIN THE BADGER
Excavations of *all* kinds, by a single
digger or 20 score.
Stone is not too hard nor mud too soft.
Ask on *Argosy* Street at the sign of the
BLIND SHOVEL
Or inquire at the Alticamelus around
the corner of Velleity.

"And that's who I am, Mistress Slops and young sieur—which I hope you won't mind my calling you, firstly because you're younger nor me, and secondly because you're a sight younger than what she is, for all you was probably born only a couple years sooner. And I'll be on my way."

I stopped him. "Before I fell in, I met an old man in a skiff who told me there was someone farther down the track who could ferry us across the lake. I think you must be the man he referred to. Will you take us?"

"Ah, the one what's lookin' for his wife, poor soul. Well, he's been a good friend to me many a time, so if he recommends you, I suppose I'd better do it. My scow will hold four in a pinch."

He strode off motioning for us to follow; I noticed that his boots, which seemed to have been greased, sank in the sedge even deeper than my own. Agia said, "She's not coming with us." Still it was obvious that she (Dorcas) was, trailing along behind Agia and looking so forlorn that I dropped behind to try to comfort her. "I'd lend you my mantle," I whispered to her, "if it weren't so wet it would make you colder than you are already. But if you'll go along this track the other way, you'll come out of here altogether and into a corridor where it's warmer and drier. Then if you'll look for a door with *Jungle Garden* on it, that will let you into a place were the sun is warm and you'll be quite comfortable."

I had no sooner spoken than I remembered the pelycosaur we had seen in the jungle. Fortunately, perhaps, Dorcas showed no sign of having heard what I said. Something in her face conveyed that she was afraid of Agia, or at least aware, in a helpless way, of having displeased her; but there was no other indication she was any more alert to her surroundings than a somnambulist.

Conscious that I had failed to relieve her misery, I began again. "There's a man in the corridor, a curator. I'm sure he'll at least try to find some clothes and a fire for you."

The wind whipped Agia's chestnut hair as she looked back at us. "There are too many of these beggar girls for anyone to be worried about one, Severian. Including yourself."

At the sound of Agia's voice, Hildegrin glanced over his shoulder. "I know a woman might take her in. Yes, and clean her up and give her some clothes. There's a high-bred shape under that mud, thin though she is."

"What are you doing here, anyway?" Agia snapped. "You contract laborers, according to your card, but what's your business here?"

"Just what you said, Mistress. My business."

Dorcas had begun to shiver. "Honestly," I told her, "all you have to do is go back. It's much warmer in the corridor. Don't go in the Jungle Garden. You might go into the Sand Garden, it's sunny and dry in there."

Something in what I had said seemed to touch a chord in her. "Yes," she whispered. "Yes."

"The Sand Garden? You'd like that?"

Very softly: "Sun."

"Here's the old scow now," Hildegrin announced. "With so many, we're going to have to be particular about the seatin'. And there's to be no movin' about—she'll be low in the water. One of the women in the bow, please, and the other and the young armiger in the stern."

I said, "I'd be happy to take an oar."

"Ever rowed before? I thought not. No, you'd best sit in the stern like I told you. It ain't much harder pullin' two oars than one, and I've done it many a time, believe me, though there was half a dozen in her with me."

His boat was like himself, wide, rough, and heavy-looking. Bow and stern were square, so much so that there was hardly any horizontal taper from the waist, where the rowlocks were, though the hull was shallower at the ends. Hildegrin got in first, and standing with one leg to either side of the bench, used an oar to nudge the boat closer to shore for us.

"You," Agia said, taking Dorcas by the arm. "You sit up there in front."

Dorcas seemed willing to obey, but Hildegrin stopped her. "If you don't mind, Mistress," he said to Agia, "I'd sooner it was you in the bow. I won't be able to keep my eye on her, you see, when I'm rowin', unless she sits behind. She's not right, which even you and me can agree on, and low as we'll be I'd like to know if she starts friskin' around."

Dorcas surprised us all by saying, "I'm not mad. It's just . . . I feel as if I've just been wakened."

Hildegrin made her sit in the stern with me nonetheless. "Now this," he said as he pushed us off, "this is something you're not likely to forget if you've never done it before. Crossin' the Lake of Birds here in the middle of the Garden of Everlastin' Sleep." His oars dipping into the water made a dull and somehow melancholy sound.

I asked why it was called the Lake of Birds.

"Because so many's found dead in the water, is what some say. But it might only be that that's because there's so many here. There's a great deal said against Death. I mean by the people that has to die, drawin' her picture like a crone with a sack, and all that. But she's a good friend to birds, Death is. Wherever there's dead men and quiet, you'll find a good many birds, that's been my experience."

Recalling how the thrushes sang in our necropolis, I nodded.

"Now if you'll look past my shoulder, you'll have a clear view of the shore ahead of us and be able to see a lot of things you couldn't before, because of the rushes growin' all around you back there. You'll notice, if it's not too misty, that the land rises farther on. The bogginess stops there, and the trees begin. Can you see 'em?''

I nodded again, and beside me Dorcas nodded as well.

"That's because this whole peep show is meant to look like the mouth of a dead volcaner. The mouth of a dead man is what some say, but that's not really so. If it was, they'd of put in teeth. You'll remember, though, that when you come in here you come up through a pipe in the ground.''

Once more, Dorcas and I nodded together. Though Agia was no more than two strides from us, she was nearly out of sight behind Hildegrin's broad shoulders and fearnought coat.

"Over there,'' he continued, jerking his square chin to show the direction, ''you ought to be able to see a spot of black. Just about halfway up, it is between the bog and the rim. Some sees it and thinks it's where they come out of, but that's behind you and lower down, and a whole lot smaller. This that you see now is the Cave of the Cumaean—the woman that knows the future and the past and everything else. There's some that say this whole place was built only for her, though I don't believe it.''

Softly, Dorcas asked, "How could that be?'' and Hildegrin misunderstood her, or at least pretended to do so.

"The Autarch wants her here, so they say, so he can come and talk without travelin' to the other side of the world. I wouldn't know about that, but sometimes I see somebody walkin' around up there, and metal or maybe a jewel or two flashin'. Who it is I wouldn't know, and since I don't want to know my future—and I know my past, I should think, better than her—I don't go near the cave. People come sometimes hopin' to know when they'll be married, or about success in trade. But I've observed they don't often come back.''

We had nearly reached the center of the lake. The Garden of Endless Sleep rose around us like the sides of a vast bowl, mossy with pines toward the lip, scummed with rushes and sedge below. I was still very cold, more so because of the inactivity of sitting in the boat while another rowed; I was beginning to worry about what the immersion in water might do to the blade of *Terminus Est* if I did not dry and oil it soon, yet even so, the spell of the place held me. (A spell there was, surely, in this garden. I could almost hear it humming over the water, voices chanting in a language I did not know but understood.) I think it held everyone, even Hildegrin, even Agia. For some time we rowed in silence; I saw geese, alive and content for all I could tell, bobbing a long way off; and once, like something in a dream, the nearly human face of a manatee looking into my own through a few spans of brownish water.

XXIV

The Flower of Dissolution

BESIDE ME, DORCAS PLUCKED A WATER HYACINTH AND PUT IT IN her hair. Except for the vague spot of white on the bank some distance ahead, it was the first flower I had seen in the Garden of Endless Sleep; I looked for others, but saw none.

Is it possible the flower came into being only because Dorcas reached for it? In daylight moments, I know as well as the next that such things are impossible; but I am writing by night, and then, when I sat in that boat with the hyacinth less than a cubit from my eyes, I wondered at the dim light and recalled Hildegrin's remark of a moment before, a remark that implied (though quite possibly he did not know it) that the seeress's cave, and thus this garden, was on the opposite side of the world. There, as Master Malrubius had taught us long ago, all was reversed: warmth to the south, cold to the north; light at night, dark by day; snow in summer. The chill I felt would be appropriate then, for it would be summer soon, with sleet riding the wind; the darkness that stood even between my eyes and the blue flowers of the water hyacinth would be appropriate then too, for it would soon be night, with light already in the sky.

The Increate maintains all things in order surely; and the theologicans say light is his shadow. Must it not be then that in darkness order grows ever less, flowers leaping from nothingness into a girl's fingers just as by light in spring they leap from mere filthiness into the air? Perhaps when night closes our eyes there is less order than we believe. Perhaps, indeed, it is this lack of order we perceive as darkness, a randomization of the waves of energy (like a sea), the fields of energy (like a farm) that appear to our deluded eyes—set by light in an order of which they themselves are incapable—to be the real world.

Mist was rising from the water, reminding me first of the swirling motes of straw in the insubstantial cathedral of the Pelerines, then of steam from the soup kettle when Brother Cook carried it into the refectory on a winter afternoon. The witches were said to stir such kettles; but I had never seen one, though their tower stood hardly a chain from ours. I remembered that we rowed across the crater of a volcano. Might it not have been the Cumaean's kettle? Urth's fires were long dead, as Master Malrubius had taught us; it was more than possible that they had cooled long before men had risen from the position of the beasts to cumber her face with their cities. But witches, it was said, raised the dead. Might not the Cumaean raise the dead fires to boil her pot? I dipped my fingers into the water; it was as cold as snow.

Hildegrin leaned toward me as he rowed, then drew away as he pulled his oars. "Goin' to your death," he said. "That's what you're thinkin'. I can see it in your face. To the Sanguin'ry Field, and he'll kill you, whoever he is."

"Are you?" Dorcas asked, and gripped my hand.

When I did not answer, Hildegrin nodded for me. "Don't have to, you know. There's them that doesn't follow the rules, and yet runs free."

"You're mistaken," I said. "I wasn't thinking about monomachy—or dying either."

In my ear, too softly, I think, even for Hildegrin to hear, Dorcas said, "Yes, you were. Your face was full of beauty, of a kind of nobility. When the world is horrible, then thoughts are high, full of grace and greatness."

I looked at her, thinking she was mocking me, but she was not.

"The world is filled half with evil and half with good. We can tilt it forward so that more good runs into our minds, or back, so that more runs into this." A movement of her eyes took in all the lake. "But the quantities are the same, we change only their proportion here or there."

"I would tilt it as far back as I can, until at last the evil runs out altogether," I said.

"It might be the good that would run out. But I am like you; I would bend time backward if I could."

"Nor do I believe that beautiful thoughts—or wise ones—are engendered by external troubles."

"I did not say beautiful thoughts, but thoughts of grace and greatness, though I suppose that is a kind of beauty. Let me show you." She lifted my hand and slipping it inside her rags pressed it to her right breast. I could feel the nipple, as firm as a cherry, and the warmth of the gentle mound beneath it, delicate, feather-soft and alive with racing blood. "Now," she said, "what are your thoughts? If I have made the external world sweet to you, aren't they less than they were?"

"Where did you learn all this?" I asked. Her face was drained of its wisdom, which condensed in crystal drops at the corners of her eyes.

The shore on which the averns grew was less marshy than the other. It seemed strange, after having walked on buoyant sedge and floated on water for so long, to set foot again on soil that was no worse than soft. We had landed at some distance from the plants; but we were near enough now that they were no longer a mere bank of white, but growths of definite color and shape, whose size could be readily estimated. I said, "They are not from here, are they? Not from our Urth." No one replied; I think I must have spoken too softly for any of the others (except perhaps Dorcas) to hear.

They had a stiffness, a geometrical precision, surely born under some other sun. The color of their leaves was that of a scarab's back, but infused with tints at once deeper and more translucent. It seemed to imply the existence of light somewhere, some inconceivable distance away, of a spectrum that would have withered or perhaps enobled the world.

As we walked nearer, Agia leading the way—I following her with Dorcas behind me, and Hildegrin following us—I saw that each leaf was like a dagger blade, stiff and pointed, with edges sharp enough to satisfy even Master Gurloes.

Above these leaves, the half-closed white blossoms we had seen from across the lake seemed creations of pure beauty, virginal fantasies guarded by a hundred knives. They were wide and lush, and their petals curled in a way that should have seemed tousled if it had not formed a complex swirling pattern that drew the eye like a spiral limned on a revolving disc.

Agia said, "Good form requires that you pick the plant yourself, Severian. But I'll go with you and show you how. The trick is to put your arm under the lowest leaves, and snap the stem off at the ground."

Hildegrin caught her by the shoulder. "That you won't, Mistress," he said. And then to me, "You go forward since you're of a mind to, young sieur. I'll take the females to safety."

I was already several strides past him, but I stopped for an instant when he spoke. Luckily Dorcas called out, "Be careful!" at that moment, and I was able to pretend it was her warning that had halted me.

The truth was otherwise. From the time we had met Hildegrin, I had felt certain I had encountered him before, though the shock of recognition that had come so swiftly when I saw Sieur Racho again was in this instance long delayed. Now it had come at last, with paralyzing force.

As I have said, I remember everything; but often I can find a fact, face, or feeling only after a long search. I suppose that in this case, the problem was that from the moment he had bent over me on the sedge track I could see him clearly, and previously I had hardly seen him at all. It was only when he said, *"I'll take these females to safety,"* that my memory closed upon his voice.

"The leaves are poisoned," Agia called. "Twisting your mantle tight about your arm will give you some protection, but try not to touch them. And watch out—you are always closer to an avern than you think."

I nodded to show I understood.

Whether the avern is deadly to the life of its own world I have no way of knowing. It may be that it is not, that it is only dangerous to us by reason of a nature accidentally inimical to our own. Whether that is so or not, the ground between and beneath the plants was covered with short and very fine grass,

grass quite different from the coarse growth elsewhere; and this short grass was littered with the curled bodies of bees and dotted with the white bones of birds.

When I was no more than a couple of paces from the plants, I stopped, suddenly aware of a problem I had given no thought to previously. The avern I selected would be my weapon in the contest to come—yet because I knew nothing as yet of the way it would be fought, I had no means of judging which plant might be best adapted to it. I could have gone back and questioned Agia, but I would have felt absurd examining a woman on such a matter, and in the end I decided to trust my judgment, since she would no doubt send me back for another if my first choice were wholly unsuitable.

The averns varied in height from seedlings of hardly more than a span to old plants of three cubits or a little less. These older plants had fewer, though larger, leaves. Those of the smaller ones were narrower, and so closely spaced that the stems were completely hidden; those of the big plants were much broader in proportion to their length, and somewhat separated on the fleshy-looking stems. If (as seemed likely) the Septentrion and I were to use our plants as maces, the largest possible plant with the longest possible stem and the stoutest possible leaves would be the best. But these all grew well away from the edges of the planting, so that it would be necessary to break down a number of smaller plants to reach them; and to do that by the method Agia had advised was clearly impossible, because the leaves of many of the smaller plants grew nearly to the ground.

In the end I chose one about two cubits high. I had knelt beside it and was reaching toward it when as though a veil had been snatched away I realized that my hand, which I had thought still several spans from the needlelike point of the nearest leaf, was about to be impaled. I drew it back hurriedly; the plant seemed almost out of reach—indeed, I was not certain I could touch its stem even by lying prone. The temptation to use my sword was very great, but I felt it would disgrace me before Agia and Dorcas to do so, and I knew I would have to handle the plant during the combat in any case.

I advanced my hand again, cautiously, this time keeping my forearm in contact with the ground, and discovered that though I had to press my shoulder against the grass as well to prevent my upper arm from being stabbed by the lowest leaves, I could touch the stem quite readily. A point that appeared to be half a cubit from my face trembled with my breath.

It was while I was snapping off the stem—no easy task— that I saw the reason only the short, soft grass flourished beneath the averns. One of the leaves of the plant I was breaking had cut half through a blade of coarse marsh grass, and the entire grass plant, almost an ell across, had begun to wither.

Once picked, the plant was an enormous nuisance, as I ought to have anticipated. It would plainly have been impossible to carry it in Hildegrin's boat as it was without killing one or more of us, so before we reembarked I had to climb the slope and cut a sapling. When the twigs had been lopped, Agia and I bound the avern to one end of its spindly trunk, so that as we made our way through the city later, I appeared to be bearing some grotesque standard.

Then Agia explained the use of the plant as a weapon; and I broke a second plant (although she objected, and at even greater risk, I fear, than before, since I was somewhat too confident) and practiced what she had told me.

The avern is not, as I had assumed, merely a viper-toothed mace. Its leaves can be detached by twisting them between the thumb and forefinger in such a way that the hand does not contact the edges or the point. The leaf is then in effect a handleless blade, envenomed and razor-sharp, ready to throw. The fighter holds the plant in his left hand by the base of the stem and plucks the lower leaves to throw with his right. Agia cautioned me, however, to keep my own plant out of my opponent's reach, since as the leaves are removed an area of bare stem appears, and this he might grasp and use to wrest my plant from me.

When I flourished the second plant and practiced striking out with it and picking and throwing the leaves, I found that my own avern was likely to be almost as great a danger to me as the Septentrion's. If I held it near me, there was a grave risk of pricking my arm or chest with the long lower leaves; and the flower with its swirling pattern held my gaze whenever I glanced down to tear off a leaf, and with the dry

lust of death sought to draw me to it. All this seemed
unpleasant enough; but when I had learned to keep my eyes
away from the half-closed blossom, I reflected that my
opponent would be exposed to the same dangers.

Throwing the leaves was easier than I had supposed. Their
surfaces were glossy, like the leaves of many of the plants I
had seen in the Jungle Garden, so that they left the fingers
readily, and they were heavy enough to fly far and true. They
could be thrown point-foremost like any knife, or made to
spin in flight to cut down anything in their path with their
deadly edges.

I was eager, of course, to question Hildegrin about
Vodalus; but no opportunity to do so came until he had
rowed us back across the silent lake. Then for a moment Agia
became so intent on driving Dorcas away that I was able to
draw him to one side and whisper that I, too, was a friend to
Vodalus.

"You've mistaken me, young sieur, for somebody else—do
you refer to Vodalus the outlaw?"

"I never forget a voice," I told him, "or anything else."
And then in my eagerness, I impulsively added what was
perhaps the worse thing I could have said: "You tried to brain
me with your shovel." His face became masklike at once, and
he stepped back into his boat and rowed out onto the brown
water.

When Agia and I left the Botanic Gardens, Dorcas was still
with us. Agia was anxious to make her go away, and for a
time I permitted her to try. I was moved in part by the fear
that with Dorcas near it would be impossible for me to
persuade Agia to lie with me; but even more by a vague
appreciation of the pain Dorcas would feel, lost and dismayed
as she was already, if she should see me die. Only a short time
before, I had poured out to Agia all my sorrow at the death of
Thecla. Now these new concerns had replaced it, and I found
I had poured it out indeed, as a man might spill sour wine on
the ground. By the use of the language of sorrow I had for the
time being obliterated my sorrow—so powerful is the charm
of words, which for us reduces to manageable entities all the
passions that would otherwise madden and destroy us.

Whatever my motives may have been, and whatever Agia's

may have been, and whatever Dorcas's may have been for following us, nothing Agia did succeeded. And in the end, I threatened to strike her if she did not desist, and called to Dorcas, who was then fifty paces or so behind us.

After that we three trudged along in silence, drawing many strange looks. I was soaked to soddenness, and no longer cared whether my mantle covered my fuligin torturer's cloak. Agia in her torn brocade must have looked nearly as strange as I. Dorcas was still smeared with mud—it dried on her in the warm spring wind that now wrapped the city, caking in her golden hair and leaving smears of powdery brown on her pale skin. Above us the avern brooded like a gonfalon; from it there drifted a myrrhic perfume. The half-closed flower still shone as white as bone, but its leaves looked nearly black in the sunlight.

XXV

The Inn of Lost Loves

IT HAS BEEN MY GOOD FORTUNE—OR EVIL FORTUNE, AS IT MAY be—that the places with which my life has been largely associated have been, with very few exceptions, of the most permanent character. I might tomorrow, if I wished, return to the Citadel and (I think) to the very cot on which I slept as an apprentice. Gyoll still rolls past my city of Nessus; the Botanic Gardens still glitter in the sun, faceted with those strange enclosures wherein a single mood is preserved for all time. When I think of the ephemera of my life, they are likely to be men and women. But there are a few houses as well, and first among these stands the inn at the margin of the Sanguinary Field.

We had walked away the afternoon, down broad avenues and up narrow byways, and always the buildings that hemmed us round were of stone and brick. At last we came to grounds that seemed no grounds at all, for there was no exalted villa at their center. I remember I warned Agia that a storm was brewing—I could feel the closeness of the air, and I saw a line of bitter black along the horizon.

She laughed at me. "What you see and what you feel too is nothing more than the City Wall. It's always like this here. The Wall impedes the movement of the air."

"That line of dark? It goes halfway to the sky."

Agia laughed again, but Dorcas pressed herself against me. "I am afraid, Severian."

Agia heard her. "Of the Wall? It won't hurt you unless it falls on you, and it has stood through a dozen ages." I looked questioningly at her, and she added, "At least it looks that old, and it may be older. Who knows?"

"It could wall out the world. Does it stretch completely around the city?"

"By definition. The city is what is enclosed, though there's open country to the north, so I've heard, and leagues and leagues of ruins in the south, where no one lives. But now, look between those poplars. Do you see the inn?"

I did not, and said so.

"Under the tree. You've promised me a meal, and that's where I want it. We should just have time to eat before you have to meet the Septentrion."

"Not now," I said. "I'll be happy to feed you when my duel is over. I'll make the arrangements now, if you like." I could still find no building, but I had come to see that there was something strange about the tree: a stair of rustic wood twined up the trunk.

"Do so. If you're killed, I'll invite the Septentrion—or if he won't come, that broken sailor who is forever inviting me. We'll drink to you."

A light kindled high in the branches of the tree, and now I saw that a path led up to the stair. Before it, a painted sign showed a weeping woman dragging a bloody sword. A monstrously fat man in an apron stepped out of the shadow and stood beside it, rubbing his hands while he waited our coming. Faintly now, I could hear the clinking of pots.

"Abban at your command," said the fat man when we

reached him. "What is your wish?" I noticed he kept a nervous eye on my avern.

"We'll have dinner for two, to be served at . . ." I looked at Agia.

"The new watch."

"Good, good. But it cannot be so soon, sieur. It will take longer to prepare. Unless you'll settle for cold meats, a salad, and a bottle of wine?"

Agia looked impatient. "We'll have a roast fowl—a young one."

"As you wish. I'll have the cook begin his preparations now, and you can amuse yourselves with baked stuff after the sieur's victory until the bird is done." Agia nodded, and a look flashed between the two that made me feel certain they had met previously. "Meanwhile," the innkeeper continued, "if you've yet time, I could provide a basin of warm water and a sponge for this other young lady, and perhaps you might all enjoy a glass of Medoc and some biscuits?"

I was suddenly conscious of having fasted since my breakfast at dawn with Baldanders and Dr. Talos, and conscious too that Agia and Dorcas might have had nothing all day. When I nodded, the innkeeper conducted us up the broad, rustic stair; the trunk it circled was a full ten paces around.

"Have you visited us before, sieur?"

I shook my head. "I was about to ask you what manner of inn this is. I've never seen anything like it."

"Nor will you, sieur, except here. But you ought to have come before—we keep a famous kitchen, and dining in the open air gives one the best appetite."

I thought that it must indeed if he maintained such a girth in a place where every room was reached by steps, but I kept the reflection to myself.

"The law, you see, sieur, forbids all buildings so near the Wall. We are permitted, having neither walls nor a roof. Those who attend the Sanguinary Field come here, the famous combatants and heroes, the spectators and physicians, even the ephors. Here's your chamber now."

It was a circular and perfectly level platform. Around and above it, pale green foliage shut out sight and sound. Agia sat

in a canvas chair, and I (very tired, I confess) threw myself
down beside Dorcas on a couch made of leather and the
linked horns of lechwes and waterbucks. When I had laid the
avern behind it, I drew *Terminus Est* and began to clean her
blade. A scullion brought water and a sponge for Dorcas and,
when she saw what I was doing, rags and oil for me. I was
soon tapping at the pommel so I could strip the blade from its
furniture for a real cleaning.

"Can't you wash yourself?" Agia asked Dorcas.

"I'd like a bath, yes, but not with you watching me."

"Severian will turn his head if you ask him. He did very
well in a place where we were this morning."

"And you, madame," Dorcas said softly. "I'd rather you
didn't watch. I'd like a private place, if I might have one."

Agia smiled at that, but I called the scullion again and gave
her an orichalk to bring a folding screen. When it was set up, I
told Dorcas I would buy her a gown if there were one to be
had at the inn.

"No," she said. In a whisper, I asked Agia what she
thought was the matter with her.

"She likes what she has, clearly. I must walk with a hand up
to hold my bodice if I wouldn't be shamed for life." She let
her hand fall, so that her high breasts gleamed in the dying
sunlight. "But those rags let her show just leg and chest
enough. There's a rent at the groin too, though I dare say you
haven't noticed it."

The innkeeper interrupted us, leading in a waiter who
carried a plate of pastries, a bottle, and glasses. I explained
that my clothing was wet, and he had a brazier brought
in—then proceeded to warm himself by it, for all the world as
if he stood in his private apartment. "Feels good, this time of
year," he said. "The sun's dead and don't know it yet, but we
do. If you're killed, you'll get to miss next winter, and if
you're hurt bad, you'll get to stay inside. That's what I always
tell them. Of course, most of the fights are around midsummer's eve, so it's more appropriate then, so to speak. I don't
know if it comforts them or not, but it does no harm."

I took off the brown mantle and my guild cloak, put my
boots on a stool near the brazier, and stood beside him to dry
my breeches and hose, asking if all those who came this way
on monomachy stopped to refresh themselves with him. Like

every man who feels himself likely to die, I would have been happy to know that I was taking part in some established tradition.

"*All?* Oh, no," he said. "May moderation and St. Amand bless you, sieur. If everyone who came tarried at my inn, why it wouldn't be my inn—I'd have sold it, and be living comfortable in a big, stone house with atroxes at the door and a few young fellows with knives hanging about me to settle my enemies. No, there's many a one goes by here without a glance, never thinking that when he comes past next time, it may be too late to drink my wine."

"Speaking of which," said Agia, and handed me a glass. It was full to the brim with a dark, crimson vintage. Not a good wine, perhaps—it made my tongue prickle, and carried with its delicious taste something of harshness. But a wonderful wine, a wine better than good, in the mouth of someone as fatigued and cold as I. Agia held a full glass of her own, but I saw by her flaming cheeks and sparkling eyes that she had already downed one other at least. I told her to save something for Dorcas, and she said, "That milk and water virgin? She won't drink it, and it's you who'll need courage—not she."

Not quite honestly, I said I was not afraid.

The innkeeper exclaimed, "That's the way! Don't you be feared, and don't fill your head with no noble thoughts about death and last days and all that. The ones that do is the ones that never come back, you may be sure. Now you was going to order a meal, I think, for you and your two young women afterward?"

"We have ordered it," I said.

"Ordered, but not paid nothing toward, that was my meaning. Also there's the wine and these here *gâteaux secs.* Those must be paid for here and now as they're eaten here and now, and drank up too. For the dinner I'll require a deposit of three orichalks, with two more to be paid when you come to eat it."

"And if I don't come?"

"Then there's no more charge, sieur. That's how I'm able to offer my dinners at such low prices."

The man's complete insensibility disarmed me; I handed over the money and he left us. Agia peeped around the side of the screen behind which Dorcas was cleansing herself with the aid of the scullion, and I sat down again on the couch and took a pastry to go with what remained of my wine.

"If we could make the hinges in this thing lock, Severian, we might enjoy ourselves for a few moments without interruption. We could put a chair against it, but no doubt those two would choose the worst possible moment to squall and knock everything over."

I was about to make some bantering reply when I noticed a scrap of paper, folded many times, that had been put beneath the waiter's tray in such a fashion that it could be seen only by someone sitting where I was. "This is really to much," I said. "A challenge, and now the mysterious note."

Agia came to look. "What are you talking about? Are you drunk already?"

I put my hand on the rounded fullness of her hip, and when she made no objection, used that pleasant handle to draw her toward me until she could see the paper. "What do you suppose it says? 'The Commonwealth has need of you—ride at once . . .' 'Your friend is he who shall say to you, camarilla . . .' 'Beware of the man with pink hair . . .'"

Falling in with the joke, Agia offered, "'Come when you hear three pebbles tap the window . . .' The *leaves*, I should say here. 'The rose hath stabbed the iris, who nectar affords . . .' That's your avern killing me, clearly. 'You will know your true love by her red pagne . . .'" She bent to kiss me, then sat in my lap. "Aren't you going to look?"

"I *am* looking." Her torn bodice had fallen again.

"Not there. Cover that with your hand, and then you can look at the note."

I did as she told me, but left the note where it was. "It's really too much, as I said a moment ago. The mysterious Septentrion and his challenge, then Hildegrin, and now this. Have I mentioned the Chatelaine Thecla to you?"

"More than once, while we were walking."

"I loved her. She read a great deal—there was really nothing for her to do when I was gone but read and sew and sleep—and when I was with her we used to laugh at the plots of some of the stories. This sort of thing was always happening to the people in them, and they were incessantly involved in high and melodramatic affairs for which they had no qualifications."

Agia laughed with me and kissed me again, a lingering kiss. When our lips parted, she said, "What's this about Hildegrin? He seemed ordinary enough."

I took another pastry, touched the note with it, then put a corner into her mouth. "Some time ago I saved the life of a man called Vodalus—"

Agia pulled away from me, spewing crumbs. "Vodalus? You're joking!"

"Not at all. That's what his friend called him. I was still hardly more than a boy, but I held back the haft of an ax for a moment. The blow would have killed him, and he gave me a chrisos."

"Wait. What has this to do with Hildegrin?"

"When I first saw Vodalus, he had a man and a woman with him. Enemies came upon them, and Vodalus remained behind to fight while the other man took the woman to safety." (I had decided it was wiser to say nothing about the corpse, or my killing of the axman.)

"I'd have fought myself—then there'd have been three fighters instead of one. Go on."

"Hildegrin was the man with Vodalus, that's all. If we had met him first, I would have had some idea, or thought I had some idea, of why a hipparch of the Septentrion Guard would want to fight me. And for that matter why someone has chosen to send me some sort of furtive message. You know, all the things the Chatelaine Thecla and I used to laugh about, spies and intrigue, masked trysts, lost heirs. What's the matter, Agia?"

"Do I revolt you? Am I so ugly?"

"You're beautiful, but you look as if you're about to be sick. I think you drank too fast."

"Here." A quick twist took Agia out of her pavonine gown; it lay about her brown, dusty feet like a heap of precious stones. I had seen her naked in the cathedral of the Pelerines, but now (whether because of the wine I had drunk or the wine she had drunk, because the light was dimmer now, or brighter, or only because she had been frightened and shamed then, covering her breasts and hiding her womanhood between her thighs) she drew me far more. I felt stupid with desire, thick-headed and thick-tongued as I pressed her warmth against my own cold flesh.

"Severian, wait. I'm not a strumpet, whatever you may think. But there's a price."

"What?"

"You must promise me you won't read that note. Throw it into the brazier."

I let go of her and stepped back.

Tears appeared in her eyes, rising as springs do among rocks. "I wish you could see the way you're looking at me now, Severian. No, I don't know what it says. It's just that—have you never heard of some women having supernatural knowledge? Premonitions? Knowing things they could not possibly have learned?"

The longing I had felt was nearly gone. I was frightened as well as angry, though I did not know why. I said, "We have a guild of such women, our sisters, in the Citadel. Neither their faces nor their bodies are like yours."

"I know I'm not like that. But that's why you must do what I advise. I've never in my life had a premonition of any strength, and I have one now. Don't you see that must mean it's something so true and so important to you that you can't and mustn't ignore it? Burn the note."

"Someone is trying to warn me, and you don't want me to see it. I asked you if the Septentrion was your lover. You told me he was not, and I believed you."

She started to speak, but I silenced her.

"I believe you still. Your voice had truth in it. Yet you are laboring to betray me in some way. Tell me now that isn't so. Tell me you are acting in my best interests, and nothing beyond."

"Severian . . ."

"Tell me."

"Severian, we met this morning. I hardly knew you and you hardly know me. What can you expect, and what would you expect if you had not just left the shelter of your guild? I've tried to help you from time to time. I'm trying to help you now."

"Put on your dress." I took the note from under the tray. She rushed at me, but it was not difficult to hold her off with one hand. The note had been penned with a crow quill, in a straggling scrawl; in the dim light I could decipher only a few words.

"I could have distracted you, and thrown it into the fire. That's what I ought to have done. Severian, let me go—"

"Be quiet."

"I had a knife, only last week. A misericorde with an ivy-root handle. We were hungry, and Agilus put it in pawn. If I had it still, I could stab you now!"

"It would be in your gown, and your gown is over there on the floor." I gave her a push that sent her staggering backward (there was wine enough in her stomach that it was not entirely from the violence of my motion) into the canvas chair, and carried the note to a spot where the last light of the sun penetrated the crowding leaves.

> The woman with you has been here before.
> Do not trust her. Trudo says the man is
> a torturer. You are my mother come again.

XXVI

Sennet

I HAD JUST HAD TIME TO ABSORB THE WORDS WHEN AGIA JUMPED from her chair, snatched the note from my hand, and threw it over the edge of the platform. For a moment she stood before me, looking from my face to *Terminus est*, which by this time leaned, reassembled, against an arm of the couch. I think she feared I was going to strike off her head and throw it after the note. When I did nothing, she said, "Did you read it? Severian, say you didn't!"

"I read it, but I don't understand it."

"Then don't think about it."

"Be calm for a moment. It wasn't even meant for me. It may have been for you, but if it was, why was it put where no one but I could see it? Agia, have you had a child? How old are you?"

"Twenty-three. That's plenty old enough, but no, I haven't. I'll let you look at my belly if you don't believe me."

I tried to make a mental calculation and discovered I did not know enough about the maturation of women. "When did you menstruate first?"

"Thirteen. If I'd got pregnant, I would have been fourteen when the baby came. Is that what you're trying to find out?"

"Yes. And the child would be nine now. If it were bright, it might be able to write a note like that. Do you want me to tell you what it said?"

"No!"

"How old would you say Dorcas is? Eighteen? Nineteen, perhaps?"

"You shouldn't think about it, Severian. Whatever it was."

"I won't play games with you now. You're a woman—how old?"

Agia pursed her full lips. "I'd say your drab little mystery's sixteen or seventeen. Hardly more than a child."

Sometimes, as I suppose everyone has noticed, talking of absent persons seems to summon them up like eidolons. So it was now. A panel of the screen swung back and Dorcas came out, no longer the muddy creature we had become accustomed to, but a round-breasted, slender girl of singular grace. I have seen skin whiter than hers, but that was not a healthy whiteness. Dorcas seemed to glow. Freed of filth, her hair was pale gold; her eyes were as they had always been: the deep blue of the world-river Uroboros in my dream. When she saw that Agia was naked, she tried to return to the shelter of the screen, but the thick body of the scullion prevented her.

Agia said, "I had better put my rags on again before your pet faints."

Dorcas murmured, "I won't look."

"I don't care if you do," Agia told her, but I noticed she turned her back to us while she put on her gown. Speaking to the wall of leaves, she added, "Now we really must go, Severian. The trumpet will sound at any moment."

"And what will that mean?"

"You don't know?" She swung about to face us. "When the machionations of the City Wall appear to touch the edge of the solar disc, a trumpet—the first—is sounded on the Sanguinary Field. Some think it's only to regulate the combats there, though that's not so. It is a signal to the guards inside the Wall to close the gates. It's also the signal to begin the fighting, and if you're there when it blows, that's when your contest will start. When the sun is below the horizon and true night comes, a trumpeter on the Wall sounds tattoo. That means the gates will not be opened again even for those who carry special passes and also that anyone who, having given or received a challenge, has not yet come to the Field is assumed to have refused satisfaction. He can be assaulted wherever he is found, and an armiger or an exultant can engage assassins without soiling his honor."

The scullion, who had been standing by the stair listening to all this and nodding, moved aside for her master, the innkeeper. "Sieur," he said, "if you indeed have a mortal appointing, I—"

"That is just what my friend was saying," I told him. "We must go."

Dorcas asked then if she might have some wine. Somewhat surprised, I nodded; the innkeeper poured her a glass, which she held in both hands like a child. I asked him if he supplied writing implements for his guests.

"You wish to make a testament, sieur? Come with me—we have a bower reserved for that purpose. There's no charge, and if you like, I will engage a boy who'll carry the document for your executor."

I picked up *Terminus Est* and followed him, leaving Agia and Dorcas to keep watch on the avern. The bower our host boasted of was perched on a small limb and hardly big enough to hold a desk, but there was a stool there, several crow-quill pens, paper, and a pot of ink. I sat down and wrote out the words of the note; so far as I could judge, the paper was the same as that on which it had been written, and the ink gave the same faded black line. When I had sanded my scribble, folded it, and tucked it away in a compartment of my sabretache I seldom used, I told the innkeeper no messenger would be required, and asked if he knew anyone named Trudo.

"Trudo, sieur?" He looked puzzled.

"Yes. It's a common enough name."

"Surely it is, sieur, I know that. It's just that I was trying to think of somebody that might be known to me and somebody, if you understand me, sieur, in your exalted position. Some armiger or—"

"Anyone," I said. "Anyone at all. It would not, for example, be the name of the waiter who served us, would it?"

"No, sieur. His name's Ouen. I had a neighbor once named Trudo, sieur, but that was years ago, before I bought this place. I don't suppose it would be him you're after? Then there's my ostler here—his name's Trudo."

"I'd like to speak to him."

The innkeeper nodded, his chin vanishing in the fat that circled his neck. "As you wish, sieur. Not that he's likely to be able to tell you much." The steps creaked beneath his weight. "He's from far south, I warn you." (He meant the southern regions of the city, not the wild and largely treeless lands abutting on the ice.) "And from across the river to boot. You're not likely to get much sense from him, though he's a hard-working fellow."

I said, "I suspect I know what part of the city he comes from."

"Do you now? Well, that's interesting, sieur. Very interesting. I've heard one or two say they could tell such things by the way a man dressed or how he spoke, but I wasn't aware you'd laid eyes on Trudo, as the saying is." We were nearing the ground now, and he bawled, *"Trudo! Tr-u-u-do!"* And then, "REINS!"

No one appeared. A single flagstone the size of a large tabletop had been laid at the foot of the stair, and we stepped out upon it.

It was just at that moment when lengthening shadows cease to be shadows at all and become instead pools of blackness, as if some fluid darker even than the waters of the Lake of Birds was rising from the ground. Hundreds of people, some alone, some in small groups, were hurrying over the grass from the direction of the city. All seemed intent, bowed by an eagerness they carried upon their backs and shoulders like a pack. Most bore no weapons I could see, but a few had cases of rapiers, and at some distance off I made out the white blossom of an avern, carried, it seemed, on a pole or staff just as mine was.

"Pity they won't stop here," the innkeeper said. "Not that I won't get some of them coming back, but a dinner before is where the money is. I speak frankly, for I can see that young as you are, sieur, you're too sensible not to know that every business is run to make a profit. I try to give good value, and as I've said, we've a famous kitchen. *Tr-u-do!* I have to have one, for no other sort of food will agree with me—I'd starve, sieur, if I had to eat what most do. *Trudo you louse farm, where are you?*"

A dirty boy appeared from somewhere behind the trunk, wiping his nose on his arm. "He's not back there, Master."

"Well, where is he? Go look for him."

I was still watching the streaming hundreds. "They are all going to the Sanguinary Field then?" For the first time, I think, I fully realized that I was liable to die before the moon shone. Accounting for the note seemed futile and childish.

"Not all to fight, you understand. Most are only going to watch, there's some come only once, because somebody they know's fighting, or just because they were told about it, or read about it, or heard a song. Usually those get taken ill, because they come here and generally put away a bottle or so when they're getting over it.

"But there's others that come every night, or anyway four or five nights out of the week. They're specialists, and only foller one weapon, or perhaps two, and they pretend to know more about those than them that use them, which perhaps some do. After your victory, sieur, two or three will want to buy you a round. If you let them, they'll tell you what you did wrong and what the other man did wrong, but you'll find they don't agree."

I said, "Our dinner is to be private," and as I spoke I heard the whisper of bare feet on the steps behind us. Agia and Dorcas were coming down, Agia carrying the avern, which seemed to me to have grown larger in the failing light.

I have already told how strongly I desired Agia. When we are talking to women, we talk as though love and desire are two separate entities; and women, who often love us and sometimes desire us, maintain the same fiction. The fact is that they are aspects of the same thing, as I might have talked to the innkeeper of the north side of his tree and the south. If we desire a woman, we soon come to love her for her condescension in submitting to us (this, indeed, had been the original foundation of my love for Thecla), and since if we desire her she always submits in imagination at least, some element of love is ever present. On the other hand, if we love her, we soon come to desire her, since attraction is one of the attributes a woman should possess, and we cannot bear to think she is without any of them; in this way men come to desire even women whose legs are locked in paralysis, and women to desire those men who are impotent save with men like themselves.

But no one can say from what it is that what we call (almost at our pleasure) *love* or *desire* is born. As Agia came down the stair, one side of her face was lit by the last light of day, and the other thrown into shadow; her skirt, split nearly to the waist, permitted a flash of silken thigh. And all I had lost in feeling for her a few moments before when I had pushed her away came back doubled and doubled again. She saw that in my face, I know, and Dorcas, hardly a step behind her, saw it too and looked away. But Agia was angry with me still (as perhaps she had a right to be), so although she smiled for policy's sake and could not have concealed the ache in her loins if she would, yet she withheld much.

I think it is in this that we find the real difference between those women to whom if we are to remain men we must offer our lives, and those who (again—if we are to remain men) we must overpower and outwit if we can, and use as we never would a beast: that the second will never permit us to give them what we give the first. Agia enjoyed my admiration and would have been moved to ecstasy by my caresses; but even if I were to pour myself into her a hundred times, we would part strangers. I understood all this as she descended the last few steps, one hand closing the bodice of her gown, the other upholding the avern, whose pole she used as a staff and carried like a baculus. And yet I loved her still, or would have loved her if I could.

The boy came running up. "Trudo's gone, cook says. She

was out fetchin' water 'cause the girl was gone, and seen him runnin' off, and his things is gone from the mews too."

"Gone for good, then," the innkeeper said. "When did he go? Just now?"

The boy nodded.

"He heard you were looking for him, sieur, that's what I'm afraid of. One of the others must have heard you asking me about the name, and run and told him. Did he steal from you?"

I shook my head. "He did me no harm, and I suspect he was trying to do good in whatever he did do. I'm sorry I cost you a servant."

The innkeeper spread his hands. "He'd some wages coming, so I won't lose by it."

As he turned away, Dorcas whispered. "And I am sorry to have taken your joy from you upstairs. I would not have deprived you. But, Severian, I love you."

From somewhere not far off, the silver voice of a trumpet called to the renascent stars.

XXVII

Is He Dead?

THE SANGUINARY FIELD, OF WHICH ALL MY READERS WILL HAVE heard, though some, I hope, will never have visited it, lies northwest of the built sections of our capital of Nessus, between a residential enclave of city armigers and the barracks and stables of the Xenagie of the Blue Dimarchi. It is near enough the Wall to seem very near to someone like myself, who had never been near it at all, yet still leagues of hard walking by twisted avenues from the actual base. How many combats can be accommodated I do not know. It may be that the railings that delimit the grounds of each—upon which the spectators lean or sit as the fancy takes them—can be moved, and are adjusted to suit the evening's needs. I have only visited the spot once, but it seemed to me, with its trampled grass and silent, languid watchers, a strange and melancholy one.

During the brief time I have occupied the throne, many issues have been of more immediate concern than monomachy. Whether it is good or evil (as I am inclined to think), it is surely ineradicable in a society such as ours, which must for its own survival hold the military virtues higher than any others, and in which so few of the armed retainers of the state can be spared to police the populace.

Yet is it evil?

Those ages that have outlawed it (and many hundreds have, by my reading) have replaced it largely with murder—and with just such murders, by and large, as monomachy seems designed to prevent: murders resulting from quarrels among families, friends, and acquaintances. In these cases two die instead of one, for the law tracks down the slayer (a person not by disposition a criminal but by chance) and slays him, as though his death would restore his victim's life. Thus if, say, a thousand legal combats between individuals resulted in a thousand deaths (which is very unlikely, since most such combats do not terminate in death) but prevented five hundred murders, the state would be no worse.

Further, the survivor of such a combat is likely to be the individual most suited to defending the state, and also the most suited to engendering healthy children; while there is no survivor of most murders, and the murderer (were he to survive) is likely to be only vicious, and not strong, quick, or intelligent.

And yet how readily this practice lends itself to intrigue.

We heard the shouted names when we were still a hundred strides away, loudly and formally announced above the trilling of the hylas.

"*Cadroe of the Seventeen Stones!*"

"*Sabas of the Parted Meadow!*"

"*Laurentia of the House of the Harp!*" (This in a woman's voice.)

"Cadroe of the Seventeen Stones!"

I asked Agia who it was who thus called.

"They have given challenges, or have been challenged themselves. By bawling their names—or having a servant do it for them—they advertise that they have come, and to the world that their opponent has not."

"Cadroe of the Seventeen Stones!"

The vanishing sun, whose disc was now a quarter concealed behind the impenetrable blackness of the Wall, had dyed the sky with gamboge and cerise, vermillion and lurid violet. These colors, falling upon the throng of monomachists and loungers much as we see the aureate beams of divine favor fall on hierarchs in art, lent them an appearance insubstantial and thaumaturgic, as though they had all been produced a moment before by the flourish of a cloth and would vanish into the air again at a whistle.

"Laurentia of the House of the Harp!"

"Agia," I said, and from somewhere nearby we heard the choking death makes in a man's throat. "Agia, you are to call out, 'Severian of the Matachin Tower.'"

"I'm not your servant. Bawl it yourself if you want it bawled."

"Cadroe of Seventeen Stones!"

"Don't look at me like that, Severian. I wish we hadn't come! *Severian! Severian of the Torturers! Severian of the Citadel! Of the Tower of Pain! Death! Death is come!*" My hand caught her just below the ear and she went sprawling, the avern on its pole beside her.

Dorcas gripped my arm. "You ought not have done that, Severian."

"It was only the flat of my hand. She'll be all right."

"She will hate you even more."

"Then you think she hates me now?"

Dorcas did not answer, and a moment later I myself forgot for the time being that I had asked the question—some distance away among the crowd, I had seen an avern.

The ground was a level circle some fifteen strides across, railed off save for an entrance at either end.

The ephor called: "The adjudication of the avern has been

offered and accepted. Here is the place. The time is now. It only remains to be decided whether you will engage as you are, naked, or otherwise. How say you?"

Before I could speak, Dorcas called, "Naked. That man is in armor."

The Septentrion's grotesque helm swung from side to side in negation. Like most cavalry helmets it left the ears bare to better hear the graisle and the shouted orders of the wearer's superiors; in the shadow behind the cheekpiece I thought I saw a narrow band of black, and tried to recall where I had seen such a thing before.

The ephor asked, "You refuse, hipparch?"

"The men of my country do not go naked save in the presence of women alone."

"He wears armor," Dorcas called again. "This man has not even a shirt." Her voice, always so soft before, rang in the twilight like a bell.

"I will remove it." The Septentrion threw back his cape and raised a gauntleted hand to the shoulder of his cuirass. It slipped from him and fell at his feet. I had expected a chest as massive as Master Gurloes's, but the one I saw was narrower than my own.

"The helmet also."

Again the Septentrion shook his head, and the ephor asked, "Your refusal is absolute?"

"It is." There was a barely perceptible hesitation. "I can only say that I am instructed not to remove it."

The ephor turned to me. "We none of us would desire, I think, to embarrass the hipparch, and still less the personage—I do not say whom it may be—that he serves. I believe the wisest course would be to allow you, sieur, some compensating advantage. Have you one to suggest?"

Agia, who had been silent since I had struck her, said, "Refuse the combat, Severian. Or reserve your advantage until you need it."

Dorcas, who was loosening the strips of rag that bound the avern, said also, "Refuse the combat."

"I've come too far to turn back now."

The ephor asked pointedly, "Have you decided, sieur?"

"I think I have." My mask was in my sabretache. Like all those used in the guild it was of thin leather stiffened with strips of bone. Whether it would keep out the thrown leaves of the avern I had no way of knowing—but it was satisfying to hear the lookers-on draw breath when I snapped it open.

"You are ready now? Hipparch? Sieur? Sieur, you must give that sword to someone to hold for you. No weapon but the avern may be carried."

I looked about for Agia, but she had vanished into the crowd. Dorcas handed me the deadly blossom, and I gave her *Terminus Est.*

"Begin!"

A leaf whizzed close to my ear. The Septentrion was advancing with an irregular motion, his avern gripped beneath the lowest leaves by his left hand, and his right thrust forward as though to wrestle mine from me. I recalled that Agia had warned me of the danger of this, and clasped it as close as I dared.

For the space of five breaths we circled. Then I struck at his outstretched hand. He countered with his plant. I raised my own above my head like a sword, and as I did so realized the position was an ideal one—it put the vulnerable stem out of my opponent's reach, permitted me to slash downward with the whole plant at will, yet allowed me to detach leaves with my right hand.

This last discovery I put to the test at once, snapping off a leaf and sending it skimming toward his face. Despite the protection his helm gave him he ducked, and the crowd behind him scattered to avoid the missile. I followed it with another. And then another, which struck his own in flight.

The result was remarkable. Instead of absorbing the other's momentum and clattering down together as inanimate blades would, the leaves appeared to writhe and wind their edged lengths about each other, slashing and striking with their points so rapidly that before they had fallen a cubit they were no more than ragged strips of blackish-green that turned to a hundred colors and spun like a child's top . . .

Something, or someone, was pressing against my back. It was as though an unknown stood close behind me, his spine against mine, exerting a slight pressure. I felt cold, and was grateful for the warmth of his body.

"Severian!" The voice was Dorcas's, but she seemed to have wandered away.

"Severian! Won't anyone help him? Let me go!"

The peal of a carillon. The colors, which I had taken to be those of the struggling leaves, were in the sky instead, where a rainbow unrolled beneath the aurora. The world was a great paschal egg, crowded with all the colors of the palette. Near my head a voice inquired, *"Is he dead?"* and someone answered matter-of-factly, *"That's it. Those things always kill. Unless you want to see them drag him off?"*

The Septentrion's voice (oddly familiar) said, "I claim victor right to his clothing and weapons. Give me that sword."

I sat up. The leaves were still faintly struggling wisps a few paces from my boots. The Septentrion stood beyond them, still holding his avern. I drew breath to ask what had happened, and something fell from my chest to my lap; it was a leaf with a bloodstained tip.

Seeing me, the Septentrion whirled and lifted his avern. The ephor stepped between us, arms extended. From the railings some spectator called, *"Gentle right! Gentle right, soldier! Let him stand up and get his weapon."*

My legs would hardly bear me. I looked around stupidly for my own avern, and found it at last only because it lay near the feet of Dorcas, who was struggling with Agia. The Septentrion shouted, "He should be dead!" The ephor said, "He is not, hipparch. When he regains his weapon, you may pursue the combat."

I touched the stem of my avern, and for an instant felt I had grasped the tail of some cold-blooded but living animal. It seemed to stir in my hand, and the leaves rattled. Agia was shouting, *"Sacrilege!"* and I paused to look at her, then picked up the avern and turned to face the Septentrion.

His eyes were shadowed by his helmet, but there was terror in every line of his body. For a moment he seemed to look from me to Agia. Then he turned and fled toward the opening in the rails at his end of the arena. The spectators blocked his way and he used his avern like a scourge, striking to right and left. There was a scream, then a crescendo of screams. My own avern was pulling me backward, or rather, my avern was gone and someone gripped me by the hand. Dorcas. Somewhere far away Agia shrieked, *"Agilus!"* and another woman called, *"Laurentia of the House of the Harp!"*

XXVIII

Carnifex

I WOKE THE NEXT MORNING IN A LAZARET, A LONG, HIGH-CEIL-
inged room where we, the sick, the injured, lay upon narrow
beds. I was naked, and for a long time, while sleep (or
perhaps it was death) tugged at my eyelids, I moved my hands
slowly over my body, searching it for injuries while I
wondered, as I might have wondered of someone in a song,
how I would live without clothing or money, how I should
explain to Master Palaemon the loss of the sword and cloak
he had given me.

For I was sure they were lost—or rather, that I was myself
in some way lost from them. An ape with the head of a dog
ran down the aisle, paused at my bed to look at me, then ran
on. That seemed no stranger to me than the light that, passing
through a window I could not see, fell upon my blanket.

I woke again, and sat up. For a moment I truly thought I
was in our dormitory again, that I was captain of apprentices,
that everything else, my masking, the death of Thecla, the
combat of the averns, had been only a dream. This was not
the last time this was to happen. Then I saw that the ceiling
was of plaster and not our familiar metal one, and that the
man in the bed next to my own was swathed in bandages. I
threw back the blanket and swung my feet to the floor.
Dorcas sat, asleep, with her back to the wall at the head of my
bed. She had wrapped herself in the brown mantle; *Terminus
Est* lay across her lap, the hilt and scabbard-tip protruding
from either side of my heaped belongings. I managed to get
my boots and hose, my breeches, my cloak, and my belt with

205

its sabretache without waking her, but when I tried to take my sword she murmured and clung to it, so I left it with her.

Many of the sick were awake and stared at me, but none spoke. A door at the end of the room opened onto a flight of steps, and these descended to a courtyard where destriers stamped. For a moment I thought I was dreaming still: the cynocephalus was climbing upon the crenelations of the wall. But it was an animal as real as the champing steeds, and when I threw a bit of rubbish at it, it bared teeth as impressive as Triskele's.

A trooper in a hauberk came out to get something from his saddlebag, and I stopped him and asked where I was. He supposed that I meant in what part of the fortress, and pointed out a turret behind which, he said, was the Hall of Justice; then told me that if I would come with him I could probably get something to eat.

As soon as he spoke, I realized I was famished. I followed him down a dark hallway into a room much lower and darker than the lazaret, where two or three score dimarchi like himself were bent over a midday meal of fresh bread, beef, and boiled greens. My new friend advised me to take a plate and tell the cooks I had been instructed to come here for my dinner. I did so, and though they looked a trifle surprised at my fuligin cloak, they served me without objection.

If the cooks were incurious, the soldiers were curiosity itself. They asked my name, and where I came from, and what my rank was (for they assumed our guild was organized like the military). They asked where my ax was, and when I told them we used the sword, where that was; and when I explained that I had a woman with me who was watching it, they cautioned me that she might run away with it, and then counseled me to carry out bread for her under my cloak, since she would not be permitted to come where we were to eat. I discovered that all the older men had supported women— camp followers of what is perhaps the most useful and least dangerous kind—at one time or another, though few had them now. They had spent the summer before in fighting in the north and had been sent to winter in Nessus, where they served to maintain order. Now they expected to go north again within a week. Their women had returned to their own villages to live with parents or relatives. I asked if the women would not have preferred to follow them south.

"Prefer it?" said my friend, "Of course they'd prefer it. But how would they do it? It's one thing to follow cavalry that's fighting its way north with army, for that doesn't make more than a league or two on the best days, and if it clears three in a week, you can bet it will lose two the next. But how would they keep up on the way back to the city? Fifteen leagues a day. And what would they eat on the way? It's better for them to wait. If a new xenagie comes to our old sector, they'll have some new men. Some new girls will come too, and some of the old ones drop out, and it gives everyone a chance to change off if they want. I heard they brought in one of you carnifexes last night, but he was nearly dead himself. Have you been to see him?"

I said I had not.

"One of our patrols reported him, and when the chiliarch heard of it he sent them back to bring him, seeing we were sure to need one in a day or so. They swear they didn't touch him, but they had to bring him back on a litter. I don't know if he's one of your comrades, but you might want to take a look."

I promised I would, and after thanking the soldiers for their hospitality, left them. I was worried about Dorcas, and their questioning, though it was clearly well meant, had made me uneasy. There were too many things I could not explain—how I had come to be injured, for example, if I had admitted I was the man who had been carried in the night before, and where Dorcas had come from. Not really understanding those things myself bothered me at least as much, and I felt, as we always feel when there is a whole sector of our lives that cannot bear light, that no matter how far the last question had been from one of the forbidden subjects, the next would pierce to the heart of it.

Dorcas was awake and standing by my bed, where someone had left a cup of steaming broth. She was so delighted to see me that I felt happy myself, as though joy were as contagious as a pestilence. "I thought you were dead," she told me. "You were gone, and your clothes were gone, and I thought they had taken them to bury you in."

"I'm all right," I said. "What happened last night?"

Dorcas became serious at once. I made her sit on the bed with me and eat the bread I had brought and drink the broth while she answered. "You remember fighting with the man who wore that strange helmet, I'm sure. You put on a mask and went into the arena with him, although I begged you not to. Almost at once he hit you in the chest, and you fell. I remember seeing the leaf, a horrible thing like a flatworm made of iron, half in your body and turning red as it drank your blood.

"Then it fell away. I don't know how to describe it. It was as though everything I had seen had been *wrong*. But it wasn't wrong—I remember what I saw. You got up again, and you looked . . . I don't know. As if you were lost, or some part of you was far away. I thought he was going to kill you at once, but the ephor protected you, saying he had to allow you to get your avern. His was quiet, the way ours had been when you pulled it up in that awful place, but yours had begun to writhe and open its flower—I thought it had been open before, the white thing with the swirl of petals, only now I believe I was thinking too much of roses, and it had not been open at all. There was something underneath, something else, a face like the face poison would have, if poison had a face.

"You didn't notice. You picked it up and it began to curl toward you, slowly, as though it were only half awake. But the other man, the hipparch, couldn't believe what he had seen. He was staring at you, and that woman Agia was shouting to him. And all at once he turned and ran away. The people who were watching didn't want him to, they wanted to see someone killed. So they tried to stop him, and he . . ."

Her eyes were brimming with tears; she turned her head to keep me from seeing them. I said, "He struck several of them with his avern, and I suppose killed them. Then what happened?"

"It wasn't just that he struck them. It struck *at* them, after the first two, like a snake. The ones who were cut with the leaves didn't die at once, they screamed, and some of them ran and fell and got up and ran again, as if they were blind, knocking other people down. And at last a big man struck him from behind and a woman who had been fighting somewhere else came with a braquemar. She cut the avern—not sidewise but down the stem so it split. Then some of the men held the hipparch and I heard her blade clash on his helmet.

"You were just standing there. I wasn't sure you even knew he was gone, and your avern was bending back toward your face. I thought of what the woman had done and hit at it with your sword. It was heavy, so very heavy at first, and then it was hardly heavy at all. But when I slashed down with it I felt as if I could have struck the head from a bison. Only I had forgotten to take off the sheath. But it knocked the avern out of your hand, and I took you and led you away . . ."

"Where?" I asked.

She shivered and dipped a piece of bread in the steaming broth. "I don't know. I didn't care. It was just so good to be walking with you, to know I was taking care of you the way you had taken care of me before we got the avern. But I was cold, terribly cold, when night came. I put your cloak all around you and fastened it in front, and you didn't seem to be cold, so I took this mantle and wrapped myself in it. My dress was falling to pieces. It still is."

I said, "I wanted to buy you another one when we were at the inn."

She shook her head, chewing the tough crust. "Do you know, I think this is the first food I've had in a long, long time. I have pains in my stomach—that's why I drank the wine there—but this makes it feel better. I hadn't realized how weak I was getting.

"But I didn't want a new dress from there because I would have had to wear it for a long time, and it would always have reminded me of that day. You can buy me a dress now, if you like, because it will remind me of this day, when I thought you were dead when you were really well.

"Anyway, we got back into the city somehow. I was hoping to find a place to stop where you could lie down, but there were only big houses with terraces and balustrades. That sort of thing. Some soldiers came galloping up and asked if you were a carnifex. I didn't know the word, but I remembered what you had told me and so I told them you were a torturer, because soldiers have always seemed to me to be a kind of torturer and I knew they would help us. They tried to get you to ride, but you fell off. So some of them tied their capes between two lances and laid you on that, and put the ends of the lances in the stirrup straps of two destriers. One of them wanted to take me up into his saddle, but I wouldn't do it. I walked beside you all the way and sometimes I talked to you, but I don't think you heard me."

She drained the last of the broth. "Now I want to ask you a question. When I was washing myself behind the screen, I could hear you and Agia whispering about a note. Later you were looking for someone in the inn. Will you tell me about that?"

"Why didn't you ask before?"

"Because Agia was with us. If you had found out anything, I didn't want her to hear what it was."

"I'm sure Agia could discover anything I discovered," I said. "I don't know her well, and in fact I don't feel I know her as well as I know you. But I know her well enough to realize that she's much cleverer than I am."

Dorcas shook her head again. "She's the sort of woman who's good at making puzzles for other people, but not at solving ones she didn't make herself. I think she thinks—I don't know—sidewise. So no one else can follow it. She's the kind of woman people say thinks like a man, but those women don't think like real men at all, in fact, they think less like real men than most women do. They just don't think like women. The way they do think is hard to follow, but that doesn't mean it's clear, or deep."

I told her about the note, and what it said, and mentioned that although it had been destroyed I had copied it out on the inn's paper and found it to be the same paper, and the same ink.

"So someone wrote it there," she said pensively. "Probably one of the inn servants, because he called the ostler by name. But what does it mean?"

"I don't know."

"I can tell you why it was put where it was. I sat there, on that horn settee, before you sat down. It made me happy, I recall, because you sat beside me. Do you remember if the waiter—he must have carried the note, whether he wrote it or not—put the tray there before I got up to bathe?"

"I can remember everything," I said, "except last night.

Agia sat in a folding canvas chair, you sat on the couch, that's right, and I sat down beside you. I had been carrying the avern on the pole as well as my sword, and I laid the avern flat behind the couch. The kitchen girl came in with water and towels for you, then she went out and got oil and rags for me."

Dorcas said, "We ought to have given her something."

"I gave her an orichalk to bring the screen. That's probably as much as she's paid for a week. Anyway, you went behind it, and a moment later the host led the waiter in with the tray and wine."

"That's why I didn't see it, then. But the waiter must have known where I was sitting, because there was no place else. So he left it under the tray, hoping I'd see it when I came out. What was the first part again?"

" 'The woman with you has been here before. Do not trust her.' "

"It must have been for me. If it had been for you, it would have distinguished between Agia and me, probably by hair color. And if it had been meant for Agia, it would have been out on the other side of the table where she would have seen it instead."

"So you reminded someone of his mother."

"Yes." Once more there were tears in her eyes.

"You're not old enough to have had a child who could have written that note."

"I don't remember," she said, and buried her face in the loose folds of the brown mantle.

XXIX

Agilus

WHEN THE PHYSICIAN IN CHARGE HAD EXAMINED ME AND FOUND I had no need of treatment, he asked us to leave the lazaret, where my cloak and sword were, as he said, upsetting to his patients.

On the opposite side of the building in which I had eaten with the troopers, we found a shop that catered to their needs. Together with false jewelry and trinkets of the sort such men give their paramours, it carried a certain amount of women's clothing; and though my money had been much depleted by the dinner we had never returned to the Inn of Lost Loves to enjoy, I was able to buy Dorcas a simar.

The entrance to the Hall of Justice was not far from this shop. A crowd of a hundred or so was milling before it, and since the people pointed and elbowed one another when they caught sight of my fuligin, we retreated again to the courtyard where the destriers were tethered. A portreeve from the Hall of Justice found us there—an imposing man with a high, white forehead like the belly of a pitcher. "You are the carnifex," he said. "I was told you are well enough to perform your office."

I told him I could do whatever was necessary today, if his master required it.

"Today? No, no, that's not possible. The trial won't be over until this afternoon."

I remarked that since he had come to make certain I was well enough to carry out the execution, he must have felt certain the prisoner would be found guilty.

"Oh, there's no question of that—not the least. Nine

212

persons died, after all, and the man was apprehended on the spot. He's of no consequence, so there's no possibility of pardon or appeal. The tribunal will reconvene at midmorning, but you won't be required until noon."

Because I had had no direct experience with judges or courts (at the Citadel, our clients had always been sent to us, and Master Gurloes dealt with those officials who occasionally came to inquire about the disposition of some case or other), and because I was eager to actually perform the act in which I had been drilled for so long, I suggested that the chiliarch might wish to consider a torchlight ceremony that same night.

"That would be impossible. He must meditate his decision. How would it look? A great many people feel already that the military magistrates are hasty and even capricious. And to be frank, a civil judge would probably have waited a week, and the case would be all the better for it, since there would have been ample time, then, for someone to come forward with fresh evidence, which of course no one will actually do."

"Tomorrow afternoon then," I said. "We'll require quarters for the night. Also I'll want to examine the scaffold and block, and ready my client. Will I need a pass to see him?"

The portreeve asked if we could not stay in the lazaret, and when I shook my head, we—the portreeve, Dorcas, and I—went there to permit him to argue with the physician in charge, who, as I had predicted, refused to have us. That was followed by a lengthy discussion with a noncommissioned officer of the xenagie, who explained that it was impossible for us to stay in the barracks with the troopers, and that if we were to use one of the rooms set aside for the higher ranks, no one would want to occupy it in the future. In the end a little, windowless storeroom was cleared out for us, and two beds and some other furniture (all of which had seen hard use) brought in. I left Dorcas there, and after assuring myself that I was unlikely to step through a rotten board at the critical moment, or to have to saw the client's head off while I held him across my knee, I went to the cells to make the call that our traditions demand.

Subjectively at least, there is a great difference between detention facilities to which one has become accustomed and those to which one has not. If I had been entering our own oubliette, I would have felt I was, quite literally, coming home—perhaps coming home to die, but coming home nevertheless. Although I would have realized in the abstract that our winding metal corridors and narrow gray doors might hold horror for the men and women confined there, I would have felt nothing of that horror myself, and if one of them had suggested I should, I would have been quick to point out their various comforts—clean sheets and ample blankets, regular meals, adequate light, privacy that was scarcely ever interrupted, and so on.

Now, going down a narrow and twisted stone stair into a facility a hundredth the size of ours, my feelings were precisely the reverse of what I would have felt there. I was oppressed by the darkness and stench as if by a weight. The thought that I might myself be confined there by some accident (a misunderstood order, for example, or some unsuspected malice on the part of the portreeve) recurred no matter how often I pushed it aside.

I heard the sobbing of a woman, and because the portreeve had spoken of a man, assumed that it came from a cell other than the one that held my client. That, I had been told, was the third from the right. I counted: one, two, and three. The door was merely wood bound with iron, but the locks (such is military efficiency!) had been oiled. Within, the sobbing hesitated and almost ceased as the bolt fell back.

Inside a naked man lay upon straw. A chain ran from the iron collar about his neck to the wall. A woman, naked too, bent over him, her long, brown hair falling past her face and his so that it seemed to unite them. She turned to look at me, and I saw that it was Agia.

She hissed, "Agilus!" and the man sat up. Their faces were so nearly alike that Agia might have been holding a mirror to her own.

"It was you," I said. "But that isn't possible." Even while I spoke, I was recalling the way Agia had behaved at the Sanguinary Field, and the strip of black I had seen by the hipparch's ear.

"You," Agia said. "Because you lived, he has to die."

I could only answer, "Is it really Agilus?"

"Of course." My client's voice was an octave lower than his

twin's, though less steady. "You still don't understand, do you?"

I could only shake my head.

"It was Agia in the shop. In the Septentrion costume. She came in through the rear entrance while I was speaking to you, and I made a sign to her when you wouldn't even talk of selling the sword."

Agia said, "I couldn't speak—you would have known it for a woman's voice—but the cuirass hid my breasts and the gauntlets my hands. Walking like a man isn't as hard as men think."

"Have you ever *looked* at that sword? The tang should be signed." Agilus's hands lifted for a moment, as though he would have taken it still if he could. Agia added in a toneless voice, "It is. By Jovinian. I saw it in the inn."

There was a tiny window high up in the wall behind them, and from it, suddenly, as though the ridge of a roof, or a cloud, had now fallen below the sun, a beam of light came to bathe them both. I looked from one aureate face to the other. "You tried to kill me. Just for my sword."

Agilus said, "I hoped you would leave it—don't you remember? I tried to persuade you to leave, to flee in disguise. I would have given the clothes to you, and as much money as I could."

"Severian, don't you understand? It was worth ten times more than our shop, and the shop was all we had."

"You've done this before. You must have. Everything went too smoothly. A legal murder, with no body to weight for Gyoll."

"You're going to kill Agilus, aren't you? That must be why you're here—but you didn't know it was us until you opened the door. What have we done that you're not going to do?"

Less stridently, her brother's voice followed Agia's. "It was a fair combat. We were equally armed, and you agreed to the conditions. Will you give me such a fight tomorrow?"

"You knew that when evening came the warmth of my hands would stimulate the avern, and that it would strike at my face. You wore gloves and you only had to wait. In reality, you didn't even have to do that, because you had thrown the leaves often before."

Agilus smiled. "So the business of the gauntlets was a side issue after all." He spread his hands. "I won. But in reality you won, by some concealed art neither my sister nor I understand. I have been wronged by you three times now, and the old law said that a man three times wronged might claim any boon of his oppressor. I grant that the old law is no longer in force, but my darling tells me you have an attachment to times past, when your guild was great and your fortress the center of the Commonwealth. I claim the boon. Set me free."

Agia rose, brushing the straw from her knees and rounded thighs. As though she realized only now that she was naked, she picked up the blue-green brocade gown I remembered so well and clasped it to her.

I said, "How have I wronged you, Agilus? It seems to me that you have wronged me, or tried to."

"First by entrapment. You carried an heirloom worth a villa about the city without knowing what it was you had. As owner it was your duty to know, and your ignorance threatens to cost me my life tomorrow unless you free me tonight. Secondly, by refusing to entertain any offer to buy. In our commercial society, one may set one's price as high as one wishes, but to refuse to sell at any price is treason. Agia and I wore the gaudy armor of a barbarian—you wore his heart. Thirdly, by the sleight with which you won our combat. Unlike you, I found myself contesting powers greater than I could comprehend. I lost my nerve, as any man would, and here I am. I call on you to free me."

Laughter came unwished-for, carrying with it the taste of gall. "You're asking me to do for you, whom I have every reason to despise, what I wouldn't do for Thecla, whom I loved almost more than my own life. No. I'm a fool, and if I was not one before, surely your darling sister has made one of me. But not such a fool as that."

Agia dropped her gown and threw herself toward me with such violence that I thought for an instant she was attacking me. Instead she covered my mouth with kisses, and seizing my hands put one on her breast and the other upon her velvet hip. There were bits of rotten straw there still, and on her back, to which I shifted both hands a moment later.

"Severian, I love you! I longed for you when we were

together, and tried to give myself to you a score of times. Don't you remember the Garden of Delectation? How much I wanted to take you there? It would have been rapture for us both, but you wouldn't go. For once be honest." (She spoke as if honesty were an abnormality like mania.) "Don't you love me? Take me now . . . here. Agilus will turn his face away, I promise you." Her fingers had slid between my waistband and my belly, and I was not aware that her other hand had lifted the flap of my sabretache until I heard the rustle of paper there.

I slapped her wrist, perhaps harder than I should, and she flew at me, clawing for my eyes as Thecla used sometimes to do when she could no longer bear the thoughts of imprisonment and pain. I pushed her away—not into a chair this time but against the wall. Her head struck the stone, and though it must have been padded by her abundant hair, the sound was as sharp as the tap of a mason's hammer. All the strength seemed to leave her knees; she slid down until she was sitting on the straw. I would never have guessed that Agia was capable of weeping, but she wept.

Agilus asked, "What did she do?" There was no emotion beyond curiosity in the question.

"You must have seen her. She tried to reach into my sabretache." I scooped what coins I possessed out of their compartment: two brass orichalks and seven copper aes. "Or perhaps she wanted to steal the letter I have to the archon of Thrax. I told her about that once, but I don't carry it in here."

"She wanted the coins, I am sure. They've fed me, but she must be dreadfully hungry."

I picked Agia up and thrust her torn gown into her arms, then opened the door and led her out. She was still dazed, but when I gave her an orichalk she threw it down and spat at it.

When I reentered the cell, Agilus was sitting cross-legged, his back propped by the wall. "Don't ask me about Agia," he said. "Everything you suspect is true—is that enough? I will be dead tomorrow, and she will wed the old man who dotes on her, or someone else. I wanted her to do it sooner. He couldn't have prevented her from seeing me, her brother. Now I will be gone, and she won't have even that to worry about."

"Yes," I said, "you will die tomorrow. That's what I've

come to talk to you about. Do you care how you look on the scaffold?"

He stared at his hands, slender and rather soft, where they lay in the narrow beam of sunlight that had given his head, and Agia's, an aureole a few moments before. "Yes," he said. "She may come. I hope she won't, but yes, I care."

I told him then (as I had been taught) to eat little in the morning so that he would not be ill when the time came, and cautioned him to empty his bladder, which relaxes at the stroke. I drilled him too in that false routine we teach to all who must die, so they will think the moment is not quite come when in fact it has come, the false routine that lets them die with something less of fear. I do not know if he believed me, though I hope he did; if ever a lie is justified in the sight of the Pancreator, it is that one.

When I left him, the orichalk was gone. In its place—and no doubt with its edge—a design had been scratched on the filthy stones. It might have been the snarling face of Jurupari, or perhaps a map, and it was wreathed with letters I did not know. I rubbed it away with my foot.

XXX

Night

THERE WERE FIVE OF THEM, THREE MEN AND TWO WOMEN. THEY waited outside the door, in a sense, but not near it, grouped a dozen strides away. Waiting, they talked among themselves, two or three talking together, almost shouting, laughing, waving arms, nudging one another. I watched them from the shadows for a time. They could not see me there, or did not, wrapped as I was in my fuligin cloak, and I was able to pretend I did not know what they were; they might have been at a party, all a little drunk.

They came eagerly yet hesitantly, afraid of being repulsed and determined to make the advance. One man was taller than I, surely the illegitimate son of some exultant, fifty or more, and nearly as fat as the host at the Inn of Lost Loves. A thin woman of twenty or so walked beside him, almost pressing against him; she had the hungriest eyes I have ever seen. When the fat man stepped in front of me, blocking my way with his bulk, she nearly (yet not quite) embraced me, coming so close it seemed almost magical that we did not touch, her long-fingered hands moving at the opening of my cloak with the desire to stroke my chest, but never quite doing so, so that I felt I was about to fall prey to some blood-drinking ghost, a succubus or lamia. The others crowded around me, hemming me against the building.

"It's tomorrow, isn't it? How does it feel?" "What's your real name?" "He's a bad one, isn't he? A monster?" None of them waited for answers to their questions, or, so far as I could see, expected or wanted any. They sought propinquity, and the experience of having spoken to me. "Will you break him first? Will there be a branding?" "Have you ever killed a woman?"

"Yes," I said. "Yes, I did, once."

One of the men, short and slight, with the high, bumpy forehead of an intellectual, was putting an asimi into my hand. "I know you fellows don't get much, and I hear he's a pauper, can't tip." A woman, gray hair straggling over her face, tried to make me take a lace-trimmed handkerchief. "Get blood on it. As much as you want, or even only a little. I'll pay you afterward."

All of them stirred me to pity even as they revolted me; but one man most of all. He was even smaller than the one who had given me the money, grayer than the gray-haired woman; and there was a madness in his dull eyes, a shadow of some half-supressed concern that had worn itself out in the prison of his mind until all its eagerness was gone and only its energy remained. He seemed to be waiting until the other four had finished speaking, and since that time clearly would never come, I quieted them with a gesture and asked him what he wanted.

"M-m-master, when I was on the *Quasar* I had a paracoita, a doll, you see, a genicon, so beautiful with her great pupils as dark as wells, her i-irises purple like asters or pansies blooming in summer, Master, whole beds of them, I thought, had b-been gathered to make those eyes, that flesh that always felt sun-warmed. Wh-wh-where is she now, my own scopolagna, my poppet? Let h-h-hooks be buried in the hands that took her! Crush them, master, beneath stones. Where has she gone from the lemon-wood box I made for her, where she never slept at all, for she lay with me all night, not in the box, the lemon-wood box where she waited all day, watch-and-watch, Master, smiling when I laid her in so she might smile when I drew her out. How soft her hands were, her little hands. Like d-d-doves. She might have flown with them about the cabin had she not chosen instead to lie with me. W-w-wind their guts about your w-windlass, stuff their eyes into their mouths. Unman them, shave them clean below so their doxies may not know them, their lemans may rebuke them, leave them to the brazen laughter of the brazen mouths of st-st-strumpets. Work your will upon those guilty. Where was their mercy on the innocent? When did they tremble, when weep? What kind of men could do as they have done—thieves, false friends, betrayers, bad shipmates, no shipmates, murderers and kidnappers. W-without you, where are their nightmares, where are their restitutions, so long promised? Where are their chains, fetters, manacles, and cangues? Where are their abacinations, that shall leave them blind? Where are the defenestrations that shall break their bones, where is the estrapade that shall grind their joints? Where is she, the beloved whom I lost?"

Dorcas had found a daisy for her hair; but as we walked about outside the walls (I wrapped in my cloak, so that to anyone more than a few paces off it must have seemed that she walked alone), it folded its petals in sleep, and she plucked instead one of those white, trumpet-shaped blossoms that are called moonflowers because they appear green in the moon's green light. Neither of us had much to say other than that we would be utterly alone save for the other. Our hands spoke of that, clasping each other tightly.

Victuallers came and went, for the soldiers were making ready to depart. To north and east the Wall hemmed us round, making the wall that enclosed the barracks and administrative buildings seem no more than children's work, a wall of sand that might be trodden down by accident. To south and west extended the Sanguinary Field. We heard the trumpet blown there, and the cries of the new monomachists who sought their foes. Both of us, I think, for a time dreaded that the other would suggest we walk there and watch the combats. Neither did.

When the last curfew had come drifting down from the Wall, we returned, with a borrowed candle, to our window-less and fireless room. There was no bolt for the door, but we put the table against it and stood the candlestick on that. I had told Dorcas she was free to go, and that forever afterward it would be said of her that she was a torturer's woman, who gave herself under the scaffold for money spotted with blood.

She had said, "That money has clothed and fed me." Now she drew off the brown mantle (which hung to her heels—and beyond, when she was not careful of it, so the hem dragged in the dust) and smoothed the raw, yellow-brown linen of her simar.

I asked if she were frightened.

"Yes," she said. Then quickly, "Oh, not of you."

"Of what then?" I was taking off my clothes. If she had asked me, I would not have touched her throughout the night. But I wanted her to ask—indeed, I wanted her to beg; and the pleasure I would have had in abstinence would then have been at least as great (as I thought) as I would have had in possession, with the additional pleasure of knowing that on the next night she would feel the more obliged because I had spared her.

"Of myself. Of what thoughts may return to me when I lie again with a man."

"Again? Do you remember a time before?"

Dorcas shook her head. "But I am certain I am no virgin. I have desired you often, yesterday and today. For whom did you believe I washed myself? Last night I held your hand while you slept, and I dreamed we sated ourselves and lay in each other's arms. But I know satiety as well as desire—so I have known one man at least. Do you wish me to remove this before I blow out the candle?"

She was slender, high-breasted and narrow-hipped,

strangely childlike to me, though fully a woman. "You seem so small," I said, and held her to me.

"And you are so big."

I knew then that however much I tried not to I would hurt her, that night and afterward. I knew too that I was incapable of sparing her. A moment before I would have refrained if she had asked. Now I could not; and just as I would have thrust forward though it had plunged my body on a spike, I would follow her later and try to cleave her to me.

But it was not my body that was impaled, but hers. We had been standing while I ran my hands over her and kissed her breasts, that were like round fruits sliced in two. Now I lifted her, and together we fell on one of the beds. She cried out, half in delight, half in pain, and pushed me away before she clutched at me. "I'm glad," she said. "I'm so glad," and bit me on the shoulder. Her body bent backward like a bow.

Later we pushed the beds together so we could lie side by side. Everything was slower the second time; she would not agree to a third. "You'll need your strength tomorrow," she said.

"Then you don't care."

"If we could have our way, no man would have to go roving or draw blood. But women did not make the world. All of you are torturers, one way or another."

It rained that night, so hard we could hear it drumming on the tiles over our heads, a cleansing, crashing, unending downpour of water. I dozed, and dreamed that the world had been turned upside down. Gyoll was overhead now, decanting all its flood of fish and filth and flowers over us. I saw the great face I had seen under the water when I had nearly drowned—a portent of coral and white seen in the sky, smiling with needle teeth.

Thrax is called the City of Windowless Rooms. This windowless room of ours, I thought, is a preparation for Thrax. Thrax will be like this. Or perhaps Dorcas and I are already there, it was not so far north as I thought, so far north as I was led to believe . . .

Dorcas got up to go out, and I went with her, knowing it would not be safe for her to go alone at night in a place where there were so many soldiers. The corridor outside our room ran along an outer wall pierced with embrasures; water splashed through each in a fine spray. I wanted to keep *Terminus Est* in her sheath, but so large a sword is slow to draw. When we were back in our room again, with the table against the door, I took out the whetstone and sharpened the man-side of the blade, honing its edge until the endmost third, the part I would use, would divide a thread tossed into the air. Then I wiped and oiled the whole blade and stood the sword against the wall near my head.

Tomorrow would be my first appearance on the scaffold, unless the chiliarch decided at the last moment to exercise clemency. That was always a possibility, always a risk. History shows that every age has some unquestioned neurosis, and Master Palaemon had taught me that clemency is ours, a way of saying that one less one is more than nothing, that since human law need not be self-consistent, justice need not be so either. There is a dialogue in the brown book somewhere between two mystes, in which one argues that culture was an outgrowth of the vision of the Increate as logical and just, bound by interior consistency to fulfill his promises and threats. If that was the case, I thought, surely we will perish now, and the invasion from the north, that so many have died to resist, is no more than the wind that topples a tree already rotten.

Justice is a high thing, and that night, when I lay beside Dorcas listening to the rain, I was young, so that I desired high things only. That, I think, was why I so desired that our guild regain the position and regard it had once possessed. (And I still desired that, even then, when I had been cast out of it.) Perhaps it was for the same reason that the love of living things, which I had felt so strongly as a child, had declined until it was hardly more than a memory when I found poor Triskele bleeding outside the Bear Tower. Life, after all, is not a high thing, and in many ways is the reverse of purity. I am wise now, if not much older, and I know it is better to have all things, high and low, than to have the high only.

Unless the chiliarch decided, then, to grant clemency, tomorrow I would take Agilus's life. No one can say what that means. The body is a colony of cells (I used to think of our oubliette when Master Palaemon said that). Divided into two major parts, it perishes. But there is no reason to mourn the destruction of a colony of cells: such a colony dies each time a loaf of bread goes into the oven. If a man is no more than such a colony, a man is nothing; but we know instinctively that a man is more. What happens, then, to that part that is more?

It may be that it perishes as well, though more slowly. There are a great many haunted buildings, tunnels, and bridges; yet I have heard that in those cases in which the spirit is that of a human being and not an elemental, its appearances grow less and less frequent and at last cease. Historiographers say that in the remote past men knew only this one world of Urth, and had no fear of such beasts as were on it then, and traveled freely from this continent to the north; but no one has ever seen even the ghosts of such men.

It may be that it perishes at once—or that it wanders among the constellations. This Urth, surely, is less than a village in the immensity of the universe. And if a man lives in a village and his neighbors burn his house, he leaves the place if he does not die in it. But then we must ask how he came.

Master Gurloes, who has performed a great many executions, used to say that only a fool worried about making some failure of ritual: slipping in the blood, or failing to perceive that the client wore a wig and attempting to lift the head by the hair. The greater dangers were a loss of nerve that would make one's arms tremble and give an awkward blow and a feeling of vindictiveness that would transform the act of justice into mere revenge. Before I slept again, I tried to steel myself against both.

XXXI

The Shadow of the Torturer

IT IS A PART OF OUR OFFICE TO STAND UNCLOAKED, MASKED, sword bared, upon the scaffold for a long time before the client is brought out. Some say this is to symbolize the unsleeping omnipresence of justice, but I believe the real reason is to give the crowd a focus, and the feeling that something is about to take place.

A crowd is not the sum of the individuals who compose it. Rather it is a species of animal, without language or real consciousness, born when they gather, dying when they depart. Before the Hall of Justice, a ring of dimarchi surrounded the scaffold with their lances, and the pistol their officer carried could, I suppose, have killed fifty or sixty before someone could snatch it from him and knock him to the cobblestones to die. Still it is better to have a focus, and some open symbol of power.

The people who had come to see the execution were by no means all, or even mostly, poor. The Sanguinary Field is near one of the better quarters of the city, and I saw plenty of red and yellow silk, and faces that had been washed with scented soap that morning. (Dorcas and I had splashed ourselves at the well in the courtyard.) Such people are much slower to violence than the poor, but once roused are far more dangerous because they are not accustomed to being over-awed by force, and despite the demagogues, have a good deal more courage.

And so I stood with my hands resting on the quillions of *Terminus Est,* and turned this way and that, and adjusted the block so that my shadow would fall across it. The chiliarch was not visible, though I discovered later that he was watching from a window. I looked for Agia in the crowd but could not find her; Dorcas was on the steps of the Hall of Justice, a position reserved for her at my request by the portreeve.

The fat man who had waylaid me the day before was as near the scaffold as he could get, with a lance-fire threatening his bulging coat. The woman of the hungry eyes was on his right and the gray-haired woman on his left; I had her handkerchief in my boot top. The short man who had given me an asimi and the dull-eyed man who stammered and talked so strangely were nowhere to be seen. I looked for them on the rooftops where they could have had a good view despite their small stature, and though I did not find them, perhaps they were there.

Four sergeants in high dress helmets led Agilus forth. I saw the crowd opening for them like the water behind Hildegrin's boat before I could see them at all. Then came the scarlet plumes, then the flash of armor, and at last Agilus's brown hair and his wide, boyish face held uptilted because the chains that bound his arms forced his shoulder blades together. I remembered how elegant he had looked in the armor of a guards officer, with the golden chimera splashed across his chest. It seemed tragic that he could not be accompanied now by men of the unit that had in some sense been his, instead of these scarred regulars in laboriously polished steel. He had been stripped of all his finery now, and I waited to receive him wearing the fuligin mask in which I had fought him. Silly old women believe the Panjudicator punishes us with defeats and rewards us with victory: I felt I had been given more reward than I desired.

A few moments later he mounted the scaffold and the brief ceremony began. When it was over, the soldiers forced him to his knees and I lifted my sword, forever blotting out the sun.

When the blade is as sharp as it should be, and the stroke is given correctly, one feels only a slight hesitation as the spinal column parts, then the solid bite of the edge into the block. I would take an oath that I smelled Agilus's blood on the rain-washed air before his head banged into the basket. The crowd drew back, then surged forward against the leveled lances. I heard the fat man's exhalation distinctly, precisely the sound he might have made at climax when he sweated over some hired woman. From far away came a scream, Agia's voice as unmistakable as a face seen by lightning. Something in its timbre made me feel she had not been watching at all, but had known nevertheless when her twin died.

The aftermath is often more troublesome than the act itself. As soon as the head has been exhibited to the crowd, it can be dropped back into the basket. But the headless body (which remains capable of losing a good deal of blood for a long time after the action of the heart has ceased) must be taken away in a manner dignified yet dishonorable. Furthermore, it must be not just taken "away," but taken to some specific spot where it will be safe from molestation. An exultant can, by custom, be laid across the saddle of his own destrier, and his remains are surrendered to his family at once. Persons of lesser rank, however, must be provided with some resting place secure from the eaters of the dead; and at least until they are safely out of sight, they must be dragged. The executioner cannot perform this task because he is already burdened with the head and with his weapon, and it is rare for anyone else involved—soldiers, officers of the court, and so on—to be willing to do so. (At the Citadel it was done by two journeymen and thus presented no difficulty.)

The chiliarch, a cavalryman by training and no doubt by inclination, had solved the problem by ordering that the body should be pulled behind a baggage sumpter. The animal had not been consulted, however, and being more of the laborer than the warrior kind, took fright at the blood and tried to bolt. We had an interesting time of it before we were able to get poor Agilus into a quadrangle from which the public was excluded.

I was cleaning off my boots when the portreeve met me there. When I saw him I supposed he had come to give me my fee, but he indicated that the chiliarch wished to pay me himself. As I told him, it was an unexpected honor.

"He watched everything," the portreeve said. "And he was quite pleased. He instructed me to tell you that you and the woman who travels with you are welcome to spend the night here, if you wish."

"We'll leave at twilight," I told him. "I believe that will be safer."

He took thought for a moment, then nodded, showing more intelligence than I would have anticipated. "The miscreant will have a family, I suppose, and friends—though no doubt you know no more of them than I. Still, it's a difficulty you must face frequently."

"I have been warned by more experienced members of my guild," I said.

I had said that we would leave at twilight, but in the event we waited until it was fully dark, in part for safety's sake and in part because it seemed wise to eat the evening meal before we left.

We could not, of course, make directly for the Wall and Thrax. The gate (of whose location I had only a vague idea in any event) would be shut, and I had been told by everyone that there were no inns between the barracks and the Wall. What we had to do, then, was first to lose ourselves, and then to find a place where we could spend the night and from which we could go without difficulty to the gate the next day. I had gotten detailed directions from the portreeve, and though we missed our way, it was some time before we realized it, and we began our walk quite cheerfully. The chiliarch had tried to hand me my fee instead of casting it on the ground at my feet (as is customary), and I had had to dissuade him for the sake of his own reputation. I gave Dorcas a detailed account of this incident, which had amused me nearly as much as it had flattered me. When I had finished, she asked practically, "He paid you well then, I suppose?"

"More than twice what he should have given for the services of a single journeyman. A master's fee. And of course I got a few tips in connection with the ceremony. Do you know, despite all I spent while Agia was with me, I have more money now than I did when I left our tower? I'm beginning to think that by practicing the mystery of our guild while you and I are traveling, I'll be able to support us."

Dorcas seemed to draw the brown mantle closer about her. "I was hoping you wouldn't have to practice it again at all. At least, not for a long time. You were so ill afterward, and I don't blame you."

"It was only nerves—I was afraid that something would go wrong."

"You pitied him. I know you did."

"I suppose so. He was Agia's brother, and like her, I think, in everything except sex."

"You miss Agia, don't you? Did you like her so much?"

"I only knew her for a day—much less time than I have known you already. If she had had her way, I'd be dead now. One of those two averns would have been the end of me."

"But the leaf didn't kill you."

I still recall the tone she used when she told me that; indeed, if I close my eyes now, I can hear her voice again and renew the shock I felt as I realized that ever since I had sat up to see Agilus still grasping his plant, I had been avoiding the thought. The leaf had not killed me, but I had turned my mind from my survival just as a man suffering from a deadly sickness manages by a thousand tricks never to look at death squarely; or rather, as a woman alone in a large house refrains from looking into mirrors, and instead busies herself with trivial errands, so that she may catch no glimpse of the thing whose feet she hears at times on the stairs.

I had survived, and I should be dead. I was haunted by my own life. I thrust one hand into my cloak and stroked my flesh, gingerly at first. There was something like a scar, and a little caked blood still adhered to the skin; but there was no bleeding and no pain. "They don't kill," I said. "That's all."

"She said they did."

"She told a great many lies." We were mounting a gentle hill bathed in pale green moonlight. Ahead of us, seeming as mountains do to be nearer than it was or could possibly be, was the pitch-black line of the Wall. Behind us the lights of Nessus created a false dawn that died bit by bit as the night advanced. I stopped at the top of the hill to admire them, and Dorcas took my arm. "So many homes. How many people are there in the city?"

"No one knows."

"And we will be leaving them all behind. Is it far to Thrax, Severian?"

"A long way, as I've told you already. At the foot of the first cataract. I'm not compelling you to go. You know that."

"I want to. But suppose . . . Severian, just suppose I wanted to go back later. Would you try and stop me?"

I said, "It would be dangerous for you to try to make the trip alone, so I might try to persuade you not to. But I wouldn't bind or imprison you, if that's what you mean."

"You told me you'd written out a copy of the note someone left for me in that inn. Do you remember? But you never showed it to me. I'd like to see it now."

"I told you exactly what it said, and it's not the real note, you know. Agia threw that away. I'm sure she thought that someone—Hildegrin, perhaps—was trying to warn me." I had already opened my sabretache; as I grasped the note, my fingers touched something else as well, something cold and strangely shaped.

Dorcas saw my expression and asked, "What is it?"

I drew it out. It was larger than an orichalk, but not by much, and only a trifle thicker. The cold material (whatever it was) flashed celestine beams back at the frigid rays of the moon. I felt I held a beacon that could be seen all over the city, and I thrust it back and dropped the closure of my sabretache.

Dorcas was clasping my arm so tightly that she might have been a bracelet of ivory and gold grown woman-sized. "What was that?" she whispered.

I shook my head to clear my thoughts. "It isn't mine. I didn't even know I had it. A gem, a precious stone . . ."

"It couldn't be. Didn't you feel the warmth? Look at your sword there—that's a gem. But what was that thing you just took out?"

I looked at the dark opal on the pommel of *Terminus Est*. It glowed in the moonlight, but it was no more like the object I had drawn from my sabretache than a lady's glass is like the sun. "The Claw of the Conciliator," I said. "Agia put it there. She must have, when we broke the altar, so it would not be found on her person if she were searched. She and Agilus would have got it again when Agilus claimed victor-right, and when I didn't die, she tried to steal it in his cell."

Dorcas was no longer staring at me. Her face was lifted and turned toward the city and the sky-glow of its myriad lamps. "Severian," she said. "It can't be."

Hanging over the city like a flying mountain in a dream was

an enormous building—a building with towers and buttresses and an arched roof. Crimson light poured from its windows. I tried to speak, to deny the miracle even as I saw it; but before I could frame a syllable, the building had vanished like a bubble in a fountain, leaving only a cascade of sparks.

XXXII

The Play

IT WAS ONLY AFTER THE VISION OF THAT GREAT BUILDING hanging, then vanishing, above the city, that I knew I had come to love Dorcas. We walked down the road—for we had found a new road just over the top of the hill—into darkness. And because our thoughts were entirely of what we had seen, our spirits embraced without hindrance, each passing through those few seconds of vision as if through a door never previously opened and never to be opened again.

I do not know just where it was we walked. I recall a winding road down the hillside, an arched bridge at the bottom, and another road, bordered for a league or so by a vagabond wooden fence. Wherever it was we went, I know we talked about ourselves not at all, but only of what we had seen and what its meaning might be. And I know that at the beginning of that walk I looked on Dorcas as no more than a chance-met companion, however desirable, however to be pitied. And at the end of it I loved Dorcas in a way that I have never loved another human being. I did not love her because I had come to love Thecla less—rather by loving Dorcas I loved Thecla more, because Dorcas was another self (as Thecla was yet to become in a fashion as terrible as the other was beautiful), and if I loved Thecla, Dorcas loved her also.

"Do you think," she asked, "that anyone saw it but us?"

I had not considered that, but I said that although the suspension of the building had endured for only a moment, yet it had taken place above the greatest of cities; and that if millions and tens of millions had failed to see it, yet hundreds must still have seen.

"Isn't it possible it was only a vision, meant only for us?"

"I have never had a vision, Dorcas."

"And I don't know whether I've had any or not. When I try to recall the time before I helped you out of the water, I can only remember being in the water myself. Everything before that is like a vision shattered to pieces, only small bright bits, a thimble I saw laid on velvet once, and the sound of a small dog barking outside a door. Nothing like this. Nothing like what we've seen."

What she said made me remember the note, which I had been searching for when my fingers touched the Claw, and that in turn suggested the brown book, which lay in the pleat of my sabretache next to it. I asked Dorcas if she would not like to see the book that had once been Thecla's, when we found a place to stop.

"Yes," she said. "When we are seated by a fire again, as we were for a moment at that inn."

"Finding that relic—which of course I will have to return before we can leave the city—and what we have been saying too remind me of something I read there once. Do you know of the key to the universe?"

Dorcas laughed softly. "No, Severian, I who scarcely know my name do not know anything about the key to the universe."

"I didn't say that as well as I should have. What I meant was, are you familiar with the idea that the universe has a secret key? A sentence, or a phrase, some say even a single word, that can be wrung from the lips of a certain statue, or read in the firmament, or that an anchorite on a world across the seas teaches his disciples?"

"Babies know it," Dorcas said. "They know it before they learn to speak, but by the time they're old enough to talk, they have forgotten most of it. At least, someone told me that once."

"That's what I mean, something like that. The brown book is a collection of the myths of the past, and it has a section listing all the keys of the universe—all the things people have said were The Secret after they had talked to mystagogues on far worlds or studied the *popul vuh* of the magicians, or fasted in the trunks of holy trees. Thecla and I used to read them and talk about them, and one of them was that everything, whatever happens, has three meanings. The first is its practical meaning, what the book calls, 'the thing the plowman sees.' The cow has taken a mouthful of grass, and it is real grass, and a real cow—that meaning is as important and as true as either of the others. The second is the reflection of the world about it. Every object is in contact with all others, and thus the wise can learn of the others by observing the first. That might be called the soothsayers' meaning, because it is the one such people use when they prophesy a fortunate meeting from the tracks of serpents or confirm the outcome of a love affair by putting the elector of one suit atop the patroness of another."

"And the third meaning?" Dorcas asked.

"The third is the transsubstantial meaning. Since all objects have their ultimate origin in the Pancreator, and all were set in motion by him, so all must express his will—which is the higher reality."

"You're saying that what we saw was a sign."

I shook my head. "The book is saying that everything is a sign. The post of that fence is a sign, and so is the way the tree leans across it. Some signs may betray the third meaning more readily than others."

For perhaps a hundred paces we were both silent. Then Dorcas said, "It seems to me that if what the Chatelaine Thecla's book says is true, then people have everything backward. We saw a great structure leap into the air and fall to nothing, didn't we?"

"I only saw it suspended over the city. Did it leap?"

Dorcas nodded. I could see the glimmer of her pale hair in the moonlight. "It seems to me that what you call the third meaning is very clear. But the second meaning is harder to find, and the first, which ought to be the easiest, is impossible."

I was about to say I understood her—at least about the first meaning—when I heard from some distance off a rumbling roar that might have been a long roll of thunder. Dorcas exclaimed, "What's that?" and took my hand in her own small, warm one, which I found very pleasant.

"I don't know, but I think it came from the copse up ahead."

She nodded. "Now I hear voices."

"Your hearing is better than mine then."

The rumbling sounded again, louder and more prolonged; and this time, perhaps only because we were a trifle nearer, I thought I saw the gleam of lights through the trunks of the grove of young beeches ahead of us.

"There!" Dorcas said and pointed in a direction somewhat to the north of the trees. "That can't be a star. It's too low and too bright, and moves too quickly."

"It's a lantern, I think. On a wagon, perhaps, or carried in someone's hand."

The rumble came once more, and this time I knew it for what it was, the rolling of a drum. I could hear voices now myself, very faintly, and particularly one voice that sounded deeper than the drum and almost as loud.

As we rounded the edge of the copse, we saw about fifty people gathered around a small platform. On it, between flaring torches, stood a giant who held a kettledrum beneath one arm like a tomtom. A much smaller man, richly dressed, stood on his right, and on his left, nearly naked, the most sensuously beautiful woman I have ever seen.

"Everyone is here," the small man was saying, loudly and very rapidly. "Everyone is here. What would you have? Love and beauty?" He pointed to the woman. "Strength? Courage?" He waved the stick he carried toward the giant. "Deception? Mystery?" He tapped his own chest. "Vice?" He pointed toward the giant again. "And look here—see who's just come! It's our old enemy Death, who always comes sooner or later." With this he pointed to me, and every face in the audience turned to stare.

It was Dr. Talos and Baldanders; their presence seemed inevitable as soon as I had recognized them. So far as I knew, I had never seen the woman.

"Death!" Dr. Talos said. "Death has come. I doubted you these past two days, old friend; I ought to have known better."

I expected the audience to laugh at this grim humor, but

they did not. A few muttered to themselves, and a crone spat into her palm and pointed two fingers toward the ground.

"And who is it he has brought with him?" Dr. Talos leaned forward to peer at Dorcas in the torchlight. "Innocence, I believe it is. Yes, it's Innocence. Now everyone is here! The show will begin in a moment or two. Not for the faint of heart! You have never seen anything like it, anything at all! Everyone is here now."

The beautiful woman was gone, and such was the magnetism of the doctor's voice that I had not noticed when she left.

If I were to describe Dr. Talos's play now, as it appeared to me (a participant), the result could only be confusion. When I describe it as it appeared to the audience (as I intend to do at a more appropriate point in this account), I will not, perhaps, be believed. In a drama with a cast of five, of whom two on this first night had not learned their parts, armies marched, orchestras played, snow fell, and Urth trembled. Dr. Talos demanded much from the imagination of his audience; but he assisted that imagination with narration, simple yet clever machinery, shadows cast upon screens, holographic projectors, recorded noises, reflecting backdrops, and every other conceivable sleight, and on the whole he succeeded admirably, as evidenced by the sobs, shouts, and sighs that floated toward us from time to time out of the dark.

Triumphing in all this, he yet failed. For his desire was to communicate, to tell a great tale that had being only in his mind and could not be reduced to common words; but no one who ever witnessed a performance—and still less we who moved across his stage and spoke at his bidding—ever left it, I think with any clear understanding of what that tale was. It could only (Dr. Talos said) be expressed in the ringing of bells and the thunder of explosions, and sometimes by the postures of ritual. Yet as it proved in the end it could not be expressed even by these. There was a scene in which Dr. Talos fought Baldanders until the blood ran down both their faces; there was another in which Baldanders searched for a terrified Jolenta (that was the name of the most beautiful woman in the world) in a room of an underground palace, and at last seated himself on the chest where she lay hidden. In the final part I held the center of the stage, presiding over a chamber of inquiry in which Baldanders, Dr. Talos, Jolenta, and Dorcas were bound in various apparatuses. As the audience watched, I inflicted the most bizarre and ineffective (had they been real) torments on each in turn. In this scene, I could not help but notice how strangely the audience began to murmur while I was preparing, as it seemed, to wrench Dorcas's legs from their sockets. Though I was unaware of it, they had been permitted to see that Baldanders was freeing himself. Several women screamed when his chain clattered to the stage; I looked covertly toward Dr. Talos for directions, but he was already springing toward the audience, having freed himself with far less effort.

"Tableau," he called. "Tableau, everyone." I froze in position, having learned that was what was meant. "Gracious people, you have watched our little show with admirable attention. Now we ask a bit of your purse as well as your time. At the conclusion of the play you will see what occurs now that the monster has freed himself at last." Dr. Talos was holding out his tall hat to the audience, and I heard several coins clink into it. Unsatisfied, he leaped from the stage and began to move among the people. "Remember that once he is free, nothing stands between him and the consummation of his brutal desires. Remember that I, his tormentor, am bound now and at his mercy. Remember that you have never as yet learned—thank you, sieur—the identity of the mysterious figure seen by the Contessa through the curtained windows. Thank you. That above the dungeon you see now the weeping statue—thank you—still digs under the rowan tree. Come now, you have been very generous with your time. We ask only that you will not be penurious with your money. A few, truly, have treated us well, but we will not perform for a few. Where are the shining asimi that should have showered into my poor hat long ago from the rest of you? The few shall not pay for the multitude! If you've no asimis, then orichalks; if you have none, surely there is no one here without an aes!"

Eventually a sufficient sum was gathered, and Dr. Talos vaulted back into his place and deftly reaffixed the fastenings that seemed to hold him in an embrace of spikes. Baldanders roared and stretched forth his long arms as though to grasp me, allowing the audience to observe that a second chain, unnoticed previously, still constrained him. "See him," Dr.

Talos prompted me *sotto voce*. "Hold him off with one of the flambeaux."

I pretended to discover for the first time that Baldanders's arms were free, and plucked one of the torches from its socket at the corner of the stage. At once both torches guttered; the flames, which had been of clear yellow above scarlet, now burned blue and pale green, spitting sparks and sputtering, doubling and tripling in size with a fearful hiss, only to sink at once as if on the point of going out. I thrust the one I had uprooted at Baldanders, shouting, "No! No! Back! Back!" prompted again by Dr. Talos. Baldanders responded by roaring more furiously than ever. He strained at the chain in a way that made the scenery wall to which he was bound creak and snap, and his mouth began quite literally to foam, a thick white liquid running from the corners of his lips to bedew his huge chin and fleck his rusty black clothes as though with snow. Someone in the audience screamed, and the chain broke with a report like the snapping of a drover's whip. By this time the giant's face was hideous in its madness, and I would no more have attempted to stand in his way than to stop an avalanche; but before I could move a step to escape him, he had wrested the torch from me and knocked me down with its iron shaft.

I got my head up in time to see him jerk the other torch from its place and make for the audience with both. The shrieking of men drowned the shrilling of women—it sounded as if our guild were exercising a hundred clients together. I pulled myself up and was about to seize Dorcas and dash for the cover of the copse when I saw Dr. Talos. He seemed filled with what I can only call malignant good humor, and though he was freeing himself from his fastenings, he was taking his time about it. Jolenta was setting herself free as well, and if there were any expression at all on that perfect face, it was one of relief.

"Very well!" Dr. Talos exclaimed. "Very well indeed. You may come back now, Baldanders. Don't leave us in the dark." To me: "Did you enjoy your maiden experience of the boards, Master Torturer? For a beginner acting without rehearsal, you played nicely enough."

I managed to nod.

"Except when Baldanders knocked you down. You must

forgive him, he could see you didn't know enough to drop.
Come with me now. Baldanders has his talents, but a fine eye
for minutiae lost in grass isn't one of them. I have some lights
backstage, and you and Innocence shall help us pick up."

I did not understand what he meant, but in a few moments
the torches were back in place and we were hunting through
the trampled area in front of the stage with dark lanterns.
"It's a gambling proposition," Dr. Talos explained. "And I
confess to loving them. The money in the hat is a sure
thing—by the close of the first act I can predict to an orichalk
how much it will be. But the dropsies! They may be no more
than two apples and a turnip, or as much as the imagination
can encompass. We have found a baby pig. Delicious, so
Baldanders told me when he ate it. We have found a baby
baby. We have found a gold-headed stick, and I retain it.
Antique brooches. Shoes . . . We frequently find shoes of all
kinds. Just now I have found a woman's parasol." He held it
up. "This will be just the thing to keep the sun from our fair
Jolenta when we go strolling tomorrow."

Jolenta straightened up as people do who are straining not
to stoop. Above the waist her creamy amplitude was such that
her spine must have been curved backward to balance the
weight. "If we're going to an inn tonight, I'd like to go now,"
she said. "I'm very tired, Doctor."

I was exhausted myself.

"An inn? Tonight? A criminal waste of funds. Look at it
this way, my dear. The nearest is a league away at the very
least, and it would take Baldanders and me a watch to pack
the scenery and properties, even with the help of this friendly
Angel of Torment. By the time we reached the inn at that rate
the horizon would be under the sun, the cocks would be
crowing, and like as not a thousand fools would be rising,
banging their doors and throwing their slops."

Baldanders grunted (I thought in confirmation), then
struck with his boot as if at some venomous thing he had
discovered in the grass.

Dr. Talos threw wide his arms to embrace the universe.
"While here, my dear, beneath stars that are the personal and
cherished property of the Increate, we have all anyone could
wish for the most salubrious rest. There's just chill enough in
the air tonight to make sleepers grateful for the warmth of

their coverings and the heat of the fire, and not a hint of rain. Here we will camp, here we will break our fast in the morning, and from here we will walk renewed in the joyful hours when the day is young."

I said, "You mentioned something about breakfast. Is there any food now? Dorcas and I are hungry."

"Of course there is. I see Baldanders has just picked up a basket of yams."

Several members of our erstwhile audience must have been farm people returning from a market with whatever produce they had been unable to sell. Besides the yams we had, eventually, a pair of squabs and several stalks of young sugar cane. There was not much bedding, but there was some, and Dr. Talos himself used none of it, saying he would sit up and watch the fire, and perhaps nap, later, in the chair that had been the Autarch's throne and the Inquisitor's bench a short time before.

XXXIII

Five Legs

FOR PERHAPS A WATCH I LAY AWAKE. I SOON REALIZED THAT DR. Talos was not going to sleep, but I clung to the hope that he would leave us for one reason or another. He sat for a time as if deep in thought, then stood and began to pace up and down before the fire. His was an immobile yet expressive face—a slight movement of one eyebrow or the cocking of his head could change it utterly, and as he passed back and forth before my half-closed eyes I saw sorrow, glee, desire, ennui, resolution, and a score of other emotions that have no names flicker across that vulpine mask.

At last he began to swing his cane at the blossoms of wild flowers. In a short time he had decapitated all those within a dozen steps of the fire. I waited until I could no longer see his erect, energetic figure and only faintly hear the whistling strokes of his cane. Then slowly I drew forth the gem.

It was as if I held a star, a thing that burned in the night. Dorcas was asleep, and though I had hoped that we could examine the gem together, I forbore from waking her. The icy blue radiance waxed until I was afraid Dr. Talos would see it, far off as he was. I held the gem to my eye with some childish idea of viewing the fire through it as through a lens, then snatched it away—the familiar world of grass and sleepers had become no more than a dance of sparks, slashed by a scimitar blade.

I am not sure how old I was when Master Malrubius died. It was a number of years before I became captain, so I must have been quite a small boy. I remember very well, however, how it was when Master Palaemon succeeded him as master of apprentices; Master Malrubius had held that position ever since I had been aware that such a thing existed, and for weeks and perhaps months it seemed to me that Master Palaemon (though I liked him as well or better) could not be our real master in the sense that Master Malrubius had been. The atmosphere of dislocation and unreality was heightened by the knowledge that Master Malrubius was not dead or even away . . . that he was, in fact, merely lying in his cabin, lying in the same bed he had slept in each night when he was still teaching and disciplining us. There is a saying that unseen is as good as unbeen; but in this case it was otherwise— unseen, Master Malrubius was more palpably present than ever before. Master Palaemon refused to assert that he would never return, and so every act was weighed in double scales: *"Would Master Palaemon permit it?"* and *"What would Master Malrubius say?"*

(In the end he said nothing. Torturers do not go to the Tower of Healing, no matter how ill; there is a belief— whether true or not I cannot say—that old scores are settled there.)

If I were writing this history to entertain or even to instruct, I would not digress here to discuss Master Malrubius, who must, at the moment when I thrust away the

Claw, have been dust for long years. But in a history, as in other things, there are necessities and necessities. I know little of literary style; but I have learned as I have progressed, and find this art not so much different from my old one as might be thought.

Many scores and sometimes many hundreds of persons come to watch an execution, and I have seen balconies torn from their walls by the weight of the watchers, killing more in their single crash than I in my career. These scores and hundreds may be likened to the readers of a written account.

But there are others besides these spectators who must be satisfied: the authority in whose name the carnifex acts; those who have given him money so that the condemned may have an easy (or a hard) death; and the carnifex himself.

The spectators will be content if there are no long delays, if the condemned is permitted to speak briefly and does it well, if the upraised blade gleams in the sun for a moment before it descends, thus giving them time to catch breath and nudge one another, and if the head falls with a satisfactory gout of blood. Similarly you, who will some day delve in Master Ultan's library, will require of me no long delays; personages who are permitted to speak only briefly yet do it well; certain dramatic pauses which shall signal to you that something of import is about to occur; excitement; and a sating quantity of blood.

The authorities for whom the carnifex acts, the chiliarchs or archons (if I may be permitted to prolong my figure of speech), will have little complaint if the condemned is prevented from escaping, or much inflaming the mob; and if he is undeniably dead at the conclusion of the proceedings. That authority, as it seems to me, in my writing is the impulse that drives me to my task. Its requirements are that the subject of this work must remain central to it—not escaping into prefaces or indexes or into another work entirely; that the rhetoric not be permitted to overwhelm it; and that it be carried to a satisfactory conclusion.

Those who have paid the carnifex to make the act a painless or a painful one may be likened to the literary traditions and accepted models to which I am compelled to bow. I recall that one winter day, when cold rain beat against the window of the room where he gave us our lessons, Master Malrubius—perhaps because he saw we were too dispirited for serious work, perhaps only because he was dispirited himself—told us of a certain Master Werenfrid of our guild who in olden times, being in grave need, accepted remuneration from the enemies of the condemned and from his friends as well; and who by stationing one party on the right of the block and the other on the left, by his great skill made it appear to each that the result was entirely satisfactory. In just this way, the contending parties of tradition pull at the writers of histories. Yes, even at autarchs. One desires ease; the other, richness of experience in the execution . . . of the writing. And I must try, in the dilemma of Master Werenfrid but lacking his abilities, to satisfy each. This I have attempted to do.

There remains the carnifex himself; I am he. It is not enough for him to earn praise from all. It is not enough, even, for him to perform his function in a way he knows to be entirely creditable and in keeping with the teaching of his masters and the ancient traditions. In addition to all this, if he is to feel full satisfaction at the moment when Time lifts his own severed head by the hair, he must add to the execution some feature however small that is entirely his own and that he will never repeat. Only thus can he feel himself a free artist.

When I shared a bed with Baldanders, I dreamed a strange dream; and in composing this history I did not hesitate to relate it, the relation of dreams being entirely in the literary tradition. At the time I write of now, when Dorcas and I slept under the stars with Baldanders and Jolenta, and Dr. Talos sat by, I experienced what may have been less or greater than a dream; and that is outside that tradition. I give warning to you who will later read this that it has little bearing on what will soon follow; I give it only because it puzzled me at the time and it will provide me with satisfaction to relate it. Yet it may be that insofar as it entered my mind and has remained there from that time to this, it affected my actions during the latter part of my narrative.

With the Claw safely hidden away, I lay stretched on an old blanket near the fire. Dorcas lay with her head near mine; Jolenta with her feet to mine; Baldanders on his back on the

opposite side of the fire, his thick-soled boots among the
embers. Dr. Talos's chair stood near the giant's hand, but it
was turned away from the fire. Whether or not he did sit in it
with his face to the night I cannot say; for parts of the time I
am going to relate I seemed conscious of his presence in the
chair, at other times I sensed that he was absent. The sky was
growing lighter, I believe, than it is at full dark.

Footfalls reached my ears yet hardly disturbed my rest,
heavy, yet softly pattering; then the sound of breath, the
snuffling of an animal. If I was awake, my eyes were open;
but I was still so nearly in sleep that I did not turn my head.
The animal approached me and sniffed at my clothes and my
face. It was Triskele, and Triskele lay down with his spine
pressed against my body. It did not seem odd then that he
had found me, though I recall feeling a certain pleasure at
seeing him again.

Once more I heard footsteps, now the slow, firm tread of a
man; I knew at once that it was Master Malrubius—I could
recall his step in the corridors under the tower on the days
when we made the rounds of the cells; the sound was the
same. He came into the circle of my vision. His cloak was
dusty, as it always was save on the most formal occasions; he
drew it about him in the old way as he seated himself on a box
of properties. "Severian. Name for me the seven principles of
governance."

It was an effort for me to speak, but I managed (in my
dream, if it was a dream) to say, "I do not recall that we have
studied such a thing, Master."

"You were always the most careless of my boys," he told
me, and fell silent.

A forboding grew on me; I sensed that if I did not reply,
some tragedy would occur. At last I began weakly,
"Anarchy . . ."

"That is not governance, but the lack of it. I taught you that
it precedes all governance. Now list the seven sorts."

"Attachment to the person of the monarch. Attachment to
a bloodline or other sequence of succession. Attachment to
the royal state. Attachment to a code legitimizing the
governing state. Attachment to the law only. Attachment to a
greater or lesser board of electors, as framers of the law.

Attachment to an abstraction conceived as including the body of electors, other bodies giving rise to them, and numerous other elements, largely ideal."

"Tolerable. Of these, which is the earliest form, and which the highest?"

"The development is in the order given, Master," I said. "But I do not recall that you ever asked before which was highest."

Master Malrubius leaned forward, his eyes burning brighter than the coals of the fire. "Which is highest, Severian?"

"The last, Master?"

"You mean attachment to an abstraction conceived as including the body of electors, other bodies giving rise to them, and numerous other elements, largely ideal?"

"Yes, Master."

"Of what kind, Severian, is your own attachment to the Divine Entity?"

I said nothing. It may have been that I was thinking; but if so, my mind was too much filled with sleep to be conscious of its thought. Instead, I became profoundly aware of my physical surroundings. The sky above my face in all its grandeur seemed to have been made solely for my benefit, and to be presented for my inspection now. I lay upon the ground as upon a woman, and the very air that surrounded me seemed a thing as admirable as crystal and as fluid as wine.

"Answer me, Severian."

"The first, if I have any."

"To the person of the monarch?"

"Yes, because there is no succession."

"The animal that rests beside you now would die for you. Of what kind is his attachment to you?"

"The first?"

There was no one there. I sat up. Malrubius and Triskele had vanished, yet my side felt faintly warm.

XXXIV

Morning

"YOU ARE AWAKE," DR. TALOS SAID. "I TRUST YOU SLEPT well?"

"I had a strange dream." I stood and looked about.

"There's no one here but ourselves." As though he were reassuring a child, Dr. Talos gestured toward Baldanders and the sleeping women.

"I dreamed my dog—he has been lost for years now—came back and lay beside me. I could still feel the warmth of his body when I woke."

"You were lying beside a fire," Dr. Talos pointed out. "There has been no dog here."

"A man, dressed much as I am."

Dr. Talos shook his head. "I could not have failed to see him."

"You might have dozed."

"Only earlier in the evening. I have been awake for the past two watches."

"I'll guard the stage and properites for you," I said, "if you'd like to sleep now." The truth was that I was afraid to lie down again.

Dr. Talos seemed to hesitate, then said, "That's very kind of you," and stiffly lowered himself onto my now dew-soaked blanket.

I took his chair, turning it so I could watch the fire. For some time I was alone with my thoughts, which were at first of my dream, then of the Claw, the mighty relic chance had dropped into my hands. I felt very glad when Jolenta began to stir and at last rose and stretched her lush limbs against the scarlet-shot sky. "Is there water?" she asked. "I want to wash."

I told her that I thought Baldanders had carried the water for our supper from the direction of the copse, and she nodded and went off to look for a stream. Her appearance, at least, distracted my thoughts; I found myself glancing from her retreating figure to Dorcas's prone one. Jolenta's beauty was perfect. No other woman I have ever seen could approach it—Thecla's towering stateliness made her seem coarse and mannish in comparison, Dorcas's blond delicacy as meager and childlike as Valeria, the forgotten girl I had encountered in the Atrium of Time.

Yet I was not attracted to Jolenta as I had been to Agia; I did not love her as I had loved Thecla; and I did not desire the intimacy of thought and feeling that had sprung up between Dorcas and me, or think it possible. Like every man who ever saw her I desired her, but I wanted her as one wants a woman in a painting. And even while I admired her, I could not help but notice (as I had on the stage the night before) how clumsily she walked, she who appeared so graceful in repose. Those round thighs chafed one another, that admirable flesh weighed her until she carried her voluptuousness as another woman would have carried a child in her belly. When she returned from the copse with drops of clear water shining in her lashes, and her face as pure and perfect as the curve of the rainbow, I felt still almost as though I were alone.

". . . I said, there's fruit if you want it. The doctor had me save some last night so we'd have something for breakfast." Her voice was husky and slightly breathless. One listened as if to music.

"I'm sorry," I told her. "I was thinking. Yes, I'd like some fruit. That's very kind of you."

"I won't get it for you, you'll have to fetch it yourself. It's there, behind that stand of armor."

The armor to which she pointed was actually of cloth stretched over a wire frame and painted silver. Behind it I found an old basket containing grapes, an apple, and a pomegranate.

"I'd like something too," Jolenta said. "Those grapes, I think."

I gave her the grapes, and considering that Dorcas would

probably prefer the apple, put it near her hand and took the pomegranate for myself.

Jolenta held up her grapes. "Grown under glass by some exultant's gardener—it's too soon for natural ones. I don't think this strolling life's going to be too bad. And I get a third of the money."

I asked if she had not trouped with the doctor and his giant before.

"You don't remember me, do you? I didn't think so." She popped a grape into her mouth and so far as I could see swallowed it whole. "No, I haven't. I did have a rehearsal, although with that girl thrust into the story so suddenly we had to change everything."

"I must have disturbed things more than she did. She was on stage much less."

"Yes, but you were supposed to be there. Dr. Talos took your roles when we practiced as well as his own, and told me what you were supposed to say."

"He depended on my meeting him, then."

The doctor himself sat up at that, almost with a snap. He looked wide awake. "Of course, of course. We told you where we'd be when we were at breakfast, and if you hadn't appeared last night, we would've presented 'Great Scenes From' and waited another day. Jolenta, you won't be getting a third of the receipts now, but a quarter—it's only fair that we share with the other woman."

Jolenta shrugged and swallowed another grape.

"Wake her now, Severian. We should be going. I'll rouse Baldanders, and we can divide the money and pack."

"I won't be going with you," I said.

Dr. Talos looked at me quizzically.

"I have to return to the city. I have business with the Order of Pelerines."

"You can remain with us until we reach the main road, then. It will be your most expeditious route back." Perhaps because he refrained from questioning me, I felt he knew more than what he had said indicated.

Ignoring our talk, Jolenta smothered a yawn. "I'll have to have more sleep before tonight, or my eyes won't look as good as they should."

I said, "I will, but when we reach the road, I must go."

Dr. Talos had already turned away to wake the giant, shaking him and striking his shoulders with his slender cane. "As you wish," he said, and I could not be sure whether he was addressing Jolenta or me. I stroked Dorcas's forehead and whispered that we would have to move on now.

"I wish you hadn't done that. I was having the most wonderful dream . . . Very detailed, very real."

"So was I—Before I woke, I mean."

"You've been awake a long time then? Is this apple mine?"

"All the breakfast you'll get, I'm afraid."

"All I need. Look at it, how round it is, how red. What is it they say? 'Red as the apples of . . .' I can't think of it. Would you like a bite?"

"I've eaten already. I had a pomegranate."

"I should have known from the stains on your mouth. I thought you'd been sucking blood all night." I must have looked shocked when she said this, because she added, "Well, you did look like a black bat bending over me."

Baldanders was sitting up now, rubbing his eyes with his hands like an unhappy child. Dorcas called across the fire, "Terrible to have to rise so early, isn't it, goodman? Were you dreaming too?"

"No dreams," Baldanders answered. "I never dream." (Dr. Talos looked toward me and shook his head as if to say, *Most unhealthy.*)

"I'll give you some of mine then. Severian says he has plenty of his own."

Though he seemed thoroughly awake, Baldanders stared at her. "Who are you?"

"I'm . . ." Dorcas turned toward me, frightened.

"Dorcas," I said.

"Yes, Dorcas. Don't you remember? We met behind the curtain last night. You . . . your friend introduced us, and said I shouldn't be afraid of you, because you would only pretend to hurt people. In the show. I said I understood, because Severian does terrible things but is really so kind." Dorcas looked at me again. "You remember, Severian, don't you?"

"Of course. I don't think you have to be anxious about Baldanders just because he's forgotten. He's big, I know, but his size is like my fuligin clothes—it makes him look much worse than he is."

Baldanders told Dorcas, "You have a wonderful memory. I wish I could recall everything like that." His voice was like the rolling of heavy stones.

While we were talking, Dr. Talos had produced the money box. He jingled it now to interrupt us. "Come, friends, I have promised you a fair and equitable distribution of the proceeds of our performance, and when that is complete, it will be time to be moving. Turn around, Baldanders, and spread your hands in your lap. Sieur Severian, ladies, will you gather around me as well?"

I had observed, of course, that when the doctor spoke earlier of dividing the contributions he had collected the night before, he had specified division into four parts; but I had assumed it was Baldanders, who seemed to be his slave, who would receive nothing. Now, however, after rummaging in the box, Dr. Talos dropped a shining asimi into the giant's hands, gave another to me, a third to Dorcas, and a fistful of orichalks to Jolenta; then he began to distribute orichalks singly. "You will notice that everything thus far is good money," he said. "I regret to report that there are a fair number of dubious coins here as well. When the undoubted specie is exhausted, you will each come in for a share of them."

Jolenta asked, "Have you already taken yours, Doctor? I think the rest of us ought to have been present."

For a moment Dr. Talos's hands, which had been darting from one of us to another as he counted out the coins, paused. "I take no share from this," he said.

Dorcas glanced toward me as if to confirm her judgment and whispered, "That doesn't seem fair."

I said, "It isn't fair. Doctor, you took as large a part in the show last night as any of us, and collected the money, and from what I have seen, you provided the stage and scenery as well. If anything, you should have a double share."

"I take nothing," Dr. Talos said slowly. It was the first time I had seen him abashed. "It is my pleasure to direct what I may now call the company. I wrote the play we perform, and like . . ." (he looked around as if at a loss for a simile)

". . . that armor there I play my part. These things are my pleasure, and all the reward I require.

"Now, friends, you will have observed that we are reduced to single orichalks, and there are not enough to make the circle again. To be specific, only two are left. Whoever wishes may have both by renouncing claim to the aes and doubtful stuff remaining. Severian? Jolenta?"

Somewhat to my surprise, Dorcas announced, "I'll take them."

"Very good. I will not presume to judge among the rest, but simply hand it out. I warn you who receive it to be careful in passing it. There are penalties for such things, though outside the Wall—What's this?"

I followed the direction of his eyes and saw a man in shabby gray advancing toward us.

XXXV

Hethor

I DO NOT KNOW WHY IT SHOULD BE HUMILIATING TO RECEIVE A stranger while sitting on the ground, but it is so. Both the women stood as the gray figure approached, and so did I. Even Baldanders lumbered to his feet, so that by the time the newcomer was within speaking distance, only Dr. Talos, who had reoccupied our one chair, remained seated.

Yet a less impressive figure would have been difficult to imagine. He was small of stature, and because his clothes were too large for him, seemed smaller still. His weak chin was covered with stubble; as he approached, he pulled a greasy cap away to show a head on which the hair had retreated at either side to leave a single wavering line like the crest of an old and dirty burginot. I knew I had seen him elsewhere, but it was a moment before I recognized him.

"Lords," he said. "O lords and mistresses of creation, silken-capped, silken-haired women, and man commanding empires and the armies of the F-f-foemen of our Ph-ph-photosphere! Tower strong as stone is strong, strong as the o-o-oak that puts forth leaves new after the fire! And my master, dark master, death's victory, viceroy over the n-night! Long I signed on the silver-sailed ships, the hundred-masted whose masts reached out to touch the st-st-stars, I, floating among their shining jibs with the Pleiades burning beyond the top-royal sp-sp-spar, but never have I seen ought like you! He-he-hethor am I, come to serve you, to scrape the mud from your cloak, whet the great sword, c-c-carry the basket with the eyes of your victims looking up at me, Master, eyes like the dead moons of Verthandi when the sun has gone out. When the sun has g-g-gone out! Where are they then, the bright players? How long will the torches burn? The f-f-freezing hands grope toward them, but the torch bowls are colder than any ice, colder than the moons of Verthandi, colder than the dead eyes! Where is the strength then that beats the lake to foam? Where is the empire, where the Armies of the Sun, long-lanced and golden-bannered? Where are the silken-haired women we loved only l-l-last night?"

"You were in our audience, I take it," said Dr. Talos. "I can well sympathize with your desire to see the performance again. But we won't be able to oblige you until evening, and by then we hope to be some distance from here."

Hethor, whom I had met outside Agilus's prison with the fat man, the hungry-eyed woman and the others, did not seem to have heard him. He was staring at me, with occasional glances toward Baldanders and Dorcas. "He hurt you, didn't he? Writhing, writhing. I saw you with the blood running, red as pentecost. Wh-wh-what honor for you! You serve him too, and your calling is higher than mine."

Dorcas shook her head and turned her face away. The giant only stared. Dr. Talos said, "Surely you understand that what you saw was a theatrical performance." (I remember thinking that if most of the audience had had a firmer grip on that idea, we would have found ourselves in an embarrassing dilemma when Baldanders jumped from the stage.)

"I u-understand more than you think, I the old captain, the old lieutenant, the old c-c-cook in his old kitchen, cooking soup, cooking broth for the dying pets! My master is real, but where are your armies? Real, and where are your empires? Sh-shall false blood run from a true wound? Where is your strength when the b-b-blood is gone, where is the luster of the silken hair? I w-will catch it in a cup of glass, I, the old c-captain of the old limping sh-ship,—with its crew black against the silver sails, and the C-c-coalstack behind it."

Perhaps I should say here that at the time I paid little attention to the rush and stumble of Hethor's words, though my ineradicable memory enables me to recreate them on paper now. He spoke a gobbling singsong, with a fine spray of spittle flying through the gaps in his teeth. In his slow way, Baldanders may have understood him. Dorcas, I feel sure, was too repelled by him to hear much of what he said. She turned aside as one turns from the mutterings and cracking bones when an alzabo savages a carcass, and Jolenta listened to nothing that did not concern herself.

"You can see for yourself that the young woman is unharmed." Dr. Talos rose and put away his money box. "It's always a pleasure to speak to someone who has appreciated our performance, but I'm afraid we've work to do. We must pack. If you'll excuse us?"

Now that his conversation had become one with Dr. Talos exclusively, Hethor put his cap on again, pulling it down until it nearly covered his eyes. "Stowage? There's no one better for it than I, the old s-supercargo, the old chandler and steward, the old st-stevedore. Who else shall put the kernels back on the cob, fit the f-fledgling into the egg again? Who shall fold the solemn-winged m-moth, with w-wings each like stuns'ls, into the broken cocoon left h-hanging like a s-s-sarcophagus? And for the love of the M-master, I'll do it, for the sake of the M-master, I'll do it. And f-f-f-follow anywhere, anywhere he goes."

I nodded, not knowing what to say. Just at the moment, Baldanders—who had apparently caught the references to packing if he had caught nothing else—scooped a backdrop from the stage and began to wind it on its pole. Hethor vaulted up with unexpected agility to fold the set for the Inquisitor's chamber and reel in the projector wires. Dr. Talos turned to me as if to say, *He's your responsibility after all, just as Baldanders is mine.*

"There are a good many of them," I told him. "They find pleasure in pain, and want to associate with us just as a normal man might want to be around Dorcas and Jolenta."

The doctor nodded. "I wondered. One can imagine an ideal servant who serves out of pure love for his master, just as one can an ideal rustic who remains a ditcher from a love of nature, or an ideal fricatrice who spreads her legs a dozen times a night from a love of copulation. But one never encounters these fabulous creatures in reality."

In about a watch we were on the road. Our small theater packed itself quite neatly into a huge barrow formed from parts of the stage, and Baldanders, who wheeled this contraption, also carried a few odds and ends on his back. Dr. Talos, with Dorcas, Jolenta, and me behind him, led the way, and Hethor followed Baldanders at a distance of perhaps a hundred paces.

"He's like me," Dorcas said, glancing back. "And the doctor is like Agia, only not as bad. Do you remember? She couldn't make me go away, and eventually you made her stop trying."

I did remember, and asked why she had followed us with such determination.

"You were the only people I knew. I was more afraid of being alone than I was of Agia."

"Then you *were* afraid of Agia."

"Yes, very much. I still am. But . . . I don't know where I've been, but I think I've been alone, wherever I was. For a long time. I didn't want to do that anymore. You won't understand this—or like it—but . . ."

"Yes?"

"If you had hated me as much as Agia did, I would have followed you anyway."

"I don't think Agia hated you."

Dorcas stared up at me, and I can see that piquant face now as well as if it were reflected in the quiet well of vermillion ink. It was, perhaps, a trifle pinched and pale, too childlike for great beauty; but the eyes were bits of the azure firmament of some hidden world waiting for Man; they could have vied with Jolenta's own. "She hated me," Dorcas said softly. "She hates me more now. Do you remember how

dazed you were after the fight? You never looked back when I
led you away. I did, and I saw her face."

Jolenta had been complaining to Dr. Talos because she had
to walk. Baldanders's deep, dull voice came from behind us
now. "I will carry you."

She glanced back at him. "What? On top of all the rest?"

He did not reply.

"When I say I want to ride, I don't mean, as you seem to
think, like a fool at a flogging."

In my imagination, I saw the giant's sad nod.

Jolenta was afraid of looking foolish, and what I am going
to write now will sound foolish indeed, though it is true. You,
my reader, may enjoy yourself at my expense. It struck me
then how fortunate I was, and how fortunate I had been since
leaving the Citadel. Dorcas I knew was my friend—more than
a lover, a true companion, though we had been together only
a few days. The giant's heavy tread behind me reminded me
of how many men there are who wander Urth utterly alone. I
knew then (or thought I did) why Baldanders chose to obey
Dr. Talos, bending his mighty strength to whatever task the
red-haired man laid on him.

A touch at my shoulder took me from my revery. It was
Hethor, who must have come up silently from his position in
the rear. "Master," he said.

I told him not to call me that, and explained that I was only
a journeyman of my guild, and would probably never attain
to mastership.

He nodded humbly. Through his open lips, I could glimpse
the broken incisors. "Master, where do we go?"

"Out the gate," I said, and told myself I said it because I
wanted him to follow Dr. Talos and not me; the truth was that
I was thinking of the preternatural beauty of the Claw, and
how sweet it would be to carry it to Thrax with me, instead of
retracing my steps to the center of Nessus. I gestured toward
the Wall, which now rose in the distance as the walls of a
common fortress must rise before a mouse. They were black
as thunderheads, and held certain clouds captive at their
summit.

"I will carry your sword, Master."

The offer seemed honestly made, though I was reminded
that the plot Agia and her brother had conceived against me

had been born of their desire for *Terminus Est*. As firmly as I could, I said, "No. Not now or ever."

"I feel pity for you, Master, seeing you walk with it on your shoulder so. It must be very heavy."

I was explaining, quite truthfully, that it was not as burdensome as it appeared, when we rounded the side of a gentle hill and saw half a league off a straight highway running toward an opening in the Wall. It was crowded with carts and wagons and traffic of all kinds, all dwarfed by the Wall and the towering gate until the people looked like mites and the beasts like ants pulling at little crumbs. Dr. Talos turned until he was walking backward and waved at the Wall as proudly as if he had built it himself.

"Some of you, I think, have never seen this. Severian? Ladies? Have you been this near before?"

Even Jolenta shook her head, and I said, "No. I've spent my life so near the middle of the city that the wall was no more than a dark line on the northern horizon when we looked from the glass-roofed room at the top of our tower. I am astounded, I admit."

"The ancients built well, did they not? Think—after so many millennia, all the open area through which we have passed today yet remains for the growth of the city. But Baldanders is shaking his head. Don't you see, my dear patient, that all these bosquets and pleasant meadows among which we have journeyed this morning will one day be displaced by buildings and streets?"

Baldanders said, "They were not for the growing of Nessus."

"Of course, of course. I'm sure you were there, and know all about it." The doctor winked at the rest of us. "Baldanders is older than I, and so believes he knows everything. Sometimes."

We were soon within a hundred paces or so of the highway, and Jolenta's attention became fixed on its traffic. "If there's a litter for hire, you must get it for me," she told Dr. Talos. "I won't be able to perform tonight if I have to walk all day."

He shook his head. "You forget, I have no money. Should you see a litter and wish to engage it, you are of course free to do so. If you cannot appear tonight, your understudy will take your role."

"My understudy?"

The doctor gestured toward Dorcas. "I'm certain she is eager to try the starring part, and that she will do famously. Why do you think I permitted her to join us and share in the proceeds? Less rewriting will be necessary than if we have two women."

"She will go with Severian, you fool. Didn't he say this morning he was going back to look for—" Jolenta wheeled on me, more beautiful than ever for being angry. "What did you call them? Pelisses?"

I said, "Pelerines." And at this a man riding a merychip at the edge of the concourse of people and animals reined his diminutive mount over. "If you're looking for the Pelerines," he said, "your way lies with mine—out the gate, not toward the city. They passed along this road last night."

I quickened my step until I could grasp the cantle of his saddle, and asked if he were sure of his information.

"I was disturbed when the other patrons of my inn rushed into the road to receive their blessing," the man on the merychip said. "I looked out the window and saw their procession. Their servants carried deeses illuminated with candles but reversed, and the priestesses themselves had torn their habits." His face, which was long and worn and humorous, split in a wry grin. "I don't know what was wrong, but believe me, their departure was impressive and unmistakable—that's what the bear said, you know, about the picnickers."

Dr. Talos whispered to Jolenta, "I think the angel of agony there, and your understudy, will remain with us a while longer."

As it proved, he was half in error. No doubt you, who have perhaps seen the Wall many times, and perhaps passed often through one or another of its gates, will be impatient with me; but before I continue this account of my life, I find I must for my own peace spend a few words on it.

I have already spoken of its height. There are few sorts of birds, I think, that would fly over it. The eagle and the great mountain teratornis, and possibly the wild geese and their allies; but few others. This height I had come to expect by the time we reached the base: the Wall had been in plain view then for many leagues, and no one who saw it, with the clouds moving across its face as ripples do across a pond, could fail to realize its altitude. It is of black metal, like the walls of the Citadel, and for this reason it seemed less terrible to me than it would have otherwise—the buildings I had seen in the city were of stone or brick, and to come now on the material I had known from earliest childhood was no unpleasant thing.

Yet to enter the gate was to enter a mine, and I could not suppress a shudder. I noticed too that everyone around me except for Dr. Talos and Baldanders seemed to feel as I did. Dorcas clasped my hand more tightly, and Hethor hung his head. Jolenta seemed to consider that the doctor, with whom she had been quarreling a moment before, might protect her; but when he paid no heed to her touch at his arm and continued to swagger forward and pound the pavement with his stick just as he had in the sunlight, she left him and to my astonishment took the stirrup strap cf the man on the merychip.

The sides of the gate rose high above us, pierced at wide intervals by windows of some material thicker, yet clearer, than glass. Behind these windows we could see the moving figures of men and women, and of creatures that were neither men nor women. Cacogens, I think, were there, beings to whom the avern was but what a marigold or a marguerite is to us. Others seemed beasts with too much of men about them, so that horned heads watched us with eyes too wise, and mouths that appeared to speak showed teeth like nails or hooks. I asked Dr. Talos what these creatures were.

"Soldiers," he said. "The pandours of the Autarch."

Jolenta, whose fear made her press the side of one full breast against the thigh of the man on the merychip, whispered, "Whose perspiration is the gold of his subjects."

"Within the Wall itself, Doctor?"

"Like mice. Although it is of immense thickness, it's honeycombed everywhere—so I am given to understand. In its passages and galleries there dwell an innumerable soldiery, ready to defend it just as termites defend their ox-high earthen nests on the pampas of the north. This is the fourth time Baldanders and I have passed through, for once, as we told you, we came south, entering Nessus by this gate and going out a year afterward through the gate called Sorrowing.

Only recently we returned from the south with what little we had won there, passing in at the other southern gate, that of Praise. On all these passages we beheld the interior of the Wall as you see it now, and the faces of these slaves of the Autarch looked out at us. I do not doubt that there are among them many who search for some particular miscreant, and that if they were to see the one they seek, they would sally out and lay hold of him."

At this the man on the merychip (whose name was Jonas, as I learned later) said, "I beg your pardon, optimate, but I could not help overhearing what you said. I can enlighten you further, if you wish."

Dr. Talos glanced at me, his eyes sparkling. "Why that would be pleasant, but we must make one proviso. We will speak only of the Wall, and those who dwell in it. Which is to say, we will ask you no questions concerning yourself. And you, likewise, will return that courtesy to us."

The stranger pushed back his battered hat, and I saw that in place of his right hand he wore a jointed contrivance of steel. "You have understood me better than I wanted, as the man said when he looked in the mirror. I admit I'd hoped to ask you why you traveled with the carnifex, and why this lady, the loveliest I've ever seen, is walking in the dust."

Jolenta released his stirrup strap and said, "You're poor, goodman, from the look of you, and no longer young. It hardly suits you to inquire of me."

Even in the shadow of the gate, I saw the flush of blood creep into the stranger's cheeks. All she had said was true. His clothes were worn and travel-stained, though not so dirty as Hethor's. His face had been lined and coarsened by the wind. For perhaps a dozen steps he did not reply, but at last he began. His voice was flat and neither high nor deep, but possessed of a dry humor.

"In the old times, the lords of this world feared no one but their own people, and to defend themselves against them built a great fortress on a hilltop to the north of the city. It was not called Nessus then, for the river was unpoisoned.

"Many of the people were angry at the building of that citadel, holding it to be their right to slay their lords without hindrance if they so desired. But others went out in the ships that ply between the stars, returning with treasure and knowledge. In time there returned a woman who had gained nothing among them but a handful of black beans."

"Ah," said Dr. Talos. "You are a professional tale-teller. I wish you had informed us of it from the beginning, for we, as you must have seen, are something the same."

Jonas shook his head. "No, this is the only tale I know—or nearly so." He looked down at Jolenta. "May I continue, most marvelous of women?"

My attention was distracted by the sight of daylight ahead of us, and by the disturbance among the vehicles that clogged the road as many sought to turn back, flailing their teams and trying to clear a path with their whips.

"—she displayed the beans to the lords of men, and told them that unless she were obeyed she would cast them into the sea and so put an end to the world. They had her seized and torn to bits, for they were a hundred times more complete in their domination than our Autarch."

"May he endure to see the New Sun," Jolenta murmured.

Dorcas tightened her grip on my arm and asked, "Why are they so frightened?" Then screamed and buried her face in her hands as the iron tip of a lash flicked her cheek. I pressed past the merychip's head, seized the ankle of the wagoneer who had struck her, and pulled him from his seat. By that time all the gate was ringing with bawling and swearing, and the cries of the injured, and the bellowings of frightened animals; and if the stranger continued his tale I could not hear it.

The driver I pulled down must have died at once. Because I had wished to impress Dorcas, I had hoped to perform the excruciation we call *two apricots;* but he had fallen under the feet of the travelers and the heavy wheels of the carts. Even his screams were lost.

Here I pause, having carried you, reader, from gate to gate—from the locked and fog-shrouded gate of our necropolis to this gate with its curling wisps of smoke, this gate which is perhaps the largest in existence, perhaps the largest ever to exist. It was by entering that first gate that I set my feet upon the road that brought me to this second gate. And surely when I entered this second gate, I began again to walk a new road. From that great gate forward, for a long time, it was to lie outside the City Imperishable and among the forests and grasslands, mountains and jungles of the north.

Here I pause. If you wish to walk no farther with me, reader, I cannot blame you. It is no easy road.

APPENDIX

A Note on the Translation

IN RENDERING THIS BOOK—ORIGINALLY COMPOSED IN A TONGUE
that has not yet achieved existence—into English, I might
easily have saved myself a great deal of labor by having
recourse to invented terms; in no case have I done so. Thus in
many instances I have been forced to replace yet undiscov-
ered concepts by their closest twentieth-century equivalents.
Such words as *peltast, androgyn,* and *exultant* are substitu-
tions of this kind, and are intended to be suggestive rather
than definitive. *Metal* is usually, but not always, employed to
designate a substance of the sort the word suggests to
contemporary minds.

When the manuscript makes reference to animal species
resulting from biogenetic manipulation or the importation of
extrasolar breeding stock, the name of a similar extinct
species has been freely substituted. (Indeed, Severian sometimes seems to assume that an extinct species has been
restored.) The nature of the riding and draft animals employed is frequently unclear in the original text. I have
scrupled to call these creatures *horses*, since I am certain the
word is not strictly correct. The "destriers" of *The Book of
the New Sun* are unquestionably swifter and more enduring
animals than those we know, and the speed of those used for
military purposes seems to permit the delivering of cavalry
charges against enemies supported by high-energy armament.

Latin is once or twice employed to indicate that inscriptions
and the like are in a language Severian appears to consider
obsolete. What the actual language may have been, I cannot
say.

To those who have preceded me in the study of the

posthistoric world, and particularly to those collectors—too numerous to name here—who have permitted me to examine artifacts surviving so many centuries of futurity, and most especially to those who have allowed me to visit and photograph the era's few extant buildings, I am truly grateful.

G.W.

RUDESIND - CURATOR
ULTAN - LIBRARIAN.
CYBY - " APPRENTICE